Chasing Rainbows

Also by Marie Anne Cope

Bonds Series

Bonds

Broken Bonds

Bonds Re-Bound

Eternal Bonds

Short Stories

Tales From a Scarygirl Series

Dark and Scary

Darkly Sinister

For Children

Writing as M. A. Cope

The Misfits

The Misfits & The Magic Stone

To Jane
Welcome to Potters Hole
Marie, xxx

Chasing Rainbows

Marie Anne Cope

Published by Scarygirl Ltd

This novel is a work of fiction. Names and characters are the product of the author's imagination and any resemblance to actual persons, living or dead is entirely coincidental.

First published in Great Britain in 2023 by Scarygirl Ltd.
Reg. No. 8336470

ISBN: 978-1-9999210-7-1

For Auntie Betty.
For introducing me to Nora.

Bluebell Cottage

Chapter 1

Jessie Ellis waited in the dusty driveway, her Audi estate crammed with the possessions she'd managed to salvage. The rest? Well, she didn't like to think about what he'd done to the rest.

Dressed in her costume of dungarees and an over-sized shirt, hiding her slender form, she rocked back and forth on her heels, waiting.

Finally! She heard a car engine rumbling along in her direction and raced out into the road to confirm the approach of perennially tardy estate agent Ben Travers. But she stopped dead, a sheen of sweat swathing her skin, her heart lurching, her hands shaking as she shook her head.

'No, no, no, no, no,' she said, tears filling her eyes as she backed away from the looming Range Rover.

How? How can he have found me? It's… it's not… Anita? Jessie's mind filled with her sister's refusal to accept the truth.

She pushed the memory aside. She couldn't let him see her. Jessie turned on her heel and ran into the driveway, dropping to the ground behind the crumbling dry-stone wall.

'Please, please, please,' she whispered, pulling her knees into her chest, hugging them close, her forehead resting on top, her eyes squeezed shut, tears making rivulets in the dry earth.

The car skidded to a halt and Jessie held her breath, her heart now thundering in her ears as she heard the door open and him climb out of the car.

'Ms Ellis? Jessie?'

Jessie's body registered the voice before her brain, and she felt the tension subside as her heart rate slowed. Still, she kept her face hidden, hoping he wouldn't find her.

'Jessie?'

Jessie screamed as his hand clutched her shoulder.

'Get away from me!' she yelled and shoved sideways, out of his reach, her hands up to shield herself.

'Jessie, it's me, Ben, Ben Travers.'

'B-Ben?' Jessie said as she finally looked up, his tousled head blurry as she blinked to clarify.

'Are you alright? What happened?'

Ben reached a hand out to Jessie, but she shied away.

'I-I'm sorry, I-I thought you w-were someone else,' she said, dropping her gaze as she felt heat suffuse her cheeks.

'Clearly,' Ben said. 'Do you need a hand?'

'No, no, I'm okay… thanks.' She pushed herself up and dusted off her clothes.

'Look, I can't stay,' Ben said, looking at his watch, 'but do you want me to call someone?'

'No, I'm fine.' Jessie squeezed her hands into fists to stop them from shaking. 'W-what do you mean you can't stay? I thought you were going to show me round?'

'I was, but I double booked, and you did buy it without

looking inside, so…'

'So…?'

'If you find something wrong, it's too late,' he said, patting down his pockets, searching for something. 'Ah, here they are.' He extracted a set of keys and tossed them to Jessie.

The keys landed in the dirt; her reflexes too sluggish to respond.

'As far as I know, all your stuff has been delivered, not that you had a lot…?'

His pause hung in the air as he raised an eyebrow in question, but Jessie ignored him.

'Is everything working? Washer? Heating? Hot water?'

'I believe so, but you'll have to wait for internet,' Ben said over his shoulder as he walked back to his car.

'I don't need internet.'

Ben stopped and looked at her. 'What do you mean you don't need wi-fi? Everyone needs wi-fi.'

'I told you, I don't do technology.'

Ben shook his head and climbed into his car. 'And here's me thinking it was just about the gamma rays.'

Jessie ignored his dig; she didn't owe him an explanation.

'Look, get in there, have a look round, and let me know if you have questions. I can put you in touch with anyone you need.' He slammed the door and gunned the engine.

'Gee, thanks,' Jessie muttered, grabbing the keys out of the path of Ben's tyres as he spun the car around, before speeding away, leaving her in a cloud of dust.

Jessie coughed, waving her hands to dispel the dust as she

watched the Range Rover disappear. He didn't have that car the first time they'd met.

Jessie leaned back against a sturdy section of wall, her free hand pressed against her chest, her eyes closed. She inhaled deeply, holding the breath for a few counts, before releasing it slowly, her body calming. Jessie repeated the process for a few minutes before holding her hand out in front of her. It still shook, but not as much.

Not ready to move yet, a quivering emptiness in her stomach, Jessie allowed herself to look up. The sight of the ramshackle cottage make her smile. She clutched the keys close to her chest, allowing a giggle to erupt amidst the chaos.

It was hers. Hers and no one else's. Hers to do with as she pleased. Hers to keep tidy or leave in a mess. It didn't matter which because it belonged to her, one hundred per cent. She'd forgotten how liberating the feeling was, and stared around her, remembering what had bewitched her about the sleepy town of Potters Hole.

It had been the remoteness of the cottage that had initially enchanted Jessie as it nestled in its own expanse of land. But as she'd stood in the road that sunny afternoon, looking from the brochure to the land, it was the cottage Jessie felt tugging at her heartstrings, pulling her forwards, through the majestic gate posts, standing alone amongst the rubble of dry-stone wall, the gateposts' etched stonework proclaiming its name—Bluebell Cottage.

'Don't be put off by the wall. I've got a local guy who can sort that for you.'

'I'm sorry?' Jessie said, dragging her gaze to Ben Travers.

'The wall? I presumed you weren't impressed by its state?'

'No, not at all,' Jessie said, her gaze tracing the tumble-down perimeter until the trees took over. 'Is that with it too?' she asked, glancing back at the brochure.

'The wood? Yes, it most certainly is,' Ben said, leading her to the left. 'It's all yours,' he added, spreading his arms wide.

'If I buy it,' she said, irritated by his confidence, and also by the fact he was right. Jessie wandered into the trees and closed her eyes, tilting her head back and inhaling the fresh air as she listened to the birds singing and the leaves rustling in the breeze. Her shoulders dropped a few inches, the tranquillity washing through her.

'It's beautiful,' she murmured, looking at the thick carpet of bluebells, odd clumps of snowdrops having yielded their position.

'Wait until you see the rest,' Ben said and headed along the earthy and overgrown driveway, curving round to the rear of the cottage.

Jessie followed, bubbles of excitement popping inside her as she feasted her gaze on the lake, shimmering in the sunshine, a dilapidated jetty jutting out into its depths, an equally dilapidated boat bobbing on the water.

'I wouldn't if I were you.'

'Wouldn't what?' Jessie asked, puzzled.

'The boat. I very much doubt it will get far, except to the bottom of the lake, and that jetty is rotten. It'll need completely rebuilding.'

'I thought you were supposed to be selling this to me?' Jessie said and laughed.

'I am, but I don't want you coming to me saying I didn't tell you about this and that. Do you know how many…'

Jessie was no longer listening as she wandered across the neatly mown lawn, a cherry blossom at its centre, and over to a walled-in garden. The garden teemed with flowers and vegetables gone to seed, yearning for the attention it once commanded.

'I'll take it,' Jessie breathed as she watched the garden come to life before her.

'But you've not seen inside?' Ben said, a perplexed look on his face as he gestured towards the cottage.

Jessie turned her gaze to the stone cottage, flora holding hostage its only way in. She followed the overhang, resting warily on a solitary post as it looked back at her, its first-floor windows weeping with condensation.

'I don't need to,' she replied, the cottage's broken exterior engulfed in forgotten wisteria and neglected rambling roses, reminding her of herself. They both needed TLC.

Jessie squeezed the keys in her hand, her emotions now somewhat under control. She pushed herself away from the wall and wandered along the driveway towards the crystal-clear lake. Standing on the shore, she slipped off her Converse, allowing the cold water to lap around her ankles, shocking her system into normal function. She inhaled the crisp air and shivered, wrapping her arms around herself as she stared into the shallow depths.

She watched, mesmerised, as the sunlight refracted in the lapping water, distorting her face and making her look like she did in the Hall of Mirrors at the funfair. Jessie rubbed her upper arms as she focused in on her sunken cheeks and shadowed eyes; they followed her wherever she went.

I wonder if he noticed? Jessie's thoughts turned to Ben and the way she'd reacted. *Of course, he noticed. How could he not?*

'What the hell is wrong with me?' she shouted up into the cloudless sky as a sob caught in her throat. But she knew what was wrong; she'd just hoped coming here would have dispelled it somewhat. She buried her face in her hands and shook her head. These things take time, she reminded herself.

Jessie raised her head, wiping away the tears that seemed to flow without warning these days, and gazed across the lake, noticing for the first time the house that occupied the opposite shore. Although not to her taste, its modernity blended into its surroundings, with its wooden structure and living roof, the vast picture windows reflecting the beauty of the lake and the sky.

Jessie noted the robust jetty, adorned with what she assumed was a functioning boat, and a sleek black SUV nestled against the house.

She closed her eyes again, her neighbour forgotten, and took another deep cleansing breath, allowing her senses to revel in the birdsong, the frantic activity of the bees, and the scents of flowers and herbs drifting on the breeze from her garden. *Hers.* There it was again, and she didn't think she'd tire of it anytime soon.

Rock music rolled across the lake towards her, and Jessie opened her eyes to see a man emerge from the house—a naked man, tall and bronzed, with muscles in all the right places. He walked to the end of his jetty, pushing back his mop of dark auburn hair.

As he looked up at her and waved, Jessie turned away, heat

colouring her cheeks at being caught staring. Quickly, she slid her feet into her shoes and turned towards the cottage.

A splash drew her attention, and she watched the man surface, flinching as he looked at her and grinned. Her body flooded with adrenaline, and Jessie crossed her arms over her chest as she hunched away from him, her heartbeat quickening, her breath becoming shallow.

Jessie focused on her breathing, elongating the inhale and slowing the exhale, to calm the panic taking over once more. Without looking back, she hurried towards the cottage, her hand shaking as she inserted the key into the rusty lock.

∞

Nate saw her watching him as he strode to the end of his jetty, ready for his daily swim. His mind registered surprise, but his body gave nothing away as he waved. He wasn't aware the cottage had been sold. Maybe he'd become complacent; it had been For Sale for a long time.

He stopped as an unfamiliar warmth flooded his chest. He pursed his lips and raised his eyebrows as he found the sale pleased him; the cottage deserved to be loved again by somebody. He could only do so much to stop it going completely wild.

'Dammit!' he grumbled, realising he'd need to change his morning routine now, as he didn't think the new owner of Bluebell Cottage would appreciate a naked man turning up every day to sunbathe on her lawn. *Or maybe she would?*

Nate grinned at the thought. Even if *she* didn't, he knew plenty who would fall over themselves for such a view.

He looked down at his tanned, muscular body and slapped his washboard stomach. Still, it took work to maintain his physique, especially given he had a "namby-pamby" job, as his mates liked to say.

Not so namby-pamby that it gives me all this. Nate turned to look at his large open-plan wood and glass home and the natural surroundings it nestled in. He shrugged, turned back to the lake, and dived in.

He surfaced to find the woman watching him again, and he smiled at her, almost choking at her reaction. He trod water, staring as she hurried to the cottage, her body almost foetal.

What the fuck? he thought, before changing direction. Nate swam the length of the lake, scouring the shore between strokes on the lookout for another sunbathing spot, curious to know if she would wonder who mowed her lawn.

Chapter 2

Jessie shoved open the oak door, the air inside whispering to her as it rushed to escape. She locked it behind her, her hand still shaking, and leaned back against it. She closed her eyes and took deep breaths to calm her still-racing heart.

This cannot be good for me!

Now somewhat composed, Jessie opened her eyes to see the disturbed dust swirling in the dappled sunlight. Steadying herself, she walked to the sink and turned on the tap, about to bend forward to splash her face, when the pipes groaned and she heard a rumbling in the depths of the cottage. Jessie stared at the dry tap, her breath held as she waited to see what would emerge. She yelped as the water burst into view, soaking her, before settling into a less pressured but, thankfully, clear flow.

As she splashed her face, Jessie considered her reactions to Ben and her new neighbour. Why had she…?

The car! her mind screamed, and she sighed.

Jessie searched for a towel, realising they were in one of the bags in her car, along with a multitude of hastily purchased paraphernalia she thought she would need.

She leaned against the sink, allowing the droplets to fall freely, gazing out across the now solitary lake.

She sighed and yawned, covering her mouth as her body sagged. All she wanted to do was crawl into bed and sleep; she was exhausted. But, as she turned to survey the kitchen before her, Jessie knew she had a lot of work to do before she could contemplate something as luxurious as sleep.

Jessie traced the toe of her shoe in the dust covering the floor, the quarry tiles peeking through as they had throughout the rest of the room, in the wake of the footsteps left by the movers.

Drag marks in the dust drew her gaze to the worn wooden dining table—a remnant of the cottage's past—with boxes containing some of her meagre possessions stacked on top. She glanced around to see a still-boxed microwave adrift on a counter, an uncovered fridge freezer, plugged in but homeless, and the requested washer-dryer snuggled into position. The packaging lay discarded beside the old Aga.

Please, please, Jessie prayed, kicking the cardboard and polythene out of the way as she approached the Aga, its gentle warmth surrounding her, her body relaxing as an image of wallowing in the claw-foot tub swam into her mind.

Drawn by the fantasy, Jessie climbed the stairs to the bathroom and peered over the edge of the tub to find a dark stain enhancing the plughole.

Nothing a good clean can't fix, she thought as she surveyed the rest of the room.

Jessie wandered through to the back bedroom, pleased to see the movers had left her bed and boxes of hastily salvaged clothes in there as requested, and gazed out of one of the picture windows.

She really was in the perfect place. Nothing but trees, the lake and Mother Nature.

And my naked neighbour… Jessie shifted her gaze to the surface of the lake but saw no sign of him. She watched his house for a while before looking down to her own lawn to make sure he hadn't decided to pay her a welcome visit. All was quiet, and Jessie smiled, allowing the tranquillity to finally wash through her.

She was safe. She was anonymous. She was home.

∞

Nate rested his palms against the granite tiles, allowing the hot water to cascade over his head and shoulders, drumming its beat into his tired muscles. He closed his eyes and turned; his face numbed by the jets; his mind on the woman across the lake.

He'd only seen her for a moment, yet the look on her face, the way she covered her body, had haunted him throughout his swim. No matter how many times he replayed it, he came to the same conclusion—her reactions were instinctive; she was afraid. But of him? *That* didn't make sense.

Nate turned off the shower, allowing himself to drip dry as he went in search of clean clothes. He needed to clear his mind of this mysterious stranger.

He hauled himself up the wrought-iron staircase two stairs at a time and plonked himself on his stool, a virgin canvas before him, awaiting instruction.

Nate grabbed a pencil and closed his eyes, conjuring the woman in his mind, his pencil dancing across the canvas. He captured the fear in her wide eyes, the panic in her creased forehead, the flight in her trembling hands, and the protection in her crossed arms. All he'd done was smile at her.

His pencil still, Nate opened his eyes and gazed upon the smoky image of his new neighbour.

'What are you afraid of, blondie?' he murmured as he pushed away from his easel and wandered over to the picture windows. The forlorn cottage across the lake was still.

Now he'd committed her to canvas, he'd purged his mind. He could focus on what he should be thinking about—pieces for his upcoming show. If he didn't get his act together and start painting, Em would skin him alive.

But try as he might, Nate couldn't focus, something enticing him back to the windows, hoping for another glimpse. Only once had Nate spent so much time thinking about one woman. He'd locked those memories away, never to be revisited.

Chapter 3

Jessie sat outside on a rickety chair she'd found in the broken-down garden shed, her feet up on a box she'd dragged outside, watching the sun igniting the evening sky as it bade farewell.

She sipped a glass of Malbec, holding the velvety wine in her mouth to savour the flavour. This simple pleasure was an indulgence she could now enjoy whenever she wanted.

Jessie's thoughts flicked back over the day, the first day of her supposedly putting the past behind her. So far, that hadn't happened. As she'd cleaned, scrubbed and disinfected a path to her bed, Jessie had pushed those thoughts away, the act of purging grime symbolic of her reason for coming to Potters Hole.

'How will I know I'm over it?' she'd asked her therapist, Dr Augur, a few months earlier.

'You'll never be over it, Jessie. What you've been through will be with you always, part of you.'

'Then why am I throwing money away coming here?'

'To learn to forgive yourself. To learn to understand that what happened wasn't your fault.'

'Of course it was. If I hadn't fallen for his charm... Ahh! I feel like I'm going around in circles!' Jessie said, jumping up and pacing the room.

'You're not. You've come a long way in the last two years, Jessie. Please stop beating yourself—'

'Then why can't I put it behind me? Why can't I chalk it up to bad judgement and move on?'

'Because he left you with more than just memories of a bad relationship. It will take time.'

'How much time?' she whispered, tugging down the cuffs of her shirt, a sob catching in her throat at Dr Augur's words.

'When you can forgive him, Jessie.'

'Are you serious? Forgive him? After what he did?'

Dr Augur looked at Jessie, and she squirmed; the chastised child unable to grasp basic information.

'All the while you feel, talk and behave like this…' Dr Augur paused, waving a hand towards Jessie as she continued to pace, '… you are giving away your power… to him.'

'What do you mean?' Jessie asked, dropping back into the chair and stilling herself.

'Who do you think you're affecting with your thoughts and behaviour?'

'Well… me… but—'

'And as long as you keep it up, he will continue to have power over you. When you stop allowing his actions to affect you, he'll lose his power.'

'But what has forgiveness got to do with that?'

'Think about it, Jessie. We can discuss it further next time.'

As it was, whilst she knew Dr Augur was right, Jessie still didn't know when, or even if, she could ever forgive him. Not after what he'd done.

Jessie sighed and leaned forward, dangling the wineglass by her fingertips as she watched the birds swooping towards the lake before disappearing to roost.

And yet it could have been so much worse. She swirled the Malbec. Maybe if it had been, her sister would have believed her.

Jessie stood, steadying herself as light-headedness washed through her. Perhaps two glasses were too much after so long. Shrugging, she picked her way along the jetty and sat down, submerging her feet in the coolness of the lake.

She stared across the water, her gaze resting on the house opposite. A light burned from the top floor, reminding her of a lighthouse. Jessie saw canvases stacked against the windows; an easel visible above them. At the easel perched her naturist neighbour, now clothed, a baseball cap turned backwards on his head. She smiled as she watched him twist his head back and forth, scrutinising what lay before him.

An artist, she mused, continuing to watch until he turned to face her. Jessie looked away quickly, the heat rising in her cheeks at being caught staring once more.

∞

The hairs on the back of Nate's neck had prickled to attention, and he'd shivered, turning to the twilight which lay beyond the windows of his studio.

As he squinted past his reflection, he saw her sitting on her jetty. She'd rolled her jeans up to her knees, revealing her slender legs, her feet immersed in the lake and a glass of wine in her hand.

Has she been watching me?

If she had, she no longer was. Her head was bowed, her dark blonde hair piled on top with loose tendrils twitching in the breeze. Her covered arms too were slender, and Nate wondered why she hid what he knew from experience would be an amazing body under such shapeless and baggy clothes?

Maybe it's just her moving outfit? Women were weird like that.

Nate shrugged and returned to the canvas before him, his second creation of the day almost complete.

'I need to know more,' he murmured, studying the oils before him as they formed a young woman standing on the shore of a crystal-clear lake, a dilapidated cottage behind her.

Nate turned back to the window. The jetty was empty. A light now burned inside the cottage. His enigmatic muse had vanished.

∞

Mellowed by the luxurious bath she'd dreamed of earlier, Jessie crawled under the new duvet, sinking into the softness of new pillows. She wrinkled her nose at the plastic smell of the bedding, which she hadn't had time to wash.

She stared through the bare windows into the inky night, her ears ringing in the silence.

Please let me sleep, she prayed as she closed her eyes and rolled onto her side, drawing her knees up into a position that had become all too familiar. Jessie allowed her body to release into the mattress as the first throes of slumber washed through her.

∞

'Get off me! Get away from me! I'll call the police this time! I swear I will! I'll—'

Jessie screamed, bolting upright and groping for the non-existent lamp. Her vision adjusting to the dark, her heart thundering against her ribs, Jessie stared around her bedroom. It was empty; she was alone.

She flopped back onto the bed, her fists releasing the duvet, her ragged breathing slowing. Jessie pushed her damp hair off her forehead and shivered, the sheen of sweat swathing her body turning frigid as she lay exposed to the darkness.

Jessie pulled the duvet around her and climbed off the bed. She had no idea of the time, her alarm clock languishing in a place unknown. She gazed out at the night sky, the moon's advancement showing she'd at least managed a few hours' sleep this time.

Better than none.

She looked back at the bed. Her one and only base sheet was soaked in the aftermath of her nightmare. Jessie hugged the duvet tight and went in search of somewhere else to rest. She knew from experience sleep would evade her for the rest of the night.

Chapter 4

As the days passed, Jessie's hours of sleep grew longer, her nightmares shorter. She didn't know if it was physical exhaustion, the fact her mind was consumed with other matters, or the tranquillity of her new surroundings. Whatever it was, she didn't care; she was grateful.

Jessie threw herself into bringing Bluebell Cottage back to life. She scrubbed away years of grease and grime to discover pastel-coloured walls, wiped oily tears from the windows to make them sparkle once more and bleached porcelain to see it regain its youth. Tearing up rotten carpets, she discovered stained and forlorn oak floors, their years of neglect disappearing as ideas danced before her. She chased dust bunnies from the corners of rooms and lost count of the spiders she re-homed as she untangled cobwebs from the brass light fittings, polishing them until they beamed.

With the filthiest jobs done, Jessie finished by washing the years of dirt from the floors and wiping what seemed like decades of dust from the surfaces, ridding, she hoped, the cottage of the mildewed smell of abandonment.

I wonder if I have a special scent. Jessie shuddered at the thought, contemplating what it might be, given everything she'd been through.

Having purged Bluebell Cottage of disuse, Jessie set about fixing shelves in the kitchen, rehanging cupboard doors, oiling the hinges of the ledge and brace doors, and suspending fallen and empty curtain poles. The bigger jobs, of which she clocked up quite a few, could wait. There was no rush, not anymore. The important thing was to create a home for herself, a sanctuary that was hers and hers alone.

Cleaning and repairing done, Jessie began to unpack her meagre possessions and dot them around her new home. It filled her with pride that she'd disobeyed him and had kept some of her beautiful things in storage—those he hadn't destroyed, at least.

Walking from room to room, Jessie settled souvenirs from her travels. The marble pyramid, which marked her diving debut in the Red Sea, found its home in the living room; the boomerang, a reminder of her surprise at the bristly koala and the downy kangaroo, she positioned in her bedroom; a forlorn shelf in the kitchen provided the perfect home for the beer stein she'd haggled for at a Berlin antiques market; and the African tribal mask guarded the stairs. Jessie smiled as she caressed them, the memories vivid and alive. Happier times.

Most of the boxes remained packed as they contained her vast collection of books, and until she had some suitable bookcases, Jessie felt it best to leave them nestled in their cocoons.

On her trips abroad, Jessie had always sought local artists, learning of their inspirations and bringing home a unique work to memorialise the city she'd visited. In each room Jessie hung these memories—of Dubrovnik before the ravages of war, of Notre Dame in its untouched splendour, of Venetian canals in quieter times and of the World Trade Centre standing tall and proud against the New York skyline.

To finish her décor, she placed a vase of flowers from her garden in the living room, invigorating the cottage with their mingling perfumes.

She smiled as she looked around at the home she'd finally created.

∞

Across the lake, Nate was making some adjustments of his own, one of which he wasn't entirely happy about.

To give the broken woman across the lake a chance to heal, Nate decided to forego his daily swim, sensing his presence was the last thing she needed.

But how do I know she's broken?

Nate had pondered this for hours as he sat in his studio, watching the activity across the lake, the realisation dawning as time wore on—it exuded from her in waves.

It made him squirm, doing what he did, but he couldn't stop; he didn't want to stop. He knew most people would call what he was doing spying, or even stalking, but Nate didn't care.

In his view, he wasn't spying on her; he was protecting her, keeping an eye out to make sure she was okay.

This desire to protect, coupled with a yearning for more than simply watching her, shocked Nate. As far as women were concerned, he didn't have thoughts and feelings. Women were there to enjoy, to have fun with, to play with, to sleep with, but never to think about, obsess about, care about, and now spy on.

Protectiveness meant attachment, and attachment meant

rejection. Once had been enough, and as long ago as it was, it had left its mark on Nate.

So, what is it about this woman?

His thoughts shifted to his mother, who he knew would be over the moon at the turmoil this stranger had evoked in her son.

Nate knew his behaviour caused his parents a great deal of sadness, especially his mother, and he felt the twinge of guilt he usually reserved for when she enquired as to the likelihood of grandchildren. He bristled whenever she mentioned this; his guilt pushed aside as his walls shot up and his heart closed down. Not wanting to upset her further, Nate would kiss her on the forehead and walk away.

Nate loved his solitary life and had no desire to change it. That was, until he'd spied the new occupant of Bluebell Cottage.

Chapter 5

With the interior of the cottage finished, or as complete as it could be without professional help, Jessie turned her attention to the garden. In a little over a week, she would be re-entering the workforce, and the thought of coming home to a pretty and tidy garden generated a warm glow.

She carried her mug of coffee outside, ready to sit and contemplate for a while, when her gaze fell upon the empty box she was still using to rest her feet on, or balance a glass of wine on, as tended to be the case.

There must be a table of some sort in that shed, she reasoned. Chairs always came with a table, just like a knife accompanied a fork; some things simply worked better together.

Sure enough, shrouded in a dusty cloth, Jessie found a wobbly table to accompany her rickety chairs. The square of slabs outside the cottage's door became her patio.

Jessie rescued her mug and refilled it before settling down on her reclaimed garden furniture. She closed her eyes and leaned her head back, allowing the sunshine to warm her pale skin.

The musical birdsong, the breeze whispering through the trees, the water lapping the shore, and the perfumes from her yet to be tamed garden filled Jessie with a sense of peace, suffusing her with warmth and unfamiliar happiness.

She sipped her coffee, savouring the bitterness and tuning into the bees buzzing around the budding wisteria above her, moulding her body to the chair as she listened.

'Meow.'

Jessie bolted upright at the incongruous sound and stared around her, her heart slamming in her chest. Picking up nothing further, she settled back, unsure if she'd imagined it.

'Meoooww!'

There was no mistaking the drawn out call this time, and she snapped round towards the wood, her gaze scouring the shadowed treeline, searching for the ball of fur that accompanied the call.

'Meow!' the cat screeched again.

She jumped at the urgency, her gaze finally settling on a young black cat observing her from the edge of her wood. She let go of the breath she'd been holding and laughed, her body relaxing once more.

'Well, hello there, little one,' Jessie said as she set her mug down and pushed out of her chair, smiling at the source of the summons.

'Come here then,' she called, crouching down and extending her arm, rubbing her fingers together to entice the stranger. The cat didn't budge, instead continuing to watch her through its slitted green eyes.

'Come on, little one. You're the one who said hello, remember,' she persisted and, keeping her body low and less threatening, Jessie took a step closer. In response, the cat yawned and stretched before taking off into the wood.

Jessie laughed as she uncurled herself. It reminded her of Fudge, her best friend from childhood.

'So, that's your game, is it?' she called, remembering how Fudge had loved to play hide and seek.

Jessie headed after the cat, but stopped, her skin prickling as a dark cloud wiped the joy from her face. She allowed the memory its moment, as her therapist had advised, before shaking away the gloom and following the cat, curious to know where it was going.

As she picked her way along an overgrown track, Jessie thrilled in the abundance of wildflowers flourishing beneath the canopy of trees. A short way into the wood, the track opened out and Jessie discovered a summer house, its paintwork peeling, its roof patchwork.

She followed the path to the front and stepped up onto the deck, its boards groaning in welcome. Two rotting wicker chairs faced the lake, their once sumptuous cushions threadbare yet inviting.

Jessie gasped as she looked out over the lake. The view took her breath away; any occupants of the wicker chairs would seem to be the only people for miles around.

This is perfect, she thought, turning back to the summer house. *Or it will be.*

She surveyed the windows, open and welcoming to all when not showing off the dazzling lake. The door was resolutely closed. Jessie crouched down to peer inside. Two green saucers stared back.

'So, this is where you live, is it?' she crooned, her gaze

taking in the dried leaves piled in a corner, bones and half-masticated rodents in another. 'This won't do, will it?'

The cat blinked before turning away and settling down on its bed of leaves.

'That's no way to treat a guest!' But her affront softened, and she smiled at the rise and fall of black fur, before retracing her steps, mentally adding the summer house to her list of repairs.

Back at the cottage, Jessie searched her cupboards until she found an old saucer left behind by a former tenant and emptied the contents of a tin of tuna onto it, mashing it up, releasing its aroma.

She hurried back to the summer house and placed the saucer inside, stirring the contents, hoping to entice the cat. No such luck. The cat merely lifted its head, reaching its nose high as it inhaled, before yawning and settling back down again.

'Have it your way,' Jessie said, 'but I will win you over… eventually.'

∞

Each day, while Jessie sat outside savouring her morning coffee, she heard the familiar call of her feline visitor.

'Good morning, and what have you got planned for the day?' she would ask, turning to the cat. A yawn and a green-eyed blink would be the response before the cat disappeared back into the wood.

And each day, Jessie filled a saucer with tuna, luring the cat, one meal at a time, towards the cottage. Finally, four days after their initial introduction, the cat seemed in no rush to leave after its morning greeting. Jessie noticed it had ventured away from the wood and was sitting much closer to her, although still far enough away to ensure an ample head start.

'Are you coming to help me at last?' she asked as the cat cleaned unseen grime from its face. It stopped and looked from Jessie to the garden and then back at her.

'Yes, with the garden, where I've been working my butt off, as you well know.' Jessie pushed herself up and stretched, the cat assuming its usual bolt position, but staying put.

'After you,' she said, gesturing for the cat to go first. It stood and stretched—the copycat movement making Jessie smile—before sauntering towards the walled-in garden.

Jessie followed, wondering if the cat really had understood her, when it changed course, flopping in a patch of sunlight with a clear view of the garden.

'Ah, so that's how it's going to be, is it? Happy to watch but not get your paws dirty?'

The cat eyed her lazily before yawning and snuggling down to sleep.

Jessie shook her head and smiled as she pulled on her gardening gloves, picking up where she'd left off the previous day.

She spent the morning finishing weeding and turning over the last flower bed, carrying the waste to a makeshift compost bin she'd started a few days before. As she worked, Jessie kept an eye on the cat as it tracked the movement of the sun, content to be in her distant company.

My first friend. The thought ignited a warm glow inside her, and memories of Fudge curled up on her knee flooded her mind.

Now finished, Jessie stood back, hands on hips, and surveyed the finished result.

'What do you think?'

At the sound of her voice, the cat lifted its head and looked at her.

'Not me, the garden.' She pointed to the treasure trove she'd discovered as she hacked, cleared, pruned and weeded.

The cat blinked, yawned, and then, to Jessie's amazement, stood and peered over the low wall. It emitted a low grumble, circled a few times, and settled back down.

'I'll take that as approval,' she said, then laughed before turning back to study the spoils of her hard work.

Stone pots and ornaments of all shapes and sizes, and a beautiful stone bird bath, had shyly greeted her over the last few days, but it was the antiquated sundial she'd fallen instantly in love with, checking its position to ensure it still reflected the time. Together with the plants, shrubs, fruit trees and flowers she'd unveiled, her garden was no longer the investment she'd worried over.

'A couple of strategically placed benches to catch the sun, and I can have your life,' she said to the cat, but her comment elicited no response.

'And some veggies,' Jessie continued as she wandered the stone paths.

Her stomach grumbled, and she glanced at the sundial to see the afternoon was marching on.

'Fancy some lunch?' she asked as she walked out of the garden. In a flash, the cat was awake, alert and retreating towards the wood.

∞

Pleased with her progress, Jessie decided to relax for the rest of the day. The sun was high, the day warm, and as she rinsed her mug and plate, she watched the branches of the cherry tree rising and falling on the breeze.

Nodding, Jessie dried her hands and headed to the only room she hadn't decided what to do with. It was too small to be anything significant, like a snug or a dining room, but it was too big to be used for storage, which was its current use, housing the multitude of boxes containing her collection of books. It also had a front-row seat to her freshly tended garden, which wrapped around the side of the cottage. Jessie felt it deserved a more appropriate use.

Opening a box at random, she pulled out a childhood memory and, making herself a glass of blackcurrant to match, she headed outside for a few hours under the cherry tree with Darrell Rivers, as she navigated her first term at Malory Towers.

'Meow.'

Jessie jolted out of the water, where Darrell was rescuing Mary Lou from Gwen's clutches, and looked towards the cottage. She smiled as she saw the cat licking its lips after devouring the latest offering.

'Come on, I've saved you a spot,' she said, patting the lawn beside her, which the sun highlighted through the branches.

The cat considered her invitation but didn't move, instead cleaning its face again.

'Your loss.' Jessie shrugged and returned to the feuding schoolgirls.

A short time later, engrossed in her book, Jessie felt a

presence and looked up to see the cat had settled down beside her. She resisted the urge to reach out and stroke it, sensing the terms of their friendship were not hers to set. Instead, she relaxed against the trunk of the tree, the cat snoring beside her, and returned to Malory Towers.

∞

When Jessie headed back to the cottage a few hours later, the cat, rather than bolting for the trees, followed her, sitting in the open doorway, its gaze boring into her as she busied herself preparing her dinner.

'Hungry again, are you?'

Jessie placed a dish of tuna further inside the kitchen, making a mental note to get some cat food. After a few moments' hesitation, the cat licked its lips and came forward, devouring the tuna in four mouthfuls.

The cat made no move to leave, hovering as Jessie ate, a soft purr resonating from it as it watched her every move.

'Would you like to stay?'

The cat blinked in response and edged a little closer.

'You'll need a bed, won't you?'

Looking around the kitchen, Jessie spotted some empty boxes and a stack of old towels she'd used for wrapping. Moving carefully, so as not to scare the cat away, she made a bed for it and placed it near the door.

As Jessie pushed the door closed, ready to lock up for the night, the cat growled, its hackles alert to the threat.

Jessie hesitated for a moment, adrenaline flooding her body at the cat's complaint. She closed her eyes and focused on her breathing, ordering her mind to take control of her body.

Calm again, she unlatched the door, pulling it ajar, expecting the cat to dart out, but it didn't. Instead, it sniffed around the makeshift bed before climbing in and lying down.

The next morning when Jessie awoke, the cat was curled up at her feet, a fluffy black ball nestled on a snowy bed.

'Cole,' she murmured as she watched the cat sleep. 'That's what I'll call you.'

Chapter 6

Jessie glanced behind her as she carried the last of the rusty but functional gardening tools back to the shed, smiling to see Cole ambling along behind her. It had been like this all day, almost as if it was afraid she would disappear.

At lunchtime, she'd coaxed Cole to come close enough to be touched, which it allowed without a flinch. But when she picked it up, Cole's claws and teeth came into play, with Jessie coming off the worst.

She looked at the scratches on her hands. The swelling had subsided after a dose of antihistamine. Cole had vanished after that, but it wasn't long before it skulked back and resumed its shadowing.

Jessie closed the shed and wiped the back of her hand across her sweaty forehead, fanning the shirt away from her body to cool down. Her gaze strayed to the shimmering water of the lake, and she bit down on her bottom lip. *Could I?*

She looked across the lake. All seemed quiet, just as it had been for days. In fact, Jessie couldn't remember seeing any sign of her new neighbour since the day she'd moved in, not that she'd been looking.

'Oh, who am I kidding?' she said to Cole, who sat out of

harm's way, looking back at her.

Jessie's mind drifted to the sight of her naked neighbour striding along his jetty, and she felt her skin prickle as heat flooded her base. She shuddered, pushing the image away, shutting the feelings down. She wasn't looking to get entangled with a man again… ever.

Jessie stalked back to the cottage, filling a glass with cold water, hoping that would be enough. But as she drank, the sun beating down, the lake drew her once more.

She studied the house opposite, fixing on each window, but she saw no movement, no sign of habitation. *Where is he?*

As the seed of solitude took root, Jessie gazed back at the lake, assessing the risk versus reward of experiencing the cool, clear waters for herself.

A few minutes later, her mind made up, she ducked back inside the cottage.

∞

It was a conundrum Nate could not wrap his head around. Why had seeing her ankle deep in the lake that first day jolted him, revealing a chink in his carefully maintained armour? It had kept him tied to the house, never wanting to leave in case he missed something.

He shook his head as he looked around his studio, at the canvases stacked deep against the windows. If anyone came up and saw them, only one word would jump to their minds.

'You're a stalker, Natey boy,' he said, but his whole being screamed out against the word he'd finally said out loud—No!

Nate's ears seemed to pop, and a hollowness preceded the

unveiling of a truth he'd never believed, especially not for him.

'The old bastard was right. I've finally found my muse,' he whispered as he stared at Bluebell Cottage, his mind taking him back to over a decade ago.

Not wanting to go to art school, Nate had won the battle with his parents and bummed his way through Europe, educating himself in the *real* world of art.

He'd met and studied with many painters, but only one had ever talked about a muse. Javier de Santos must have been in his seventies, given his white hair held back by a leather thong, his luminous rheumy eyes and the deep creases in his tanned face, but his enthusiasm and vitality belonged to a much younger man.

'Why do you always paint the same woman?' Nate asked.

Javier shrugged, the corners of his mouth turning down in a Robert De Niro "what you gonna do" expression. 'I have not painted her all the time.'

Nate frowned and spread his arms, indicating the single subject adorning Javier's studio.

'Ah, yes, but before Sofia, I painted many things. Yet, alas, no matter the subject, nothing brought the need to paint until the night I saw her.'

Nate watched as Javier's gaze looked beyond the walls of his studio, to a time gone by. Tears rimmed his dark eyes. Nate cleared his throat, jolting the old man back to the present.

'So, why her? Why Sofia? What was… is so special about her?'

'Was, I am sad to say.' Javier smiled sadly and patted Nate's hand. 'She was my muse.'

'Your what?'

'My muse. My inspiration. My reason to paint.'

'But you painted before her.'

'I did, but not as well. All artists spend their lives searching for their muse. Some are lucky enough to find it, others not so much. Still more give up long before.'

'How will I know if I find mine?'

'You will know. If painting is truly the desire of your heart, you will find yours, and when you do, ahh…' Javier broke off, turning in circles, his arms wide, '… like me, it will be a tap you can no longer turn off. You will not be able to paint fast enough!'

Nate remembered laughing at what the old artist said, not taking him seriously, but now…?

Again, Nate looked around his studio, proof the guy had been right—he couldn't paint fast enough.

Each canvas was part-complete, the images and ideas coming too quickly for him to finish anything. An outline of her body, a silhouette, a tear forming in the corner of her eye, a rare smile, a faraway look. All he could do was capture the essence; the rest would come when he had time.

And when will that be? Maybe when he stopped spying on her! But the thought turned him cold. He was addicted, and the thought of giving her up… well, it was something Nate refused to contemplate.

Chapter 7

Jessie stood before the antique mottled mirror, the unworn swimsuit vibrant against her ashen complexion. She traced her fingertips across her puckered skin, the angriness still visible, though dimming. A memory pushed forward.

'What've you bought that for?' he'd snapped when she held up the navy swimsuit, the hot pink edging having drawn her.

'F-for beside the pool. It'll be hot.'

'You're not going to the pool dressed in that!'

'B-but why not? Th-this is how everyone—'

'And I won't have everyone staring at my wife! You'll wear what I tell you.'

'B-but I—'

'But nothing. Give me that!'

He'd snatched the costume out of her hand and thrown it in the rubbish.

A moment later he'd struck her cheek, dazing her. Jessie danced her fingertips across the memory. Shivering, she pulled a robe around herself and peered out at the water shimmering below.

Is this a good idea?

She looked at the wood and glass house again, staring at the top floor where she'd last seen him, but the easel stood alone.

Taking a deep breath, Jessie padded outside and picked her way along the jetty. She sat on the edge and eased her feet into the lake, shuddering as the cold water sent goosebumps rippling across her skin.

Jessie untied her robe, slipping from it and into the water in one smooth movement. She gasped as the icy temperature took her breath away, before kicking her legs and settling into a gentle freestyle, her body acclimatising as she cut through the water.

Her heart pounding at the unaccustomed exertion, Jessie slowed and rolled onto her back, floating as the sun warmed her body and the fish nibbled her fingertips.

Jessie saw Cole perched on the end of the jetty and smiled. The cat scanned the lake, its green gaze resting on the house opposite before sweeping back to her, and then repeating the cycle.

Feeling protected by Cole's watchfulness, Jessie closed her eyes. Her mind wandered to the following day, and a pang of sadness jockeyed for position with the bubbles of excitement.

When she'd met him, Jessie had been Deputy Head of her local primary school, on course to becoming Head Teacher. But as their relationship intensified, her hopes and dreams had yielded to him. Now, she was about to take a step back to doing something she loved.

'The only vacancy I have is for a teaching assistant,' Bev Parker, Head Teacher at Potters Hole primary school, had told her almost as soon as she'd sat down.

'I know,' Jessie had responded, smiling at the older woman.

'But Jessie, you're much too over-qualified. Hell, you should be vying for my job!'

'Yes, I know, but I've been away from teaching for so long, I…'

Bev glanced at Jessie's CV. 'Ten years, it would seem.'

'Yes.' Jessie looked at her hands and swallowed the memories, hoping they wouldn't make themselves known. 'I can't expect to pick up where I left off. I know that. And, if I'm honest, I don't want to.' She looked Bev in the eye as she spoke. Bev held her gaze for a moment and nodded.

'Okay then. Well, the job is yours if you want it?'

'Really? Yes, yes, yes. That's fantastic! Thank you,' Jessie said, fighting the urge to jump up and hug Bev.

'Just for the record, though,' Bev said, and Jessie sobered at the stiff look on Bev's face.

'Yes,' Jessie almost whispered.

'I'm not planning on going anywhere anytime soon.'

The statement hung in the air. Jessie didn't know how to respond, but then Bev's features softened, and she grinned.

'But when I do, Jessie, I have a feeling this place would be in safe hands with you.'

Bev stood, and Jessie followed suit, thrusting out her hand.

'Thank you so much, Mrs Parker. You don't know what this means to me.'

'It's Bev,' she said, waving Jessie's hand away and hugging her, before stepping back and holding Jessie at arm's length as she studied her. 'And, I think I do.'

Jessie remembered the understanding look in the older woman's eyes and how she hadn't pressed her on the reason for her decade-long absence.

Maybe I have more than Cole as a friend, she thought, gazing at Bluebell Cottage from her watery vantage point. She would miss the alone time she'd become used to over the past few weeks, but it was time she introduced herself into Potters Hole society.

∞

As he watched her slip out of her robe and into the water, the swiftness revealing her self-consciousness, for the first time in a fortnight Nate felt like a Peeping Tom. But, it wasn't the feeling of nausea the thought brought with it that disturbed him the most, it was the vulnerability she'd revealed in that moment; his heart ached for her.

Never, not since meeting his birth mother when he was a child, had any woman evoked such emotion in him. Yet this stranger, whom he'd yet to meet, had.

Ever since the night he'd captured her staring out of the window, the images had poured from Nate like blood from an open wound.

The phone echoed from the living space downstairs, and Nate pulled his mobile from his pocket to see a string of missed calls and voicemails. He winced as the answering machine kicked in and Em's taut voice hissed through the air.

'Where the fuck are you? We're in the middle of planning a show and you go fucking AWOL! You better have a damn good excuse, Nate. Now call me back, or I *will* come and find you, rules or not!'

He jumped as she slammed the phone down, in no doubt she would carry out her threat if he didn't check in soon; he couldn't have that.

No one was allowed to visit him at home, not even his parents. The Lake House, the unimaginative monocle for his home, was his private space, and everyone respected that, except Em. Em was a law unto herself.

At least she'll be pleased I've been painting.

Or he hoped she would be, praying his productive spurt would somewhat mollify her anger about his lack of communication.

It certainly wasn't uncommon for Nate to go off the grid, but he usually agreed on a set period. This time he'd just gone on radio silence.

Em was right, though; they had a show to organise, one he'd been excited about until a few of weeks ago.

Now, all Nate could think about was the willowy blonde across the lake, and all he could paint was her. He was especially captivated by the time and effort she'd taken to befriend the black cat.

Nate knew where it came from—Greyling Farm—but he'd never known one roam so far. He could see it was little more than a kitten, so maybe it had got lost.

A lost soul seeking a lost soul, he thought as he looked at his latest creation of her with the cat on her knee. Nate laughed, as a few seconds after he witnessed that huge step, she screamed as the cat fought for its life, before charging off into the wood.

He captured her whenever she set foot outside the cottage: having coffee or wine, when she was clean or grubby, gardening, enticing the cat, walking wistfully across the lawn to the water, sitting under the cherry tree reading, the cat curled beside her, and sitting on the jetty with her feet stirring the lake.

Nate leaned against a pillar in his studio and looked out at the lake, seeing her floating on her back, her hair fanning in the water. He allowed his gaze to travel along her slender legs as she gently kicked the water, her knees breaching a steady rhythm, her arms distorted by the water as they danced beside her.

He shuddered as desire raced through him, and he turned away, pressing his back against the pillar. Nate closed his eyes and focused on his breathing, fighting to calm the rush of blood through his veins. He had to snap out of this obsession, or whatever had settled over him. He needed to get back to his life.

He grabbed his mobile and searched for the number.

'Em, it's me.'

'Well, wonders never fucking cease! Where the hell have you been? Don't you know we have a show—?'

Nate tuned out, and pictured Emily Nicholls, feet planted wide, free hand gesticulating as she tore strips off him. At five foot nothing, Em was a force to be reckoned with, and the only woman he'd come across immune to his charms. That's why they got on so well. Em called it how it was, Nate included, and he loved her for it.

'I've been working, Em, I promise,' he said when she finally ran out of steam.

'Working on pieces for this show, I hope?'

'Not exactly.'

'What the—?'

'Em, let me finish. They are pieces for a show, just not this show, and I promise you, you will love them.'

'When can I see them?'

Nate smiled at the excitement in her voice. Sometimes he thought she loved his work more than he did. At least he'd averted her wrath, which was always a good thing.

'Not until they're finished, you know the rules, and…'

'And what?'

'And I get permission.'

'What? Why would you need permission?'

'I kinda found my muse, Em,' Nate said, and waited for her squeal of excitement; it didn't come.

'I'm sensing a but?' Em said instead.

'She kinda doesn't know I painted her.'

'What do you mean "kinda"? She either does or she doesn't.'

'Okay then, she doesn't.'

'Nate!'

'I know, I know, but it's not as bad as it sounds, I promise.'

'What? So, you haven't been watching this girl without her knowledge and then painting her?'

'Well, when you put it like that… Look, it'll be fine, I promise. I'll see you tomorrow. We'll plan the show. Bye.'

Nate ended the call before Em launched into a lecture about invasion of privacy, or some other lawsuit she thought he would open himself up to.

Then, for the first time in two weeks, Nate left the house. He went for a run. He needed to clear his head.

Blank Canvas

Chapter 8

Jessie scrutinised her appearance, turning from side to side. She'd decided on loose-fitting navy trousers, a long-sleeved, high-necked cream blouse—to hide the scars on her collarbone and arms—and navy court shoes. She'd then piled her blonde hair on top of her head and applied light make-up.

I look, well, nondescript, she decided, which was what she was going for. She didn't want to stand out and be noticed; she wanted to blend in.

'What do you think, bud?' She turned to Cole, who'd allowed her a cuddle the previous night—albeit grudgingly—and revealed himself to be a boy.

Cole stared at Jessie before blinking his green eyes and commencing his morning grooming.

'As good as that, hey?' Jessie picked up the cat and buried her face in his fur. He grumbled at the interruption, so she deposited him back onto her bed before he added a slash of red to her outfit.

'Wish me luck.'

∞

Waves of nausea prevented Jessie from stepping out of the

car—she didn't want vomiting on her first day to follow her around for the next six years. From her seat she stared at the cheerful edifice of Potters Hole Primary School.

'Argh!' Her hand flew to her mouth as a sharp rap on her window broke through her thoughts.

Jessie turned to see Bev Parker bent down, a concerned look on her face, and she forced a smile, pressing her hands into her lap to stop them shaking.

'Oh my God, Jessie, I'm so sorry. I didn't mean to scare you,' Bev blustered when Jessie buzzed down the window.

'No, no, don't be silly. I was miles away, that's all.'

'First day nerves?' Bev nodded and stood back to let Jessie out of the car.

'Something like that.'

'Would an escort into the building help calm you?' Bev said, smiling at Jessie.

'Do you know what, Bev? It just might,' she replied, and both women smiled.

As she retrieved her briefcase from the back seat, Jessie observed Bev. Dressed in a black business suit, Bev Parker was roughly Jessie's height and looked the part of a scary headteacher, but Jessie knew differently. If Bev showed the kids as much compassion as she'd shown Jessie in the short time they'd known each other, Jessie had no doubt she was a hit with them… and their parents.

'Ready?'

Taking a deep breath and locking the car, Jessie nodded, before the two women walked towards the school building.

'I'm covering for one of my teachers who's on maternity leave, until I can get a reliable substitute, and thought you might like to assist me?'

Jessie stopped walking, her insides tensing. 'What, so you can keep an eye on me?' she blurted before she could stop herself.

'Of course not. Why ever would you think that?' Bev faced Jessie, frowning.

Heat flooded Jessie's cheeks, and she stared at her feet before looking back up at Bev. 'I'm so sorry, Bev. I didn't mean it to come out like that. I just…'

Bev took Jessie's hand, squeezed it, and smiled. 'It's fine, you have nothing to apologise for. You're safe here, Jessie. I hope you know that?'

Jessie looked into Bev's eyes and felt tears fill her own.

'Come here,' Bev said, and pulled Jessie into her arms. 'I thought you'd like a familiar face while you settled in, that's all. You have nothing to prove to me. Your CV is tantamount to that.'

Jessie closed her eyes as she hugged Bev back, trying to prevent tears from spilling and ruining her make-up. The scent of jasmine reminded Jessie of her mother, and her heart ached. Not wanting fresh tears to well up, she pulled away and smiled at Bev.

'Ready?' Bev repeated.

'Ready.'

The two women walked arm in arm into the school.

Chapter 9

Nate was up before dawn the following day, wanting to get on the road before his resolve crumbled. The other advantage of being up and out early was avoiding the rush hour, a necessary pitfall of having his gallery in the city. The benefit was a steady stream of customers only too happy to part with their cash.

Setting up the gallery had been his father's idea. Ray took great pride in being the Potters Hole doctor, with his name above the door, and he wanted something similar for his adopted son. He felt it would be a way for Nate to prove to the world he was somebody, that he was worthy. Bev, of course, had been outraged by Ray's clumsy way of explaining it to their son, but Nate had understood. Not being worthy was an issue he'd struggled with all his life, exacerbated when his birth mother had rejected him a second time.

To a certain extent, his father was right. Seeing "The Nathaniel Parker Gallery" filled Nate with a sense of pride and achievement every time, as did being widely sought after for his art, but it wasn't the all-encompassing cure Ray had hoped for.

The double rejection by his birth mother had cut deep, and it was one thing Nate knew for certain he never wanted to feel again. As such, he avoided romantic entanglement at all costs.

Love 'em and leave 'em was his philosophy, and it had served him well… until now.

Nate pushed all thoughts of his muse to one side, as thinking of her defeated the object of coming into the city.

He parked in the vacant car park behind the gallery, pleased the place would be empty and knowing how annoyed Em would be he'd beaten her in.

Nate grinned as he set Em's Americano on the counter, remembering her response when he'd asked what coffee she'd like at her interview.

'I like my coffee how I like my men,' she'd said, with no further explanation. He hadn't understood, until she introduced him to her partner Chase, and Nate had howled with laughter.

He heard the gallery door swoosh shut; the air seemed to fizz, making Nate shiver. *Em.* He turned to greet her, his arms outstretched and a useless disarming smile on his face. He braced himself for the onslaught.

With dyed black hair cropped close to her head, blood-red lips and nails, and an hourglass figure, Em reminded Nate of Betty Boop… with an attitude.

He held his arms up in front of his face, and pretended he was dying from the bullets she was firing at him, until she broke into laughter and punched him in the arm.

'Bloody hell, Em, that hurt!' Nate grumbled, rubbing his dead arm to get some life back into it.

'Serves you right for going AWOL on me. Believe me when I say I'd take great pleasure in doing far worse, but it is your talent that keeps the punters coming in, not mine. Mind you, what is it they say about the work of dead artists?'

'Gee, thanks, Em, missed you too.'

'Well, you wouldn't have to miss me if you showed up like you're supposed to.'

'Whoa! It's not like I've been swanning off around the world. I have been working, you know.'

'Ah yes, your new occupation as a stalker. How's that working out for you?' Em fixed him with one of her stares, which seemed to bore straight through him.

Nate looked at the floor and kicked the toe of his shoe against the tiles.

'I see, so you still haven't spoken to her then?' Em watched him over the top of her Americano.

'Of course I haven't. I only spoke to *you* last night, then I went to bed, got up early and came in here, as promised.'

'Hmmm,' Em replied and turned her back on him. 'You do realise being a Peeping Tom is a felony, don't you, and you can't use any of the paintings without her permission? I'm assuming you have several paintings?'

Nate rolled his eyes. 'You said all this last night, remember?'

'Not the felony part.' Em spun around, her index finger extended to emphasise her point.

'I get the message. Permission needed. Understood. But, Em, you're missing the excitement of it all… I found my muse! I never believed such a thing existed, but I've found mine.' He whooped and grabbed Em's coffee, depositing it on the counter before whirling her around, laughing.

'Okay, okay, you've made your point,' Em said, and

laughed. 'You can put me down now.'

Nate wasn't listening, lost in thoughts of his new neighbour and the stack of paintings she'd inspired.

'Now, Nate!'

'Sorry, sorry,' Nate said and set Em back on her feet, both grabbing the counter to steady themselves. 'I've just never been this compelled to paint before. The images come so fast, I have to get as much down as I can, and then go on to the next.'

'And how many of these part-finished paintings do you have?' Em asked, frowning.

Nate shrugged. 'I don't know. Twenty. Thirty. More than enough for a show.'

'They have to be finished for that.'

'I know, I know.'

'When? When are you going to finish them? You still have pieces to do for the show we're supposed to be having. How are you going to do that if your head is full of this bloody woman?'

Nate watched Em fold her arms over her ample chest and pout, a move which usually got him to do her bidding.

'Have no fear, fair maiden, our show is not in jeopardy. That's why I'm here, to get ready for *that* very show. I have no plans to leave until I've completed every piece.'

'Great! Just what I need, you cluttering the place up.'

'Ouch!' Nate said and blew her a kiss before disappearing upstairs to his studio.

∞

If he was honest, Nate was grateful for the distraction. Hiding away in his studio, painting additional pieces for a show, was where he was comfortable. That was his normal. Despite Em haranguing him about still painting, sometimes up to a few days before a show opened, it was how he'd always produced some of his best work—last minute and under pressure.

A feverish compulsion to record every look, every movement, every smile, every tear… *that* he wasn't used to, and as much as he didn't want to stop, it made him uncomfortable. It was different; it was new, and change was something Nate took time to adjust to.

Losing himself in a world away from the haunting stranger across the water was the best idea, especially if he wanted to keep Em off his back. Maybe the distraction would break the spell, or whatever it was, she'd cast over him.

Chapter 10

The day whizzed by and Jessie was all smiles as she collapsed into a chair in Bev's office once all the kids had left.

As soon as they'd got inside, Bev had showed Jessie around before they both headed to the morning staff meeting. Here Jessie met her colleagues and soon felt part of the team as they discussed the stars and the problems, the pushy parents and the ones who couldn't care less.

'It's like I've never been away,' Jessie said as she accepted a mug of coffee from Bev.

'Well, the children certainly took to you,' Bev said, smiling as she settled into a chair opposite Jessie.

'That's the great thing when they're this age, and they're a fantastic class!'

'Yes, well, you know from this morning that doesn't apply to every class.'

Jessie nodded and sipped her coffee, unable to stop grinning.

'I have to say, Jessie, you are very at ease with the children. Are you sure you've had a ten-year break?'

Bev laughed, so Jessie knew it wasn't a question about her honesty. Still, she couldn't stop the clouds from the past smothering her happiness, even if only for a moment.

'I didn't realise how much I've missed it all, to be honest,' she replied, not looking at Bev.

'Well, hopefully those nerves will keep away now. What're your plans for this evening? Would you like to come for dinner, to celebrate a successful first day?'

Jessie was aware she was shaking her head before she answered. 'I can't. I have an appointment at the vet for Cole.'

'I told you Randall would be only too happy for you to keep him.'

Bev had called Greyling Farm earlier to ask about the cat. Randall Greyling hadn't noticed he was a cat down and was pleased he'd found a home.

'I don't know what I'd have done if he'd said no. I've got used to having him around. Although he may leave after his vet's visit,' Jessie said, then chuckled.

'You could come by later. I could warm a plate for you?'

'Thanks, Bev, I really appreciate it, but I have a feeling I'll be grovelling to a four-legged ball of angry fur later. Another time?'

'Of course. You're welcome whenever you're ready,' Bev said, raising her eyebrows.

Jessie was about to protest that she really did have plans, but decided to leave it. Bev seemed to understand far more than Jessie had shared.

∞

Jessie was not wrong about Cole. When she collected him a few hours later, having been neutered, de-flead, micro-chipped, and thoroughly checked over, Cole sulked all the way home, growling each time Jessie spoke to him.

Having experience of grumpy cats, Jessie knew exactly how to win him back, cooking him a fillet of salmon, just as she did for herself.

'Don't get used to this, young man,' she said as Cole decided she was taking the appropriate steps to forgiveness, and rubbed against her legs, purring at full volume.

Jessie spent the rest of the evening fussing over the black cat as she lost herself in Cathy and Heathcliff's yearning, and by the time she switched her bedside lamp off, Cole had forgiven her.

Still smiling following her first day back in the world, Jessie fell into the first dreamless sleep she'd had in a very long time.

Chapter 11

Over the following weeks, Nate spent his time holed up in his studio at the gallery. As was his norm when preparing for a show, he barely slept, not wanting the interruption to appear in whichever painting he was creating.

Em, on the other hand, refused to have Nate's "man smell" permeating the gallery, and kicked him out periodically to go back to the Lake House and shower. While he was there, Nate took a nap, knowing he wouldn't when he returned to the studio.

Another interruption to his self-imposed isolation were his bi-weekly dinners at his parents'. He'd tried in the past to avoid these in the lead up to a show, but all it did was force his mother to bring dinner to him, disturbing his flow and passing comments on paintings that were yet to be finished.

Nate had decided long ago that his existence was far less stressful if he obeyed the women in his life.

∞

Over the next few weeks, Jessie settled into a comforting routine. For three days a week she revelled in the laughter, tears and tantrums of Potters Hole's youngest inhabitants, and the rest she spent with Cole and her renovations, as she termed the fixing up of Bluebell Cottage.

By saying renovations, Jessie could imagine scaffolding, tradespeople, sheets of plastic hanging throughout her home, and endless clouds of plaster dust. It made her feel better about turning down Bev's offer of dinner, which came at the end of each workday.

Jessie didn't want to admit the reason she declined Bev's invitations was because all she wanted to do was go home to Cole and spend the evening reading. On her non-work days, she did carry on doing up the cottage, but she also explored the wood and the surrounding area, familiarising herself with her new home. She felt bad about declining Bev, but Jessie wasn't ready to take that next step; she wanted her solitude for a while longer.

Unfortunately, as with best laid plans, Bev didn't see things the way Jessie did. As they were enjoying a fruity Merlot in Bev's office, to celebrate Jessie's first month, Bev made her announcement.

'I think it's high time you got out and about and made a few friends,' she said after they'd toasted with their paper cups.

Jessie thought she might be sick, as the bottom seemed to fall out of her stomach and her hands shook.

'I do go out, and besides, I have friends,' she lied, putting her cup down to hide her hands, hoping Bev hadn't noticed.

∞

Bev watched Jessie as her gaze darted around the room and she clasped her hands together, wringing them as she seemed to process Bev's statement.

What did that man do to you? Bev wondered, because she had no doubt a man was responsible for the decade-long gap in

Jessie's life, which she evaded talking about, no matter how gently Bev had prodded. If it wasn't for the physical reactions and the way Jessie dressed, Bev may have let it go as simply a bad break-up. She was certain now, though; it was a lot more than that, and a lot worse.

'Cole and I don't really count as friends, Jessie,' she said, watching the younger woman.

'You do for me,' Jessie replied and smiled, but it didn't reach her eyes, eyes now rimmed with unshed tears.

Most definitely something terrible, Bev thought, and went to Jessie, taking hold of her still shaking hands.

'Okay, if you're not ready for that, how about taking a night school class and learning something new?' Bev suggested, deciding not to pick at the festering wound of Jessie's past.

'To do what?' Jessie shrugged as she tried and failed to hold Bev's gaze, the tears inching over the edges.

'Well, let's see. What do you like to do?' Bev let go of Jessie's hands and retrieved her wine. Jessie did the same, taking a big gulp before she replied.

'Reading. I love books. *Wuthering Heights* is my favourite. Heathcliff is so…' she drifted off, and Bev smiled at the change in Jessie's demeanour as she stared wistfully out of the window.

Bev contemplated inviting her to the book club she was a member of, but it was a place frequented by people Bev's age. She wanted Jessie to mix with people more her own age. She wrinkled her nose and shook her head. 'Anything else?'

'Well, I could do with learning how to grow my own vegetables, given the wonderful garden I've uncovered.'

Bev pondered this, but it wasn't what she was after. She would introduce Jessie to the Old Wrinklies Gardening Club, as it was known, but they wouldn't help her meet people her own age.

Before Bev could prompt her again, a brief light shone in Jessie's eyes as she continued. 'What would be great, is to capture the gorgeousness of the cottage and the lake, but I was never any good at art in school, and my photography skills don't really give me what I'm after.'

We got there in the end, Bev thought, and smiled. 'How about an art class, then?' she said matter-of-factly.

'Are you mad? When I said I was never any good I was being kind. I was useless! My art teacher used to put his head in his hands and pretend to sob when he looked at my efforts,' Jessie said, shaking her head.

Bev bit down on her lip. She hated hearing about such things. Some people should never be allowed to teach!

'Most teachers are more supportive than that,' she said instead, opting for tact. 'How about a watercolours class? Impressionism is always welcome there.' She winked at Jessie, making her laugh.

'I'm certainly good at that! My impression of what it should be.' Jessie doubled over, laughing, and Bev felt a lightness in her chest at the sight. She didn't think laughter had featured in Jessie's life in recent years.

Deciding to seize the opportunity, Bev got to the point. 'There's a beginner's watercolours course due to start at the community centre. It's in the village, so you won't have to travel far. What do you think?'

'Oh, I don't know, I wouldn't be any good and—'

'The tutor is brilliant,' Bev interrupted. 'He starts with the basics and goes from there. He's very patient.'

Jessie pressed her lips together and shook her head.

'Please, Jessie. I'm worried about you spending so much time alone. Give it a try. You can always stop if you really don't like it, and who knows, you may end up decorating your walls instead.'

'Okay, fine. If it'll stop you going on about my life of chastity, I'll do it,' Jessie said and laughed as Bev felt the heat rise in her cheeks. 'I don't have any stuff though—paints, brushes… you know.'

'You don't need to. It's all provided. Anyway, there's no point in investing in something until you're sure you like it.'

'Great, so when does this class start?'

'Tomorrow night,' Bev said, and watched the colour drain from Jessie's face.

Chapter 12

It was a few days before the show and Nate still had so much to do, he could have done without a parental dinner. But, as was expected, he arrived at his parents, albeit just in time to sit down to eat.

'You could have showered first!' his mother said, wrinkling her nose as she set Nate's dinner in front of him. His father wisely put his head down and tucked in.

'Don't start, Mum, you know there're only a few days until the show and I still have so much to do.'

'Well, you will leave everything until the last minute, so what do you expect?'

'Mum, don't,' Nate warned, clenching his fists around his cutlery, not having the patience for the familiar ritual.

'I'm just saying—'

'Bev, listen to the lad,' his father interjected, causing both Nate and his mother to look at him in astonishment. His father *never* stepped into the middle of one of their *discussions*.

'Fine, I'll keep my opinions to myself,' his mother sniffed, drawing a snort of laughter from Nate. His father glared at him.

'You'll need to smarten yourself up by tomorrow, and a shave wouldn't go amiss,' his mother said.

'Why? What's happening tomorrow?' Nate's body tensed as

his mind raced through his diary but came up short.

'For goodness' sake, Nate, I wish you'd write these things down. You have a class starting tomorrow, remember?'

'Ah, shit!'

'Nathaniel Parker!'

'Sorry, Mum, but there's just no way—'

'You need to find a way. Those classes are extremely popular and besides, I've persuaded my new teaching assistant to attend, so you can't cancel it. Aside from that, it isn't professional to cancel…'

Nate tuned out. Knowing he couldn't win the argument, his mind sifted through what he had left to do for the show. The painting was finished; he'd applied the final strokes before leaving that evening, hence his tardiness. Nate still needed to select which pieces he wanted to exhibit. He tended to leave that to the last minute because he often changed his mind, which was one reason he painted more than he included. The other was so he would always have paintings to sell on the night. He'd learned that lesson after his first show sold out in less than an hour.

Once he'd made his selection, he would need to frame and hang them in the room above the main gallery, which Nate used for all his shows. Em did everything else, from the planning and marketing to the invites and catering, but the framing and hanging Nate did himself. Until the painting sold, no one touched it but him; it was one superstition he had.

'… anyway, it's only a couple of hours and the break will do you good. Plus, you'll be able to invite the class to your show;

they'd like that,' his mother continued, oblivious to the fact he'd missed most of what she'd said.

Nate shook his head at the last remark and looked at his father, who winked at him.

Nate *never* invited his classes to his shows. His mother knew that, so he was at a loss why she'd mentioned it. The shows were for serious buyers, collectors with the means to part with the price tags commanded by his work, not the looky-loos who came to gawk at him.

'You'll need to smarten yourself up, though, Nate. You can't teach a class looking like that.' His mother nodded towards him, frowning.

Nate looked down at his torn, paint-smeared clothing. He scratched his stubbly chin and lifted his arm to sniff his armpit, drawing a sharp "tut" from his mother.

'I don't see why not. At least they'll see what serious art does to a person,' he said, winking at his father whilst keeping a straight face. His mother, however, didn't see the funny side.

'Don't you dare! Those people all know me and I will not have you humiliating me, especially in front of my new assistant. I can't believe—'

'Mum, I'm joking,' Nate interrupted, holding his hands up. 'I'd never do anything to ruin your good name.' He pushed away from the table and kissed her on the cheek as she swatted his arm.

'Stop teasing,' she said, chuckling.

'Gotta go. Thanks for dinner, Mum. Love you both,' Nate said, patting his father on the shoulder as he passed.

He had a class to plan.

Chapter 13

Jessie nestled into the Audi's well-worn leather seat. She had made it to the community centre for the art class Bev had pushed her into, but she wasn't sure she wanted to go in. She'd only said yes so Bev would stop quizzing her. Starting again meant finding new things to like, and she hadn't got there yet.

Part of her promise to herself when she decided to make a new start in Potters Hole was that no one would tell her what to do, or make her do something she didn't want to, ever again.

A stab of guilt punctured her chest as Bev's understanding smile filled her mind, and Jessie looked down at her hands, shaking her head.

Bev did say that if she didn't like it, she didn't have to come again, but enjoy it, she just might.

It's about trying new things. I won't know what I like if I don't try.

With one decision made, Jessie moved on to the next—when to go in? She certainly didn't want to be first as she would feel obliged to make conversation with the tutor, and *that* she knew she didn't want to do.

'One step at a time, Jessie, one step at a time,' she said as she heard voices outside.

Jessie turned to see a gaggle of women laughing and chatting as they locked up their cars and walked towards the entrance.

Perfect!

Jessie jumped out of her car and hurried to catch up, disguising herself as one of them as they walked inside.

Detaching herself from the group, Jessie slipped to the back of the room, locating a seat in the far corner and positioning the easel to afford her the protection she desired.

'Jeez, Jessie, pull yourself together; it's only an art class,' she muttered as she watched the women squabbling over places at the front, before hugging and air-kissing one another.

Only to be expected, Jessie thought, *Potters Hole is a small place.*

But as she inadvertently eavesdropped, it became apparent they weren't from Potters Hole. Not only that, but this wasn't the first time they'd attended Introduction to Watercolours, either.

This tutor can't be much good if they keep coming back, Jessie mused, looking at her watch—7.05pm; he was late. As she flopped back in her chair, contemplating a more desirable evening curled up with Cole and a novel, the flighty group became agitated, and Jessie watched in amusement as compacts were snapped open, lips were smacked, hair was plumped and low-cut tops were adjusted for best effect.

Or maybe he's just hot?

The thought caused a stutter in her belly, and she sat up straight, quashing the sensation. She was *not* there to meet a man; she was there to try new things; all part of starting over. Besides, she had hardly dressed to impress, having donned her habitual attire of shapeless dungarees over a long-sleeved T-shirt. Her days of trying to impress anyone were well and truly behind her.

'Sorry I'm late, guys,' the tutor said, making his entrance. 'I left something very important in the car. We won't get far without these, will we?' He brandished a handful of paintbrushes as he looked up at the class.

Jessie's stomach flipped, a rush of heat racing through her body and settling in her cheeks as she stared at the unfamiliar state of her new neighbour. *You have got to be kidding*, she thought, sliding down in her seat, hoping he hadn't seen her.

'Can you hand these around?'

'Yes, Nate, anything for you,' replied a giggly voice, and Jessie groaned.

'Yes, right, well, it would appear I've seen most of you before… *several* times.'

Oh, is that a hint of disdain? Jessie wondered.

'Though why you keep wasting your money is beyond me.'

Jessie snorted, his sarcasm falling on a wave of fresh giggling, and she clamped her hand over her mouth as she peeked over the top of her easel to see if he'd heard her. His gaze met hers and he winked.

Oh, he heard me all right.

Jessie grimaced, her heart skipping and her cheeks warming again, unable to stop herself following his movements. She bit down on her lip as he ran long graceful fingers through his thick auburn hair, and her gaze lingered on his full lips, formed into an Elvis smile, his head cocked to one side, appraising her.

'Well, class, it appears we *do* have some fresh blood… thank God.' Raised eyebrows punctuated the last two words, a deep sigh drawing Jessie's attention to his broad chest, now shrouded in a paint-spattered t-shirt. Her body throbbed in recollection of what lay beneath.

'Welcome, neighbour. Don't you recognise me like this?' He plucked at his t-shirt. 'I'm Nate… Nate Parker.'

Shit!

Jessie's mind jumped to Bev, her urging Jessie to join the class becoming clear.

No, no, no, Bev, I thought you understood? The fires inside her instantly doused, and her exit at break time was now a done deal.

∞

At break time, Nate ushered everyone outside, picking his phone up and turning his back, pretending he had a call so his fan club wouldn't hang around.

Once the innate chattering had died down, he put his phone in his pocket and turned around. His muse still sat at the back of the room, her brow furrowed, chewing her bottom lip, engrossed in her painting.

Maybe she didn't hear me say it was break time?

Deciding to grasp the opportunity, and at least find out her name, Nate sauntered over. Still, she didn't look up.

Feeling a little foolish standing there, Nate cleared his throat, making her jump.

'Dammit!' she said as her brush skidded across her painting.

'Sorry, sorry, here, let me.'

She moved out of the way to allow Nate to remove the smear of cobalt from her trees.

'There, you can't even tell they've had an unfortunate

encounter,' he said, stepping back to show the greenery in all its non-blue glory.

She didn't respond, her gaze focused on the photographic guide he'd provided for the class.

'Is something wrong?' he asked when she remained glued to the photograph, studying it. 'Do you need help? Because, looking at it, I'd say you'd give me a run for my money.' He laughed, but still she didn't respond, and Nate felt a bead of sweat trickle between his shoulder blades as he rubbed his clammy palms on his battered jeans.

I've never had to work this hard… ever.

Shaking her head at last, and without looking at him, she said, 'No, nothing's wrong. This lake'—she pointed at the photograph—'it looks so familiar.'

'It's the lake in front of my house.

'Interesting,' she said, and Nate watched her trace her finger across the photograph to the left. 'That would mean my cottage would be just out of shot, here,' she said, cocking her head to one side and tapping the photo.

Silence fell between them. She remained still, her gaze fixed on the photograph. Nate, always uncomfortable with silence, especially when coupled with awkward moments, as this clearly was, shifted from one foot to the other, running a hand back and forth through his hair.

'Look, I'm sorry if I scared you—'

'I must apologise for staring. I didn't—'

They both blurted and laughed. Nate was caught by the mesmerising grey eyes of his muse.

'Hi, I'm Nate Parker.' He thrust his hand out, unable to stop staring into her face, her eyes; committing it all to memory.

'I know, you introduced yourself earlier.'

Nate nodded.

'Jessie,' she said, 'I'm Jessie Ellis. I work with your mum. She's the one who made me come… I'm sorry, I didn't mean that to sound…'

'It's fine, don't worry. I know exactly what my mother's like. She virtually held me at gunpoint to not cancel the class because you were coming.'

'Oh, so you knew who I was?'

'No, no, no,' Nate said hurriedly, seeing a shadow pass over Jessie's face. 'She referred to her "new assistant", that's all. To be honest, I was expecting one of her book club cronies.'

'Hey! I'm one of her book club cronies!'

Nate felt heat rise into his cheeks. *Jeez, am I ever going to say the right thing?*

He glanced at the floor for a moment, and when he looked back at her, she was grinning, her eyebrows raised.

'Good one. You had me there. For a minute, I thought I'd actually offended you!'

'Well, I *do* go to her book club, or I will, but I'd like to think I'm not a crony.'

'No, not by a long way,' Nate said, the heat increasing in his face. He coughed and looked away, taking a deep breath to compose himself. 'So, how long have you been painting?' he asked, turning back to her and pointing at her rather accurate depiction of the lake.

Jessie looked at her watch and shrugged. 'A couple of hours, give or take.'

'Well, I have to say, you're a natural. What made you come tonight?'

'Your mum.'

'My mother.'

They had spoken at the same time again and laughed.

'Sorry, you've already said that. Sorry if Mum coerced you, she can be rather pushy when she wants something. I seem to be apologising a lot, sorry. Ah! There I go again, and now I'm babbling…'

'It's fine, don't worry,' Jessie said and touched his arm, sending a shock wave through him. She yanked her hand away as if she too felt the static, and Nate watched as her face clouded over again.

'She means well, your mum, she just wants me to meet people from the village, like those ladies,' Jessie said, indicating the empty seats in front of her.

Nate blushed again and looked back at the floor as he massaged his forehead.

'Yeah, my class doesn't tend to be inhabited by many local people, unfortunately.' He looked back at her and smiled ruefully, pleased to see her smiling again. 'They're more a fan club than avid painters.'

'So I see, but why—?'

But Jessie was interrupted by the returning fan club, and Nate groaned.

'I'll see you later?' he asked as he backed towards the front of the room, but he received only a smile in response.

Chapter 14

Jessie was smiling as she walked into Bluebell Cottage later that evening. She was surprised by how much she'd enjoyed losing herself in painting, not thinking of anything else except ensuring her colour mixes did justice to the photograph she was recreating. She'd finished it before the class ended, and had to admit Nate's comments about her first attempt made her glow. And, as his adoring fans had mobbed Nate, Jessie had sneaked out; she'd done enough socialising for one day.

'What do you think?' Jessie said to Cole, who sat waiting on the kitchen table, something she'd given up telling him off for.

To his credit, Cole looked down his nose at the painting, narrowing his green eyes, before looking up at her and stalking off.

Clearly, not a good enough reason to have abandoned him, Jessie thought, and laughed.

Humming to herself, she carried the painting into the living room and propped it on the mantelpiece, making a mental note to add a trip to the framers to her "to do" list; it *was* her lake, after all.

Jessie wandered back into the kitchen and, deciding it was too late for coffee, she made herself a mug of Earl Grey tea, before curling up in her armchair. Cole—having forgiven her—

perched on her knee as she ran through her list of jobs for the next day. Her gaze settled on her painting and she smiled at the thought of having something *she'd* created hanging on the wall in *her* home.

∞

Nate watched her through the window, the soft light illuminating her face as she held a steaming mug close to her mouth, a faraway look in her eyes, an enigmatic smile on her lips—a far cry from the haunted looks he'd borne witness to.

Christ, another image for me to paint, he thought as he watched the once feral black cat stand up and stretch before settling back down on her knee.

Nate had to fight against the alien, yet natural, urge to join them; every cell in his body screamed for him to do just that.

After wading through the adoration, Nate had been crestfallen to find her gone. He knew his actions, more than his talent and fame, brought on these women, but for the first time, he didn't want it, didn't want any of them.

All he wanted was Jessie.

Nate shook his head and laughed before leaning back against the headrest and staring up at the roof of his truck. He shrugged, letting his palms slap against his thighs. *Why? Why do I have these feelings for her?* And why had he rushed out of the community centre, packing nothing up, and driven like a man possessed to Bluebell Cottage?

He hung his head and stared at his paint-stained hands.

'What did you think would happen, Nate?' he whispered, before looking back at her. It's not like she'd have invited him in if he'd knocked, not if he'd read her correctly.

Jessie Ellis was strong, he'd seen that, but there was a fragility to her. She was rebuilding, but from what he didn't know—not yet.

Finally, feeling like a Peeping Tom, Nate pulled away and headed back to the community centre. He had to clear up, and then he had a show to focus on.

Chapter 15

With the art class and Nate Parker forgotten, and with four work-free days ahead of her, Jessie focused her attention on Bluebell Cottage.

The day after art class, she ventured into the centre of Potters Hole for a long overdue visit, and was surprised by what she found. She had thought she'd have to go further afield, but everything she needed was on her doorstep.

With a smile on her face, her painting stowed in the Audi for now, Jessie pulled out her list and set about crossing off the items.

She hired a sander to strip the floors, bought paint, lining paper and paste for the walls and hired a work bench and a selection of other tools. She even bought some beautiful planks of oak for her biggest project—building bookcases into every alcove, nook and cranny of the cottage, as well as the obligatory collection of free-standing ones.

Jessie couldn't wait to unpack and surround herself with her beloved books once more. They had been in storage for so long that unboxing them would be like feasting her eyes on them for the first time. Bubbles of excitement fizzed through her body, and Jessie giggled at the thought, the giddiness making her head spin.

Slamming the hatch on her Audi, the old car packed solid once more—the equipment and wood being delivered later—Jessie retrieved her work of art from the passenger seat.

As she'd been exploring Potters Hole, she'd noticed a bookshop, which included a stationers, an art supply store and a coffee house called Bennett's. Given they seemed to do most things, Jessie hoped they'd be able to frame her painting.

The good thing about small towns were these hybrid shops, and Jessie decided she'd buy a book and sit and enjoy a frothy coffee while she waited for her painting, should they be able to acquiesce.

But, as she set foot inside the store, all thought of burying her nose in a book evaporated as the collection of paintings on display drew her into their midst, each seeming to reflect an aspect of her new home.

She surrendered her own lake scene to the young lad behind the counter, who assured her it wouldn't take long, and lost herself in the woods. Jessie inhaled the fragrance of the flowers, heard the whisper of the water over the pebbles, and listened to the chatter of the dawn chorus as she held her breath, waiting for the kingfisher to make his move.

Budget forgotten, Jessie wandered through Bluebell Cottage, selecting the paintings as she went, leaving the store laden with packages and a precariously balanced takeaway coffee.

Back home, Jessie unwrapped her own painting and took it into the living room, holding it above the fireplace.

Perfect!

At least now she had a place to start.

Chapter 16

Nate's show was entitled *Stillness*, the opposite of the gallery on Saturday evening, as bodies swirled through, taking in each of his creations in the sequence he'd mapped out. If he could observe from above, Nate knew the movement of art lovers would resemble the symbol for infinity—the lemniscate—which was his intention; to mirror the endless stillness of his paintings.

'I can't believe it!' Em said, squealing, making Nate jump.

'Jeez, Em, turn the volume down!' Nate winced as she squealed again.

'I hope I've got enough of these.' She brandished her swathe of what used to be red sticky dots. 'We've only a few left! You're a sell-out, Nate!' she shouted, punching his arm.

'Ouch!' Nate grumbled, rubbing the blooming bruise. 'I hope you mean that in a good way, Em?'

She squealed again, and Nate flinched, the sound piercing his eardrums. 'Volume, Em! Volume!'

'Talk later. Gotta run. Another sale,' she said and pecked him on the cheek, her latest red sticker already between her thumb and forefinger, ready to strike.

I'm not sure who's more excited, Nate thought, watching Em bouncing up and down as she spoke to the latest buyer.

He'd done his fair share of talking: answering questions about his technique and inspiration, accepting praise for his paintings, and sending people Em's way when they wanted to buy. He had to admit, despite all the distractions—or maybe because of them—the pieces he'd turned out for the show had sold faster than any other show before.

Em was right; tonight would be a sell-out, and he knew through his conversations he could have sold some of his work several times over. This only meant one thing: Em would be taking commissions. Nate just wasn't sure he'd be able to paint anything other than his muse… for a while, anyway.

The thought of Jessie caused him to scour the room, but he didn't see her. He was unsure why he thought he would.

Because I told the class about the show.

And he'd only done that in the hope Jessie would come.

Nate glanced towards the bar and saw his giggling fan club preoccupied with the barman.

God bless Em!

He smiled as his gaze settled on his parents, also hovering by the bar. They came to every show without fail, and Nate had hoped they'd get used to the arty set who attended, but they never had. He saw their stiff stances and bewildered looks and made his way over.

'Hey, you guys,' he said, and hugged his father before kissing his mother on the forehead, whispering in her ear, 'You look ravishing tonight, Mrs Parker. I do hope Mr Parker sees that, too.'

'Oh, Nate, stop it, you're making me blush!' his mother said, giggling as colour flooded her cheeks.

'I'm not surprised he has all these hangers-on, if that's the drivel he fills their heads with,' his father grumbled, winking at Nate.

'Oh, Ray, stop being such a stick-in-the-mud!' his mother admonished, swatting his arm and making them both laugh.

Nate stiffened at his father's light-hearted barb, but forced a smile, knowing he meant nothing by it.

'We're so proud of you, son,' his father said, patting his shoulder.

'Yes, Emily said the paintings have almost sold out. Is that true?' his mother added.

'Looks that way,' Nate said and hung his head, looking up at his mother and grinning. 'I'm a sell-out, Mum, as Em so eloquently put it.'

'That's fantastic, darling! I'm so happy for you.' His mother hugged him and he squeezed her back, clearing his throat.

'Erm, is Jessie here, by any chance?' he asked, hoping he sounded more casual than he felt. The elbow to his father's ribs didn't go unnoticed.

'I haven't seen her. Why? Did you invite her?'

Nate shifted under his mother's scrutiny, gazed around the room, and shrugged. 'Not specifically. I invited the class and thought she may have tagged along.' He nodded towards the gaggle of women at the bar.

His parents followed his gaze, his father tutting, and his mother shaking her head.

'I'm not sure those young ladies have much in common with Jessie, do you?' she said, and Nate shrugged.

'I thought, maybe, you might have invited her with you, like you *encouraged* her to come to my class.' Nate watched as his mother set her jaw and rolled her shoulders back. His father chuckled; his mother didn't like being told she was interfering, no matter how subtly.

'I merely thought it would be good for her to meet people her own age. Clearly, she wouldn't do that at one of your classes,' his mother retorted.

'Ouch! Touché, Mum. Truce?' Nate pretended to wave a white flag, which made her laugh.

'I would've invited her, but I haven't seen her since Wednesday. She only works part time.'

Disappointment; an alien feeling. He was disappointed Jessie wasn't there to share in his success. Nate had pinned his hopes on his mother, as she was the master of getting people to do things; probably why she was such a great teacher.

Nate sighed as he escorted his parents around the gallery, introducing them to people as he always did, but his heart was no longer in it; it was at Bluebell Cottage, waiting to be heard.

Chapter 17

It was two in the morning by the time Nate pushed open his front door, having dropped off his parents, declining the invitation of champagne and feigning exhaustion.

He'd seen the look of disappointment on his mother's face, but what else could he have done? If he'd toasted his success, as they always did after a show—ever since the beginning—she would have grilled him over his despondency and he could do without it; he had no answers to give to her or himself.

What would he have said? Tell them the truth? That, despite selling every painting in the show, plus half of the gallery—a record even for him—it meant nothing, because a woman he didn't even know hadn't been there.

Nate slumped onto the sofa and shook his head. He picked up the tennis ball lying next to him and juggled it between his hands as his mind drifted to his parents' reactions… had he done just that.

His father would have hunched his shoulders and ducked his head, scurrying off to find a newspaper or a book to hide behind; matters of the heart always made him uncomfortable.

His mother would have raised her eyebrows and nodded, patting a seat at the breakfast bar for him to sit while she busied herself producing healing tea and sugary biscuits. She would then have begun her investigation, extracting from him the reasons for such melancholy.

Huh! She wouldn't have got far.

Nate threw the tennis ball against the wall and caught it, the scuff marks in the paint evidence of his part-time occupation. His mind wandered back to the conversation he'd had all those years ago about muses.

'It will take your appetite, your sleep, your will, and your desire to paint any other thing. It will possess you, enslave you, and you will have no power to stop it,' Javier had said. 'I tell you the truth,' he'd added when Nate scoffed at his prediction.

The old bastard was right.

'But I *have* to paint other things,' he said aloud, as he thought of the list of commissions Em had been beside herself to show him.

Not only that, but he also had a gallery to refill. Nate sighed and let his head fall back on the sofa, allowing him a view of his bed on the mezzanine floor.

Fill with what?

That was the big question. What on earth could he replenish the gallery with when all he could think about was Jessie? The only reason he'd managed to pull together this show was because he had a theme, and, as was his way, plenty of paintings he'd started. But now?

He hurled the ball away in frustration, not caring at the wreckage it left in its wake, and climbed the wooden stairs to his studio. Nate gazed at the stacks of part-finished canvases, all with one thing in common—Jessie. He could fill the gallery three times over with them, but there was one thing—one extremely important thing—standing in his way; he needed permission to share them with the world, and how the hell could he justify such an invasion of her privacy?

Hands on his hips, Nate hung his head and sighed. Where was the old painter now he needed his advice?

Nate wandered over to the picture window and stared across the lake at the snug cottage, illuminated by the dappled light of the moon.

I wonder what she's doing? he thought, before laughing out loud as he remembered the time. *Lucky her!*

Too wired to sleep, Nate's gaze settled on the shimmering waters, and he grinned.

∞

Across the lake, Jessie lay staring at the moon as she waited for Cole to settle himself down. He'd woken her about half an hour earlier, his paddy-pawing resulting in his claws sinking into her bare flesh, jolting her awake with a yelp.

The black cat had looked at her through half-closed eyes as she'd told him off, his pleasure clear, and Jessie wondered whether he'd woken her on purpose.

Although she loved having Cole curl up with her every night, she certainly didn't get much sleep. As was the will of a cat, their human fitted around them and not the other way around.

'For goodness' sake, Cole, surely it's plumped up enough!' she said, observing the cosy nest he was constructing around himself.

A splash drew Jessie's attention back to the window, and she eased out of bed to investigate, careful not to disturb Cole's nest-building.

Veiled by the voile she'd draped across the windows, Jessie gazed down at the lake, her breath catching as she saw Nate cutting through the water, the moonlight glinting off the droplets clinging to his muscular arms.

A flutter in her belly made her gasp, and she clamped her hand across her middle, shutting it down. She couldn't. That wasn't why she'd come to Potters Hole.

How could she share her damage with someone else? She'd promised herself she would never relive what he'd done to her; she'd rather remain alone.

A sadness squeezing her heart and pulling her towards the lake, Jessie turned and climbed back into bed, pulling Cole close, no longer bothered about disturbing him. Jessie tuned into his rhythmic purr and allowed him to sing her his lullaby.

Chapter 18

'What on earth have you been doing?' Bev asked, as she grabbed Jessie's arm and helped her out of the car.

'DIY,' Jessie replied, stretching her back, thinking she'd probably overdone things the last few days.

'You can't do that cottage up yourself; it's too much. I'll get Nate to come and help, he's very—'

'No, Bev, I'm fine,' Jessie snapped, but seeing the look on Bev's face, she realised her retort was a little too abrupt. 'Thanks, Bev. I do appreciate the offer, but I want to do as much of it as I can myself; I need to, you know?'

Bev smiled and nodded. 'I understand. Let me at least carry that bag for you, and you can tell me how you got on at art class.'

Jessie relinquished her bag before following Bev into the school building.

'I loved it,' Jessie said, smiling and easing into a chair in Bev's office.

'You sound surprised. Coffee?'

'Please. To be honest, I am. I didn't think I'd be any good, but I was. I've even had my painting framed to take pride of place on my chimney breast!' Jessie grinned at Bev, feeling a rush of energy and lightness surge through her.

Bev laughed, saying, 'I take it you'll be giving Nate a run for his money soon, then?'

'Funny, he said the same thing, but no, his crown is safe. I won't be going again.' Jessie reached for the proffered mug, wincing at the overstretch.

'Why ever not? You said you loved it,' Bev said, a puzzled look on her face.

Jessie stopped herself just in time as she almost blurted, 'Because of Nate.' Instead, she took a moment before saying, 'And I did, but the idea, as pointed out by you, was to meet local people, to get to know them, but there was no one local there. Besides, I have the cottage…'

'No one local except Nate,' Bev said, and Jessie felt the heat creep into her cheeks. 'He's about your age and he knows everyone. He could—'

'Is this why you didn't tell me he was the tutor? *Or* my new neighbour?' The heat vanished as her flight mode notched up a gear.

'I don't follow.'

'Because he's your son, and you were hoping to play matchmak—' Jessie broke off as the older woman's brow furrowed. 'I-I think he has his hands full with his fan club anyway,' she finished, her cheeks heating again.

'Ah, yes,' Bev said after a few moments, and rolled her eyes, shaking her head before sipping her coffee. 'I warned him about this, but did he listen to me?'

'Warned him?'

'I know I'm his mother, but Nate is rather attractive.' Bev

paused and looked at Jessie, who couldn't help but nod in agreement. Smiling, Bev continued, 'Well, he's always used it to his advantage, never being short of a pretty girl on his arm, a different one every night, I might add.' Bev frowned. 'Anyway, when his art took off, I told him he needed to change his behaviour. Of course, he didn't listen to me. I'm only his mother, so what do I know?'

Bev paused again, and Jessie watched the conflicting emotions on the older woman's face.

'Needless to say, the fame that came with his art only made things worse. I don't understand what these women find so appealing about being a notch on his bedpost.' Bev wrinkled her nose and looked at Jessie.

'Fame,' Jessie said, shifting in her seat, uncomfortable at the image Bev was creating of Nate.

'Obviously—'

The door banged open, cutting Bev off, and a screaming child burst in. His knees were bloody, and snot hung from his nose.

'Not again, Bradley,' Bev said, teacher pose assumed as both she and Jessie went to soothe the clumsy child.

∞

Jessie hurried to her car, eager to get home and enjoy a glass of Malbec after a fraught day of injured children—Bradley having been the first of many—when a hand on her arm caused her to scream and recoil, almost losing her balance.

'Oh my God! I'm sorry, Jessie. I didn't mean to startle you. Are you all right?'

Jessie turned, heart hammering and her skin now swathed

in a sheen of sweat. Tears brimmed her eyes as she saw Bev, her hands covering her mouth, eyes wide. Taking a deep breath, Jessie closed her eyes. She waited for her adrenaline to subside and her breathing to return to normal before opening her eyes and offering Bev a quivering smile.

'I'm sorry, Bev, you startled me. Have I forgotten to do something?'

'No, nothing like that. Are you sure you're okay? It looked—'

'Honestly, I'm fine. I was in a world of my own, thinking about my list of jobs at home.' Jessie reached out and squeezed Bev's hand, hoping she didn't notice Jessie's shaking one. 'What's up?'

Bev stared at her for a short while but, deciding to take Jessie's word for it, she said, 'Nothing's up. We just didn't get to finish our conversation this morning, and I feel I may have done Nate an injustice with what I said.'

'I think you painted a very clear picture of him, no pun intended.' Jessie straightened up, her smile vanishing.

'That's what I was afraid of. I don't want to hold you up any longer, so I'll be brief. Don't give up on art class, Jessie, not yet. You clearly love it and, from what you've said, you have a natural talent. If nothing else, it gets you out of the house and gives you a break from DIY, which can only be a good thing.' She winked at Jessie as she finished.

'Okay,' Jessie said, feeling there was more to come, but that it wouldn't be quite so benign.

'And don't give up on Nate… please.'

'I wasn't aware I was on Nate,' Jessie said, a little too curtly, as she stiffened.

'You're not, but… look at me, Jessie.' Bev turned her around, making Jessie look her in the eye. 'There is a reason behind everyone's behaviour, as you know only too well.'

Bev hugged her and bade her goodnight, leaving Jessie standing in the car park, staring after her, an unasked question on her lips.

Chapter 19

Jessie thought about Bev's words as she drove home, conflicting feelings jostling for position within her. Bev's description of Nate's behaviour had repulsed her, that she would be nothing more than a one-night stand, making her uncomfortable. Those feelings led to pangs of guilt about judging someone she didn't even know. Bev was right; people often wore masks, or behaved a certain way, to protect themselves from something, or to stop people finding out who they truly were.

She smiled as she turned into the driveway. She spotted Cole perched on the wall, waiting for her. As she parked and gathered her bag, Cole sauntered over, pretending it was nothing more than coincidence.

Jessie scooped him up and nuzzled her face into his fur. The purring her affection unleashed in him made her heart swell. Having had enough attention, Cole pushed his front paws against Jessie's chest and turned his head away.

'Okay, okay, point taken,' she said and released him, the black cat racing to the door, eager for a full belly.

Dumping her bag on the kitchen table, Jessie busied herself feeding a complaining Cole as her mind drifted back to Nate.

She would be furious for people to pass judgement on her demeanour when they had no idea what had caused it.

But I'm not judging Nate, am I? she pondered as she got changed into her scruffs, ready for another night of DIY. *Then why does the thought of being one of many bother me so much?*

Jessie shuddered at the thought of being intimate with someone again, yet her body disagreed, an ache forming in the pit of her stomach; a feeling which brought Nate's handsome face and toned muscular body to mind.

'No! Absolutely not,' she chastised herself. 'I'm not ready.'

It was more than two years ago, but still the nightmares plagued her. The feeling she was being watched made her constantly look over her shoulder.

'Have you put the restraining order in place?' Dr Augur had asked a nervous and sleep-deprived Jessie.

'Y-yes, but it hasn't helped. You said it would help.'

'I did, and it will, but it won't happen overnight. Your mind needs time to recognise that you are safe. He won't come after you now.'

'He might.'

'What makes you say that, Jessie?'

'Well, it's hardly a tangible barrier, so there's nothing to physically stop him, is there?'

'No, there isn't, but have you seen or heard from him since?'

Jessie shook her head.

'Then trust it is doing its job.'

'I-I'm trying but…'

'Give it time. Focus on something else to distract your mind.'

Jessie looked around her as she recalled Dr Augur's words. Having the cottage to do up helped, but time was slow to acquiesce with Dr Augur. Jessie worked herself to exhaustion each night, the nightmares finding it impossible to rouse her. On the nights when sleep evaded her, despite her best efforts, she had the lake. Sitting on the jetty, her feet in the cool water, had a way of soothing her soul, of purging her mind of the past, allowing the sandman to come.

Jessie wondered what tonight would bring as she looked at the freshly buffed floor in her living room, remembering the suffocating, irrational panic of a few nights ago, and the sleepless night that followed.

She'd got home late and by the time she'd fed herself and Cole, there was very little light left and she wanted to get the walls painted. Going against her better judgement, Jessie hadn't covered the newly stripped and finished floor. Nor had she opened her stepladder properly. As she climbed onto it, the ladder jolted into place, unsettling the tin of paint balanced on the top. Jessie lunged forward to stop it falling, but succeeded only in sending it into the air, paint flying everywhere as the can bounced down the other side of the ladder and crashed to the floor, paint pooling around it.

Jessie stood rooted to the spot, her hand against her open mouth, a pain in her chest as her heart paused and her breath caught. The shaking followed, the tears soon after as she stared at the mess, impotent, as Matthew stomped into her mind to see what all the noise was.

'What the fuck have you done now?' he screamed, and

Jessie turned to see him filling the doorway, fists clenched as he looked from her to the expanding stain on the carpet.

'I'm s-sorry. It was an a-accident. I—'

'It wasn't an accident! You're just a clumsy bitch! Now get it cleaned up.' He grabbed her by the hair and shoved her towards the mess, the wine glass a dribbling waterfall.

'I-I need to get s-something to—'

'You can lick it up first. I'm not having expensive wine going to waste because of your incompetence!'

Jessie had closed her eyes and inhaled slowly, counting to ten, before holding it and then slowly releasing the breath. When she re-opened her eyes, both Matthew and the offending scene were gone. She'd managed to clean the paint up and buff out the residue, so no harm had been done, but the nightmares hadn't agreed.

To make sure there wasn't a repeat performance, Jessie took time to secure the covers in place over the floor, and prepared for a few hours of painting to aid her journey to the land of Nod, her mind drifting back to Bev's words.

What had happened to Nate for him to behave the way he did? It was more than a broken heart, Jessie was sure of it.

Chapter 20

Nate perched on his stool at the front of the class, his easel a barrier keeping his fan club at bay. As he smiled and nodded at their barrage of questions, his gaze drifted to the vacant easel at the back of the room. *Will she come?* Nate glanced at the clock on the wall and his shoulders slumped; he would have to kick things off in a few minutes.

His mind drifted to the previous evening, to his obligatory weekly dinner with his parents.

'So, how's your new assistant measuring up?' he'd asked as he pecked his mother on the cheek and stuck his finger in the potatoes she was mashing, scooping a dollop into his mouth.

'Why would you use the term *measuring up*?' she said, swatting his arm and pushing him away from the food.

'It's just a turn of phrase, Mum, nothing more.'

'But it isn't, is it? Is this how you think of your conquests? Seeing if they *measure up*? But measure up to what?'

'Jeez, Mum, I'm just curious to know how she's getting on, that's all,' Nate said, throwing his arms in the air.

'Nate, you should know better by now,' his father said as he brought his empty mug into the kitchen and set it by the sink.

'That doesn't live there, does it?' Nate's mother snapped,

and his father rolled his eyes as he put the offending mug in the dishwasher and retreated.

'Don't take it out on Dad. In fact, why are you mad at me? I only asked—'

'I'm *mad* because Jessie is a lovely woman and your flagrant reputation is scaring her off.'

'Hang on, how on earth does she know about this reputation of mine? Mum? What the hell have you told her?' Nate faced his mother, hands on hips, jaw clenched, a knot forming in his stomach at the damage his mother may have inflicted.

'I told her the truth, Nathaniel. She deserves that, so she can make up her own mind about you.'

'Why would she need… Mum? What have you been doing?'

'Nothing. Jessie is like a wounded animal, Nate, and you need to approach her with care. She's not one of your floozies, do you hear me?'

'Why, what's happened to her?' Nate's need to know more about Jessie's past outweighed his annoyance at his mother, but she didn't reply, having wandered into the living room.

Nate overheard his father telling her to stop interfering. Her response was typical: 'Never. They're perfect for each other.'

He reached out to grab the worktop to steady himself, the knot in his belly tightening as adrenaline surged through his body. Flight was his usual response to his mother's matchmaking, but his body wanted to do the exact opposite; his fear being doused by his curiosity.

His mother knew how to manipulate him, she always had; it was like a sixth sense. She knew that by portraying Jessie the way she did, Nate would want to know more, rather than run for the hills, which was his usual response to the possibility of something going beyond the night arranged.

Yet why was he even thinking this way about Jessie? He barely knew her, had spoken to her once, and yet his mother had also seen something more, just as he had the first time he'd laid eyes on her.

Nate craved to know her better, to know what had caused the pain and fear he saw in her eyes as he watched her standing in her bedroom window at night, pain his mother had also alluded to.

Guilt stabbed at his heart for invading Jessie's privacy, but he pushed it away. He meant her no harm; he would never let anything hurt her again.

He was so lost in his thoughts, Nate almost missed her slip into the room at the last minute, hiding herself at the back of the class. A surge of joy took his breath away.

∞

At break time, Nate waited for the gaggle of girls to leave the room before he approached Jessie, who was still engrossed in the evening's project.

Not wanting to ruin her painting again, Nate watched her, smiling as her brow furrowed and she moved closer to the canvas. He wished all his students took the class as seriously.

He waited until she looked away, her concentration now on choosing a different colour, before he cleared his throat to announce his presence. A part of him wondered if she knew he was there, but had opted to ignore him.

Nate got the answer when Jessie jumped, one hand flying to

her mouth as the other shook, a look of terror filling her grey eyes.

'Shit, I'm sorry. I thought you knew I was here,' Nate said. 'I don't mean to make a habit out of scaring you, honestly,' he continued and smiled, watching her face soften as she acknowledged him.

He saw her cheeks redden, and she looked away before looking back at him with cloudless eyes.

'It would appear I owe *you* an apology. How long was I actually ignoring you? Sorry, I didn't mean to be rude.'

'Not long, don't worry. It's all good,' Nate said, and reached out to touch her arm, to reassure her, but she flinched and pulled away.

'Sorry,' they both said before lapsing into silence.

'I wish all my students concentrated as much as you.' Nate watched her as he spoke, and she smiled and rolled her eyes.

'Oh, they concentrate all right, just not on the painting.'

It was his turn to blush at the frankness of her words. They continued to look at each other before bursting out laughing.

'A little bird tells me last week's painting now has pride of place above your mantelpiece?'

Jessie's averted her eyes and groaned. 'I know, sounds a bit vain of me to consider my work for such a lofty position.'

'Not in the slightest. It's a great painting. You're right to be proud of it.'

Jessie smiled and looked down at her hands, picking the paint from her fingernails.

Nate thrust his hands into his pockets, unused to being lost for words with women.

'So, I presume you have wall space picked out for tonight's work of art too, then?' he said, desperate to keep the conversation going.

'Ha! Hardly,' she replied and laughed, a throaty laugh that made Nate shiver as something stirred in his belly.

Jessie turned her painting towards him, adding, 'Somehow, I don't think animals are my forte, do you?'

Nate stared at the oddly shaped pig on the paper in front of him, scanning his vocabulary for something positive to say, when she said, 'Impressionist or not,' and erupted in laughter again.

God, how I love that sound, he thought, saying, 'Well, as long as you're enjoying the class…?'

'I am, but…' Jessie fell silent and looked away, playing with her brush.

'But what?' Nate managed, his body gripped by a sudden fear of what she might say.

'Please don't be offended, but the only reason I came was to meet people from the village, to make some friends. Your mum said I really ought to make some.'

Nate bristled at the mention of his mother and her interfering.

'Yeah, I'm sorry about that,' he said, glancing at the empty row at the front. 'But if I don't let them come, I wouldn't have the numbers and the class wouldn't run.'

Jessie didn't respond, so Nate continued, 'I'm local. I could show you around, if you like?'

She opened her mouth to reply, but seemed to decide better of it, smiling at him instead.

'We are neighbours, after all. A step closer to friendship,

perhaps?' he urged, regretting it as Jessie reddened and shifted in her seat—backwards, away from him.

Every cell in his body screamed for him to stop talking, but his mouth hadn't got the memo. 'I could even pop round to see if you've hung your painting, so it's shown in the best light?'

Too far, Nate, too far, he thought, and held his breath as he watched her look anywhere but at him.

Jessie shrugged and gave him a half smile, saying, 'It looks perfect where it is.'

Nate registered the chatter of the rest of the class returning from break and panicked, desperate to salvage the situation.

'Have a drink with me after class,' he blurted.

'I can't; I have things to do.'

'How about tomorrow?'

But Jessie shook her head. 'I've got my hands full doing my house up.'

Not knowing what else to say, Nate nodded and returned to the front of the room, vowing to try again after class.

But, by the time he'd appeased his groupies when the class was over, Jessie had gone.

Chapter 21

Jessie closed the door and leaned against it, feasting her eyes on her dilapidated kitchen as she inhaled the scent of fresh paint, varnish and goodness knows how many other smells that would make her head spin without proper ventilation.

Her gaze settled on the bright green eyes staring back at her. She loved this; coming home to Cole and closing the door against the outside world, existing inside her own little bubble.

Although she loved her new job, art class, and even the book club Bev had finally introduced her to, coming home on a Wednesday evening after art class, knowing she didn't have to speak to anyone until Monday, filled Jessie with excitement.

Her space, her time, it was as simple as that. Cole was the only one permitted to share it.

As if he'd read her thoughts, Cole yawned and stretched, before reaching his nose out towards her for the expected return home fuss.

Jessie laughed and picked him up instead, cuddling him and eliciting a meow of protest at the break in routine. She plonked him on the worktop as she reached for the bottle of Malbec and poured herself a large glass.

With Cole in tow, Jessie carried her glass outside and settled herself on her little patio to listen to the sounds of the lake evening.

Jessie shifted position, disturbing Cole, who had settled more quickly. The chairs she'd uncovered in the shed weren't the slightest bit comfortable, and, not for the first time, Jessie found her mind wandering to thoughts of a swing under the overhang of the cottage.

The overhang itself created a sheltered porch, and Jessie was toying with the idea of making it more of a year-round porch—closed to the elements in the winter, but open and airy in the summer. Such a project, however, was way beyond her skill set and her current budget. It would have to remain a dream for now until she could afford a contractor to come and build it.

As she watched the birds swooping down to the surface of the lake, their actions playful, their song melodious, Jessie's thoughts drifted to her earlier conversation with Bev and her offering of Nate's services to help with the renovations.

That was the reason she'd hesitated when he'd mentioned coming over; she was going to ask for his help, but thought better of it as the rest of what Bev had said filled her mind.

No, stick with plan A. That was the best thing to do. Plan A involved hiring a contractor to do everything she couldn't do herself; it just had to wait until she could afford it.

Yes, but that swing would be so good right about now, she thought, and her mind drifted to Nate again.

'I'd still need to pay him, wouldn't I, bud?' she said to Cole as she sipped her wine, savouring the velvety flavour on her tongue before letting it slip down her throat, under no illusion as to the type of payment he'd be willing to accept.

A tingling sensation between her legs at this thought startled her and dislodged Cole, who grumbled as he settled himself close by.

Where did that come from? she wondered, and her gaze strayed to the house across the lake. A light burned from the top floor windows and she could see him bent over his easel, a basketball cap holding back his floppy auburn hair.

Jessie wondered what he was working on, realising she hadn't thought to ask either him or Bev about his work.

Probably nudes.

She reached down to stroke Cole as he rubbed around her legs.

He'd certainly have no shortage of willing models, she mused, as the girls from art class crowded into her mind.

Distracted by her thoughts, Jessie didn't notice Nate come to the window, staring across the lake at her.

Startled, she froze as he raised his hand and waved to her. Jessie raised her glass in return, aware that she'd told him she had things to do that evening.

Nate turned and grabbed a bottle of beer from behind him, toasting her back, before disappearing from view.

Worried he might see her toast as an invitation, Jessie went inside and locked the door, taking Cole and the rest of her wine up to bed.

Chapter 22

Cradling her morning coffee, Jessie assessed the alcoves on either side of the fireplace. She'd marked up, drilled holes, and secured the shelf rests on one side of the alcoves, but there she'd had to stop.

In her head, drilling holes and making bookshelves was easy. In reality, boring into a stone wall was too much for her battered shoulder, and she'd had to break off, resigned to the job taking much longer than expected.

Not wanting to waste her free time, Jessie had turned her attention to the lengths of wood she'd bought for the shelving. She'd marked the correct width; all she needed to do was cut them to size.

Draining the now lukewarm coffee, Jessie deposited the mug in the kitchen as she headed outside, a handsaw and multiple lengths of wood awaiting her attention.

I can do this. Just take my time and keep changing hands.

She laid a length of oak on the sawhorse and secured it in place, before taking the saw and drawing it backwards along the mark to make the first cut, ensuring it didn't slip and damage the rest of the wood.

An hour later, her hands bloodied after her blisters had burst,

Jessie gave up. She wasn't even halfway through the first plank! She had not thought it through.

As she was heading back into the cottage to clean her wounds, she heard a car pull up in the driveway. Thinking it might be the postman, Jessie decided it was time she introduced herself.

She wiped her hands on her dungarees, blood smears adding to the paint, and walked around the corner with a smile on her face; a smile which vanished when she saw Nate walking towards her.

'Hi,' he said, waving as he stopped. 'I've got your mail for you.'

'Why?' Jessie blurted.

'Well, because I was coming to see you and said I'd save the postie the journey.' Nate looked back towards the road as he shifted position, one hand resting on his hip.

'I meant, why are you here?' Jessie made no move towards him, and Nate's smile faltered as he glanced at the mail in his hand. He looked up at her, pursing his lips.

Jessie saw the discomfort in his face, and guilt stabbed at her belly. 'I'm sorry, that was rude. Thank you for bringing the post,' she said and retrieved the proffered letters.

She glanced down and gasped, the hairs on the back of her neck rising as the familiar fear surged through her at the sight of the handwritten envelope on top of the pile. She recoiled, almost losing her balance, but Nate grabbed hold of her.

'Jeez, Jessie, are you okay? What's wrong?'

But Jessie couldn't find the words, staring back at him as she fought her emotions.

'Come on, let's get you to a chair.' Nate steered her to the back of the house and urged her into one of the reclaimed garden chairs.

'Do you need anything? Water? Do you feel faint? What can I do?' Nate hovered in front of her, his hands now thrust into the pockets of his snug jeans.

Jessie continued to stare, before dropping her gaze back to the letter. 'I'm fine.'

'Something tells me that's not entirely true, is it? Who's the letter from? It's clearly upset you.'

'No one important. Honestly, I'm fine. It was just a bit of a shock, that's all.'

Nate said nothing, looking at her, his eyebrows raised in question and hands back on his hips. Jessie rolled her eyes; she wouldn't be able to fob him off.

'It's from my sister, okay?'

'Bit of a strange reaction if it's from your sister. Don't you get on or something? And why doesn't she email or text like a normal person?'

'*I* don't do technology, Mr Nosey. Now, why *are* you here? You clearly came over for something?'

Nate continued to study her, and she held his gaze, but offered nothing more. Nate was the first to look away as he toed the gravel.

'Like I mentioned in class, I've come to check on that painting of yours…' He paused and looked around at the wood, the sawhorse and the tools. 'What on earth are you doing?'

Jessie looked at her poor attempt at sawing the wood and sighed. 'Today, I'm trying to build bookcases, but as you can see, I'm not getting very far.' She brandished her bloody palms, and Nate winced.

'Ouch,' he said as he inspected the lengths of wood she'd marked up. 'You were going to cut all these?'

Jessie nodded. 'I was, and I'd wanted to get them done today, but—'

'I can finish them for you, if you like?' he said, the saw already grasped in his hand.

'No, no, I can't ask you to do that. I'll—'

'You haven't asked, I'm offering. Now, get your hands cleaned up while I make a start on these.'

∞

'Where do you want these?

Jessie jumped, and the antiseptic cream she was packing back into the first aid box fell to the floor.

'You frightened the life out of me!' she said, turning to face Nate, heat rushing to her cheeks as she met his bare chest, freshly cut shelves balanced on his shoulder.

'Oh, er, um… in there.' She gestured towards the living room, unable to tear her gaze away from his tanned torso, a throbbing in her base warming her cheeks further.

Jessie took a few minutes to splash some cold water on her face, hoping to cool herself down, before she followed him.

'Not bad,' he said, looking over his shoulder and inclining his head towards her part-mounted shelf supports. 'But these shelves will need some shaping before they'll fit in there.'

'Why? Haven't I measured them correctly?' Jessie picked up a shelf from where he'd propped them against the wall. She slid it into the alcove, but it came to a halt halfway in, and no amount of shoving would make it budge any further.

'Old houses,' Nate said as he extricated the wedged shelf. 'You'll still get your shelves, don't worry, I just need to shape these for you. I'll need to nip home and get my tools, though.'

Jessie groaned and covered her face with her hands, shaking her head. 'Why do I start these things?'

'Because it's important to you,' Nate said, and Jessie opened her fingers to look at him, her whole body relaxing at his words. Not sure how to respond, she released her hands and smiled at him. 'It is.'

'Right, I won't be long,' he said before her painting drew his attention. He stared at it, moving from side to side to view it from different angles.

'Yep, you're right. It does look good there.'

∞

For the rest of the afternoon, Nate and Jessie worked side by side, she assisting him as he drilled and cut, before sliding the shelves flush into the alcoves. All the while, she chattered about her love of books. To her surprise, Nate had read many of the novels she talked about.

'So, how many books have you got?' Nate laughed as they stood back and admired the finished alcoves.

'Oh, I don't know… hundreds… I like to say I have a library,' she replied, feeling herself blush again.

'Well, I hate to tell you this, but they ain't all gonna fit on these.' He raised his eyebrows as he nodded towards the shelves, and Jessie laughed.

'I know that,' she said, shoving him playfully before sobering. 'I, er, I want bookcases everywhere. In every nook and cranny, and as many free-standing ones as I can fit in.'

'Blimey, you really *do* want a library! I'll have to check with Em to see if she can loan me out.' He laughed and Jessie looked at the floor, a knot forming in her stomach.

'Oh… er… no… erm, I didn't mean for you to do it. I'll get someone in.'

'Why the hell would you do that when you have a talented neighbour who will do it for a fraction of the cost?' Nate spread his arms wide before taking a bow.

Mortified, Jessie said, 'Yes, yes, of course, sorry, I didn't expect you to do all this for free. How much do I owe you?'

'Let me see,' Nate said, scratching his head as he looked at his handiwork. 'Well, there're the hours, how many… say five, multiplied by my rate, plus the use of my tools… erm, let me see…'

Jessie shifted from foot to foot, chastising herself for not asking for a cost up front. Of course he'd want paying. Nothing came for free. Her mind flicked to her overdraft, and she prayed she had enough leeway.

'… how does a coffee and the pleasure of your company sound?' Nate said, looking at her, his eyebrows raised.

'What?'

'Payment for today. If you insist on paying me, that is my bill.'

'I, er… I don't know what to say,' she stammered as she stared at him, her insides churning.

'How about a simple "yes"?'

'Yes, of course, I'll put the kettle—'

'No, I meant a proper coffee, at a café, just you and me.'

'Oh,' was all Jessie could manage, her mind whirring, her body screaming for her to run. She looked up at him and he smiled, spreading his hands.

'It's just a coffee, Jessie.'

Jessie felt herself nodding. He *had* helped her out. The least she could do was buy him a coffee.

'Okay, w-when?'

'How about right now?'

Chapter 23

Nate held his breath as he watched the myriad emotions play across her face. He didn't know what she would say and was both surprised and disappointed when she responded.

'Okay.' Jessie shrugged, her body language conveying to Nate the opposite message. A weight settled in his chest.

'Fantastic!' He forced a smile, sad she was compelling herself to do something she didn't want to do. Maybe he should—?

'I'll just change,' she said, a little light coming into her grey eyes; a glimmer of hope.

Afraid she'd change her mind and back out, Nate shook his head. 'It's only coffee. We'll be fine as we are,' he said, hoping to ease whatever concerned her.

Jessie raised an eyebrow, one side of her mouth curling into a genuine smile as she looked him up and down.

'Really? I kinda think even the coffee shop has a dress code involving actual clothes.'

Nate looked down at his naked torso and burst out laughing, the tension snapping as he did so. 'Don't worry, I'll grab it on the way out. You ready?'

Jessie looked down at her paint- and blood-spattered dungarees and laughed. 'If you're sure? I just need to lock up.

You go ahead, I'll meet you there.'

Panic clutched Nate's heart as another escape route opened up. 'I… I thought we could go together?' He followed her into the kitchen.

'Oh… erm… I… I've got things to do afterwards, so it makes more sense to take both cars,' she lied, opening a drawer and pulling out her car keys.

Nate was about to say it hardly made a difference, but decided against it. He didn't want to scare her off.

'You go,' Jessie said, nudging him towards the door. 'I need to grab some money. I won't be far behind you.'

Nate stared at her retreating back, wondering if that would be true.

∞

Nate sat in the booth, staring out of the plate-glass window of Bennett's, the stillness of his upper body belying the agitation beneath the table. He glanced at the clock again. *Where is she?*

'You sure I can't get you something, Nate?' Al Bennett called over.

'Nah, waiting for someone first. Thanks, Al.'

'Not like you to wait for anyone,' Al replied, chuckling.

Nate stared at the table and clenched his jaw. Al was right. Waiting for anyone, let alone a woman, was definitely alien to Nate Parker.

He heard the bell as someone entered the café, but he didn't look up this time, until a waft of perfume and a "whoomph" accompanied an arrival at his table.

'I'm so sorry I took so long,' a breathless Jessie said.

Nate looked up, a grin spreading across his face. *She got changed for me*, he noted, as he took in her clean shirt and dusky lipstick, a warm glow igniting inside him.

'You look nice,' he said, wincing at the banality of the word. 'What can I get you?' he added, so she didn't feel obliged to respond to his first comment.

'Aren't I supposed to by buying you the coffee?' she said, laughing.

'Pay at the end. It's just ordering, darlin'.'

'Ah, okay. Just a latte for me, please, a skinny one if they do it.'

'One skinny latte coming right up,' Nate said, and wandered over to the counter to order.

'Ah, damn, I was hoping I'd finally see the *amazing* Nate Parker stood up on a date,' Al said as he made their coffees.

'Oh, cheers, Al, love you too. And this is not a date.'

'Really?' Al turned and looked at Nate, his eyebrows raised. 'Since when do you go out with a woman without getting something out of it at the end?' He winked and carried on making their coffees.

Nate didn't respond; the light-hearted barb stung, the truth in it irrelevant.

'Oh, while you're here, can you bring in some more of your paintings? Someone cleaned me out the other day.'

Nate turned to see the bare walls. 'Wow, and that was all one sale? Looks like *someone* owes me a big fat cheque.'

'Yeah, yeah, you'll get your money. Most of it was one person. Seemed very taken by your work. Right, here you go. Anything else?'

'Not right now. Thanks, Al, and yes, I'll get some more paintings over to you. Anything in particular?'

'Nah, your work sells whatever it is, so I'll leave the subject to you. You know what I like.'

'I do,' Nate replied, rolling his eyes as he carried the coffees back to the table and set Jessie's down in front of her.

'Sorry for being so long. It seems I have another fan. Completely cleaned Al out of all my paintings, so he was asking me for some more.'

Jessie groaned and hid her face in her hands.

'I'm sorry, I didn't mean to bring up the fan club, I was just…' Nate stopped as Jessie held up her hand.

'No, no, that's not what I meant,' she said, uncovering her face. 'I'm the new fan. I bought most of them.' She spread her arms and shrugged before continuing. 'In my defence, I didn't know they were yours.'

'In your defence?' Nate said, sitting back in his seat, feigning affront. 'So, if you'd known they were mine, you wouldn't have bought them?'

'No, no, that's not what I'm saying. God, this isn't coming out right.'

Jessie stopped and took a deep breath. 'I bought them for the subject; they reminded me of my new home, which, now I know you painted them, makes perfect sense.' She cocked her head, giving him a half smile.

'It's fine. I was only joking with the whole insulted thing. I'm actually flattered. Thanks.' He smiled, placing his hand over hers.

Jessie withdrew it, her face sobering as she wrapped both hands around her mug.

Hoping to diffuse the awkwardness his gesture had created,

Nate blurted, 'I tend to paint scenes on and around the lake; it brings me a lot of pleasure sharing elements of home with others.'

'I guess you could say the lake is your muse, then? I hear all artists have one.' Jessie looked at him, a hint of caution clear in her eyes.

'Not at all. I didn't actually believe in muses until recently; thought they were the great myth of the art world.'

'Really? What changed your mind? Has your elusive muse finally put in an appearance?'

Nate watched the light dance in Jessie's grey eyes as curiosity pushed everything else aside, making her irises a kaleidoscope of colours.

'Yes, sh… my muse has hit me with both barrels, shall we say. Ah, ah, nope, not ready to share yet,' he said as Jessie made to interrupt. 'Let's just say, there are plenty more paintings of the lake in progress.'

'Is that what you're working on up in your studio?'

Nate nodded, raising an eyebrow. 'Sounds like someone's been watching me?'

'Ha, no, not at all. I just see a light burning late at night and assumed…' She tailed off as her cheeks flushed in a colour he was trying to commit to memory.

Silence fell between them, and Jessie played with her near-empty mug.

Worried she might leave, and not ready to be without her, Nate said, 'So, what brought you to Potters Hole?'

He immediately wished he hadn't; as her body stiffened, a shadow extinguished the light in her eyes.

Chapter 24

Jessie looked down at her empty mug. She could get up and leave now, feign jobs to do, tiredness, but she had to face this question at some point if she was going to make new friends. After all, there's always a reason strangers move to small towns and villages, while those born there can't wait to escape.

'A fresh start,' she said, shrugging as she fiddled with the handle of her mug, not daring to look up at him in case her face gave more away.

'Ah, the famous fresh start. I'm not sure Potters Hole would be my first choice for that; it's a bit small and out of the way with not much going on.'

Hence the nature of its appeal, thought Jessie, but added nothing more.

'So, what's this fresh start from, the proverbial crappy break-up?' he said, his voice light and teasing.

Jessie's muscles went rigid, and she dropped her hands to her sides so he wouldn't see the whites of her knuckles.

Oh, if only you knew, she thought, saying instead, 'Something like that.'

She stared out of the window, hoping he would grow bored with her flat responses, but luck didn't appear to be on her side.

'Don't tell me it involved your sister?' he said, his voice taking on an element of concern.

Jessie turned to look at him, frowning. 'What would make you say that?'

'The letter you got earlier… from your sister… it seemed to upset you… so I just put two and two together.'

And came up with five.

She'd forgotten all about the letter, but now the all too familiar weight settled across her chest. Jessie shifted and took a deep breath to dislodge it, but it had buried its hooks deep.

As she looked at Nate, clearly waiting for her to spill her guts, all Jessie wanted to do was scream, *"My past is none of your damn business; it's none of anyone's business"*, which was true, but she also knew that to make friends she needed to share some of herself; she just hadn't had time to sanitise her story.

'How about you tell me something about you?' she deflected, smiling at Nate. 'If this is such a small insignificant place, why are you still here? You could afford to go anywhere, couldn't you?'

'I guess,' he said, his gaze drifting off. 'I have travelled pretty much all over the world, but I'm always drawn back here. No matter how far I go, there comes a point when I wake up and say, "time to go home".'

'Why do you think that is?' she asked, leaning forward as she settled in to get a first insight into the famous Nate Parker.

'I honestly don't know. Maybe because I was born here. Well, I think I was. I'm adopted, so it's never been that clear…'

A sheen of sweat washed over Jessie's skin at his words,

and she looked down as her expression slackened, hoping he hadn't noticed. His voice became distant and echoey, as though she was submerged in water. She felt a hand clamp over her arm and she wrenched it away, jumping back and hitting the back of the booth.

'Hey, hey, it's only me,' Nate said, a look of concern on his face. 'Are you feeling okay? Your skin looks clammy. I thought you were going to faint. I—'

'I'm fine, I'm fine, honestly. I think I'm just a little warm. What were you saying?' Jessie plastered a smile on her face as she straightened up, shaking off his words. 'Honestly, I'm okay. Please, go on.'

'I was just saying I grew up in Potters Hole, explored every inch of the woods and the lake as a child, so I guess you could say it's in my blood.' He smiled at her, and she could see his childhood in his eyes.

'That's why you paint it so well,' she said, 'bringing it to life so people can see it the way you do.'

Nate looked away, laughing.

'Is that why you bought the house on the lake? To keep yourself immersed in your childhood, so to speak?'

'Built the house, and yeah, I suppose it is.'

'You *built* that house?' Jessie asked, wide-eyed.

'Not physically. Friends of mine did the hard work. I just drew them a picture.' He laughed and drained the last of his coffee, pulling a face as he did so.

'Is there no end to your talents, Mr Parker?'

'It is double-edged,' he said with a shrug.

'What do you mean? The house is gorgeous.'

'I know. That's the double-edged bit.'

'I don't follow.'

'My mates Mac and Johnny, the guys who built it, have photos in their portfolio and they have generated so much interest they want me to design houses for other clients.'

'Wow, that's brilliant... isn't it?' she asked, noticing his expression.

Nate shrugged. 'It is, but...'

'You think it will take you away from your painting too much?'

'No, it's not just that; it won't be that often. It's that the guys want me to join the company, be an equal partner.'

Jessie watched his face as he spoke. She could see the uneasiness in his eyes, the nervousness in his movements. For the life of her, she couldn't understand why.

'That sounds more than fair, if you ask me. I'm sensing you don't see it that way, though?'

'No, it's more than fair. It's amazing. It's just the thought of going into business with someone else. I've only ever relied on myself; I can trust myself. I don't feel I can apply this to others. I can't, I...'

He looked at her, his gaze seeming to reach into her soul, making her shudder, and she looked away.

'I... I can understand that,' she said, focusing on the dregs of her coffee as she searched for something useful to say. 'But why do you need to jump into such a commitment straight away?'

Nate didn't respond, and when she looked up, she saw he was waiting for her to elaborate.

'If something so permanent unnerves you, why not do a few freelance jobs first? That way, you stay your own boss and can see if you're comfortable working with them before you take the plunge.'

'True enough. I hadn't really thought about it like that. Thanks.'

'Any time,' Jessie said, and seeing a question on his lips, she jumped in with one of her own. 'So, the gallery… Bev,' she added when he looked at her quizzically.

'Ah, yes, of course, Mum. She does like to talk about me.'

'Well, you're a celebrity. You're her celebrity.'

'Hardly,' he said and laughed. 'What do you want to know?'

'Oh, ah, erm…' Jessie stalled as she tried to think of an art-related question that wouldn't make her look like an idiot. 'Do you put on many shows?'

'A few. You've just missed one, last weekend.'

'Oh, and how was it?'

'A sell out,' Nate said. 'But that was down to Em's knack as a saleswoman.'

Jessie watched Nate's face light up as he spoke of Em, his eyes widening at some remembered memory. A pang of jealousy stabbed at her heart and her smile disappeared. 'Oh,' she said, shifting in her seat.

Nate burst out laughing, and Jessie frowned, his mirth dying in an instant.

'Em's a friend, nothing more, and she's far better at managing the gallery than I ever was. We make a great team. Besides, she only has eyes for Chase; she wouldn't touch me with a barge pole.'

'Is the barge pole down to your harem, then?' Jessie blurted, to cover her own embarrassment.

Nate's face sobered at her words.

'Oh, God, I'm so sorry, I didn't—'

'It's fine, I'm used to it from my mother,' he said, his expression belying his words. 'My *harem* is only because I'm local and well known.'

'I'm surprised, given your propensity for one-night stands,' Jessie said, immediately clamping a hand over her mouth, but it was too late; the hurt in his eyes showed the low blow. 'Nate, I'm sorry, I didn't mean… I don't know what's wrong with me. I'm never rude. I-I think I should go before I say something I'll regret… regret more. Oh, God!'

Jessie pushed herself out of the booth, knocking her mug over, the dregs of her coffee dribbling on to her clothes. She didn't care. She had to get away. She needed to escape.

'No, no, don't go, Jessie, it's fine, honestly. I know you didn't… Jessie, please don't go,' Nate pleaded and grabbed hold of her wrist.

Jessie screamed and snatched her arm away, her eyes filling with tears at the look of shock on Nate's face, before she turned and fled.

It was only when she reached her car she realised she hadn't paid for the coffees.

Chapter 25

Oh God, Jessie thought, and rested her head against the door as she pushed it closed. *What was I thinking?* She relived the hurt on Nate's face as she delivered her blows and buried her face in her hands. Why did she say such awful things? It wasn't like her. How on earth could she face him again after that?

Maybe I won't have to? She only saw him at art class, and she could avoid that. But Jessie's sense of morality weighed in and thudded in her chest.

That's what a coward would do. She owed him an apology. After the help he'd given her earlier, he didn't deserve such cruelty. The very least she could do was say she was sorry.

But what am I going to say? How could she explain away her behaviour? She was in no doubt he would want to know why.

Jessie sighed and looked up, eager for Cole's green eyes to cheer her up, but her gaze came to rest on the letter from her sister instead, and her heart sank. It was too soon.

Picking up an expectant and ever-patient Cole, Jessie sat at the table, the letter lying on the surface, waiting to impart its news. Jessie cuddled the cat, his purring easing her tension somewhat.

Releasing Cole, Jessie picked up the envelope and traced her fingertips over Anita's precise script before slitting it open and removing the letter. Her hands shook as she unfolded it, fresh tears filling her eyes as she read her sister's curt note.

Half an hour later, with fat dollops of water dripping onto an uncomplaining Cole, Jessie stared at the now discarded letter. She scratched Cole absently under his chin, her mind ricocheting from one scenario to another, Anita's words both vague and frightening.

A knock at the door jarred her out of her trance.

'Wh-who is it?' she croaked, without looking away from the letter.

'It's me… Nate. Can I come in?'

Jessie's body spasmed as, not for the first time, it urged her to flight, but she didn't move; she didn't trust her legs to hold her.

'I-I'm tired, Nate. Can we do this an—?' But her voice broke, a sob escaping before she could finish.

The door swung open, and Nate strode in. Without a word, he pulled her into his arms and held her as she sobbed. A dislodged and disgruntled Cole adopted a lofty position to monitor his mistress.

Jessie buried her face against Nate's chest, allowing the past to roll through. All the while, Nate crooned to her and stroked her hair.

When the sobs had progressed to hiccups, Nate spoke. 'Please, please tell me this isn't about what happened in the café?'

Jessie shook her head, regretting it as the question she didn't want to answer, wasn't ready to answer, couldn't answer, followed.

'Then what on earth has done this to you?'

Jessie buried her face deeper against his chest, inhaling the slightly sweaty muskiness of him, triggering the longing in her base again, hoping he would just hold her; that's all she wanted, all she needed.

But Nate, it would seem, was a man of action, a man who needed answers, who wanted to fix, to help. She felt his arms relinquish their support and his hands grip her upper arms, rubbing them.

'Hey, Jessie, you can tell me. Whatever it is, you can talk to me.' He pushed away from her, tilting her chin as he bent to meet her.

Jessie gazed into his handsome face, marred only by his concern for her, and clenched her fists to stop herself from reaching up to brush away the lock of auburn hair that had fallen across his liquid brown eyes.

There is more to you than meets the eye, Nate Parker.

Jessie opened her mouth to tell him, to purge herself, to have another human being share the burden she carried, but she stopped. She couldn't tell him, couldn't bear the horror, the judgement, the recoiling. She'd had it all before; she never wanted it again.

'It's the letter from my sister, that's all,' she said instead, shrugging as she pulled away from him, burying her hands in her pockets as she stared at the floor.

'Do you want to talk about it?'

Jessie shook her head and looked up at him. 'Honestly, I'm fine.' She offered him a smile, and after a brief hesitation, he nodded, seeming to accept this.

Silence hung between them until Jessie, wanting to be alone, said, 'What brought you round, Nate? After the way I was, I—'

'I wanted to make sure you were okay. Plus, and only if you're interested, no pressure, I wanted to offer you my bookcase building services.' He took a bow, making Jessie smile.

'You still want to help me after I was so awful to you? No, I couldn't ask—'

'You haven't, I've offered, and let's forget about what we said earlier, shall we?'

'I-I don't think I can. I don't know where it came from. I'm never mean. I-I'm so sorry, Nate, really, I am. I—'

'I know, and you're forgiven. It's not like what you said doesn't have an element of truth to it.'

'Still, I—'

'Sh! Let's forget about it. So, what do you say?'

Before she could respond, Nate stepped forward and grabbed her hands, inspecting her wounded palms.

'Let's face it, Jess, it's not like your delicate constitution can do it, is it?' he said, dodging out of the way as she swatted him.

'Hey, I'm not as delicate as I look!'

'I don't doubt it. So, what's it to be? I'm happy to work for coffee,' he said, spreading his arms wide and cocking his head to one side.

'Fine, fine, I give in.' Jessie threw her hands in the air, enjoying the ease with which Nate had distracted her. 'But you'll have to improve your debt collection skills, as I didn't pay for the last one.'

Nate shrugged, and winked as he said, 'I'll invoice you. So, what time do you want me in the morning?'

'I thought you had a muse commanding all your time now?' Jessie watched as Nate seemed to freeze, his initial response dying on his lips, a battle of wills playing behind his eyes. Instead, he looked at the floor, a smile just visible as he nodded, hands now resting on his hips.

'Yeah, I do,' he said, looking up at her from beneath his floppy fringe. 'But I think my muse would approve of me offering my services to you for as long as you need them. I am at your disposal, mademoiselle,' he said, bowing again.

Who is this understanding muse? Jessie wondered, certain it was a person, as she pushed him out the door.

Nate gripped the door frame, stopping Jessie shoving him out, and raised his eyebrows. 'I cannot leave without an answer, my lady.'

Jessie rolled her eyes and swatted his chest. 'Fine. If you want to help, who am I to refuse?'

Nate closed his eyes and brought his palms together, giving a slight bow, before opening his eyes and looking around the kitchen. 'And this,' he said, gesturing to encompass the entire room, 'we'll talk about this tomorrow.'

He surprised her with a kiss on the forehead before allowing her to close the door on him.

Jessie was grinning as she leaned back against the door, her face sobering as she saw Anita's letter, its contents causing a knot to form in her stomach.

She walked over to the table and picked it up, skimming the

contents again. She folded it and put it back in the envelope, before scooping up Cole and burying her face in his fur, inhaling the mossy scent of his nocturnal ramble.

Jessie carried both Cole and the letter upstairs, hiding Anita's words on the Yorkshire moors, somewhere between Thrushcross Grange and *Wuthering Heights*. Then, as she did every night, she stood at her bedroom window and gazed out over the lake. Her gaze moved to the house on the other side, its huge windows still in darkness.

There was more to Nate than the persona he'd created; she'd seen as much that evening.

As her body relived the feel of his muscular arms around her, Jessie climbed into bed and nestled under her duvet. With Cole curled up beside her, she stepped into Cathy's turmoil as she wrestled with love and life.

∞

Nate raced upstairs as soon as he got home, not even bothering to close the front door. He grabbed a pencil and his sketchbook and went to work. He needed to catch the rawness of what he'd seen while it was still fresh in his mind.

A couple of hours later, he stood up and stretched, his muscles complaining at being asked to change position, and stepped back to observe his latest creation.

His body shuddered and his heart ached as he relived what he'd seen. The pain, the hurt, the sadness, the guilt, were all staring back at him from Jessie's face, just as they'd been when he walked into her kitchen to find tears coursing down her cheeks.

I didn't like that.

Seeing Jessie in so much pain made him want to destroy the person who'd caused it.

That sister of hers must be a real piece of work.

How could anyone want to cause pain to someone who took the time and effort to win over a feral cat? Nate shook his head in disbelief.

Something else was bothering him, too. The strength of his reaction to Jessie's distress was something he had never experienced before, and he didn't know what shocked him more—his desire to destroy Jessie's sister, or the fact he wanted to protect Jessie from harm and upset… at all costs.

He walked over to the window and stared across the lake, but Bluebell Cottage was in darkness. Nate wrapped his arms around himself and closed his eyes, remembering the feel of her body against his, of her tears soaking through his shirt and electrifying his skin.

Christ, how I wish I was there with her right now.

What the hell was happening to him? He released his arms and turned away from the window, shaking his head. He'd never had feelings like this before about anyone, and more importantly, he'd never wanted to.

Now, though?

He snorted out a laugh. Now though, what, exactly? He didn't know.

There was one person who would be over the moon to see the state he was in—his mother. As his thoughts drifted to her, Nate couldn't help but wonder if *she* knew Jessie's story.

Chapter 26

Nate arrived at Bluebell Cottage at what he considered an acceptably early hour, armed with coffees and a selection of pastries so they could enjoy breakfast together before getting stuck in.

Not early enough, it would appear.

He observed an empty mug and plate on the patio table, Cole sitting sentry like on a chair, staring down his nose at Nate through hooded eyes.

'We're both on the same side, you know,' Nate said, ruffling the black cat's head before walking through the open door, offerings in hand.

He paused in the kitchen, deciding its emptiness was the perfect time to make his assessment. He wandered around, capturing the angles and features while his mind created. The sound of out of tune singing coming from the living room, however, proved too distracting.

He ambled through and leaned against the door frame, a grin spreading across his face.

Ear buds in, her back to him, Jessie gyrated her hips to what Nate interpreted as a Latin beat. Her terrible singing punctuated the air as she picked up the odd word, all the while rubbing beeswax on the shelves they'd put up the previous day.

Now, this is an image I want to capture, Nate thought, his fingers itching to record what he was watching.

Unable to take his eyes off her undulating hips, Nate had to adjust his jeans to make them more comfortable as desire flooded his body.

Jessie's singing reduced to a hum as her hips slowed. Nate cleared his throat, but got no response, so he coughed as loudly as he could.

Startled, Jessie whirled around, one hand on her chest, the other pulling the ear buds from her ears. The look on her face doused the flames in Nate.

'I'm sorry, I didn't mean to startle you, but there was no easy way to get your attention with those in,' he said, pointing to her ear buds. 'I brought energy.' He held out the bag of pastries.

'What're you doing here?' Jessie snapped, deflating Nate's mood. He saw his fantasy day dissipate as Jessie stared at him, a none-too-welcoming frown on her face.

'I-I've come to help… like we agreed last night.' His cheeks flushed as he spoke.

Jeez, what is wrong with me?

'I'm fine. I don't need any more help,' Jessie said, turning her back on him.

What the hell happened after I left? Nate wondered. 'Let me see your hands.'

'What?'

'Your hands, the one's you messed up yesterday. Let me see them.'

Jessie turned back to him and reluctantly held out her hands, palms down. Nate turned them over, one at a time, and traced his finger over the damp, stained bandages, making Jessie shudder.

He looked up at her, a half smile on his lips. 'And how far do you think you'll get with these?' He watched as the corners of her mouth twitched. 'Besides, how often do you have a slave willing to do your bidding? A slave bearing gifts, no less, gifts which are going to be cold and gooey if we don't eat them soon.' He held up the bag again, the darker bottom supporting his plea.

Jessie stared at him, and he could see the warring emotions playing across her face. After a few moments of silence, Nate was ready to give up, when it was as if she suddenly awoke from a hypnotic state. Her body relaxed as she smiled.

'I *would* get more done with your help,' she conceded.

She led him back into the kitchen, where she opened and closed cupboards and drawers, extracting plates and cutlery. All the while, Nate noticed, her hands shook.

'Are you okay?' he asked as they sat at the kitchen table.

'Yeah, why?'

'Well, you just seem on edge, that's all. You forgot about today and I…' He tailed off and looked at her, but she didn't meet his gaze.

'I didn't sleep well,' she said, offering him a smile as she picked up the bag of pastries.

'The letter?'

Jessie nodded, but said nothing more.

∞

'Bloody hell, did you buy enough?' Jessie asked as she stared into the bag. She wasn't in the least bit hungry, but she needed to steer the conversation in a different direction.

'Well, I wasn't sure what you liked.'

'So you bought the entire shop?'

'Almost, yeah.'

They both smiled before stuffing buttered delights into their mouths, looking anywhere but at each other.

Jessie hadn't forgotten Nate was coming to help; she'd been looking forward to it—as the singing and dancing would testify.

The problem was, he'd startled her. He'd been watching her and then he'd announced his presence, just like Matthew used to do, triggering a memory, and her response had been instinctive, defensive, protective.

Jessie had been so excited, she'd been beside herself as she'd watched the confirmation appear on the laptop screen. She opened her email to see the tickets already waiting, and she printed them off, wanting something tangible to give to him, convinced he'd be pleased with what she'd done.

How can he not be? Jessie thought as she stared at the tickets in her hand. She'd initially wanted to surprise him on his birthday, but she knew she wouldn't be able to keep it a secret until then.

'What the hell do you think you're doing?' Matthew said, startling Jessie. She spun round in her chair to find him leaning against the door frame.

'H-how long have you been there?'

'Long enough,' he said, uncrossing his arms and advancing towards her. He leaned down, resting his hands on the arms of her chair, his face inches from hers.

'Care to tell me why you were on the computer?'

'I-I have a surprise for you,' she said as a lump rose in her throat, but she swallowed it down and forced a smile into place.

'Really? And did I give you permission for whatever this is?' Matthew sneered, spittle landing on her face. Jessie recoiled and Matthew growled, grabbing her chin and forcing her to look at him.

'Don't you dare turn away from me when I'm talking to you.'

'Y-you're h-hurting me,' Jessie managed, a tear running from the corner of her eye.

'Am I now? Well, that's no more than you deserve, given your disobedience.'

'B-but it wouldn't be a surprise if you knew…'

'And that's just how I like things. No surprises.'

'But it's for your b-birthday.'

'I told you what I want for my birthday.'

'I know, but I th-thought I'd… argh!' Jessie's head snapped back, and she clutched her cheek at the blow.

'I don't want you to think!' Matthew snarled.

Jessie held her hands up, protecting her face, the tickets still clutched in her hand. Matthew snatched them away as he loomed over her.

Jessie shuddered as she remembered him taking the tickets. He'd gone to the concert, just not with her.

She looked up at Nate and smiled. She couldn't tell him why she'd reacted that way. She couldn't tell him any of it. He wouldn't understand. He wouldn't believe her; no one did.

'These are delicious, thank you,' she said instead, leaning back and patting her belly. 'But I'm stuffed, I can't eat any more.'

'Not to worry, I'm sure our avian friends will enjoy a treat too.' He peered into the still full bag. 'And you're welcome, by the way. Any time. So, what's on the agenda for today, boss?' he asked, winking at her.

'More of the same, I'm afraid, but in here this time, and in my bedroom. I want all the alcoves full of books.'

'Hold that thought for a moment,' Nate said, holding up his hand. 'Before we start, could I share a few thoughts I've had about this room?'

Jessie bristled, her defences lining up at the perceived criticism, but she killed the retort this time. She shrugged and nodded instead.

She crossed her arms as he talked, deciding she'd be polite and listen, but stick to what she wanted, But, as he described how he would move cupboards, change the position of the sink, and put in patio doors which opened out onto a covered porch, complete with a swing, Jessie couldn't stop the smile spreading across her face.

He gets it! He completely gets it!

Jessie's smile vanished as her thoughts shifted, and Nate's plans stuttered to a halt.

'What's wrong? What did I say? You were smiling and now you're not.'

'Nothing's wrong, honestly. I love it. You've described pretty much exactly what I want to do, but…'

'But what?'

'Money. I just can't afford it, so it's going to have to remain a dream until my bank balance says otherwise.'

'Don't worry about the money. I can do most of the labour, and I can get the materials at cost, so it'll be a fraction of a contractor.'

'I know and, believe me, I am grateful, but I wouldn't even have enough to pay you. And, before you say anything, payment in coffee is not an option for a project this big.'

'If you don't mind it taking a bit longer, well, a lot longer, I'd be happy to do it for you for free, in exchange for allowing the designs to be part of my portfolio.'

'What about your painting, your design work with your friends, your muse? I couldn't take advantage of you like that, Nate. It wouldn't be fair, and I don't want to feel indebted to you. Besides, I didn't think you were a builder?'

'I'm not, but I can turn my hand to most things. It wouldn't affect my other work, hence why I said about the timescale—I'd fit it around the other stuff,' he said, smiling at her before dropping his gaze and fiddling with his hands.

'As for my muse, as I said last night, my muse would be fine with me helping you, and you wouldn't be taking advantage of me, Jessie, far from it…' Nate paused and Jessie watched him grinding his teeth as he formed his next words.

'You'd actually be allowing *me* to repay a debt.'

'What do you mean?'

Nate looked up at her, his face flushed. 'It's you.'

Chapter 27

Jessie stared at him, her body stiffening as if frigid air had blown across it, a feverish sheen left in its wake. 'What's me?' she whispered.

Nate looked down at his hands, and she watched his embarrassment spread to his ears as he shifted his weight in his seat.

'Remember, I said at the café I'd recently found my muse?'

'I remember,' Jessie said, waiting for him to have the good grace to look at her.

'It's you, Jessie. My muse is you. You are my muse.' He looked at her and the honesty and innocence in his eyes started the thaw.

'Why me?' She rested her elbows on the table, her curiosity pushing her fear aside.

Nate shrugged. 'It wasn't intended, I promise. When I saw you that first day, your feet in the lake, a faraway look on your face, the pain and sadness were palpable. It took my breath away. *You* took my breath away, and I couldn't stop. I…'

'You've been spying on me?' Jessie couldn't help the edge that crept into her voice, the mention of her pain putting her on her guard.

'I'm sorry, I'm sorry. I know I shouldn't have, but you

looked so vulnerable, so mesmerising, so beautiful. No matter what I see you do, I haven't been able to stop painting you. I—'

'So you *have* been spying on me?'

'No, no, it's not like that, it's…' Nate hung his head, his shoulders slumping. 'I guess I have, haven't I?' he sighed, looking up. 'I'm sorry, I should have told you. Hell, I should have asked. I… why are you smiling?' he asked, frowning, a look of utter bewilderment on his face. 'I thought you were pissed off?'

Jessie pondered his question, asking herself the same thing. While she should be livid at the intrusion on her privacy, she wasn't. As she'd listened to Nate justify his actions, her body had relaxed, the feeling of being interesting and desired far more potent… and welcoming.

'I am, or at least, I should be. But, for some reason, I'm more flattered than pissed off. And intrigued. When can I see them?'

Nate stared at her, open-mouthed, before stammering, 'A-as soon as they're finished. Really? You're okay with it? You're not mad?'

'Don't get me wrong, you should have asked me first, but no, I'm not mad.'

'I will, one hundred per cent, in future, I promise.'

'So, you're hoping to keep this up, are you?' Jessie raised an eyebrow.

'Well, yeah, that's kind of how having a muse works,' he said, cracking a half smile as he looked up at her.

'It would seem I'm in credit when it comes to your services then?'

'Yes, you are.' Nate smiled. 'Does that mean I can bring my ideas for your kitchen to life?'

'Er, they're my ideas. You just happen to think the same way,' Jessie corrected.

'Yes, ma'am,' he said, holding up his hands and making her laugh.

'Before all that, though, I'd like the shelves put up in my bedroom.'

'Your wish is my command,' Nate said and saluted. 'Show me the way and I'll measure up.'

Jessie's body went cold at the thought of being alone in her bedroom with a man, and she shook her head. 'Y-you don't need me. It's pretty obvious where they should go,' she said, forcing a smile, but not meeting his gaze. 'Besides, I want to finish waxing these down here.'

Nate stared at her for a moment, but said nothing. He nodded and disappeared into the hallway.

∞

It was mid-afternoon when Nate came clumping downstairs, pulling his t-shirt down over his head.

'All done,' he said, setting his tools on the worktop. Jessie had to drag her gaze away from the flash of toned torso as she proffered a cup of coffee.

'That was quick,' she said, hiding her face behind her mug and inhaling the rich coffee aroma.

'You can check if you don't believe me,' he said, lifting the mug to his lips.

'Careful, that's…'

'Ouch! Yeah, hot, I got it.' Nate set the mug on the counter.

'Sorry, I've only just made it.'

'My fault. So, you coming up so I can show you what I've done, make sure it's right?'

'I'm sure it's fine,' Jessie said, not shifting from her position leaning against the sink. 'I'll have a look later when I go up.'

'It'd be better if you looked now so I can make any adjustments before I go, otherwise it'll be next weekend as—'

'I said I'll look later!' she snapped, the words out before she could stop them, a surge of anger racing through her at his pushing.

'Have it your way,' Nate said, holding his hands up in defence. 'But if it's wrong…' He didn't finish the sentence, instead gathering up his tools.

Jessie didn't respond. She watched as he moved towards the door, not daring to speak, not trusting what might come out. But as Nate said goodbye to Cole, panic took over.

'Nate!'

Nate paused in the doorway and turned to look at her, his opinion of the way she'd spoken to him clear on his face.

'I… I'm sorry. I-I shouldn't have snapped at you. It's no excuse. There is no excuse for being rude to you, not after everything you've done, but…' Her words died on her lips as she looked at him; she couldn't tell him.

Nate shook his head and walked out.

Jessie burst into tears.

Chapter 28

It's no excuse, but what? What is it she so clearly wants to tell me, but just as clearly can't?

Nate shook his head as he walked to his truck. He took his time packing his tools away, hoping she'd come out, hoping she'd finally open up and tell him what she'd been on the verge of telling him so many times, but she didn't.

Cole did. He sauntered over and plonked himself down, staring at Nate, his green eyes wide, as though imploring Nate to make the first move.

'I can't,' Nate said, and picked up the cat. Cole stiffened, but then settled down, butting Nate's chest as he purred.

'It's not me that's in the wrong, mate,' he said as he put Cole back down. 'I'll see you next weekend, assuming I'll be welcome, of course.'

The cat meowed and rubbed around Nate's legs before sauntering away.

As Nate backed out of the driveway, Cole watched, and he waved to the cat as he pulled away. His heart jolted as he glimpsed Jessie at the living room window, half-hidden as she peered out. He slammed on the brakes and reversed back, but when he turned to look, she was nowhere to be seen.

Shaking his head, Nate put the truck into gear and headed home, questions filling his mind. What was it about her Jekyll and Hyde personality that kept him coming back for more? He'd always headed for the hills at the first sign of trouble, but not this time.

What is it about you, Jessie Ellis?

∞

Jessie pressed herself back against the wall, her heart thudding in her chest. *Did he see me?* He must have, he reversed back. She barely dared breathe as she listened, waiting to see what his decision would be. Would he drive away, or would he come back, throw the door open and demand she tell him why she'd been such a bitch to him, why she kept tormenting him?

She stared wide-eyed at the door, almost wishing he would come back and force it out of her. At least it would be done then. But his tyres crunching on the gravel gave her the only answer she knew in her heart was fitting.

Nate Parker would *never* force her to do anything she wasn't ready, or didn't want, to do.

So, why do I keep reacting as if he would?

Her glassy stare still fixed on the door, she suddenly snorted with laughter. Maybe if she'd *reacted* to Matthew, things would have been different.

What the hell must Nate think of me?

Jessie pushed herself away from the wall and collapsed into the armchair, burying her face in her hands.

Groaning, she sat back up, and found Cole sitting watching her, his head cocked to one side.

'What does it matter what Nate thinks, hey?' But deep down it did matter, the knot in her belly serving as evidence.

Nate was a good man. She'd borne witness to that. Yes, he had his demons, but he didn't take them out on her.

Jessie thought about the time they'd spent together, about what he'd shared with her, and, despite her promise to herself, she liked him… a lot. She shivered, her skin prickling at the thought that this time, he might not come back.

I have to tell him.

Part of her wanted to, despite her vow never to tell anyone, but telling him about Matthew was one thing, the rest… She shuddered as she contemplated his reaction.

Nate had shared some of his past with her, was even cheery and upbeat about it, but Jessie had seen his jaw clench. She knew there was more to his story, and she'd bet it wasn't as rosy.

Memories of the past tugged her thoughts back to the letter from Anita, the only person from her former life who knew where she was. Jessie pulled the letter from its hiding place inside her well-read copy of *Wuthering Heights* and stared at it.

A letter in the twenty-first century. Jessie chuckled as she recalled Nate's reaction to it, but then she sobered. Snail mail was all Jessie was willing to accept, the only way she could keep her location confined to those who needed to know. As for the rest, Matthew had turned her against technology by tracking her every move through her mobile phone and her email. She didn't even want a landline connected, which meant any apologising to Nate would need to be face to face.

Jessie shook her head, pushing the thought aside, and re-

read the letter. A sob escaped her throat, startling Cole from his slumber on her lap, and she squeezed her eyes closed.

Why does this have to happen?

If she did what Anita said, it could blow the life she'd worked so hard to build for herself apart. And he might find her

But how can I refuse?

If she didn't do it, the fallout would be far worse than Matthew finding her. *That* she could live with. *That* she could survive. The other? Jessie shuddered at the thought as her heart ached for what she'd done.

Anita didn't understand; never had.

'You're a heartless bitch, you know that, Jessie? You only ever think of yourself!' Anita had screamed at her when Jessie had shared her plans.

'This isn't about me, dammit!'

'Of course it is. It's always about you. As long as you're okay, no one else matters.'

'How dare you! You know damn well why I'm doing this. Why can't you just support me, like I need you to?'

'Because you're wrong, and you'll see that when this blows over.'

Jessie shook her head as she recalled the row. Anita had never believed her. She looked at the letter again. If she was the one, she'd have to go back. Matthew would know then. He'd know where she was. He'd come after her, restraining order or not. He'd…

But would he? If he was so desperate to find her, he could hire a Private Detective, but would he risk his career on her?

Besides, Jessie thought, glancing at her sister's script, *he has a pretty new wife.* Jessie snorted, shaking her head. It hadn't taken him long to replace someone he would *never* let go of.

Pushing Matthew from her mind, Jessie looked at Anita's order, and made her decision; she needed to register with the doctors, anyway.

Jessie tucked the letter back inside the book and gathered Cole into her arms. His protests at being disturbed again soon subsided as Jessie carried him upstairs.

She stood at her bedroom window, Cole purring in her arms, and stared across the lake. His truck was there, but the house was in darkness. Even his studio stared blankly back at her.

How will I ever find the words to tell you?

Chapter 29

Nate gave up on sleep and padded to the coffee maker.

Today will require the hard stuff.

As his rocket fuel armed itself, Nate stared across the lake at a slumbering Bluebell Cottage.

He'd lain awake all night, wrestling with why Jessie captured him so much, but he was still no closer to an answer.

A distraction is what he needed. He had paintings to deliver to Al Bennett, and also to Em. He decided to concentrate on the easier of the two—Al. Nate gave him whatever he hadn't been able to sell in the gallery.

'As long as it's not too big. I don't want to be suffocated,' Al had grumbled when Nate had approached him years earlier. His response still made Nate chuckle, as he always referred to the size of the paintings, despite all the money Nate had paid him in commission over the years.

Smiling at the image of Al the art connoisseur, approving or dismissing his work, Nate carried a steaming mug of nectar into his garage where he kept some of his excess stock. He whiled away a few hours sorting through his paintings, selecting ones he knew Al would like.

He also made a mental note to photograph the rest. It was

about time he did what he'd been wanting to do for ages and set up an online shop to sell them through. His only dilemma was whether to sell them through the gallery's website, or to set up a new one and tap into a different demographic.

Maybe I'll ask Jessie and see…

Nate stopped what he was doing and nipped the thought of Jessie in the bud.

What does it matter what she thinks?

'Oh, who am I kidding?' he snorted, shaking his head. Of course, it mattered; he'd taken her advice about working independently with his friends on a trial basis. Besides, he liked the idea of her opinion. He wanted her opinion.

Nate tried to push thoughts of Jessie aside, focusing on the canvases before him. He hadn't been up to his studio deliberately; he wanted to avoid seeing her, or spying on her, to be more precise.

The thought of spying brought back to him how well Jessie had taken the news she had a Peeping Tom. Given how she flew off the handle at what he would term trivial things, her calm acceptance of his crime puzzled him.

Most women would have been incensed, and, in all honesty, would have probably reported him to the police, but not Jessie. Jessie struck him as being flattered by his actions, as though no one had thought her worthy of attention in the past.

Nate shrugged and shook his head.

Women!

He winced as Em marched into his mind to put him in his place. Nate groaned. He had to get some paintings to her before she started pecking at him.

He could finish some of those he'd been doing of Jessie, as there were several close enough to completion; they wouldn't take too much time. But he'd promised Jessie he wouldn't show them to anyone else before she'd seen them, and he definitely wouldn't put them in a show without her say so.

Nope. He couldn't face seeing Jessie right now, not with the angst, or whatever it was, between them.

A lightness bubbled up through him, making the hairs on the back of his neck stand on end, as an idea for his next collection took root—one based on the turmoil he currently felt.

If he was to bring it to fruition, it would involve a road trip, which would involve cancelling his art class. He pondered this, knowing his mother would be none too pleased, but then shrugged—it wasn't like he hadn't done it before.

Cheered by this well-needed focus, Nate packed the paintings for Al into his truck—he'd drop them off on the way—before racing upstairs to pack some clothes; his "go bag" with all his painting and drawing supplies forever in his truck.

Humming to himself, his mind at ease for the first time since he'd laid eyes on Jessie, Nate set off for Rock Cliff Falls—the perfect reflection of his inner turmoil.

Chapter 30

Jessie's heart sank as she stared at the plaque on the wall outside Potters Hole Medical Practice. There was only one name on the plaque—Ray Parker.

Of course it is!

She looked around, toeing the ground as she did so, wrestling with the decision. Questions would be asked if she ventured further afield, unless, of course, she had no choice.

With a bubble of hope, Jessie stepped into the doctor's office, only to have it popped by the receptionist, who not only informed her they had space on their books but also that Dr Parker had a cancellation and could see her straight away.

As soon as she'd completed the required registration paperwork, Jessie was ushered into Dr Parker's office—Bev's husband, Nate's father.

'Jessie! It's so good to meet you at last,' Dr Parker said, coming around from behind his desk and enveloping Jessie in a hug. 'Bev's told me so much about you; I feel I know you already.' He laughed as he released her and sat back down. 'What can I do for you today?'

Jessie stared at the tall, yet stooped, man.

He's in great shape, like his son.

Jessie felt her cheeks warming at the thought of Nate and she turned away, hoping he wouldn't notice.

Regaining control, Jessie looked back at Ray Parker, who was smiling at her, his mischievous blue eyes creasing with genuine emotion.

'I'll tell you what, why don't you sit down first?' he said, running a hand through his thick white hair, a mannerism she'd seen Nate adopt too.

'Jessie? Are you okay? What's troubling you?' he asked, leaning forward on his desk, his face tinged with concern as he watched her through his rounded glasses.

Jessie cleared her throat. 'I… I… need, Doctor—'

'Call me Ray, please. Everyone does.'

'Um, okay… Ray… I, er, I need a blood test,' Jessie rushed out before flopping back in the chair, as though having unloaded an enormous weight.

'Do you want to tell me why you think you need a blood test?' Ray frowned as he looked at her.

'I don't *think* I need one; I *know* I do, so would you be able to do it for me, please?'

'Jessie, I can't take your blood without knowing what it's for.'

Jessie looked at him, at his kind, gentle face, and opened her mouth to speak, before remembering Bev was his wife, and Nate was his son. She closed her mouth and looked down at her hands.

'Whatever you tell me remains between us, Jessie. Everything between me and my patients is confidential, irrespective of how well they know my wife,' Ray said, his voice soothing.

Jessie looked at him, chewing on her bottom lip as she pondered how little she could tell him to enable him to do the test.

'I need to know if I'm a match so I can help someone… in my family.'

'A match for what?' Ray asked, but Jessie shook her head.

'Look, you're going to have to tell me a bit more so I can help you, Jessie.'

'L-leukaemia. They have leukaemia.'

'I see. I'm afraid I can't do that here. You need to go to the hospital where they can do all the required… Why're you shaking your head?'

'I can't go to the hospital.'

'Why on earth not?'

'I just can't,' Jessie snapped. 'I… I'm sorry, I can't go to the hospital. Please, can you help me? The letter said all I need is a simple blood test at this stage. Please. I might not even be a match, but I have… I have to try.' Jessie looked up at Ray, her eyes wide as she struggled to stop the tears from spilling.

Ray stared at her for what seemed an age, the dilemma playing across his handsome face. Finally, he nodded.

'Can you come back later, after school?'

'Yes, yes, of course, but why—?'

'I need to speak to the hospital—'

'I can't go!'

'Jessie, it's okay. I won't make you go, but I do need to find out exactly what I need to do, okay?'

Jessie nodded. 'Thank you. I really appreciate you doing this for me.'

Ray stood up and came around and perched on his desk. 'Is

there anything else you want to tell me? You're safe here, Jessie. I can help you.'

'No, I-I'm fine, honestly,' she said, standing up. 'I… I'll see you later.' She turned and left before he could say anything more.

∞

Jessie closed the door behind her and leaned against it, savouring the essence of Bluebell Cottage. She was glad to be home. Dodging probing questions, especially those artfully woven into the conversation, was exhausting, but worth it. Ray had promised her he would deal with everything, and send the results to the hospital Anita had advised her of in the letter.

Too exhausted to cook, Jessie poured herself a glass of wine, and after changing into some jeans and a t-shirt, she carried her wine down to the jetty. As she picked her way along the rotten structure, she wondered if Nate could bring it back to life.

Thoughts of her neighbour drew her gaze to the house across the lake. Once again, it lay in darkness, but this time, his truck was missing.

As Jessie settled herself at the end of the jetty, bare feet dangling in the cool water, she wondered where Nate had disappeared to.

Chapter 31

'Is Nate okay?' Jessie asked, her back to Bev as she tidied up the daily mess Potters Hole's youngest members had left. Nate's truck still hadn't been back in its usual place when Jessie wandered down to the lake to enjoy her morning coffee.

After a pause Bev, replied. 'Yes, as far as I know, why?'

'No reason, I was just wondering.'

'And why would you just be wondering?'

As she turned to face Bev, the older woman's eyebrows raised in question, Jessie felt her cheeks burning.

'I... I haven't seen his truck since... for a while,' she corrected, opting not to say anything further in case she prompted questions she couldn't answer.

After several uncomfortable minutes, Bev responded, 'He's gone off on one of his painting trips.'

'Oh?'

'He does this every so often, giving no one any notice; very inconsiderate. Which reminds me, art class is cancelled tonight. I need to let them know.' Bev grabbed her phone.

'Oh,' Jessie repeated, a weight settling itself in her stomach. 'How long will he be away for?'

Bev shrugged as she put the phone to her ear, but then

looked at Jessie, narrowing her eyes. 'Why?'

It was Jessie's turn to shrug as she fought down unexpected tears. 'No reason. I-I was just curious.' She turned away, the tears having won through.

'Hey, hey,' Bev said, grabbing Jessie's arm as she cut her call, pulling Jessie around to face her. 'What's wrong? Why are you crying? Has Nate done something—?'

'No, no, nothing's wrong, honestly. I was… I was suppressing a sneeze, that's all,' Jessie said, giving Bev a weak smile. 'Right, you have a class to cancel, and I have a house that still needs attention. I'll see you Monday.' Jessie turned and walked away before Bev could question her further.

∞

To stave off thoughts of Nate and whether she would see him again, Jessie busied herself tidying up the cottage and finishing any minor jobs. The kitchen, however, she left, just in case.

Her biggest thrill, and the only thing which pushed Nate from her mind, was unpacking and arranging her books. As she gently peeled the packing tape from the boxes, memories surfaced once more.

'What the fuck do you need so many damn books for?' Matthew had stormed as the movers brought in the last of her boxes.

'Because they're what I love. You know this. You—'

'Yeah, well, *I'm* what you love now. You won't be needing all this.'

'What are you saying?' Jessie had asked, puzzled at his reaction to the passion he'd shown so much interest in when they first started dating.

'Isn't it obvious? Do you need me to spell it out for you? Are you really that dumb?' Matthew glared at her, jamming his forefinger into her temple. Jessie shrugged away from him, rubbing her head.

'But you kn-know they're my p-passion.'

'Not anymore, baby. All you need is me.'

'But they m-make a home…'

'They make a home smell musty and old, you mean? They're not coming in my house, end of discussion.'

'B-but it's our home… argh!' Jessie screamed as Matthew punched her, her central incisors slicing through her bottom lip.

Jessie clamped her hand over her mouth, the blood dripping through her fingers, tears stinging her eyes as she stared at him.

'W-what am I su-supposed to do with them?'

'Bin them for all I care, just get rid of them… before I get back!'

He'd left at that point and Jessie hadn't seen him until the early hours, when he'd returned stinking of booze

Jessie shuddered as she remembered what he'd done to her when he got home and focused her attention on uncovering the books she hadn't laid eyes on for over a decade. Despite Matthew's wishes, a friend of Jessie's had agreed to keep the boxes until she could arrange proper storage.

Caressing each volume as she unwrapped it, Jessie spent hours arranging her collection, in author order, in the room she felt each book best suited, reflecting the reading mood she would be in when curled up in that room. Romance, classics and books from her childhood found a home in her bedroom, whilst thrillers, suspense, mystery and biography took pride of place in the living room. The only volume which defied these rules was *Wuthering Heights*, the book she'd never let down, hiding it under her mattress where Matthew wouldn't find it. Heathcliff and Cathy were welcome anywhere. To give her books space to breathe, Jessie interspersed them with the objects she'd unwrapped from her travels.

Any books she found that best suited the kitchen—cooking, birds, art, gardening—she boxed them back up. She even emptied all the kitchen cupboards, the boxes joining the others, just in case. If Nate didn't come, Jessie had decided to sand down the cupboard doors and paint them in soft shades of buttermilk.

The very last job on her list for the inside of the cottage was to hang the paintings she'd bought at Bennett's, Nate's paintings.

Jessie unwrapped each one and lined them up, drinking in the richness of the detail and the vibrancy of the colours. They were all so lifelike, and Jessie hunted out a magnifying glass, scrutinising each, proving to her brain they weren't the photographs her mind was trying to convince her they were.

Wanting to ensure each painting captured both the light and her eye in the most breathtaking way, Jessie spent the best part of an afternoon carrying them from room to room. As it turned out, Mother Nature had decided for her, and Jessie laughed as she observed her decisions—the paintings of the lake, wild flowers and birds waited in anticipation in her bedroom and the hallway, with a couple set aside for the kitchen; those of the wood and wildlife lingered patiently in the living room.

Pleased with the interior of Bluebell Cottage, and with time to fill in before the weekend, Jessie turned her attention to the garden.

She'd already determined she needed little, so she took a trip to the out-of-town garden centre and browsed the selection of plants, pots, ornaments and furniture, allowing herself to be drawn to certain things, purchasing two wooden benches, some evening-scented phlox and some pots and compost in which to plant them.

As she tied down the hatch of her trusty Audi, securing the flat-packed benches in place for their journey to Potters Hole, Jessie contemplated paying a visit to Nate's gallery. She climbed behind the wheel, the thought bouncing around in her mind.

What if he's there? What will I say?

Jessie leaned back and stared at the roof of the car, lips pursed.

No! Let's see if he turns up tomorrow.

She hadn't decided what to say to him, anyway.

Decision made, Jessie headed home.

Chapter 32

Nate slid his truck into its space close to the house and turned the engine off. He leaned his head against the headrest and closed his eyes, savouring the quiet that enveloped him, his ears ringing with the silence.

He'd had a hell of a week, and part of him hadn't wanted to come home. Yet another part of him was eager to see her.

He'd spent five days lost in his art, and it was just what he'd needed. The sheer power of the water at Rock Cliff Falls had restored him. The thundering waterfalls drowned out everything else, allowing him to focus and capture the beauty of the movement. He'd created so much new material that Em would be over the moon.

And hopefully off my back for a while.

Nate dug his phone out of the glove compartment, where it had languished for his week of seclusion, and powered it on. As he waited for the onslaught, Nate let his gaze drift across the lake.

As distracting as his week had been, at night, while he'd lain in bed, the only thing he'd seen, the only thing he'd wanted to see, was Jessie. Nate had certainly gained clarity while he'd been away, just not in the way he'd expected.

He'd missed her; a feeling he'd only ever experienced for

his art, never for another person, especially a woman.

The incessant pinging of his phone interrupted his thoughts, and he checked through his messages—the expected barrage from Em, whom he'd not told about his trip, plus a string of messages from Mac and Johnny with details about the first project they wanted him to design.

Well, I've certainly got plenty of excuses not to see you again, Jessie Ellis.

Nate looked out across the lake again, his stomach turning sour at the thought. He wanted to see her, more than anything; he wanted to take away the pain she tried so hard to hide.

I need to find out what it is, though, first.

Chapter 33

Leaning against the stone wall of Bluebell Cottage, Nate smiled as he watched Jessie manhandling the pieces of a garden bench, cursing as she tried to put them together.

He squeezed the cardboard tube in his hand, hoping she'd like what was inside; he'd been up most of the night finishing them for her.

Nate cleared his throat, but Jessie didn't flinch.

Ear buds again.

He cleared his throat again, calling out, 'Do you need a hand with that?'

Jessie jumped and whirled around, Nate flinching as he braced himself for a reprimand. What he received was the most beautiful smile he'd ever seen.

'You came,' Jessie breathed, stepping forward and reaching out to him before she stopped herself. Nate watched her smile falter, and she looked away as she thrust her hands in her pockets instead.

'Of course I did,' he said, bridging some of the space between them. 'I said I would, and I always keep my promises.' He grinned, and she smiled before sobering again.

'I've been looking forward to seeing you,' Nate ventured, holding his breath, hoping he hadn't said the wrong thing.

Jessie stared at him for what seemed an age, her grey eyes probing into him before she relaxed and grinned. 'Me too,' she said. 'I'm glad you came.'

Jessie lapsed into silence, looking towards the lake. Not knowing what to say next, Nate thrust the cardboard tube at her.

'I hope you like these. I hope you like what I've done.'

'What is it?' she asked, accepting the tube and peering inside.

'Open it and find out!' he said and laughed, and Jessie let out a squeal as she hurried into the kitchen.

Nate stayed where he was, hopping from foot to foot as he watched her pull the contents from the tube. She spread them on the table before stepping back and studying them.

He watched her trace her finger across the depictions of how he saw her kitchen and porch, designs he'd turned into works of art, just for her.

When she lifted her head and looked at him, there were tears in her eyes, and Nate's heart sank.

She hates them.

He stood, rooted to the spot, not knowing what to do or say. He looked down at the ground and almost lost his footing as Jessie ran out of the kitchen and threw her arms around him.

'I love them. I love them. Thank you so, so much,' she enthused, her eyes sparkling, a broad grin on her face. 'It's as if you've been inside my head. I can't believe it!'

Relieved, Nate wrapped his arms around her, pulling her close, laughing as he kissed the top of her head.

Jessie went rigid in his arms, and Nate released her, as if she'd stung him.

'Would you like some coffee? I was just about to make some when you came,' Jessie said before he could question her.

Nate nodded, staring after her as she disappeared back into the kitchen.

'How was your painting trip?' she called.

'How did you—?' Nate started, stepping into the kitchen.

'Your mum, who else?' Jessie smiled, and Nate laughed, rolling his eyes.

'Of course,' he said, the tension between them broken. 'It was inspiring. Got loads of new material, which will please Em. What've you been up to?'

'Come with me.' Jessie handed him his coffee, before leading him from room to room, including the two bedrooms.

'Soooo, what do you think?' she asked a short while later, as they deposited their empty mugs in the sink.

'I think it looks fantastic. You've made a cosy home out of this old place.' He smiled as she blushed. 'Plus, you have great taste in art!' He winked at her.

'Like there was anything else to choose from!'

Nate felt as if she'd sucker-punched him. He turned away quickly, hoping she didn't notice the hurt.

After a few moments of silence, his composure restored, Nate looked back at her and saw the glint in her eyes and the half smile on her lips.

'Why, you little…' He let the sentence tail off as he chased her out of the cottage, catching her and throwing her over his shoulder, before running to the end of the precarious jetty. His heart swelled at her shrieks and laughter, her fists pounding his back.

He had every intention of throwing her in the lake, or jumping them both in, but his instincts warned him not to ruin the moment. Instead, he deposited her on the jetty, catching her as she almost lost her balance.

'Nearly,' he said, holding her arm as she steadied herself. 'Well, I guess we best get emptying your cupboards and make a start. That kitchen won't remodel itself, you know.'

'I'll have you know, Mr Parker, I've already packed it all away. We're good to go,' she said primly, hands on her hips, chin held high.

Nate burst out laughing. 'Well, all right then, Ms Ellis, so lead the way.' He bowed, gesturing for her to take the lead. 'Would you like me to finish erecting those benches for you?'

'Nah, I'll do it another day,' Jessie said, primness forgotten. 'Race you,' she yelled, punching him in the arm, before running gazelle-like along the jetty and back to the cottage.

Deciding not to question this new playfulness, Nate raced after her.

∞

Who knew smashing up kitchen units would feel so good?

Jessie brought the hammer down for the umpteenth time, a thrill shivering through her as the cupboard splintered, shrapnel exploding in all directions.

'Enjoying yourself?'

Jessie started at his voice, lost in her own destructive fantasy. When she turned, she saw him grinning as he leaned against the door frame.

'Have you been watching me?' she asked, laughter tingeing her voice.

'Not for long, but long enough to know I wouldn't want to be on the receiving end.' He winked at her. 'I thought maybe you were ready for a break?'

Jessie nodded, relinquishing her hammer as Nate ambled outside with two mugs of coffee. They settled in the old garden chairs and stared out over the lake in silence.

'Tell me about your trip,' Jessie eventually said, looking at him over the top of her mug. She watched his features soften and a faraway look appear on his face.

'What do you want to know?' He turned his melted-chocolate gaze on her and she shivered.

'I want to know why it does this,' she said, indicating his current demeanour. When he looked puzzled, she added, 'Why it makes you all relaxed and dreamlike.'

'Ah, well, that's easy. When I'm working on something, I like to immerse myself in the subject, to the exclusion of everything else. In that way, I can paint the subject in the most alive and visceral way.'

'I get that,' Jessie said, nodding. 'So, Mr Parker, how are you planning to immerse yourself in me?' As soon as the words were out of her mouth, Jessie regretted them, cursing the playful bubble still bouncing around inside her.

Her question hung unanswered in mid-air, and Jessie hid behind her mug as she sneaked a peek at Nate.

He had turned a deeper shade of red than she thought possible, and she hunkered down as low as she could in her chair, wishing the ground would open up and swallow her.

'So,' Nate said, clearing his throat, his colour receding, 'I took you up on your advice, and have agreed to do a job with the lads, but on my own terms, as you suggested. They were more than happy, just glad I said yes! So, thanks for that.' He smiled and toasted her with his mug.

'You're more than welcome,' Jessie said, toasting him back, thrilled he'd taken her advice. 'I'm really pleased for you, Nate.'

'Thanks. I'm looking forward to in in all fairness. Can't wait to flex my design skills… again,' he said, laughing as he acknowledged her kitchen. 'So, what else have you been up to while I've been gone?'

'Well, I me… made myself focus on work and this place,' Jessie said, catching herself before she told Nate she'd met his dad; that would lead to questions she wasn't ready to answer.

Feeling agitation taking root, Jessie put her mug down and rubbed her palms on her dungarees before jumping up. 'What's next?'

'Wow, someone's keen,' Nate said, chuckling. 'The only thing left, for now, is to knock out the wall where you want the patio doors.'

Jessie clapped her hands. 'Whoop! Let's do this!'

'Are you sure you want to do it today? The doors won't be here for a few days, so—'

'Can you board up the hole and make it secure?'

'Yes, of course.'

'Well, what're we waiting for? Let's get to it,' Jessie urged, the need to smash still with her. She grabbed a sledgehammer, Nate howling with laughter as she struggled to lift it.

'Why don't you let me do this?' he said, prising the tool

from her hands. 'This isn't a demolition derby, Ms Ellis. We have to do it carefully, and in stages, so as not to damage the rest of the cottage.'

Embarrassed by her hot-headedness, Jessie nodded, allowing Nate to show her how to demolish a wall.

∞

By the end of the day, Jessie's kitchen was unrecognisable—bare of units and with a huge boarded-up hole in the wall, the room was completely unusable.

'Who knew destroying a room would be so easy, and sooo satisfying,' she said, wiping a plaster dust-covered hand across her dirt-streaked forehead.

Nate laughed, saying, 'Controlled demolition is good. If I'd left it to you, though, we might be standing amidst a pile of debris now.'

'Hey, that's just mean!' Jessie pouted and swatted his arm. 'Beer?' Nate nodded.

'Well, now I have no kitchen, it looks like it's microwave meals and takeaways for me.' She handed him a beer from the now dusty fridge.

'And what may I ask is wrong with takeaway food?' Nate frowned as he spread his arms wide.

Jessie rolled her eyes. 'I'm not sure your mum would be too impressed to hear that!'

Nate shrugged and pointed his beer bottle towards the door. 'Shall we get out of the dust for a while and get some fresh air?'

'Good plan.' Jessie followed him down to the lake, taking

off her shoes and submerging her feet, allowing the cool water to weave its magic.

'Mmmm, this feels so good,' she murmured and closed her eyes. 'Hey! What the—?' she spluttered, spitting beer out of her mouth.

'I thought you said the water felt good?' Nate said, splashing more water on her.

'Hey! How dare you… you… I'll…' Jessie dissolved into squeals of laughter as Nate covered her in water.

Setting her bottle down, she pushed up her sleeves. 'Right, you've asked for it, Parker.' And, crouching down, she used both her hands to heave as much water over Nate as she could.

The look on his face had her roaring with laughter as she turned and ran, Nate hot on her heels.

It didn't take him long to catch her, and, throwing her over his shoulder, Nate charged into the lake.

'Someone's in for a dunking,' he threatened as Jessie wriggled and screamed, kicking her legs and punching his back. 'No one splashes me and gets away… whoa!'

Jessie felt Nate's legs go out from under him and they both disappeared beneath the water, emerging coughing and spluttering, Jessie laughing at his backfired plan.

Before she knew what was happening, Nate grabbed her waist and pulled her towards him, leaning down and crushing his lips to hers as he wrapped his arms around her, moulding her body to his.

Jessie froze, her lips refusing to return his kiss.

What's he doing? I'm not ready. It's not supposed to happen like this.

Nate released her, recoiling. 'Jessie, what's wrong? I thought… But, you…'

Jessie shook her head, backing away from him, her lips pressed together as she waved away his protests and his confusion. She turned away, unable to bear the look of hurt on his handsome face, and waded back to shore.

Slipping her wet feet into her shoes, she raced back to the cottage without looking back, locking the door behind her, praying he wouldn't follow.

What the hell do I do now?

Chapter 34

With her back against the door, Jessie slid to the floor, pulling her knees against her chest and resting her forehead on top.

'No, no, no, no, no,' she whispered, tears spilling down her cheeks.

Why did I do that? Why did I pull away from his kiss? And oh, such a beautiful kiss it was…

But Jessie knew why. She also knew it wasn't his kiss she'd pulled away from, it was his embrace; the feel of his body pressed against hers. Matthew hadn't been a fan of kissing—too intimate, too personal—but grabbing hold of her was another thing; he'd ruined it for her. With Matthew's roughness and demands, and the pain that came with them, Jessie's mind had shut down her gullible body the moment Nate touched her.

What does it matter? I didn't want to get involved with anyone again, anyway.

But she'd never expected to meet Nate, either.

'What am I going to do?' she sobbed as she lifted her head and rested it back against the door. Her tear-filled gaze found Cole sitting at her feet, his green eyes boring into her, his head cocked to one side.

'Come and give me a cuddle, Coley Moley,' she said, reaching out for him. Cole allowed himself to be pulled into her embrace, permitting Jessie to bury her face in his fur as she sobbed.

'Oh, Cole, what do I do? I have to fix it. He didn't deserve… I don't know what to say.'

Cole purred as he nestled in her lap, the resonating sound comforting Jessie as she wrestled with her options.

'I have to tell him.' Cole meowed, and she sighed. She had to explain; she owed him that much after her behaviour. But what would he think? Would he understand?

'Oh, God, I hope so,' Jessie murmured, brushing her fingertips over her lips, recalling the feel of him as he'd kissed her, of his large hands on her hips… She shivered as a throbbing started in her base.

Oh, please let him understand.

Jessie got to her feet, holding Cole close. She stared at the door, her heart racing as she contemplated how to bridge the gap she'd created, when she heard his tyres crunching on the driveway.

'No!' she cried, and yanked open the door, ready to chase after him, prepared to do whatever it took to repair the damage she'd done, when a gasp caught in her throat and she almost dropped Cole.

In front of her, set ready for use, were two completed benches, flowers from her garden arranged across the seats. Tears sprang to Jessie's eyes again as she read the words:

I'm sorry x

Chapter 35

Jessie hammered on Nate's front door. Her palms were sweating and her stomach was doing back flips as her heart thudded in her chest, the panic almost choking her, her brain issuing opposing messages to her body.

Her pounding went unanswered, her hand, raw and sore. Jessie wondered if he'd even come home. She'd just presumed he had, but he could just as easily have gone to Bev's, or even gone to seek solace in the arms of… Jessie shook her head, shutting down the thought.

She walked round the side of the house to find his truck in its usual place.

So, he is home.

Seeing no sign of him in the unlit interior, Jessie stepped back and looked up to see a light burning in his studio on the top floor. Maybe he hadn't heard her?

Jessie walked back and banged on the door with her fist, calling his name. Still, there was no answer.

Cursing under her breath and shaking her hand to relieve the pain, Jessie cupped her face and peered through the glass. Nate was sitting on the stairs. Her heart sank at the look of hurt and sadness on his face.

'Open the door, Nate!' she yelled, peering through the glass.

That did it.

Nate shot off the stairs, and Jessie stepped back as he yanked the door open, the rush of air pulling against her.

'Sh! Someone will hear you,' Nate hissed.

Jessie looked around and was about to issue a smart retort when she turned back and looked into his eyes; the eyes of a child who didn't understand what he'd done wrong.

'Oh, Nate,' she said, closing the distance between them, before standing on her tiptoes and pulling him into a kiss.

Nate didn't respond, his body stiff, and Jessie fought the urge to flee, instead pressing her lips against his, the tip of her tongue encouraging his lips to part.

A low moan escaped him, sending spikes of electricity through Jessie's body, and he pulled her close, desire spiralling through her at his need.

Nate lifted her off her feet, and Jessie wrapped her legs around his waist as he closed the door.

∞

Nate carried Jessie towards the stairs, stopping and pulling away from her as he took the first step.

'Are you sure?' he whispered, his voice hoarse.

Jessie nodded. 'I am,' she said, biting her bottom lip and nodding again, confirming to herself she was ready.

He kissed her so softly, Jessie thought she would explode, before he carried her up to his bedroom.

Laying her on the bed as if she were a flower whose petals he didn't want to damage, Nate stood, staring down at her, a wistful look on his face.

'Stop staring at me and kiss me.' Jessie grabbed his shirt and pulled him down on top of her, crushing her lips against his.

She fumbled with his t-shirt, her hands shaking, and Nate placed his hand on hers before pulling away from her and tugging his shirt over his head.

Jessie couldn't stop the grin as she ran her fingertips over his tanned, muscular torso, lingering on his hairless chest, giggling at the goosebumps chasing her touch. She allowed her index finger to tease his nipples, drawing a gasp, his nipples hardening.

Jessie sat up, her tongue replacing her fingertip. Nate groaned in response.

After a few minutes, Nate pushed her back onto the bed. 'Your turn,' he murmured, unhooking her dungarees as he spoke. But as he went to lift her t-shirt, Jessie stopped him.

'Let me.' Her heart thundered in her ears; it was time to show him the mess that was her body. Her mind screamed at her, telling her she could still run away.

Instead, Jessie fixed her gaze on Nate's face, wanting to see his first reaction to the physical damage Matthew had done. She sat forward, removing her t-shirt and her bra, before laying back down.

Jessie watched as Nate's gaze roamed her upper body, lingering on the places she'd been ashamed of for so long. She waited for the revulsion to show, as she fought the urge to cover herself with her arms, but it never came.

'Beautiful,' he murmured, and Jessie's eyes filled with tears.

Nate bent his head, peppering her body with butterfly kisses, his fingertips tracing her, committing her to memory.

Jessie closed her eyes, her nipples hardening as Nate's lips caressed the parts of her she'd thought ugly—the scar on her collarbone where a plate was inserted after he threw her down the stairs; the scar on her throat where they'd intubated her after he'd punched her in the chest, breaking her sternum and collapsing her lungs; the slash down her ribs where a chest tube was inserted, re-inflating another collapsed lung; the cigarette burns because he didn't like what she said, what she wore, what she did; the scar zigzagging her left arm where another plate was inserted after he'd shattered her elbow, wrenching her arm up her back.

Jessie cried—silent tears, tears of relief, tears of happiness—as Nate brushed his lips across every one of her scars.

'Beautiful,' he whispered each time.

When he reached her belly, his tongue dancing across her soft flesh, he looked up at her, his eyes hooded, and said, 'May I?' Jessie nodded, the desire throbbing inside her as he slid her dungarees and panties down, throwing them to one side.

Jessie gasped as he bent his head and cupped her with his mouth, allowing his tongue to dance, registering when she groaned and bucked and whispered his name.

Jessie wanted him like she'd wanted no one before. She grabbed for him, trying to pull him on top of her.

'Not yet,' he murmured, and resumed his discovery. Jessie cried out as his tongue circled, flicking from side to side before repeating the cycle. She bunched the bedclothes in her hands, breathing deeply to slow her racing heart, to take control of the orgasm charging through her. It had been so long since anyone had considered her needs, Jessie was struggling to keep the wave from breaking.

As if sensing her impending explosion, Nate withdrew his tongue, choosing to explore with his fingers instead.

Jessie felt him watching her, but she couldn't open her eyes, was afraid to, instead focusing on his fingers as they caressed and penetrated.

She cried out his name as his fingertip massaged her, his tongue resuming its taunting, pulling her towards her peak until she could hold back no longer. Jessie's eyes rolled back in her head as she released her orgasm, savouring the igniting of her nerve endings as it surged through her, crashing ashore.

Jessie's body shuddered as wave after wave tore through her, sweat peppering her skin as she relaxed into the afterglow.

Smiling, Nate kissed the insides of her thighs, working his way back up her body until he pressed his lips against hers once more.

'Make love to me,' she whispered, biting her lip as she looked into his eyes.

'Are you sure?' he murmured, and Jessie nodded as she reached for him, her shaking hands fumbling with the button fly of his jeans.

Nate kissed her, before standing up and removing his jeans, revealing his glistening anticipation. He reached past her and into a drawer beside the bed, pulling out a condom.

'Let me.' Jessie took it from him and unrolled it over his twitching shaft, her hand moving up and down, her grip tightening.

Nate pushed her back down, bracing himself on his arms as he leaned down, his lips meeting hers, his tongue pushing into her mouth.

Jessie felt the tip of him nudging her and she shuddered, desire arching her upwards towards him. Wrapping her legs around his waist, Jessie guided him, gasping as he entered her.

Knowing he wouldn't want to hurt her, Jessie drew Nate deep inside her, directing him, savouring the feel of his body moving with hers as she rhythmically circled her hips.

'You're gonna make me come,' Nate groaned, so Jessie continued, enjoying the sounds of pleasure emanating from him, until he took over, his need dismissing everything else as he drove into her, over and over.

Jessie felt his heart racing to keep up, and as he climaxed, Nate arched away from her with a final thrust, his body shuddering as his orgasm surged through him.

As his spasms slowed, Nate opened his eyes and looked down at her. Jessie met his gaze, smiling, and pulled him towards her, her lips meeting his, dissolving into a long, lingering kiss.

As Nate lay down beside her and pulled her close, Jessie laid her head on his chest as she moulded her body to his.

She couldn't stop the grin spreading across her face as she stared out at the star-studded sky, the steady beat of Nate's heart a welcoming lullaby.

Jessie sighed as Nate ran his fingers through her hair.

'Do you want to tell me what happened?' he whispered.

Chapter 36

A huge mug of tea in her hands and one of Nate's flannel shirts covering her naked body, Jessie sat cross-legged in bed facing Nate.

Christ, how do I do this? How do I tell him everything, without telling him everything?

'You don't have to tell me, not if you're not ready,' he said, smiling at her.

Jessie studied him over the rim of her mug. 'I was married. For eight years.' Nate said nothing, waiting for her to go on. 'H-he beat me,' she whispered as she watched him.

Nate closed his eyes and shook his head, exhaling in a huff as he dropped his chin, his shoulders slumping.

Panic sent goosebumps racing across Jessie's skin, and her stomach clenched. She jumped off the bed, backing away from him, tears filling her eyes.

I thought he might understand, that he would be okay. I was wrong.

Nate lunged forward, grabbing her arm, and Jessie screamed, jerking it away from him, the past flashing through her mind.

She dropped the mug, staring open-mouthed as it shattered on the wooden floor, hot tea scalding her legs and feet. She gasped for breath as her heart contracted, her eyes wide in fear.

'I'm s-sorry,' she said, her body shaking as she knelt down, gathering the shards of the mug.

Nate jumped off the bed and Jessie screamed again, cowering, her hands raised to shield herself as she shrank away from him.

But the blows never came.

'Hey, hey, it's okay, baby. I'm not going to hurt you,' Nate crooned as he crouched beside her. 'Jessie, it's okay. No one's going to hurt you again, I promise.'

Jessie flinched as Nate touched her shoulder, but she didn't pull away, instead allowing him to draw her into the warmth of his embrace.

They sat, Nate resting against the bed, Jessie nestled in his arms as he rocked her. He whispered to her as he stroked her hair.

'You don't have to tell me any more, Jessie. I've seen the scars. Did you prosecute him?' he asked, his voice neutral.

Jessie shook her head. 'I just left,' she muttered, feeling Nate tense beneath her.

∞

Nate didn't know what to say. How could he say anything, really? He hadn't been there, he wasn't Jessie. His gut told him there was more to her story, but he wasn't going to push her; nothing could erase what had happened to her. All he could do was reassure her nothing like that would ever happen to her again.

Jeez, if I get my hands on that bastard, I'll…

But that wouldn't help Jessie. She'd gone to great lengths to get away from him.

He sighed and kissed the top of her head. He'd never been

one to let wrongs lie, but maybe he needed to, in this case, for both their sakes.

Nate noticed Jessie had quietened and, not wanting to do anything to upset her, he decided to do something he'd never done before… for anyone.

'Would you like to see your paintings?' He held his breath, wondering if she'd changed her mind about his voyeurism.

Jessie sniffed and nodded, shivering in his arms.

Nate stood and helped her up before searching out a pair of sweatpants for her to wear.

Jessie looked so forlorn in his oversized clothes, Nate's heart lurched as he hugged her to him, kissing the top of her head again, before leading her up the spiral staircase to his studio.

He let go of her hand, his heart pounding as he hoped she'd like what he'd done.

Chapter 37

Jessie stepped forward into Nate's studio, her fingers trailing away from his, her breath catching as her gaze swept over the paintings lining the room. They were all part-finished, but all shared one thing, one element that was complete—her.

Approaching each painting, Jessie paused to study them, crouching down before two in particular. Not daring to touch, she traced her finger along the delicate brush strokes; the intimacy bringing back to her those precious moments, seeing herself as Nate had, staring out across the lake that first night, and laughing as Cole finally allowed her to touch him.

From the composition of each painting, Jessie realised Nate had done more than watch her; he'd studied her, capturing each mannerism, translating each mood. She felt revered, and for the first time in a long time, interesting.

'They're beautiful, Nate,' Jessie breathed, turning to face him, tears in her eyes. 'They're so real.'

'They simply tell the truth,' he said, releasing a long-held breath and grinning.

Jessie blushed as he pulled her close, and they stared across the lake at a starlit Bluebell Cottage.

'So, you're not annoyed?' he ventured, and Jessie shook her head.

'Why would I be annoyed, especially when they are so breathtaking?'

'Well, I did spy on you without your knowledge.' He shrugged, and Jessie laughed.

'True, but I'm not entirely innocent in the whole game of voyeurism,' she said, leaning against him.

'Oh, really?'

'Well, if you're going to go skinny dipping, what do you expect?'

'Fair enough,' he said, resting his chin on the top of her head.

Jessie felt his heart race against her cheek as he took a deep breath, and the hairs on the back of her neck bristled.

'Are you okay?' she asked, alarmed.

Nate didn't respond and Jessie pulled away from him, her brow furrowed, her heart racing.

'How would you feel about me hanging those paintings in the gallery… as a show… all together?' he finally stumbled.

'Seriously?' She stared at him, open-mouthed, adrenaline washing ashore as she processed his question.

Nate stepped back, his hands up. 'I'm sorry, you're right. It's a stupid idea. What was I thinking? I'm sorry, Jessie, I just thought...' He stopped talking, his shoulders slumping as he looked at her.

'What are you wittering on about?' she said, shaking her head before planting a kiss on his lips. She smiled at the puzzled look on his face. 'What I meant was, I can't believe you'd want to show paintings of *me*.'

'Why wouldn't I want to share with the world how beautiful you are?'

Jessie shrugged and looked at the floor.

Nate pulled her to him and kissed the top of her head again. 'You *are* beautiful, Jessie Ellis, *and* intriguing *and* mysterious. Why wouldn't I want to exhibit them?'

Jessie shrugged again, uncomfortable under his flattery.

'I have one condition,' she finally said.

'Name it.'

'I want first pick of the paintings.'

'Done!' Nate scooped her up, spinning her around in circles.

'Put me down! Put me down!' Jessie squealed, nausea threatening as she grew dizzy.

Nate deposited her back on her feet, and she grabbed his hand to steady herself.

'Drink?' he asked, and Jessie nodded, allowing him to lead her down the stairs.

'Where's your dustpan and brush?' she asked as they passed the mezzanine. 'I'll clean up my mess while you make the drinks.'

'Don't be daft. I'll sort it later. Make yourself comfortable.' He waved her towards the sofa.

When they were both settled on his huge corner sofa, Jessie turned the spotlight on him, and not knowing how best to phrase it, she blurted, 'So, what's with you and the whole "love 'em and leave 'em" philosophy? Is this what's going to happen to me?'

Chapter 38

'One day, Nate, you'll meet someone who'll change all this,' his mother had said to him as she'd indicated his dishevelled appearance early one morning.

'Change all what?' he'd said through a yawn, emptying the contents of the cafetiere into a mug.

'This… you… out all night with goodness knows who, someone you'll never see again.' His mother curled her lip in disdain.

'Don't start, Mum. This is how I like things.'

'For now.'

'Mum!'

'I'm just saying, one day you'll meet the person who'll repair the damage that woman did to you, who'll enable you to feel, and who'll teach you to love and to be loved. Mark my words, Nate—'

'I'm not listening, Mum. I've got to go,' he'd said and left, pushing her words from his mind.

Until now.

Nate looked at Jessie snuggled down into the corner of the sofa, her knees pulled up, her mug balanced on top of them, hiding her reddening cheeks at the question she'd just asked him.

She looked so perfect there, like she belonged, like she'd

always belonged, as no one had before. Warmth suffused Nate's body at the thought of Jessie being there… with him… in his house… regularly, and a smile spread across his face.

Maybe Mum was right.

If Jessie *was* the one to open him up to the prospect of love, she deserved to know the truth about him. After all, she'd shared the horrors of her past with him. His scars weren't as visible as hers, but they were there, keeping him safe.

Nate looked up into the kaleidoscope of her eyes and, taking a deep breath, he began.

'Do you remember me telling you I was adopted?'

Jessie nodded.

'Well, I was abandoned on the steps of the doctor's surgery—Dad's surgery. Ray found me and took me home. Bev took care of me while Ray worked with the police to find my birth mother.'

Nate watched as Jessie's face closed down as he spoke, as if someone had switched the power off, her features frozen in a neutral look. Unsure how to interpret her reaction, and wanting to get his tale told now he'd started, Nate continued.

'They found my birth mother but, unsurprisingly, she wanted nothing to do with me. She'd left me on Ray's doorstep on purpose, she said, because he'd always been kind to her when she was younger. She was more than happy to sign the papers and give me over to Ray and Bev.'

Jessie reached out towards him, her small hand squeezing his, her expression alive again as she cocked her head to one side, frowning as she listened. Nate shivered, shocked by how cold her hand was, given she had wrapped it around a hot mug. More than that, he was surprised by how her touch made him feel—safe and vulnerable.

He looked down at her hand, covering it with his other one, rubbing it gently to warm it before taking another deep breath as he prepared to share with her something he'd never told another living soul.

He couldn't look at her as he spoke, so acute was the impact it'd had on him.

'Mum and Dad told me I was adopted. They've always believed in being up front about things, and so as soon as I was old enough to understand, they told me.

'When I asked if I could meet her, I could see the hurt in their eyes, Mum's especially, but they said without hesitation they would see if she was willing to meet me. I knew how hard this was for them, but, as young as I was, I needed to know why she hadn't wanted me.'

A sob escaped Jessie's throat, and Nate looked up to see tears running down her face. He squeezed her hand and gave her a half smile before averting his gaze and continuing his story.

'My birth mother agreed to meet me, but to this day I wish she hadn't. The whole meeting lasted less than five minutes and left me…' Nate's voice broke as the memory that haunted his life resurfaced. 'She made me feel ashamed, Jessie, ashamed and… and unlovable.' He broke off, squeezing his eyes shut, refusing to let the tears fall. She didn't deserve his tears, not after all this time, not after what she'd done to him, how she'd made him feel.

'What happened, Nate? Tell me what happened.' Jessie's small voice broke through the silence, and he looked up at her, saw the love and concern in her eyes, and he sighed.

'The agreed meeting place was the park, so Mum and Dad left me on a bench, standing far enough away to give me privacy, but also so they could see me and intervene if necessary. She came, but she never sat down. She stood about six feet away from me, shaking her head, saying she should never have agreed to come. I remember the revulsion on her face, Jessie, as she looked at me. All I could think was what must be wrong with me for her to look at me like that. She never spoke to me, just shouted across to Mum and Dad, saying I looked exactly like my lying, abusive bastard of a father…'

Nate paused as he felt Jessie's hand flinch at what he said, but she said nothing, so he continued.

'She carried on ranting about my birth father, things I must've blocked out because I can't remember what else she said. All I remember is crying. I was crying so hard I could barely catch my breath. Mum came rushing over, pulling me into her arms and shielding me from her. I remember the anger on Dad's face as he stood between us and her. It's the only time I've ever heard Dad raise his voice, the only time I've ever seen him angry.

'He told her to be quiet, that enough was enough, but she just carried on hurling abuse… at me. She said why would she want the offspring of a man who'd beaten her and left her with a brat she'd never wanted in the first place? She said why would she want to see a reminder of that every day? The last thing I remember her saying was that she never wanted to lay eyes on me again. She spat at us. Then she left.'

Nate fell silent, venturing a look at Jessie to see tears spilling down her cheeks.

'It was a long time ago,' Nate said, squeezing her hand again. 'Time heals, as they say. I'm past it now.'

'Except you're not, not really, are you? Be honest,' Jessie whispered.

Nate looked into her tear-filled eyes, his heart aching at the understanding he saw there, and shrugged.

'Mum would agree with you,' he said and laughed. 'According to her, my behaviour is proof of that.' He gave Jessie a half smile as he raised an eyebrow. 'They've given me a fantastic life, probably even perfect. They've showered me with love, supported me in everything I've wanted to do, even when they didn't agree with it. They've given me everything, and I'm sure there are times I didn't deserve it, trying to make up for what she did. I owe them my life. They didn't have to do any of it, but they did, without question, and wanting nothing in return.'

'Because they love you,' Jessie said, squeezing his hand, and Nate nodded, smiling.

'I know they do, and the feeling is mutual, it's just… what she did… rejecting me… in such a vicious and public way… Ah, shit, I just couldn't let it go.' He sighed, the admission like a weight being lifted.

'That's understandable, but she is only one person, one opinion,' Jessie said, shaking his hand to get him to look at her. 'You also know it's not true, don't you, deep down?'

Nate shrugged and sighed. 'I don't know. I do, but I also never want to feel again the way she made me feel. I was five years old, Jessie. Five. After that day, I shut myself down. I had to. I couldn't let anyone make me feel like that again.

'Only Mum and Dad receive any love from me. They took me in, without question, and treated me as their own, always. It takes a special person to do that. I've let no one else get close to me, never allowed myself to care about anyone else… until now.' Nate held his breath and looked at her, but she hadn't registered his words.

'So, that's why you have a string of one-night stands and flings,' Jessie stated.

'Jeez, Jessie,' Nate said, then laughed and rolled his eyes. 'When you say it out loud, it does sound seedy, but, yes, I guess… *until now*,' he said, squeezing her hand as he emphasised the last two words.

He heard her breath catch in her throat, and she looked at him, myriad emotions crossing her face—sadness, fear, anger, and back to sadness.

'W-what do you mean?'

∞

Jessie watched the flush creeping up his neck and into his face at her question. She hadn't known what else to say. Her heart had skipped a beat at his words, but could he mean what her heart believed?

Is he telling me I'm the one to heal him?

'Until you, Jessie.'

Those three little words, so unremarkable, yet so full of

hope and certainty, were too much, and Jessie burst into tears; huge, gulping sobs. After all he'd shared with her, he was letting her know *she* was his saviour.

'Oh God, Jessie, I'm sorry!' Nate said, a horrified look on his face as he pulled her into his arms, running his fingers through her hair as he rocked her. 'I'm so sorry. I never meant to upset you. I just wanted you to know that you're not alone, that I know…' His sentence tailed off as he told her over and over he was sorry.

But his apologies, his words, his tenderness, only brought the tears harder and faster. Her heart broke for him, for the pain his birth mother had caused, but her tears weren't for that; they were for a future that could never be, not with him, not now.

He would never understand, not after what he'd been through.

But do I have to tell him?

There was no reason he should find out… why would he? And didn't she deserve some happiness after everything she'd been through, after everything Matthew had put her through?

Jessie's mind drifted to Anita's letter and the blood test, the results of which she still didn't know, but she pushed them away.

Her past was her past. Nate represented her future, a future she deserved. If she told him the truth, if she told him what *she'd* done, that future would disappear, and Matthew would win… again. She wasn't about to let that happen.

'Stay with me tonight… here,' Nate whispered.

After a moment, Jessie nodded, snuggling closer against him, her sadness and despair calm, her heart opening itself up to a new possibility.

Blending

Chapter 39

Inhaling the flora-scented air, Jessie stepped outside. The day was young, but the sun was already warm, and Jessie smiled, her cheeks aching as they familiarised themselves with the action. Her happiness hadn't gone unnoticed.

'Thank you, Jessie,' Bev had said to her one morning as they'd shared their customary pre-class cup of coffee, and Jessie had frowned as she looked at her friend… and boss.

'What're you thanking me for?'

'Well, let's put it this way, I've never, and I mean *never*, seen Nate so peaceful, and I have a feeling you're everything to do with it.'

'What's he said to you?' Jessie asked, wondering how much Nate had told his parents.

'Absolutely nothing, but that's not unusual. Nate has always kept his personal life to himself. But, over the years I've learned to read him, and the fact I can see the same change in you means it wouldn't take Poirot to deduce something was going on between the two of you.' Bev winked at her as she sipped her coffee.

Jessie turned away, not wanting Bev to witness the blush that was making her feel clammy on what was going to be a scorcher of a day.

Her emotions under control, Jessie looked at Bev and said, 'We're healing each other.' She'd added nothing further, instead leaving the room for a day of shaping young minds.

Jessie set her mug on the table and busied herself dead-heading the flowers adorning her small patio, letting her mind roam.

It had been weeks since she'd submitted her blood and she'd heard nothing from Anita, so either she wasn't a match or he was responding to the treatment and was no longer in need of her. Jessie hoped it was the latter, as she couldn't bear the thought of him suffering; he didn't deserve that.

Guilt stabbed at her heart, and Jessie felt her smile falter as the past invaded her thoughts. It had been the hardest thing she'd ever had to do, but she knew, deep down, she'd done the right thing, done what was best for him, despite Anita's opinion; Jessie could live with her sister's hatred.

Her thoughts shifted to Nate and all he'd shared with her that night, and shame smothered the guilt. He didn't know she'd held anything back, assuming it was too painful for her to talk about, wrongly accepting the damaged canvas of her body as the full picture. Every day she remained silent made it worse, yet the more time that passed, the harder it became.

"Why rock the boat when you don't need to?" her mum used to say. *"It does no good to anyone. Some things are better left unsaid."*

Jessie hoped that was true and wished her parents were still alive; she needed their counsel right now. She sighed and settled back in the rickety chair, pushing the dark thoughts aside and listening to the morning birdsong, the aroma of fresh coffee filling her nostrils as she held her mug to her lips.

The day had arrived. They were finally starting on the porch, and Jessie allowed the bubbles of excitement to fizz through her, dispelling the clouds in an instant.

She heard the purr of Nate's engine and let out a squeal, her stomach doing somersaults as she raced to meet him.

'Wow! Any chance I can get this welcome every morning?' he said, laughing, and Jessie swatted his arm as she bounced up and down.

'You do know we won't finish it today, don't you?' he said, raising his eyebrows and smiling as he watched her.

'I know, I know, but the sooner we start…'

'You're the boss. Oh, here, I picked this up for you.' He dropped her mail on the patio table.

Jessie froze, emitting a cry as she spotted Anita's handwriting.

Chapter 40

'Are you okay?' Nate asked after Jessie stiffened at the sight of the letter. Her smile vanished. 'Jessie?' he urged when she didn't respond, and touched her shoulder. She jerked away from him with such force, the hairs on Nate's arms bristled.

Something's wrong.

He knew who the letter was from; he recognised the handwriting from the last one.

'Talk to me, Jessie. What's going on?'

'I'm fine,' she said, her tone flat, but offered nothing more.

'Look, what the hell happened between you two?' Nate asked, deciding on a different approach, but Jessie was somewhere else when she looked at him, her brows furrowed. Nate nodded towards the letter. 'You and your sister. What happened?'

Jessie looked down at the letter as she clenched and unclenched her hands, her jaw set.

'Sister stuff. You wouldn't understand.' Her voice was devoid of emotion, yet so full of sorrow Nate's heart ached for her.

'Ouch, that was below the belt.'

He watched as she slid the letter into one of the buttermilk-coloured drawers in her new kitchen, her back to him, her head bowed as she leaned against the units.

Finally, she turned to face him, her eyes full of tears. 'I'm sorry. I-I didn't mean to be rude. I…'

But Nate hushed her by pulling her into his arms; the pain he'd seen on her face was proof she still had skeletons she'd yet to share.

Nate held her while she cried, her tears soaking through his flannel shirt, making him shiver. He murmured to her as he stroked her hair, rocking back and forth, soothing her.

Her sobs had abated, so Nate pulled away and held her head in his hands as he kissed her softly on the lips. Brushing stray tears from her cheeks, he said, 'Do you want to tell me about it?'

Jessie paused and opened her mouth to speak. He saw a cloud cross her eyes before she changed her mind and shook her head.

'I can't,' she whispered, before looking up at him and smiling. Taking a deep breath, she said, 'So, what do you have in store for me today, then?'

Nate studied her for a few seconds, but she'd hidden all signs of the pain and sadness from view once more. He didn't like it. The pause only confirmed there was something she wasn't telling him. But he knew better than to push. Pushing someone before they were ready never ended well. She would tell him in her own time.

Smiling as Jessie bobbed up and down once more, he put his arm around her shoulders and led her outside.

'Today, little lady, we build us a porch.'

Chapter 41

'Bloody hell, Nate. Are you sure you've got enough wood?' Jessie said as she inspected the back of his truck.

'You may jest, but wait until I tell you what I have in mind.' He turned her to face the cottage. 'Picture this…'

Jessie snorted as Nate spread his legs and framed the cottage with his hands. She bit down on her lip as he looked at her.

'Are you taking this seriously, Ms Ellis?'

'Sorry. Do continue, Mr Parker.'

Nate nodded and started again. 'Picture this.' He paused, but Jessie resisted the urge to make fun, instead stepping forward and focusing on the cottage, her mind constructing images as Nate spoke.

'I think we put a row of posts along the length of the cottage. We'll fix them into the overhang of your bedroom, where I'm pretty sure I'll find where a similar structure used to be. Then what I propose is laying reclaimed oak boards to create the wooden porch look you've mentioned. Last but not least, I suggest fitting retractable screens which wouldn't block your view, and would create the illusion of being outside in the elements, whilst actually being shielded from them. All I need to know from you is where you want the swing? What do you think?' He turned to look at her, his face questioning.

Jessie didn't acknowledge him; instead she walked from one end of the cottage to the other, looking at it from multiple angles. Finally, she put him out of his misery and grinned. 'I love it!'

'Thank God!' Nate exhaled in relief, and Jessie burst out laughing.

'I'm surprised you had your doubts, given what I said when you first mentioned it.'

'Well, being a woman, I wasn't sure if you'd exert your right to change your mind.'

'Ouch!' Jessie said, feigning a blow to the stomach.

'We're even now.' Nate winked before handing her a spade and a tape measure. 'Right, we best get started then, as I want to get the posts cemented into the ground today before I have to disappear, and we've got a good few holes to dig before we can do that.'

Jessie took the spade and measure and followed him. 'Where're you disappearing to?'

'Oh, you know how I said I'd taken your advice vis-à-vis working with Mac and Johnny?'

Jessie nodded.

'Well, they called the other night. Our first commission starts tomorrow, down south somewhere, Cambridge, I think.'

Jessie squealed, and, abandoning her tools, she threw her arms around his neck. 'Nate, that's fantastic! I'm so pleased for you. How long will you be away?'

'A week to start with. I'm doing the design, so I need to get a feel for the place and then do as much as I can while I'm there.

If I need to, I'll finish it when I get back. I can't be away too long; Em would do her nut.'

He picked up Jessie's tools and handed them back to her.

'Oh, I almost forgot, I got something for you.' He ran to his truck, grabbing something off the front seat.

A present, already?

Excitement bubbled up inside until he showed it to her. Jessie groaned and shook her head.

'No, absolutely not. You know my feelings about those.' She planted her hands on her hips as she stared at the proffered mobile phone.

'How else are we going to stay in touch while I'm gone? Besides, it's a pay as you go, and it's in my name.'

Before she could comment further, he marched into the kitchen and plonked it on the table.

'Now, let's get to work,' he said as he emerged.

Chapter 42

Jessie waved as Nate drove away, a rush of exhaustion sweeping through her, making her eyelids droop. He was a punishing taskmaster, but they'd got the posts fixed and cemented. Now she could relax.

It'll probably take me a week to recover, she thought, stretching out her back and spying two slitted green eyes staring at her from under a bush.

'Oh dear, is someone feeling left out?' Jessie said, and bent down to retrieve a sulking Cole, wincing as her back protested against further exertion. 'Don't worry, mister, you have me all to yourself now.' Jessie held the cat close, smiling at his efforts to resist her. By the time she was back in the kitchen, he'd given in and his purrs vibrated against her chest.

'One good thing about manual labour, Cole, it keeps your mind occupied.'

Jessie stood, rubbing Cole under his chin as she stared down at the drawer containing Anita's letter. It had to bring bad news. Her sister wouldn't have got in touch otherwise; she'd have saved it for her monthly update.

Her heart heavy, Jessie retrieved the letter and sat at the kitchen table to read it. As Cole busied himself kneading Jessie's legs to make them more comfortable, Jessie stared at her sister's handwriting, unwilling to learn what was inside, but knowing she had to, for him.

Jessie's mind drifted to the last time she'd seen Anita.

'You're doing what?' Anita had screeched.

'Nita, it's my decision, and I'm doing what I feel is best for—'

'For who? You? Because you're certainly not thinking about anyone else. You've always been a selfish bitch, expecting everyone to bow down and pander to you. Poor Matthew. I don't know how he—'

'Don't you dare, Anita!'

'Someone has to! You can't keep treating people like they don't matter, throwing them away because you're bored.'

'How dare you! You know exactly what—'

'No, I know what you've said. Matthew tells a diff—'

'To hell with Matthew! You're my sister. You're supposed to be on my side!'

'Never! All you do is lie and make everyone else the bad guy. You make me sick, and this latest… Well, I hope you rot in hell for what you're going to do!'

'I'm doing what's best for him!'

'No, you're not! You just want an excuse to make yourself feel better. Well, tough! You'll get your comeuppance. Manipulative, lying scum like you always do. You must be dead inside; it's the only explanation!'

Jessie put her head in her hands, taking deep breaths to calm herself, to block out the memory. The only thing Anita had got right in that last confrontation was about her being dead inside, because she was, or she had been, until Nate.

Anita hadn't believed a word Jessie had told her, especially about what Matthew had done. Her sister had always carried a torch for Jessie's ex-husband; he'd charmed Anita just as he charmed everyone he met.

No one knew the real Matthew, no one but Jessie. It was true what people said, that no one knows what goes on inside a relationship except the people actually in it. But that hadn't moved Anita. Jessie only hoped Matthew's new wife wasn't in the living hell she had been, that Matthew was treating her better.

"Leopard's never change their spots", her mum always said, but Anita would retort that it wasn't the leopard's fault.

Jessie had tried multiple times to talk to Anita about her decision, but her sister refused to listen, refused to see it had torn Jessie apart to do what she'd done, but she'd done it for him.

Jessie sighed and opened the letter, reading her sister's poisonous words as tears pooled on the table.

His life hung in the balance. He needed her. She would not let him down, not ever.

Chapter 43

Cole sat on the bed watching her, his ears back, his eyes wide, as Jessie threw clothes into a bag.

'You're only going to stay with Auntie Bev for a few days,' she told him, and scooped him up, bundling him into his cat carrier and muttering, 'I hope.'

She looked around one last time before locking up Bluebell Cottage and settling them both into her Audi.

As she hurtled along the still unfamiliar roads, Cole protested his incarceration to such a level, Jessie's head ached. She prayed Bev would be home; she hadn't thought about anything else except getting to him as fast as she could.

'Thank God,' Jessie muttered as she pulled up behind Bev's car and jumped out, racing to the front door and knocking until Bev opened up.

'Jessie! What on earth's the matter? Is everything okay? What's happened? Oh my God, is it Nate?' Bev's hand flew to her chest, but Jessie reached out to stop it.

'No, no, Nate's fine, don't worry, and if he weren't going away tomorrow, I'd be asking him to help me.'

'Jessie, what's the matter? Come in, come in.'

'I can't, Bev, I'm sorry. I'm in a hurry. I just need your help.

I—' Jessie's voice broke, and she stopped. Bev reached out and grabbed hold of Jessie's hands.

'Jessie, what's wrong? You can tell me.'

Jessie looked into Bev's eyes, the urge to pour her heart out overwhelming, but she couldn't. If Bev knew, she'd tell Nate, and… Jessie didn't have time to think about that. Instead, she took a deep breath and told Bev the story she'd decided on as she drove.

'It's my sister. She's sick and needs an operation. She needs me with her, so I have to go up to Scotland for a few days. I'm so, so sorry to leave you in the lurch at school, but it's life or death; I wouldn't do it otherwise. I wondered, well, more like hoped, you'd be able to take Cole for me until I get back? I can't take him with me, I…' She tailed off as she looked at Bev, the older woman staring at her as though trying to determine whether she was telling the truth. 'Please, Bev. I have no one else,' Jessie said after a few minutes of silence.

'Yes, yes, of course I'll take him. How rude of me to pause like that. It's just I didn't know… never mind, it can wait. Where is he?'

Jessie retrieved a still protesting Cole and handed him, in his carrier, to Bev, deciding against trying to kiss him, the mood he was in.

'He will quieten down, I promise. He just isn't a fan of confined spaces.'

'Who is?' Bev said as she looked in on Cole. 'He'll be safe with us.'

'Thanks, Bev. I really appreciate it. You be good for Auntie

Bev, Cole, and I'll see you both in a few days,' Jessie said, heading to her car.

'Jessie?'

'Yep?'

'Drive carefully, and let me know how things go. I'm here when you need me.'

Jessie looked into Bev's knowing eyes and turned away before she let it all out.

'I will. Thanks, Bev. I owe you.'

'You owe me nothing, Jessie. You only owe yourself. Now, let me know when you get there, okay?'

Jessie nodded and jumped into the car, waving as she drove away.

It was only as she sped along the motorway that she realised she'd left the mobile phone on the kitchen table. She'd have to figure something out when she got there, if she arrived in one piece.

'Focus, Ellis,' she muttered as she sped through the darkness.

Chapter 44

Racing into the hospital, Jessie berated herself for the umpteenth time.

Why didn't I open the letter straight away?

If she had, she could have been checked in by now, and had the procedure the following day. As it was, she'd wasted a day, and now would prolong his pain.

The reception desk was in darkness when she got there, and Jessie cursed under her breath. Again, if she'd only read the letter sooner… She looked round, catching sight of a list of departments through a set of open double doors. Racing over, Jessie scoured the list until she saw the one Anita had highlighted in her letter… multiple times.

As if I could forget.

Jessie was out of breath by the time she reached her destination, her heart hammering in her chest. She reached out to grab the desk as light-headedness overcame her.

'Hey, are you okay?' a passing nurse asked as she reached out to steady Jessie.

'Yes, yes, sorry. I've been rushing to get here, been driving for hours…'

'Have you eaten anything?'

'No, I-I didn't want to waste any more time. I…'

'Okay, take a deep breath and let's get you to a chair.'

'No, not yet. I-I'm Jessie Ellis, I'm here for Owen…' Jessie stopped, her mind searching for his last name, horrified she'd never wanted to find out.

'McKenna,' the nurse finished, smiling at her. 'You must be his… mother.'

Chapter 45

When Jessie awoke she was in a hospital bed, monitors and a drip attached to her, her head throbbing. She groaned and reached up, feeling the dressing on her forehead.

What the…?

'Knocked yourself out when you fainted. You just had to make it about you, didn't you? Typical Jessie.'

Jessie clenched her jaw. 'What are you doing he—?'

'Oh, you're awake are you?' a nurse said, bustling into the room. 'You gave us a wee fright, you did.'

'W… what happened?' Jessie asked.

'Passed out cold, you did. When I said you must be Owen's mother, you came over all funny and—'

But Jessie was no longer listening. The word "mother" echoed in her head, and the unchecked memories came crashing in one after the other; memories she'd fought hard to come to terms with; a decision that had ripped her apart.

'Are you feeling alright, Jessie? You've gone a wee bit pale again,' the nurse said, placing her hand against Jessie's forehead. 'Let me go and fetch some fresh water.'

'W… what's she doing here?' Jessie asked, but the nurse had already left.

'They called me, as I'd asked them to, in case you had the good grace to show up.'

'Of course I came!' Jessie snapped and turned to face her sister, regretting it as pain shot through her temple. 'But it's the middle of the night.'

Anita smirked and stood up, going to the window and yanking the curtains back, grinning as Jessie yelped and shied away from the harsh sunlight, which seared through her skull.

'For God's sake, shut the damn curtains!'

Anita complied and retook her seat, the sisters staring at each other in silence.

'How bad is he?' Jessie whispered.

'It's bad. You should've come sooner.'

Jessie gritted her teeth and took a breath before she asked, 'Why hasn't Matthew stepped up? He lives much closer than me.'

'And whose choice is that?' Anita retorted, but Jessie ignored her, raising an eyebrow despite the pain.

'He would've come, but he had an important business trip he couldn't rearrange,' Anita added eventually.

'Likely story!'

'He said you were the one who should be here to help him, anyway; you're his mother.'

'Why are you here, Anita?' Jessie sighed, ignoring the barb.

'I've already told you.'

'But you didn't actually have to come down, did you? So why are you really here?'

'Why do you think? Someone has to make sure you don't change your mind and abandon your son... *again!*'

'I didn't abandon him, as you well know! I found him parents who would give him security and the love I mightn't have been able to… I made sure he was safe.'

'Of course you would have loved him. I told you I'd take him until you got over it and pulled yourself together.'

Jessie stared at her sister, who sat with her arms folded, her nose in the air, the air of superiority she surrounded herself with choking Jessie. But try as she might, she couldn't resist. Anita always knew which buttons to press.

'Get over it! Pull myself together! That bastard beat me half to death… more than once.'

'You probably provoked him, just like you provoke me!'

'How dare you! It's hardly the same thing.'

'If it was as bad as you say, why didn't you leave him, hey? Why didn't you press charges? I know why. Because you're a liar!'

Jessie sighed and looked away. They'd had this argument so many times, and she didn't want to dredge it up again; she'd worked too hard to move forward.

'Do you know how all this will work?' she asked, opting to change the subject, watching Anita work her jaw. Her annoyance at Jessie's lack of fight was all too clear.

After a few minutes, Anita said, 'Not really. Not the details. All I know is they'll monitor you today, because of your convenient fall, and if everything is normal they'll do the procedure tomorrow.'

'Procedure!' Jessie laughed. 'I'm sure donating bone marrow is more than just a procedure.'

'Well, it's hardly an operation, is it? They don't even anaesthetise you!' Anita snapped.

The sisters sat in silence until a doctor came in to talk Jessie through what would happen.

'I'll leave you to it,' Anita said, her tone polite in front of the doctor. She pecked Jessie on the cheek, something she'd never done before, and left.

Jessie didn't know if she would come back, and she didn't care.

Chapter 46

Nate lay awake, staring at the ceiling, the rumbles of the hotel coming to life drifting up from below. He looked at his phone, but all it showed him was the earliness of the hour.

Why hasn't she replied?

He'd travelled down the previous evening to make sure he was fresh to meet the client with Mac and Johnny. He'd texted Jessie to let her know and to wish her goodnight, and had lain in bed awaiting a reply, finally drifting off into a fitful sleep.

When he awoke, unfamiliar bubbles of excitement had erupted, only to turn flat at the uninterrupted screen of his phone.

Maybe she just hasn't switched it on yet.

Mollified by this likely scenario, Nate hopped out of bed to get ready for the day.

∞

'What do you think then, Natey boy?' Mac asked as the three of them stood staring at the limestone façade of Eddlestone House.

Nate didn't respond immediately, taking in the huge sash windows, imposing columns and sweeping steps before him.

'And Nick wants an exact replica of the mansion?' he asked.

'A smaller version, but yeah,' Johnny said.

'No shit, Sherlock,' said Nate, shaking his head.

'Well, you said replica, and a replica is—'

'He knows what a replica is. Jeez. So, is it doable?' Mac said as he punched Johnny in the arm.

'It's doable,' Nate replied, 'but I don't think it's the right thing.'

'How do you mean?' Johnny asked, massaging his injured arm.

'Where did he say he wanted it?'

'Over there, close to the wood,' Mac said.

'Away from prying eyes,' said a sniggering Johnny, nudging Mac, who rolled his eyes.

'Mmmm, I have a better idea. Just leave it with—'

'Whoa, hang on a minute, mate,' Mac said, holding his hands up. 'Nick Eddlestone is our first *big* client. Do you get that?'

'Yeah, I know,' Nate replied, frowning. 'That's why I want to do something special.'

'Yeah, but is it not better to just do what he asked, you know, to keep him happy?' Mac persisted.

'Guys, you asked me to join you for a reason, yeah?'

'Because your gaff is awesome,' replied Johnny.'

'Agreed,' said Mac, 'And we respect your eye for these things, but…'

'But what? Don't you trust me?'

'Oh, come on, it's not about that and you know it,' Mac said, shaking his head at Nate.

'So, before you jump to conclusions—'

'He does that… a lot.' Johnny nodded.

'Let me do what I do and come up with an idea. If Nick doesn't like it, then we'll stick with a repli… a scaled-down version of the original. What do you say?'

'Fine by me,' said Johnny, without hesitation.

Nate and Johnny both turned to look at Mac, who looked from Nate to the house and back, before throwing his hands up and shrugging.

'Go for it.'

'What have we got to lose, hey?' Nate smiled and slapped Mac on the back.

'Just our most prestigious client,' grumbled Mac as he and Johnny headed away from the house, leaving Nate to his own devices.

∞

'Pick up, pick up,' muttered Nate as he paced before the sash windows, the wooden shutters muting the sunlight into hexagonal patterns on the carpet. He cursed as his call diverted to voicemail, deciding to leave a message:

'Jessie, it's me... Nate. You'll never guess where I am. I'm surrounded by your favourite things in the entire world... books. You'd love it, you really would. I'll take some pictures for you. Anyway, I hope you're okay. I... I won't lie. I'm getting worried. Call me, yeah? Or text or something. Just let me know you're okay.'

Nate cut the call, shaking his head. He'd never left a message like that; he'd never had to.

Damn you, Jessie!

He took a deep breath and walked around the room, capturing images of the floor-to-ceiling bookcases as best he could, the shutters doing a sterling job of keeping the sun away.

Pictures captured for Jessie, Nate slid his phone in his

pocket and did what he'd done in all the other rooms in the house: he closed his eyes and tuned into his other senses, picking up the smells, the sounds and the feel of the space, before opening them again and inspecting the details.

Unlike many of the others, the library was a room Nick used. Nate traced his fingers over the wing-backed leather chair in a corner, a wool blanket thrown over the arm, a volume lying discarded on the walnut coffee table, classic car magazines for company. Unlike the other windows, the one beside the chair was devoid of shuttering, allowing the light to spill over the armchair, creating the perfect conditions to curl up with a book.

Jessie would love this.

The hearth next to the chair was swept clean, the firewood set for when Nick wanted to light it. Nate visualised Jessie snuggled under the blanket, Cole curled up on her knee and her attention absorbed in one of the many volumes.

Out of curiosity, Nate wandered along the bookshelves, tracing his finger along the dust-free oak shelves, seeing the names of authors with whom he was acquainted, as well as those who remained strangers. Suddenly he stopped and hooked his finger over the spine of a dark grey volume, the intricate gilt design catching his eye. He eased the book out of its place, the cloth binding slightly darker on the front than the spine. He traced his fingertips across the etched cover, jumping as the door clicked open, almost dropping the book as he hurried to return it.

'I-I'm sorry, I didn't mean to be nosy, it's…' Nate stammered as he turned to see Nick walking into the room.

'It's a library full of books all meant to be read,' Nick said, smiling. 'A favourite of yours?' He nodded towards the book Nate still had his hand on.

'Yes, well no, not mine… my girlfriend's…' Nate paused, his reference to Jessie taking him by surprise.

'And does she own a first edition?'

'First edition? Wow, really? I'm sorry. I hope I haven't reduced its value by putting my sticky mitts on it?'

'I'm sure it'll be fine,' Nick said, and winked. 'She must have several copies if it's her favourite?'

'No, not Jessie. Just one. A well-read, battered copy she keeps close by.'

'Well then, you must take that one to her, so she can have one that's not so well read. It seems she would give it a good home.'

'That's very generous of you, Nick, but aren't first editions rare and valuable?'

'Some are, some aren't.'

'And this?'

'How would you feel about painting some bespoke pieces for the new house in exchange?'

'Well, of course I'll paint for you, but my work nowhere near compares in value to this,' Nate said, holding up the beautifully preserved novel.

'Maybe, maybe not, but I always feel value is relative. What is valuable to me may not be to you. And I would imagine your lady friend will see immense value in the book, just as I do in your work.'

'Are you sure? You haven't seen my designs for the house yet, and you may not—'

'I insist. And as to your ideas for the house, well, as I told Mac when he came to me panicking about you going off plan—'

Nate chuckled. 'Sounds like Mac.'

'Well, I put his mind at rest.'

'Really? How?'

'I simply told him that any creation by Nathaniel Parker was worth having.'

'Wow, thanks, I… um… I really don't know what to say.'

'You don't need to say anything. Just let me know what your girlfriend thinks of your gift.'

∞

Nate shoved his plate away and grabbed his beer bottle, gulping the cool liquid before setting the bottle back down, his attention again drawn to the label he'd been picking at with his thumbnail. He'd had no response from Jessie to any of his messages, and a heavy, ominous feeling was taking root in his stomach.

'Not like you to leave a perfectly good steak, Natey boy. What's eating you?' Mac asked as he shovelled an overfull fork into his mouth.

'Girl trouble?' proffered Johnny, burping as he slammed his empty bottle back on the table. 'Anyone for another?'

Nate shook his head, but Mac nodded as he swallowed his latest shovel of food.

'Natey boy doesn't have girl trouble. Ain't that right, Nate?'

Nate looked at Mac, who was grinning; the four bottles of beer he'd consumed were taking effect.

'Ah, yeah, I forgot. Nate does the heart breaking, not the other way around,' Johnny said and laughed.

'So, what's eating you, Nate? Seriously? Is it the job? I thought Nick was on board with whatever you come up with?' Mac said, his face becoming serious at the thought of business, and he leaned forward on the table.

'He is, don't worry, it's nothing to do with the job, it's…' But he couldn't finish. As he looked into the half-drunk faces of his long-term friends, Nate realised he couldn't tell them about Jessie; they wouldn't take him seriously.

And whose fault is that?

'So, what is it? Spill,' Mac pushed, but Nate shook his head.

'It's fine. I'm just tired.'

'Don't make me laugh. You're never tired,' Mac snorted.

'Maybe he is, just not the tired you're thinking about,' Johnny said, winking. Both Mac and Johnny burst out laughing. Nate shifted in his seat.

'Look, I've got a lot to think about after today, and I want to get another look early tomorrow, so I think I'll hit the hay,' he said and stood up.

'But I thought we were going to paint the town?' Johnny complained.

'You guys go, but I need to get my head together if you're to have these designs.'

Nate left Mac and Johnny gaping after him. Neither had ever seen Nate Parker turn down a night on the town.

Chapter 47

The next day, not long after the nurse had left after prepping her for the procedure, Jessie heard a knock at the door to her room. She looked up to see a couple she didn't recognise standing in the doorway.

'Hi,' Jessie said when they didn't introduce themselves. 'Who're you looking for? I think you'd be best to ask the nurse.'

The couple looked at one another, and Jessie watched as they nodded and squeezed their clasped hands. Her stomach turned sour as the couple ushered into her room. Clearly, they had come to see her.

Jessie reached towards the panic button tied to her bed, clutching it in her hand in case she needed it. She stayed silent as she watched the couple deciding who would do the talking.

Finally, the woman looked at Jessie. 'Hi, I'm Beth McKenna, and this is my husband, Adam,' she said, gesturing to the man beside her, who raised his hand in acknowledgement.

Jessie stared at them, waiting for them to expand, as she was still in the dark.

'W… we're Owen's parents… adoptive parents.'

Jessie felt heat rush to her cheeks, and she looked down, shifting in the bed, her thumb massaging the red button. Her heart raced as her mind sought a way to escape, but there was nowhere to go, not this time.

She closed her eyes and took a deep breath, focusing on settling her body down before she replied.

'I-I'm sorry, I didn't recognise the name,' she eventually said as she looked at them.

'Why would you?' Beth said and smiled. 'I hope you don't mind us coming to see you?'

Jessie didn't reply, looking down at the loose blanket thread she'd been worrying.

'We just wanted to thank you from the bottom of our hearts for what you're doing for our son… for Owen,' Adam said, stepping forward.

Beth picked up from him. 'We both got tested, just in case, but it wasn't a surprise we weren't a match. We would never have put you through this if…' Her voice broke, and Adam pulled her into his arms as she wept.

A lump formed in Jessie's throat as she watched them, her own eyes filling with tears.

'It's… it's okay. I'm happy to help. It's the least I can do after what you've done for me, for Owen,' Jessie said, her voice choked as she battled with her emotions.

Beth pulled away from Adam and went to Jessie's bedside, taking her hand, stopping it toying with the blanket. Jessie flinched, the urge to pull away overpowering, but she forced herself to remain at Beth's disposal.

'I understand why you did it; we both do, and Owen will too one day.'

Jessie was shaking her head as Beth spoke and said, 'No! It's best he never knows about me, about being adopted.'

'Absolutely not. We want him to know who his mother is, how brave and strong she was to walk away from her abuser,' Beth said, squeezing Jessie's hand.

'Not brave and strong enough to keep my son, though.' Jessie's voice broke and tears flowed down her cheeks as she met Beth's gaze.

'Of course you are. I know why you did it, Jessie. I've been in a situation not too dissimilar, but my baby didn't survive. I got away too, and eventually I met Adam, and then we found you.' Tears were flowing down Beth's cheeks as she looked at Jessie. 'I couldn't have any more children after what my ex did to me, so you gave us the most valuable gift. Please know that.'

Jessie bit down on her lip and nodded as she battled the sobs that demanded release.

'We told your sister all of this in the emails we sent her, but I'm sensing she didn't pass any of it on to you?' Adam asked, coming to embrace his wife and pat Jessie's hand.

Jessie shook her head, and Adam sighed. 'I told you she wouldn't, didn't I?'

Beth nodded and looked at Jessie, squeezing her hand. 'Would you like to see him?'

Jessie froze, an echo starting in her ears as she felt the breath sucked out of her, memories rushing in of his scrunched-up pink face and shock of dark hair as she handed him to the doctor.

'I… I…' Jessie started, but got no further.

Beth pulled a photograph out of her handbag and gave it to Jessie.

Jessie stared at the familiar face, the same one she looked at every day in the mirror, and she could no longer hold back.

The grief she'd carefully hidden away broke free, and Jessie sobbed into the arms of a woman she'd just met; a woman who'd healed many of Jessie's open wounds with her kind words.

'H-he's so beautiful,' Jessie sobbed, wiping her eyes so she could take in the photo and imprint it on her memory. 'He looks so happy.'

Adam and Beth grinned.

'He is. He is pure sunshine. He loves books and having stories read to him, and he loves the outdoors. He drives us crazy with his questions.'

Beth's words stabbed Jessie through the heart. Owen was all her, not Matthew.

'Th-thank you both for taking him in, and for loving him as parents should, something I wasn't sure if I'd be able to do if he looked like…'

Before Beth could respond, a nurse appeared in the doorway.

'Okay Jessie, we'll be ready for you shortly. I'm just waiting on the porter,' the nurse said, smiling at Beth and Adam. Jessie nodded, and the nurse withdrew.

Jessie handed the photo back to Beth, but she shook her head.

'That's for you, and there are plenty more should you decide you want them. Our address and phone number are on the back… if you would prefer to hear from *us* about Owen.'

Jessie's eyes filled with tears again and a lump rose in her throat, blocking a response. Beth hugged her.

'Just remember, Jessie, you're the hero in all this, and we're eternally grateful to you… for everything.'

The two women smiled at each other as they waved goodbye.

After the McKennas had left, Jessie stared at the photograph of her son, tracing her finger over his mop of blond hair, his grey eyes and his gummy grin.

Owen was the image of her. How could she ever have thought she wouldn't be able to love him?

'Right, time to go, Jessie. Are you ready?' the nurse asked as she returned with a porter.

Jessie nodded and tucked the photo in a drawer.

As the porter wheeled her bed out of the room, Jessie saw Anita at the nurses' station. Her back was to Jessie, and she wasn't alone. Beside her, his back also to Jessie, stood a tall, dark-haired man.

Hmm, I wonder who that is.

It certainly wasn't Roland, Anita's husband, as he had red hair.

Jessie grinned at the thought of her sister being not so perfect after all.

Chapter 48

Jessie groaned as she woke up. Her body ached, not from the procedure, but due to the angle someone had propped her following her bone marrow donation. She cried out as she tried to find a more comfortable position.

'Here, let me help.'

Jessie froze, pain and discomfort forgotten, as her body shifted gears, flooding her with adrenaline. Her skin turned clammy, her heart raced and the hairs on the back of her neck bristled.

The image of the tall, dark-haired man with Anita filled her mind; an image now all too familiar.

'Don't you touch me!' Jessie hissed and tried to turn to face him, but the pain crashing through her body thwarted her.

'Now, now, that's no way to talk to your concerned husband, is it, Jessica?'

Jessie shuddered as he said her name and finally stepped into her field of vision.

Matthew Barton was an arresting sight. Even after everything he'd done to her, Jessie had to admit it. Dressed in his customary designer suit and wire-rimmed glasses, his chiselled jaw and bright blue eyes hid the viciousness which lay within.

He smoothed a hand through his slicked-back hair and

folded his tall, gym-honed frame into a chair facing Jessie, smiling his disarming smile that conned so many.

'*Ex*-husband!' Jessie snapped. 'What do you want, Matthew? You shouldn't be here.' Jessie sought her panic button, but the nurse must have forgotten to put it within reach when they brought her back to her room.

'Looking for this?' Matthew said, holding up her lifeline.

Jessie glanced towards the door to find he had closed it, then up at the clock—fifteen minutes until rounds. Jessie swallowed, her mouth suddenly dry. She knew what Matthew could do in fifteen minutes.

'Let me get you some water,' he said, and refilled her glass from the jug before holding the straw to her lips for her to take a sip.

Jessie complied, just like she always had.

'Good girl,' Matthew said, and put the glass down.

'I said you shouldn't be here,' Jessie repeated, bracing herself for the blow.

Matthew leaned in close to her face, his hand on her freshly operated-upon hip, and he squeezed.

Jessie cried out.

He smiled and sighed. 'Oh, I have missed that sound, but you had to ruin it all, didn't you? Had to get the damn restraining order?'

Jessie whimpered as he rested his weight on her hip, pushing himself up.

'It didn't take you long to get over me, though,' she whispered.

Matthew rounded on her, his hand raised, and Jessie curled

in on herself as much as she could, shielding her head. Matthew burst out laughing.

'I've changed, Jessica, and it's all thanks to Rachel. She understands me, you see. If only you'd done the same.'

'Then what? You wouldn't have beaten me half to death? You wouldn't have pushed me down the stairs? You wouldn't ha—' But she couldn't continue.

'And still, after all this time, you can't see that if you'd done as I asked, none of it would've happened.'

'That's just it, though, Matthew. I *did* everything you wanted. You just never thought it was good enough.' Jessie glanced at the clock—ten minutes until rounds. 'What do you want, Matthew? Or shall I call security and have you thrown in jail?'

'Even if you were quick enough, before I stopped you, of course, they won't do anything.'

'Of course they will.'

'They won't throw out a man who's come to see his newborn, and just happened to bump into an old friend… by accident.'

'You stay away from him! You wouldn't…' The sentence died on Jessie's lips as she realised what he'd said. 'What? But you never wanted children.'

'True, with you. I didn't want them to inherit your whiny weakness, which, by the look of it, he has.'

'Get out!' Jessie snarled, an unfamiliar maternal protectiveness washing through her.

Matthew ignored her. 'Rachel, on the other hand, will make the perfectly compliant mother.'

'I said get out!' Jessie raged. 'How *dare* you judge our son!

He is stronger than you'll ever be; he survived your best attempt to kill him, after all!'

Jessie bolted upright, numb to the pain slicing through her, her hands formed into claws, ready for him for the first time.

'Still as unhinged as you always were, I see. If you think hard, I believe you'll find you're responsible for that too. Once again, you disobeyed me.' He laughed.

'Get out! Nurse!' Jessie yelled as loud as she could. 'You stay away from him, you bastard! You've done enough!'

Jessie heard footsteps hurrying along the corridor, and she saw Matthew edging towards the door.

Holding his hands up, he said, 'Have no fear. I have no interest in your decrepit offspring, or in you, for that matter.'

Jessie was about to respond when a nurse burst in.

'What on earth are you doing out of bed? For goodness' sake, you…' The nurse drifted off as she saw Jessie's stance, and then looked at Matthew. 'Jessie, are you okay? Do I need to call security?'

'Not at all, I was just leaving,' Matthew said, his coercive tone back as he smiled at the nurse and left.

Jessie allowed the nurse to settle her back down, her gaze never leaving the door, the shock of finally standing up to Matthew rendering her mute.

I protected my son. Maybe I would have been a good mother after all.

Chapter 49

Nate stared through the windscreen, the tarmac melting past him, his mind elsewhere. He knew Mac and Johnny wouldn't be happy, but he had no choice. He wanted to get home. He wanted to see Jessie. He was worried.

After another sleepless night, he'd left Mac and Johnny snoring off their hangovers, and had returned to Eddlestone Hall. The remit from Nick was to build a house away from the main hall and out of sight of it. As a bachelor, the hall was too big for just him, so he'd decided to open it up to the public, wanting a separate residence to protect his privacy.

Nate thought he'd be able to immerse himself in the project, pushing his worries over Jessie aside, but that wasn't to be. As soon as he'd settled with his sketchbook, the only image he conjured before him was Jessie. After two hours, and almost a sketchbook full of gouged out drawings, he gave up.

He knew she shied away from technology, but he'd hoped she'd want to stay in touch with him as much as he did with her. He hurtled up the motorway, anxious to see her, to understand why she hadn't responded.

She must've changed her mind.

It was the only explanation he could think of that made

sense, especially given he remembered *he'd* switched the phone on before he left.

Except one.

The acidic taste hovered in his throat as his mind wandered beyond Potters Hole.

What if that bastard of an ex has found her?

Nate's stomach convulsed, and he swallowed quickly.

'I shouldn't have left her,' he admonished himself, slamming the heel of his hand against the steering wheel.

If anything happens to her…

But he refused to finish the thought.

Nate had considered ringing his mother to ask her to check on Jessie, but decided against it. He didn't want her knowing how he felt about Jessie, especially if she had changed her mind. He didn't want his mother to know he'd fallen for her.

He glanced at the book lying on the passenger seat and smiled. If she wasn't convinced by him yet, maybe that would help.

Nate chuckled as he pictured Jessie squealing and jumping up and down with excitement. Regardless of how she felt about him, Nate knew she would love the book, and he couldn't wait to give it to her.

∞

Nate patted the book as he pulled into Jessie's driveway. Bluebell Cottage was quiet, and there was no sign of her car.

She may just be out, Nate reminded himself, taking a deep breath to calm his racing heart.

He climbed down from the truck, walked around to the back of the cottage and knocked on the door, just in case. While he waited, he called out for Cole, but there was no sign of the once-feral cat… or his owner.

Unsure why, given her track record, Nate called her phone again. From somewhere inside the cottage, he heard a faint ring, and he peered through the new patio doors to see the phone glowing on the kitchen table.

Well, that explains why you haven't answered me.

Nate sighed and stared at his phone. He was all out of options. He found the number and put the phone to his ear, waiting for it to be answered.

'Just keep it casual,' he murmured and then puffed; there wouldn't be much chance of that.

'Hey, Mum,' Nate said when the call connected. He knew it would be his mother, as his father never answered the phone; he never had much to say except to his patients.

'Nate!' his mother said, surprise in her sultry voice. 'I didn't expect to hear from you. I thought you were away?'

'I was… I am…'

Nate groaned. He was terrible at lying to her.

'Is everything all right? You've not all had a falling out already, have you?'

'No, no, everything's fine. I've got what I need, so just thought I'd come home. I always work better in my own space.' Nate paused, but, as usual, his mother's silence when she knew there was more to tell—a teacher tactic—worked its magic on him. 'Ummm, I wanted to surprise Jessie as I've not been able to get hold of her…'

Dammit! Another admission. Nate stared up at the sky before he shrugged. *What the hell!*

'… but she's not home, and there's no sign of Cole, and the house—'

'Cole's here with us,' his mother interrupted. 'He's taken a liking to your father, sits on his lap all the time.'

'Cole's with you? Why? Where's Jessie?'

'She's gone up to Scotland. Didn't she tell you?'

Nate's stomach went hollow, and his mother's words echoed in his ears as his fear of Jessie's ex resurfaced; her scars burned into his memory.

In as measured a voice as he could muster, Nate said, 'No, no, she didn't.'

'Well, don't worry, it seemed to be a bit of a last-minute thing.'

'When did she go?'

'Oh, it was a few of days ago. She said her sister was ill and—'

'When exactly?' Nate interrupted, more abruptly than he intended.

'It was Saturday night, quite late. She said she had to go, as if she had no choice. She apologised for leaving me in the lurch at school and asked if we'd watch Cole, as you were going away.'

Nate didn't respond, recalling the letter Jessie had received that same morning. She must have read it after he'd left, and forgot all about the phone in her haste.

'She did seem rather distraught,' his mother added, which puzzled Nate, as Jessie gave him the impression there was no love lost between her and her sister.

'Thanks, Mum,' he said eventually.

'Don't worry, I'm sure she's fine.'

Nate didn't respond.

'So, will we see you tonight?'

Nate rolled his eyes at the tone in her voice. 'Yes, as you always do.'

'Mmmm, well, bye for now then.'

'Bye, Mum. Love you.'

Nate cut the call and pondered what his mother had told him. No matter which way he looked at it, Jessie could have let him know.

Would I have?

He shrugged and, wanting her to have something to make her smile when she got back, Nate decided he would leave the book.

He returned to his truck and scribbled a note on a scrap of paper:

For my Cathy,

H x

Nate let himself into the cottage with the key Jessie had given him, and placed the book on the table next to the forgotten phone; the letter from her sister lay open beside it.

Contemplating what it might contain, Nate reached out to pick it up, but paused, wrestling with the invasion of her privacy.

Deciding to leave it to Jessie, he turned to go, but a niggling voice in his head made him stop. It was the same voice which had informed him she hadn't told him the full story about her past.

Nate picked up the letter and gazed at the stilted script, his eyes scanning the words before his mind had decided.

As he read, a chill washed through him and he clenched his jaw as the door Jessie had inexplicably opened to his heart slammed shut.

Chapter 50

The shock of seeing Matthew, of standing up to him, had wiped Jessie out, and she was dozing when her senses detected the tapping foot and imperceptible clearing of the throat; her heart sank.

'What do you want, Anita?' she said without opening her eyes.

'How dare—?'

'How dare *I*?' Jessie snapped, cutting Anita off as she pushed herself up as much as she could in bed.

She stared at her older sister, itching to unleash her fury on her, taking in the petite stature and dark colouring, so different from her own.

'What're you talking about?' Anita retorted, fiddling with the rope of pearls at the neck of her twin-set.

'Oh, don't play coy with me, Anita. You know exactly what I'm talking about. Matthew!'

'What about him?'

'I saw the two of you together here, before my surgery, so stop pretending you don't know what I'm talking about.'

'Well, he's been asking after you,' Anita said, dropping her hands to her hips—her defensive posture.

'So you told him where to find me?' Jessie stared, wide-eyed, at Anita, shaking her head.

'Well, why wouldn't I? He's always asking for an update, so I thought, as you were here, he could see for himself.'

'I don't believe you!'

'What?'

'What do you mean, "what?"? After everything he put me through, everything he did to me.'

'Well, according to you. Matthew has a decidedly different viewpoint,' Anita said and huffed.

'I'm sure he does,' Jessie muttered. 'And what else have you shared with him about me, exactly?'

'Nothing,' Anita said, glaring at Jessie.

'Really? So you've not told him anything about my new life then?'

'Hardly, because you haven't told *me* anything about it!'

'And for very good reason, by the sound of it!' Jessie snapped, watching Anita curl her top lip back. 'Please tell me you haven't told him where I live?' Her voice was taut as her heart contracted, a hollowness forming in her stomach.

'It's not as if he's going to waste his time chasing after you; he has a new wife now and a ba—'

'Yes, a baby you conveniently kept quiet about. You better hope he doesn't come looking for me!'

'How can he when you slapped the poor man with a restraining order?'

'That didn't stop him today, did it?' Jessie glared at Anita, who had the good grace to look away.

Jessie sighed as a decision she wished she'd made a long time ago made itself known.

'I stayed in touch with you, Anita, because it's what Mum and Dad would have wanted, and because, deep down, I hoped one day we would be as close as we were before Matthew.' Jessie paused, holding up her hand to stop Anita interrupting. 'But what's happened today, and your stubborn refusal to see that Matthew was in the wrong, has clarified that's never going to happen. I want you to leave, Anita, and I don't want to see or hear from you again.' Jessie felt the weight lift from her as she delivered the words.

'What? Not ever?' Anita said, her voice indignant.

'That's what I said,' Jessie confirmed, a feeling of calm washing through her.

'But what about updates on Owen?'

'The McKennas will tell me everything I want to know.'

'When did you…?'

'Not that it's any of your business, but they came and introduced themselves yesterday.'

'But…'

'Just leave, Anita, before I call security and have you removed.'

'What about your nephews, and Roland?'

'They are nothing to do with this, and are welcome to stay in my life, provided they don't share it with you. Go, Anita,' Jessie said when her sister made no move to leave.

Jessie watched as Anita nodded before finally turning and walking away.

As Jessie lay back against her pillows, an overwhelming need to be wrapped in Nate's arms suffused her.

∞

'When can I leave?' Jessie all but pounced on the nurse as she came to check on her half an hour later.

'Not until at least tomorrow, but only after the doctor has seen you and is happy to release you.'

'How's Owen? Is he out of surgery yet?' Jessie asked, her fingers crossed, her breath held.

'He is, just, and he did really well. The doctors are optimistic.'

'Thank you,' Jessie whispered.

'Now, lie yourself down and get some rest,' the nurse said, patting Jessie's hand before she left.

Jessie lay on her side, staring at the wall, her mind in turmoil. She had to tell Nate the truth. She had to tell him about Owen. But would he understand? Would he even listen? Would he give her the chance to tell him her story?

Her eyelids heavy, Jessie drifted off to sleep as images of Nate and Owen filled her mind.

Chapter 51

The last thing Nate wanted to do was have dinner with his parents. He wanted time to think, time to calm down, but more than anything, he wanted an explanation.

He'd thought about cancelling, feigning a headache, or something else easy to recover from, but he'd promised his mother and he never let her down; he wouldn't dare.

'A late night was it last night, son?' his father commented when he opened the door, Cole in his arms.

'Didn't sleep,' Nate grumbled and walked inside, taking his shoes off at the door.

Cole meowed and reached his front paws out towards Nate as he stretched in Ray's arms.

Nate obliged, scratching the downy belly as Cole purred his appreciation. A lump formed in Nate's throat as he remembered how Jessie had spent days befriending the feral cat.

'What's for dinner?' he asked, clearing his throat and wandering into the living room, flopping onto the sofa and planting his feet on the coffee table.

'Ask your mother,' his father said, sitting back in his armchair. Cole settled himself back down and closed his eyes. 'After you've said hello,' he added, staring at Nate.

Feeling like a naughty teenager, Nate gave a half smile before pushing himself off the sofa and going to find his mother.

'Hey, Mum,' he said, kissing her on the cheek while she chopped vegetables. 'Something smells good.'

'I thought we'd have a treat—a roast.' She looked at Nate. 'You look dreadful. Are you all right?' His mother stopped what she was doing and laid the back of her hand against his forehead, just as she used to do when Nate was a child.

'I didn't sleep much last night, that's all.' Nate shrugged away from her.

'I thought everything was fine,' she commented as she set the vegetables cooking on the hob.

'It is.'

'Then what?' She turned to face him, crossing her arms as Nate tossed a forgotten piece of carrot into his mouth.

Nate looked away from her and shrugged, not wanting to have the conversation he already knew was inevitable.

'Jessie, perhaps?' she nudged.

Nate felt the tears rush forward and clenched his jaw, willing them away as he stared out of the kitchen window.

'Nathaniel Parker, look at me when I'm talking to you!'

∞

As Nate turned his tear-filled gaze towards her, Bev's heart lurched.

'Oh, Nate, what's happened?' she asked, pulling her son into her arms, feeling his tears fall onto her hair as she held him tight.

'Talk to me, Nate. What's happened?' Bev crooned, feeling his heart thudding in his chest, his body shuddering as he fought back his sobs. There was only one other time she'd seen him cry; he'd been five years old.

Bev pulled away from him and held his face in her hands, looking into his pain-filled eyes. A rush of panic took over, racing through her as her own heart picked up its pace at the sudden thought.

'Has something happened to Jessie?' she blurted.

'I wouldn't know.' Nate pulled away from her and walked to the other side of the kitchen. 'She lied to me, Mum.'

Bev watched the change in her son as his tears vanished, the long-ago hurt taking their place.

'In what way?' Bev prompted when it didn't appear he was going to say anything more.

'She hasn't gone to Scotland to help her sister.'

'What do you mean? Why—?'

'She's gone to help a little boy… her little boy.'

Bev paused for a moment before responding. Of all the scenarios she had speculated upon about Jessie's past, a child hadn't been part of them.

'How do you know? Have you spoken to her?' she finally asked.

'I read it in a letter from her sister. It came on Saturday morning, but she didn't open it. It agitated her and—'

'You read a private letter? How did you—?'

'Yes, I read the letter! It was lying there, on the table, next to the mobile phone I bought her, which she *conveniently* didn't take with her.' Nate kicked the cupboard doors, the contents rattling.

'Nate!'

'Sorry.'

'What on earth were you doing in her house? More to the point, how did you get in? Please tell me you didn't break in?'

'Of course I didn't break in! What do you take me for?'

'I'm not sure you should be asking me that at the moment, are you?' Bev stared at Nate, but he looked away.

'She gave me a key so I could work on her kitchen when she wasn't home...'

'But you've finished the kitchen, so what were you doing in Jessie's house? And snooping at her private mail?'

'I wasn't snooping!' Nate snapped. 'It was just there. I saw it when I was leaving the book I got for her as a surprise.'

'Just because it was there doesn't make it okay to read it. I raised you better than that, Nate.'

Nate hung his head, nodding. 'I know. I was just worried after she told me about her past, and then when I couldn't get hold of her… and she wasn't home.'

'What did she tell you about her past?'

'Only that she was married to this guy who used to beat the crap out of her. You should see her scars, Mum.' Nate's voice broke, and Bev's heart went out to him. He looked lost and confused.

'I take it she never mentioned a baby?' she asked.

Nate shook his head. 'She abandoned him, just like *she* abandoned me!'

And there it is, Bev thought.

'Nate, shouldn't you give Jessie a chance to explain? You don't know the circum—'

'What's to know? She was abused, like that bitch. She had a kid, like that bitch. She abandoned her kid, like that bitch!'

Nate thumped the counter and turned on his heel. 'I'm not hungry,' he muttered, pushing past Ray as he left.

∞

Nate sat in his truck in his parents' driveway, his breath coming hard and fast as his emotions raged. He couldn't go home, not yet. He needed to vent, to let off steam, and he didn't trust what he would do if he went home.

Decision made, he started the engine and headed to the place he always went when he needed to be alone and brood—his gallery. There he had a room that he'd even banned Em from entering. Inside, he created art he never sold; it was far too personal, and would share more of himself than he was willing.

As Nate unlocked the door, the plastic-lined floor and walls greeted him in their psychedelic way. Blank canvases lined the walls—he always left it ready for the next time—and tins of paint sat in the centre of the room awaiting instruction; paint brushes standing to attention, their orders not yet issued.

Nate stepped out of his clothes and into the waiting overalls, then picked up the remote control and pressed play; *Linkin Park* filled the room. He gritted his teeth, slapped his hands together and walked forward, ready for battle.

He prised the lids off all the paint cans, picked up a brush in each hand and thrust them into random tins, before turning to face his canvas.

Lowering his chin, Nate looked up at the pristine surface, paint running from the brushes he held by his sides like swords. The rumble started in his belly, travelling up through his body, erupting as a roar from his throat as he launched forward, hurling paint at the canvases as he danced around to the music until he collapsed, exhausted, and slept.

Chapter 52

Anxious to be home and to talk to Nate, Jessie was up before the bustle of the hospital commenced the following day. Berating herself again for leaving the phone behind, she hoped Nate had asked Bev where she was, worried he'd take her silence as a sign she'd changed her mind.

It's not as if my behaviour doesn't support this, she thought as she paced her room, bag packed and waiting for the doctor.

'Going somewhere, Ms Ellis?' the doctor asked, making Jessie jump as he came in. The look of disapproval on his face caused her to sit on the bed, chastened.

'Is there a particular reason Ms Ellis thinks she'll be leaving today, nurse?'

Jessie's heart sank.

'Well, I said yesterday that, provided you are happy, she'll be able to leave, and she has responded well and is showing no signs—'

'I think I'll be the judge of Ms Ellis' condition, don't you?'

'Yes, doctor,' the nurse said, and pulled a face behind his back. Jessie had to bite the insides of her cheeks to stop herself from laughing.

The doctor checked her chart, listened to her heart, checked her temperature and blood pressure, and finally asked the nurse to uncover her wound so he could inspect it.

Nodding all the while, and not even making eye contact with Jessie, never mind speaking to her, the doctor finished his assessment before finally looking at her.

'Well, Ms Ellis, today's your lucky day. Everything looks in order, so once the nurse has given you the after-care instructions, you're free to leave.'

'Thank you,' Jessie murmured.

'Who will pick you up?' he asked, his eyebrows raised as he looked at her.

'Er… my sister,' Jessie said, knowing the truth would meet with disapproval.

'Good, well, safe trip, and take care of that wound. Any problems, call us.' And with that, he turned and left.

'I won't be long,' the nurse said, and hurried out after the doctor.

Jessie resumed pacing as she awaited the nurse's return. As soon as she had the after-care instructions, Jessie grabbed her bag and turned to go, hesitating in the doorway.

'Do you know where I can find Owen?'

Chapter 53

Jessie stood outside his room, peering through the window, her view obscured by Beth and Adam.

What am I doing here?

Her heart was racing as she pondered the reception she'd get. Beth and Adam had been friendly when they came to see her, but how would they feel about her being outside Owen's room?

Only one way to find out. Jessie raised her hand to knock, but a nurse squeezing past interrupted her.

Beth looked around as the door opened. At the same time, Jessie turned to leave, deciding they'd have invited her if they wanted her to meet Owen.

'Jessie!'

She stopped, turning back and smiling at Beth.

'Hey,' Jessie said before Beth enveloped her in an enormous hug, a hug she wasn't sure how to return.

'How are you?' Beth asked, releasing Jessie and stepping back to look at her.

'I'm good. A bit sore, but otherwise okay.' She hoisted her bag up onto her shoulder.

'Heading home now, then?' Beth indicated the bag, and Jessie nodded.

'I—'

'Would you like to meet Owen?'

'I was hoping to just catch a glimpse of him before I left, that's all. You don't—'

'Don't be silly. Come on,' Beth said, holding out her hand. 'Let me introduce Owen to his lifesaver.'

Jessie reached out her shaking hand, taking hold of Beth's, and allowed Beth to pull her into the room.

Her heart hammered against her ribcage and her senses jumped up a notch as her all too familiar fight or flight kicked in, yet this time she responded differently.

Beth urged her forward, the nurse stepping out of the way. Then, Jessie's breath caught as, for the first time since giving birth to him, Jessie gazed upon her son.

Owen's eyes were closed, tubes coming out of his tiny frame, machines beeping all around him. But those faded into the background as Jessie stared down at her son, tears streaming down her cheeks.

The shock of black hair from birth had turned dark blond, like her own, and stopped below his ears, his fringe interrupted by the same cow-lick she'd battled as a child. His lips, already full and pouting, conjured images of Jessie's mother blowing her a kiss as she left for school.

Before she could stop it, a sob escaped her throat, causing Owen's eyes to flutter open.

He looked at Jessie, and as their eyes locked, a wave of love crashed through her body. She gazed into her father's eyes, the same ones she shared.

The little boy, her little boy, reached his hand towards her and she responded, wrapping hers around his and stepping forward.

'Owen,' Beth said. 'This is Jessie. Jessie's the lady who's helping you get better.'

Owen looked at his mother and then back at Jessie, and smiled, dimples forming in his cheeks—Matthew's dimples.

'Do you have something you'd like to say to Jessie?' Adam said, and Owen nodded, but looked at his father. 'Thank you, Jessie,' Adam continued.

Owen turned his deep grey eyes to Jessie, and in a baby voice still struggling to form words, he said, 'Thank you, Jessie.'

Hearing his tiny, broken voice proved too much for her, and just about holding it together, she said, 'You're welcome, and I hope you feel better soon,' before running from the room and bursting into tears.

Beth raced out after her, rubbing Jessie's back as she fought to bring her sobs under control.

'I am so s-sorry, he didn't s-see me cry, d-did he?'

'Everything's fine, don't worry,' Beth said, taking Jessie in her arms and allowing her time to cry.

Once her emotions were back under control, Jessie pulled away from Beth and dried her eyes.

'Would you like to grab a coffee?' Beth asked, rubbing Jessie's arm.

'I can't. I've got a long drive, so I need to get on the road.'

'Is that a good idea?' Beth asked, frowning. 'You're still too upset, not to mention what you've just undergone. I don't think driving right now is a good idea.'

'I'll be fine, honestly. I just want to get home, and I promise I'll take regular breaks.'

'Mmmm,' Beth mused and Jessie laughed.

Sobering, Jessie said, 'Thank you for coming to see me, both of you, and for letting me see Owen. Y-you've helped me to heal.' Her voice broke as she finished, and Beth hugged her again.

'I'm glad we've helped. Thank you for coming, Jessie. It took a lot of courage for you to come back, and I will never forget it. Please stay in touch. We'd very much like you to be part of Owen's life, but only if you want to.'

Jessie's eyes filled with tears again, and, not trusting herself to speak, she nodded. The two women embraced before going their separate ways.

Chapter 54

Jessie pulled into her driveway, a sense of calm washing through her as she turned off the engine and closed her eyes, resting back against the headrest.

Despite her promise to Beth, she hadn't stopped. She'd wanted to get home. She'd wanted to hear Nate's voice. She'd wanted to snuggle under the duvet with Cole. Most of all, though, she'd wanted to get away from Anita, and from Matthew, as quickly as possible.

Owen was a different matter. Seeing his dimples, so much like Matthew's, hadn't brought the revulsion she'd expected. Instead, all she'd felt was love, and a longing she knew would never go away.

Jessie sighed and opened her eyes, staring into the inky blackness of the slumbering wood.

All I have to do is tell Nate… and hope he understands why I didn't tell him sooner.

Smiling ruefully, Jessie opened the car door and swivelled round to get out, crying out as she did so, pain shooting through her hip. She leaned to one side and massaged her hip, wincing.

Perhaps driving straight home was a bad idea.

She eased herself out of the car and tentatively settled the weight on her right leg.

Nope.

Trying to keep the pressure off her injured hip, Jessie retrieved her bag from the back seat and limped inside Bluebell Cottage and flipped on the kitchen light.

She saw the book lying beside the phone she'd left behind.

∞

Dropping her bag in the open doorway, Jessie hobbled to the table and steadied herself against it. She reached out and gently touched the cover, her fingertips tracing the impression stamped into the cloth, before she gathered the volume up. The gilt lettering and intricate floral decoration on the spine were almost perfect, and as she opened the cover, a slip of paper whispered to the floor.

Placing the book back on the table, Jessie perched on a chair and bent to rescue the fallen note. Her heart skipped a beat as she read Nate's words:

For my Cathy,

H x

Jessie felt herself grinning as she read it over and over, before she picked up the book again and turned the pages one by one, seeing how Heathcliff's and Cathy's story was originally presented. When she saw the publication date, her breath caught, as she knew without a doubt that the novel before her was a first edition.

How…?

Jessie grabbed the phone and was about to dial Nate's number when she saw the missed calls, voicemails and text messages. She looked from the book to the phone and back again, unsure what to do next.

How does he know?

She'd never told Nate it was her favourite book, and yet, somehow, he knew.

He pays attention… unlike me.

Guilt stabbed at her as she placed the phone to her ear and listened to Nate's messages.

∞

'C'mon, pick up, pick up,' Jessie muttered as she limped back and forth in the kitchen. But, once again, all she got was Nate's voicemail. She looked through the window towards the house across the lake, but the cloudy night didn't do her any favours.

'Where are you, dammit?!' she grumbled and dropped the phone on the table in frustration.

Jessie rested her hands on the back of the chair and leaned forward, stretching out her right hip, flinching as she did. It wasn't far to Nate's, but the terrain was rutted, and Jessie didn't relish the thought of bouncing along the lane he refused to level.

What choice do I have?

Gritting her teeth, Jessie grabbed her keys and phone and made her way to her car, her hip protesting at being forced back into the unforgiving seat.

As she drove, she kept calling, but Nate didn't pick up. It was his last message that had spurred her into frantic action.

"I… I just don't understand, Jessie. I thought everything was fine… good… great, even. So, why won't you answer me? If you have changed your mind, just tell me… please."

His voice had broken, and the message had ended, leaving Jessie's happiness on finding the book in tatters.

Why think I've changed my mind? Why assume the worst?

'Bloody technology,' Jessie cursed as she skidded to a halt at the entrance to the lane that led to Nate's.

Shifting position, so her good hip endured the remaining journey, Jessie put the Audi in first gear and began to crawl to the Lake House, anxiety and impatience at boiling point by the time she rolled to a stop.

Sweat peppered her forehead and Jessie pushed her damp hair out of the way as she eased out of the car, her right hip drumming its own beat.

I'll check it later.

Right now, she needed to find Nate. She needed to put his mind at rest. She needed to assure him she hadn't changed her mind. She needed to show him how much his gift meant to her.

But Nate wasn't at home.

Jessie left another voicemail and sent a text message, for good measure, before getting back in her car.

Maybe I should call Bev?

But when she glanced at the clock on her dashboard, she saw it was far too late to call, let alone collect Cole.

Her heart heavy, and her stomach in knots, Jessie headed home.

Tomorrow I'll sort everything out.

Chapter 55

Jessie stepped back after ringing the doorbell, settling her weight so as not to aggravate her hip any further. When she'd inspected it the previous night, it was swollen, the puncture mark inflamed. She'd put a fresh dressing on it and tried to put it out of her mind, which had proved impossible. She pressed her palm against her belly to quell the anger at her negligence. Having given up on sleep, and still with no response from Nate, Jessie had forgone breakfast, keen to dispel any misunderstanding. First, though, she had to find out where he was.

'Jessie! You're back!' Bev said. 'I didn't even know if you'd got there.'

Jessie felt her cheeks heat at the gentle admonishment. 'I know, Bev, I'm so sorry. I forgot to take the phone Nate got for me and… I'm sorry. I didn't mean to worry you.' She finished babbling and looked up at Bev.

Bev studied her for a minute before nodding and stepping aside. 'Come on in. When did you get back?'

'Thanks. Last night, but it was too late to call. I didn't think… How's he been?'

'Nate?' Bev asked, and Jessie felt herself flush again.

'No, Cole. Has he behaved himself? But… speaking of

Nate… ummm, do you… do you know where he is?'

Bev looked at her again, making Jessie feel uncomfortable, before she said, 'You best come through.'

'Is Cole okay?' Jessie asked, grabbing Bev's arm as panic gripped her; the thought of something having happened to him made her nauseous.

Bev laughed and patted Jessie's hand. 'Relax, Cole's fine. Look,' she said, nodding towards the living room.

Jessie peered into the room to find Cole curled up on Ray's lap, both of them snoring away.

'Oh, thank God for that,' Jessie said, her hand pressed against her chest. 'You scared me then. For a minute I thought…' But she didn't finish as tears welled up and she swallowed them back down. She cleared her throat before saying any more. 'I feel guilty disturbing him when he looks so cosy.'

'Well, it's a good thing you don't have to then, isn't it? We need to talk.' Bev turned and headed towards the kitchen.

Jessie paused, the hairs on her arms alerting her as her body made its preparations. 'What's wrong?' Jessie ventured, forcing herself to follow Bev.

'It's Nate.' Bev's tone was flat.

Jessie gasped as the adrenaline surged forward and she reached out to steady herself. 'What's happened?' Is he hurt? Is he in hospital?' All thoughts of hiding her feelings vanished as fear squeezed her heart.

Bev turned and hurried towards her, concern etched on her face as she held Jessie's shoulders. 'Jessie, look at me.'

Jessie obeyed the older woman, tears spilling, her breath

coming far too quickly.

'Jessie! Breathe. Nice and slow.'

Jessie followed Bev's actions as she took long, deep breaths. After a few minutes, Jessie's heart slowed in time with her breathing, and her body relaxed and settled itself down.

Bev, still holding Jessie's shoulders, pulled her into her arms and sighed. 'Nate is safe, don't worry.'

Jessie felt the tension ebbing away until Bev spoke again.

'I had every intention of giving you a piece of my mind for what you've done to my son, but seeing you now, so upset, I realise how much you care, and that you must have your reasons.'

Jessie pulled away from Bev's embrace. 'What're you talking about? I haven't hurt Nate. I—'

'How's your sister?' Bev interrupted, studying Jessie once more.

Jessie felt heat reach her cheeks again, and she looked away. 'She'll be okay, thanks.'

'I think you should sit. I'll make some coffee and then you're going to be honest with me.' Bev pointed Jessie towards a stool at the breakfast bar.

Jessie nodded, the chastised schoolgirl once more, and sat at the bar. She watched in silence as Bev made coffee and even placed a plate of home-made muffins in front of her. All the while, Jessie tried to figure out how he'd found out, and also *what* he'd found out.

Her heart lurched as she remembered Matthew might know where she lived. Was it him? But how would he know about Nate? Had he bumped into him when Nate left the book? But why would Matthew come when his new wife was still in the hospital?

Jessie was staring into space as the thoughts ricocheted around inside her head, and she didn't notice Bev settle down opposite.

'What on earth happened to you, Jessie?' Bev finally said, reaching her hand out to take Jessie's shaking one.

Chapter 56

Over an hour later, Jessie stopped talking and picked up her cold coffee. For the first time, she'd told her story in full. She felt a weight had lifted, albeit replaced by another.

'Why didn't you tell Nate the full story? You showed him your scars. You could've told him everything.'

'He told you about that?' she whispered, her cheeks burning at the thought of how much Nate might have shared. She looked at Bev's sympathetic face over the rim of her mug.

Bev nodded. 'You had the perfect opportunity. Why did you hold back?'

Jessie put her mug down and sighed, stretching out her hunched back and shoulders. 'I wanted to, Bev, believe me, but I was too scared.' She paused before continuing. 'And then he told me about his mother—sorry, his birth mother—and what she'd done, how she'd treated him when they met, and I just couldn't. Our stories were so similar that I was more than scared. I was terrified, terrified of losing him, terrified that he would never understand.

'But when I came home and found this…' Jessie broke off again and reached for her bag, pulling out the first edition of *Wuthering Heights* and handing it to Bev.

'… and the note with it,' she added, opening the cover, to where she'd returned the note. 'I knew in my heart he would. You see, I've never told him how much this book means to me; he just knew.'

Bev looked at Jessie and smiled, patting her hand. 'I think if you'd been completely honest with him at the time, I agree, with time, he probably would—'

'But I didn't want anyone to know. That's why I came to Potters Hole, for a fresh start.' Jessie shrugged as fresh tears plopped onto the counter and into her discarded coffee.

'I know, sweetheart, but we can never escape our pasts, only learn and move forward from them.' Bev squeezed Jessie's hand.

'How did he find out?' Jessie asked, holding her breath, praying her worst nightmare hadn't come true.

'He found your sister's letter when he left this.' Bev pointed to the book.

'But how?' Jessie murmured, racking her brain as to how he could possibly have read something she'd hidden... 'Oh no.' She put her head in her hands, remembering seeing the open letter next to the phone. In her haste to leave, she'd forgotten.

'I have to see him!' she blurted, jumping up. 'He has to know I didn't mean for him to find out this way…'

'He won't see you, Jessie.'

'Maybe not, but I have to try. He has to know the truth about why I gave up Owen.'

Chapter 57

Jessie drove into the gallery car park and pulled up beside Nate's truck. She switched off the engine and leaned against the headrest, taking a moment to savour the peace and calm before facing the imminent storm.

She looked down at her hands, recognising the quiver that had plagued her throughout her married life; now they shook for a different reason.

You don't have to go in.

The words repeated in Jessie's mind. It would be so easy to leave and go home, to forget about Nate and stick with her original plan, but deep down, she knew it was too late for that.

Jessie couldn't bear the thought of him hating her for the wrong reason. If she told him the full story, at least then, if he still hated her, it would be… well, maybe he wasn't the man he'd painted himself to be.

Here goes nothing.

She slid out of the car and walked to the front of the gallery, knocking on the glass door, as Bev had instructed, praying she'd got hold of Em.

When there was no response, Jessie banged on the door with her fist, before cupping her hands to peer through the glass and into the darkened gallery. A short curvaceous woman in a rockabilly dress made her way to the door and opened it. Her hair was as black as Cole and styled close to her head, her eyelashes thick and dark, and her lips shone a cherry red.

The woman stared at Jessie for a moment, and then said, 'I'm Em. You must be Jessie?'

'Y-yes,' Jessie stammered. Em's scrutiny made her uncomfortable.

'Okay, you can come in.' Em stepped aside to allow Jessie to enter the gallery. 'No matter what Mrs P says, no one is left in this gallery without my approval.'

Unsure of what to say, Jessie nodded.

'Here, this is for you.' Em held out a key towards Jessie. 'It's for his room upstairs… where the music is blaring from.'

Jessie angled her head, but couldn't hear any music, prompting Em to continue. 'Trust me, you'll hear it. He may think I obey his rule of not going into his space, but someone has to clean up after his binges. You'll find the remote for the music system just inside the door.'

'I'm sorry,' Jessie said, sensing Em's last comment was a dig at her, and twisted the key between her fingers, unsure how to talk to this fierce woman.

'Look, don't get me wrong, Nate's no angel, but I love him like a brother, and I want him to be happy. If that happiness is you, then I'll love you too, but you've got your work cut out.'

Jessie followed Em's gaze. 'How mad is he?' she finally asked.

'You'll find out. The gallery's closed today, so let yourself out this way if you need to. The door will lock.' Em showed Jessie what she meant, and Jessie nodded.

'Right then. Well, good luck.' Em kissed Jessie on the cheek and left.

Chapter 58

After Em's departure, Jessie remained where she was, staring absently around the gallery and trying to work out how to get upstairs.

Unable to see any obvious exits, Jessie headed towards the back of the gallery from where Em had emerged and studied what appeared to be a wall decorated to resemble an abstract painting. Jessie reached out, tracing the lines until her fingertips detected a defect in the image and she pushed. As the invisible door swung open, heavy metal assailed her ears, and she winced.

Jessie followed the music to the bottom of a wrought iron staircase. As she climbed, the music grew louder.

How is he not deaf?

At the top of the stairs, a narrow landing led to a wooden door. She looked at the key in her hand, its impression vivid on her palm. As she stood before the door, Jessie squeezed her eyes shut for a moment.

Please, please, please let him listen.

Her prayer sent, Jessie inserted the key in the lock and, twisting the knob, she opened the door.

Jessie gasped as she took in the scene before her. Paint, in sharp slashes and smears of colour, daubed the floor and walls.

The smell of stale sweat, leftover pizza and alcohol permeated the paint-infused air. In the centre of it all was Nate, his bare chest splattered with colour, his face unshaven, his hair lank, hurling paint at the walls as if he was throwing a dagger.

Jessie glanced to the right and saw his clothes piled on a chair beside an unmade camp bed, hidden in the only paint-free area of the room. On a shelf, as Em had said, sat a remote control.

Before she could overthink the situation, Jessie plucked the remote and, locating the power button, she shut off the noise.

Silence sliced through the air, and Nate whirled around, the anger and hate etched on his face making every cell in her body want to flee.

Instead, Jessie gritted her teeth and stood her ground.

Chapter 59

'What the hell are you doing here?' Nate snapped as he stood, feet spread wide, fists clenched around paint-laden brushes, glaring at her.

'I… I…' Her voice was so small, Jessie could barely hear it herself. She cleared her throat and tried again. 'I've come to explain,' she said, the confidence in her words belying the storm raging inside her.

'Explain what? Why you lied to me?'

'I didn't lie to you, Nate. I –'

'How can you say that?' he interrupted, his voice catching, his brows drawn together, the hurt clear for Jessie to see.

Nate cleared his throat and looked away, and Jessie watched his jaw flexing as he considered his words. When he turned back to her, tears glistening amber as they rimmed his eyes, Jessie reached out to him, but he shook his head and backed away.

'After *everything* I told you, *everything* I shared with you… you didn't think I should know what you… what you did?'

He glared at her, chewing on his lip and wrestling with his emotions.

'Nate, I…' But words failed her, and Jessie turned away as a sob threatened to escape.

'You did to your own son *exactly* what that bitch did to me? Don't I… didn't I deserve to know the truth, before I…' He fell silent, his chest heaving, his weight shifting from foot to foot.

'Before what?'

But he didn't respond, shaking his head and refusing to look at her.

'I didn't lie to you, Nate,' Jessie repeated, walking towards him, the bitterness in his next words stopping her.

'Didn't you? You believe that not telling me something isn't lying?'

'But I *was* going to tell you, I was just—'

'When? In a week? In a month? When we got married? When he came looking for you?'

Jessie's heart skipped a beat as Nate said "married", and a spark of hope ignited inside her.

'I was scared, terrified, to be more precise. I didn't know how you would…'

'What? How I would take it? Well, now you do! And whether I would understand, the answer is… How could a mother abandon her child and never look back? How could she say she never wanted to see him again?' Nate's voice broke, and tears spilled down Jessie's cheeks as she watched him.

'I didn't abandon him, Nate. I would *never* do that. Please, you have to believe me.'

'Do I? Why? Just because you tell me to? I don't know you! I know nothing about you!'

Jessie flinched; his words felt sharp, as if he'd slapped her. 'You *do* know me.'

'No,' he said, shaking his head. 'I thought I did. After seeing what that bastard did to you, I believed you'd shared the worst. Even seeing your reaction to your sister's letter, I convinced myself that whatever you had to tell me couldn't be worse than what I'd seen. I was wrong.'

Nate snorted and balanced his fists on his hips, paint slumping to the floor.

'You're no better than her.'

'Don't say that, Nate, please, just listen to me, let me—'

'Listen to what? More lies? I don't know what to believe anymore. Just leave me alone.'

'Nate, please, let me—'

'I said go!'

'What?'

'Go! Get out!' He paused before adding, 'I *never* want to see you again.'

Jessie burst into tears at the venom in his voice and turned and fled, the pain in her hip paling against her need to escape.

∞

As her feet hit the bottom of the stairs, the loud music crashed against her once more. She kept going, stumbling as tears blurred her way.

She turned the lock on the front door, about to pull it open, when she stopped.

This is not how I want to leave things.

Jessie rested her forehead against the cool glass and closed her eyes. As she did so, Matthew's smug smile filled her mind.

'No!' she said, stamping her foot, ignoring the burning in

her hip as his face dissipated. 'You will *not* ruin this life for me, too. You will *not* win!'

Her mind made up, Jessie turned and marched back upstairs.

The door stood ajar, and she shoved it open, silencing the music once more.

'I told you to get out!' Nate bellowed, rounding on her.

'Not until you know the truth,' she said, standing her ground.

'The truth? It hardly matters now, does it?' he said, glaring down his nose at her, snuffing out her spark of hope.

I've nothing left to lose now.

Jessie squared her shoulders and stared at him.

'Hate me if you want to, but I'll be damned if you'll hate me for the wrong reason. I came here to tell you the full story. If you still feel the same way after I've finished, so be it.'

Nate turned his back on her without replying and went back to hurling paint.

Chapter 60

To compose herself and assemble her thoughts into some kind of order, Jessie sat down on the camp bed, leaning to one side to ease the throbbing in her hip.

She stared down at her hands; her gaze caught by a scar—a sign of the life she'd signed up to; a sign she'd ignored.

'You've seen my scars,' she said, looking up at Nate. 'You've seen the life I lived with him.'

Nate kept his back to her, the slap of paint all she could hear. She glanced down again, casting her mind back to a time she'd hoped she'd never have to revisit.

'I've always wanted children, couldn't wait to have my own. It's the reason I became a teacher. Children give me so much pleasure, so much hope.' She took a breath. 'Matthew didn't want them. He was an only child, spoiled by his parents, and used to their undivided attention; that's what he expected from me.'

She paused and cleared her throat before she continued, massaging her hip unconsciously, attempting to sooth away the pain.

'He made me take the pill, literally fed it to me every night.' Again she paused as a memory surfaced: Matthew holding her down as he forced the little pill down her throat, making her gag.

'I have no doubt if hysterectomies were a matter of choice,

he would have made me have one. Perhaps this is why they're not. Anyway, when I found out I was pregnant, I was terrified. I spent days trying to figure out how it could have happened. I know contraception isn't one hundred per cent, but Matthew would never have accepted that. As it turned out, he didn't accept the more likely truth, either. You see, I had been quite sick with food poisoning—another fun past-time of his, so I didn't get "fat and ugly".'

She inhaled, letting it go slowly. Nate hadn't flinched.

'This particular time, though,' she continued, 'was different. As well as making me ill, he decided he still deserved his marital rights. And he took them… without my consent. I… I was too sick to stop him.'

Jessie turned away, the shame flaring in her cheeks. She sniffed and brushed away a stray tear before continuing.

'An abortion would have been the easy way out for me, but I couldn't do that. I would rather face his wrath than kill my own child. When I told him about the baby, when I explained to him how it happened, he punched me, breaking my nose and busting my lip.'

Jessie heard the hollowness in her voice as she replayed the scene in her mind, her body shutting down once more.

'As I lay on the floor, he kicked me repeatedly, calling me a whore… a liar… a cheat, never once believing I was telling the truth. I curled myself into the tightest ball I could, wanting only to protect my ba—' Her voice broke as she sobbed, shuddering at the reminder. She took a deep breath and cleared her throat before she spoke again.

'You see, in his mind, the baby wasn't his. I'd obviously cheated on him and deserved to be treated like the whoring scum I was. Not content with beating me, he dragged me into the bedroom and gave me "what I clearly wanted". He raped me, Nate.'

Jessie paused and looked up, but Nate didn't respond, and she sighed.

'He left then, and somehow, and I'll never know how, I dragged myself to the neighbour's, people who knew of me, but whom I'd never even met. They took me to the hospital. Six broken ribs, a ruptured spleen, a broken arm, nose and cheekbone. That's what my husband gave me for telling him I was pregnant with his child. He didn't kill my baby, though, of that I'm grateful. But, because of the extent of my injuries, the doctors advised me to terminate my pregnancy, but I refused.

'I made a decision then, one I should have made a long time before. I left him. My sister Anita took me in, but she'd always had a soft spot for Matthew and tried to reconcile us. I had to get a restraining order in the end to keep him away. Anita never forgave me for that—one of many things.

'When the baby came, I looked into his eyes and instantly fell in love. But I knew I couldn't keep him. Not because I didn't love him, but because I did.' Jessie sobbed as Owen's face swam into her mind.

'Anita went berserk, said I was just depressed, said she'd take him until I came to my senses. She didn't get it, refused to understand, hated me for giving him up. I know what you're probably thinking—if I loved him, how could I give him up? I did it to protect him. Restraining order or not, Matthew would have found me, and I would *never* have put my son in danger. There was also another reason, one I'm not proud of. I-I was… I was… afraid, afraid that if he grew up to look like Matthew, I would stop loving him. I c-couldn't do that to him.'

Jessie watched as Nate continued to fire at the walls.

'It turns out, though, he's the image of me. I wasn't wrong about Matthew. He came to the hospital, and I have a feeling he knows where I live, thanks to Anita. The irony is, he was visiting his new wife and their baby. I only hope he treats her better, but I doubt he does.'

She shook her head, hoping for some response from Nate, though none was forthcoming.

'Owen, that's my son's name, has leukaemia. That's why I went; it's the only reason I went. I wanted to help, had to help, especially after Matthew refused. And I met him, you know—Owen. Beth and Adam, his adoptive parents, wanted me to meet him. He is such a beautiful, brave and strong little boy.

'They want me to stay in touch. When Owen is older, they will tell him the truth about me. They want him to know how much I love him, that I did what I did to save him, because I love him, and I always will. I was so excited. I couldn't wait to get back and tell you. I wanted you to meet him too, I still do… but, I guess I've blown that now?'

Nate didn't respond.

Jessie sighed, feeling both lighter and overwhelmed from purging. She pushed herself off the bed and limped to the door.

'I never meant to hurt you, Nate. I had hoped my past

would stay buried, but when I knew it wouldn't, I was going to tell you. I just didn't know how. I hope you can see that I am nothing like your birth mother. I would *never* abandon anyone, especially my own child.'

Jessie finished and waited, giving him a chance to return, but he remained silent, consumed with his art.

What more can I do?

With tears streaming down her cheeks, she left the studio, closing the door behind her.

Finishing Touches

Chapter 61

As the gallery door slammed in Jessie's wake, Nate finally allowed his legs to buckle. The paint brushes clattered to the floor and his knees connected with the unyielding concrete.

He buried his face in his hands; the sobs coming in huge gulps, like waves crashing on the shore trying to outrun the storm. But there was no outrunning the past—not his, and not Jessie's.

Spent, Nate sat back on his haunches and stared at the chaos in front of him; a reflection of everything she'd told him.

He'd wanted to go to her, to hold her, to stop her pain, but he couldn't. He'd been impotent, tears running down his face, teeth gritted, heaving paint in response to her words.

If he'd stopped, he'd have walked out, he'd have driven up to Scotland, he'd have paid that loving sister of hers a visit, and then…? And that's where all sense of reason stopped, because Nate knew he would have torn that man limb from limb for what he'd done to Jessie.

Man… ha!

Nate snorted. No man would ever do what that bastard had done.

Nate shook his head to clear the image of him pulverising

her ex from his mind. Jessie didn't need to deal with the results of his anger.

He pushed himself up and went to sit on the bed. Jessie's perfume lingered in the air.

How the hell am I going to fix this?

He lay back and stared up at the ceiling, running his hand through his hair, and sighed. How could he have tarred Jessie with the same brush as his birth mother? They were poles apart.

'How can I have been so damn blind?' he shouted into the silence.

I just let her walk away. I should have gone after her. I should have told her I was sorry. I…

Nate jumped off the bed. Needing an outlet for his anger, for his self-loathing, and for his shame, he punched the wall, savouring the punishment as it radiated through his fist.

He rested his forehead against the brickwork as he continued to pummel it. He didn't care about the potential damage to his future, for his mind had come to rest on the real reason for his inaction, the reason he'd allowed the only woman he'd ever cared about to walk away—shame.

Nate was ashamed of his behaviour, ashamed of passing judgement on Jessie without giving her a chance to explain, and ashamed of the hateful thoughts he'd had about her since he'd found the letter.

Most of all, though, he was ashamed of letting her relive the most difficult time of her life, without acknowledging her and without consoling her. He hung his head, his hands on his hips, his injured fist already stiff and swollen.

Without looking back, Nate walked out of the room, locking the gallery behind him.

I have to make this right.

He only hoped Jessie would give him the very thing he'd denied her—a chance.

Chapter 62

It's going to take forever to get home at this rate.

Jessie edge the Audi away from the curb and back into traffic. How many stops was that—two, three? But what else could she do? She couldn't very well carry on driving, blinded by tears, could she? An accident was the last thing she needed.

She winced, shifting position to alleviate the pressure on her hip, but it did no good. Reaching down, she felt the dampness and, not wanting them to stick, Jessie pulled her clothes away from the wound. She checked her fingers to see them covered in blood and swallowed down a sudden wave of nausea.

This is not good.

Wiping her tarnished fingers on her jeans, Jessie took a breath to calm herself, her skin suddenly clammy in the confines of the car. She buzzed the window down, allowing the breeze to wash over her, chasing the beads of perspiration away.

Her stomach chose that moment to weigh in and remind her she hadn't eaten anything; the muffins at Bev's went untouched.

When was the last time I ate?

Jessie cast her mind back to the hospital, recalling how she'd left her dinner untouched, the encounter with Matthew having soured her stomach. *When was that? Yesterday, the day before? It's not surprising I feel like crap.*

Her thoughts turned to the humiliation she'd just put herself through, revealing her darkest secret to a man she'd believed would understand; a man who didn't give a damn.

Why did I think I owed him an explanation?

Jessie shook her head, succeeding only in making herself feel light-headed. She pulled the car over again and rested her forehead against the steering wheel, taking slow deep breaths as she waited for the dizziness to pass.

All she wanted to do was pick up Cole, go home, crawl into bed, and sleep.

Jessie raised her head and opened her eyes. When the street didn't teeter, she set off again.

∞

Jessie extricated herself from the car and shuffled to the front door. As she rang the doorbell, a wave of dizziness swept through her again. She reached out to steady herself just as Bev opened the door.

'Oh my God, Jessie!' Bev screamed as she broke Jessie's fall. 'Ray! Ray! Get here quickly!'

Jessie was vaguely aware of being half led, half carried into the living room and laid on the sofa. She cried out at the excess pressure on her hip.

'Let me look at that,' Ray said, urging Jessie onto her left side. 'Bev, grab my case,' he instructed, his voice calm as he stroked Jessie's hair.

'What have I done?' she mumbled.

'Nothing I can't fix,' Ray said as he peeled the soaked

dressing away and tutted.

'W-what is it?' Jessie whispered

'Looks like constant friction has aggravated the injection site. It's weeping and angry, but I'll clean it up, don't worry. Didn't they tell you to take it easy, to give yourself a chance to heal?' Ray glanced over his glasses at her as he cleaned and re-dressed the puncture wound.

'Had to get back, had to—'

'Meooowww!'

Jessie managed a weak smile as Cole appeared and nuzzled her fingers.

'Hey, Coley Moley,' she murmured, running her fingers along his ebony back.

'Did you mange to speak to Nate?' Bev asked gently as Ray finished and packed up his case.

'For all the good it did,' Jessie muttered, gritting her teeth as she pushed herself up.

'You really need to lie down and rest,' Ray admonished.

'I will, I promise. I just came to get Cole and go home.' Jessie hauled herself off the sofa, a wave of dizziness sending her straight back down, causing her to cry out.

'Is it the wound again?' Bev asked, placing a hand on Jessie's shoulder, urging her to stay put.

Ray shook his head. 'Jessie, when was the last time you ate?'

Jessie shrugged. 'A couple of days ago… maybe. I honestly don't know.'

'Bev, can you get her something? And some hot, sweet tea too, please?'

'No, no, I just want to go home. I'll get something there. Please,' Jessie pleaded, tears filling her eyes again. She didn't want to be there in case Nate showed up.

'You can, after some food,' Bev said.

'But I'll drive the two of you home,' Ray added. 'No arguing.'

Chapter 63

'Where is she? Where's Jessie?' Nate demanded, walking in as soon as his mother answered the door. 'Jessie?' he called.

'She's not here,' his mother said, folding her arms as she looked at Nate.

'She must be. Her car's outside. Jessie?' he said, calling upstairs.

'Your father's taken her home.'

'Why? What's happened? Is she okay?' Nate stopped and stared, his eyes wide, his breath held.

'She will be, no thanks to you.' His mother pushed past him into the kitchen.

'What's that supposed to mean? I didn't hurt her, not…' Nate stopped himself in his lie.

'What do you mean, you didn't hurt her?' His mother rounded on him. 'You may not have struck her, but by God, you *have* hurt her!'

Nate stared at his mother. Bev Parker never lost her temper, not unless there was a good reason. He hung his head as his heart sank.

'You might well hang your head, Nathaniel Parker. I raised you to be respectful and compassionate! What you did to Jessie is unforgivable. Do you hear me?'

'But, I—'

'You ignored her as she told you every little detail about the very worst part of her life. You kept your back to her as she told you about the very thing she came to Potters Hole to escape! Do you have any idea what it took for her to tell you?'

Nate didn't reply.

'Do you?' his mother snapped.

'I just thought—'

'I know what you "just thought". It's what you always think. It's the excuse you've used all your life, but enough is enough!'

Nate stared at his mother, her eyes blazing as she glared at him.

'Jessie is *not* your birth mother, not even close, and it's time—'

'Look, Mum, I know.'

'If you know that, why did you—?'

'I just did! I didn't know what to say, how to respond. I was so angry at that bastard for what he did, I didn't trust—'

'Why are you telling *me* this?'

'What?' Nate frowned as he observed his mother's about turn in her relaxed demeanour.

'I'm not the one who needs to hear this, am I?'

'I know, but she wasn't home, so I came here and… oh God, is she okay?' Nate felt a hollowness in the pit of his stomach as he remembered Jessie's car parked outside.

'She'll be fine. Your father needed to re-dress her wound from the operation. I gave her something to eat, as the silly girl hadn't eaten for days; too concerned with getting back to you… to explain.'

Nate felt his cheeks burn at the dig.

'What are you waiting for? Go.' His mother shooed him towards the door, but Nate stopped and looked at her.

'But what do I say? How do I…? I love her, Mum,' Nate said, his voice breaking.

'Just that.'

Chapter 64

'Okay, in you go, and hold on to the units as you go as I've got my hands full,' Ray instructed as he held the door to Bluebell Cottage open for Jessie. Cole, knowing he was home, was growing restless and Ray struggled to keep from dropping his carrier.

'I told you to let him out when we got out of the car,' Jessie said, laughing, as Ray finally relinquished the carrier and opened the door. The freed Cole shot from captivity as though his life depended on it.

'Got no patience, that one,' Ray grumbled as he massaged his arm. 'How much does he weigh?'

'I know, he's soon put it on.' Jessie pushed away from the counter she'd been holding on to and teetered, making a lunge for the table as Ray caught her.

'I told you to hold on to things,' he admonished.

'I know, I just thought…' But she didn't finish. She hadn't thought, and that was the problem.

'Right, let's get you upstairs and into bed, shall we?' Ray tucked her arm in his and patted her hand, but didn't move forward.

'I'm afraid you'll have to lead.'

After a moment, Jessie caught on. 'Of course, I'm sorry. Straight ahead and to the left.'

Ray guided Jessie through the cottage and up to her bedroom, lowering her onto her bed. He leaned down and lifted her feet, but Jessie reached a hand out to stop him.

'I think I'd like to take a shower first.'

Ray stood up and appraised her. 'I don't think a shower is a priority over a good night's sleep, Jessie.'

'I know, but I can't even remember when I last showered. I… I just want to wash away the last few days…'

Ray studied her for a few moments and then nodded his head. 'Fine, but I'm not leaving until I know you're safely tucked up in bed for the night.'

Jessie felt a warmth radiate through her at his words, and she smiled. 'That's fine. Would you do me a favour then and feed Cole?'

'No need, he's had more than enough at ours.'

'I find a little tuna always helps to salve his affronted sensibilities.' She winked as she eased off the bed, waving Ray away as he stepped forward to help. 'You're not coming in the bathroom with me, so I best figure this out for myself.'

'Yes, yes, of course,' blustered Ray, who turned on his heels and left.

∞

Jessie sat on the edge of her bed, towelling her hair dry as she stared absently across the lake at Nate's dark house. She smiled as she listened to Ray talking to Cole. His voice grew louder, and the stairs creaked, announcing his imminent arrival.

A tap on the door was followed by, 'Are you decent?'

'Come in.' Jessie double-checked she'd fastened all the buttons on her pyjamas.

'Come on, Cole, let me pass, will you?'

Jessie watched as Cole shot into the room with a growl, followed by Ray carrying a tray laden with tea things and some biscuits Jessie wasn't aware she had.

'I'm not sure they're palatable,' Jessie said as he placed the tray beside her.

'It's irrelevant if you're going to dunk.' He grinned as he took one mug and a biscuit and promptly demonstrated, before settling into the armchair opposite Jessie.

'I never thought about it like that.' Jessie followed suit, laughing when only half her biscuit re-emerged.

'It takes practice.'

The two lapsed into silence.

'Why didn't you tell me about Owen when you came to see me?' Ray asked, breaching the peace.

Jessie looked at him over the rim of her mug, using the tea as an excuse to take her time to respond. Lowering the mug, she glanced down at her hands before looking back at Ray.

'I could have warned you about Nate, about how he would react.'

'Why would you? You didn't know about us… I didn't even know about us…'

'Now, I don't think that's entirely true.'

Jessie shrugged. 'Maybe, maybe not.'

'So, why didn't you tell me why you needed that test?'

Jessie sighed. 'I didn't want anyone to know. I moved here for a fresh start, to put the past behind me, but…'

'The past never stays hidden, and secrets have a way of surfacing, as hard as you might try to prevent that.'

'I didn't know he was sick when I left. I would never have come here if I'd known. I feel terrible for—'

'For what? Saving his life?'

'But if I'd stayed, I could have been there sooner, could've stopped his pain.'

'Jessie, look at me.' Ray paused until Jessie dragged her gaze away from the dregs of tea. 'You have absolutely nothing to feel guilty about as far as Owen is concerned…'

Jessie waited for Ray to finish his sentence, but he seemed to have thought better of it.

'Buuuut…?'

Cole chose that moment to jump up on the bed, sitting equidistant between Ray and Jessie, before proceeding to groom himself.

'You feel I should have told Nate?' Jessie pushed when Ray watched Cole instead of responding.

'You would have had to tell him, eventually. I just feel it would've been better if you'd been more open. Secrets between couples—'

'But we weren't a couple then… and we're not now!' Jessie jumped up, startling Cole, who dived off the bed. She regretted the sudden movement as the room tilted on its axis.

'Careful!' Ray lunged forward and grabbed her arm as her legs buckled, helping her back onto the bed.

'You might not be a couple, but there is definitely something between you. I have never seen Nate like this, and I think you should have told him, that's all, especially after he told you about his background.'

Jessie felt the heat flood her cheeks as Ray called her out on the very thing she'd chickened out of doing.

'I didn't know how,' she said, 'but he knows now, and he's made his views pretty clear, so maybe you're right, I should've told him sooner, then I wouldn't have got my hopes up…'

When Ray didn't respond, Jessie found him studying her.

'He'll come round.'

Jessie shook her head. 'I don't think he will.'

'He will, believe me.'

'But you didn't see him… the way he spoke to me, the way he looked at me.'

'He's hurt, Jessie. He let you in. The first woman he's ever let in, I can assure you, and he feels betrayed. Give him time.'

Jessie sighed and gingerly pushed herself up and walked over to the window. She stared into the darkening evening to see the Lake House looking lost and forlorn.

'It doesn't matter now,' she finally said.

'What do you mean?'

Jessie turned from the window to see the concern etched on Ray's handsome face.

'The things he said, the way he acted… he reminded me of Matthew, and I never—'

'Did he hit you?' Ray interrupted, jumping up.

'No, not physically,' Jessie said, shaking her head. Ray relaxed back into the chair. 'But his words… his tone… his anger… they've left their marks, and I… I… I came to Potters Hole to rebuild my life… alone, and I think it's best I do that… if I stay.' She whispered the last three words, her subconscious having added them, taking her by surprise.

'Why wouldn't you stay, Jessie? This thing with Nate is nothing the two of you can't resolve, and believe me when I say Nate doesn't have a violent bone in his body, so please don't worry that he'll ever hurt you.'

'Hurt isn't just physical, Ray. As a doctor, you know this.'

'I know, but—'

'Owen is why I might not stay. I met his adoptive parents, and they invited me to be part of his life.'

'Jessie, that's wonderful, but are you sure it's something you feel up to doing?'

'I… I don't know. I need to think, which is why I need to forget about everything else.'

'But you don't need to move away to be part of Owen's life.'

'No, I don't, but it would be easier to live closer.'

'But what about your ex? I thought you left to get away from him?'

'I did, but thanks to my sister, I think he knows where I am anyway, so what difference does it make?'

Jessie watched Ray's face crease with concern as he clenched his fists.

'Do you think he'll come looking for you?'

'Honestly, I don't know. He made a point of coming to see me in the hospital, but I'm not sure if it was to rub my nose in the fact he now has a child; something he never wanted with me. But I never could predict his actions. If I could, maybe things would've turned out differently.'

Jessie shrugged and yawned, making her way back to the

bed as she felt the strength draining from her.

'What would you do if you left? Stay with your sister?'

Jessie snorted as she replied, 'No chance, not after all she's done.'

Jessie yawned again and pulled the duvet back, looking longingly at her pillow.

'What happened between you?'

Jessie's shoulders sagged at the weight of the question, and she could feel her eyelids drooping.

'Let's just say she's Matthew's number one fan, and leave it at that.' Jessie climbed into bed and snuggled down under the duvet, Cole jumping up and hunkering down beside her, having chosen his side.

'What about your parents?'

Shaking her head, Jessie said, 'Both dead.'

Nodding, Ray pushed himself to his feet. 'Promise me something?'

'What?' Jessie only just covered her mouth as an enormous yawn took over. 'Sorry.'

'No apologies needed. I'll leave you to get some sleep. Just promise me you won't make any hasty decisions.'

'Mmmm,' Jessie mumbled, her eyes already closed.

'I'll check on you tomorrow, but if you need me, call me on this. Our home number's programmed in.'

Jessie opened one eye to see Ray place the mobile phone Nate had given her on the bedside table.

'It doesn't matter what time it is or what you need, just call.'

''Kay,' Jessie murmured, Ray's footsteps fading as she succumbed to the sandman.

Chapter 65

It had hammered down with rain while his mother had read him the riot act, and the truck jolted against the puddles as Nate sped towards Jessie's, hoping his father wouldn't be there. He didn't need an audience while he fell on his sword before the woman he loved; the only woman he'd ever loved.

Goosebumps erupted across his skin, as they had when the realisation hit him on the drive back from the gallery. He'd been turning things over in his mind, trying to figure out why it all mattered to him, why she mattered to him, when no one ever had before. That's when it had hit him. He finally knew the answer to the question that had plagued him since he first saw Jessie—why her?

It had come to him as he listened to her pour out her heart in his studio. As she told him of the pain of giving up her son, the pieces slotted into place; he just hadn't paid attention.

Jessie was his balm to heal the wounds of the past, and he was hers. Their shared pain gave them an understanding of each other that he had never had before.

This dawning brought a calmness to his soul, and with it, the weight of his birth mother's abandonment finally lifted. And Nate knew he owed it all to Jessie, to the bravery she showed in sharing her past.

Nate thought back to that first day, to the pain and vulnerability he'd seen in her eyes. His heart had gone out to her then, in more ways than one. Just as he hadn't believed in muses, Nate certainly hadn't believed in love, especially not at first sight.

Until Jessie. Everything came back to Jessie.

As he turned onto the road to Bluebell Cottage, the sun broke through the clouds, chasing the last of the rain away.

Nate smiled as he saw a rainbow shimmering in the blue-grey sky and, as he always did, ever since he was a child, he followed the arc to see where his pot of gold lay.

Nate laughed out loud, nodding his head as the rainbow ended at Bluebell Cottage.

If that wasn't a sign, he didn't know what was. But, as he drew closer, he saw his father's car pulling out of Jessie's driveway, and he groaned.

∞

Nate watched as his father drew to a stop, ensuring his car blocked Nate's access, and mirrored his father's movements as he buzzed down the window.

'Where do you think you're going?' his father asked.

'To see Jessie, where else… Ummm, to apologise.'

His father nodded his head as he rubbed his chin. 'Not tonight, you're not. Jessie needs her rest.'

'But I have to see her,' Nate protested, feeling like a child asking for something denied to him.

'I'm sure you do, but you should have thought of that when the poor girl poured her heart out to you, shouldn't you?'

'Don't start, Dad, please, I've already had Mum laying into

me about it.' Nate looked away, through the windscreen into the darkening evening, not daring to look his father in the eye.

'You're lucky that's all she did. Have you any idea how Jessie interpreted your behaviour?'

Nate dragged his gaze back to his father, who was frowning at him as he glared over the top of his glasses. Nate's shoulders slumped as he shook his head.

'Her ex.'

'What?' Nate jerked upright.

'Your disgusting behaviour reminded Jessie of her ex-husband.'

'But, I—'

'It doesn't matter what you did or didn't do, it's how Jessie interpreted it that matters. And now, thanks to you, she's pondering leaving Potters Hole! She's only just bloody got here.'

'Leave? I don't understand. Why on earth would she leave because of me? She can't leave!' Nate smacked the steering wheel to emphasise his last point, causing his father to raise his eyebrows.

'And why is that? Jessie is her own person. She's already escaped one rather nasty relationship, from what I can gather, so why on earth would she open herself up to another?'

Nate stared open-mouthed at his father, his words stinging as if he'd slapped Nate across the face.

'Is that what you think of me? That I would hurt Jessie? That I would hurt anyone?'

'No, no, of course not,' his father said, shaking his head as he reached through the window to pat Nate's hand. 'But, it's not about what I think, it's about what Jessie thinks. And right now, she's not thinking a lot of good things about you.'

'But she can't leave,' Nate said again, his blood pounding in his ears as it raced through his system.

'Why can't she?'

Nate looked at his father and felt the emotion rise and threaten to breach. He swallowed it down before replying, 'Because I love her.'

A grin spread across his father's face, melting away the stern look he'd been wearing since Nate pulled up. 'Well, well, well, it would seem Cupid got you in the end then, but you've got your work cut out with Jessie.'

'I know. That's why I need to see her. I need to fix it. I need to explain.'

'Not tonight, you don't. She's already asleep. She's been through a tremendous amount in the last few days, mentally and physically, and she needs time to rest.'

'But, Dad, she thinks I hate her.'

His father nodded in agreement.

'I have to fix this. I have to let her know it's not her I hate.'

His father studied him for a minute and nodded again. 'You better hope she gives you a chance to explain, unlike what you gave her.'

'Do you think she will?'

'I don't know.'

The two men looked at each other, neither moving from their position.

'You're not seeing her tonight, Nate. I've already told you this. She's asleep. Now, go home.'

'But—'

'Go home.'

Nate sighed and bumped his head back against the headrest. He stared through the windscreen for a few moments and then, without saying goodbye to his father, he drove away.

∞

Nate raced up to his studio and over to the picture windows, his palms against the glass as he stared across at Bluebell Cottage. All was in darkness.

He rested his forehead against the cool salve of the window and closed his eyes, replaying Jessie's words, the anger rolling through him like a fireball. He clenched his fists against the glass, his injured hand crying out as he did so.

Nate eased away from the window and studied the bruising now decorating his swollen knuckles. He flexed his hand as he turned to his easel, his solace, and sat down, picking up a pencil. His hand protested but maintained its grip.

His mind filled with the hurt and determination he'd seen on Jessie's face as he'd screamed at her. His hand went to work to capture the last image he had of her.

Half an hour later, spent, his neck and back aching, and his hand throbbing because of its cramped position, Nate sat back and stared at his latest creation, and a sob caught in his throat.

How could I have been so stupid? How could I turn my back on her? Tar her with the same brush as my birth mother? How could I think she's lying to me?

The truth lay before him on the canvas—the honesty clear in her eyes, in her body language, in her openness.

Nate hung his head as he massaged his eyes.

What if I've blown it?

He pushed away from the easel and switched off the light, deciding he better ice his hand, when the hairs on the back of his neck rippled. He returned to the window and squinted across the lake, the moon offering no help as it played hide and seek with the clouds. The cottage was still shrouded in darkness, but as he stared, he swore he saw the voile twitch.

Is she watching me?

Nate's heart leapt as hope surged through him.

∞

Across the lake, Jessie lay staring at the ceiling. Despite her exhaustion, after Ray had left she woke up, images of Nate as he'd studiously ignored her playing on repeat in her mind. All she could see was the tension in his body, and the viciousness with which he hurled the paint as she told her story. His shoulders only sagged as she talked about Owen. But, was that a response to her pain, or merely his waning strength? Jessie didn't know.

Maybe I've had a lucky escape?

She'd expected her experience with Matthew to make her more savvy with men, but maybe it didn't work that way. After all, Matthew had been perfectly charming and attentive when they'd first met.

Maybe Nate is just another Matthew?

As this thought filled her mind, Jessie shook her head, conjuring an image of Bev and Ray. There was no way two people so good and kind could have raised anyone other than a decent son. But then she remembered what Nate had told her about his birth mother and what she, in turn, had said about his father.

Is abusiveness a product of DNA, environment, or both?

Jessie screwed her face up as she tried to remember what Matthew's parents were like, but she drew a blank. She'd only met them once, at their wedding; the day she'd met umpteen people she'd never seen since.

Did he do that deliberately?

As the questions churned up her mind, Jessie eased out of bed and pulled on her robe, padding over to the window. Cole didn't budge, as was the wont of a slumbering feline.

A light burned across the lake, and Jessie parted the voile covering her windows to see Nate hunched over his easel, leaning in close as he worked on whatever he was creating.

Jessie's heart sank. Part of her had clung to the hope that, despite his appalling behaviour, she's got through to him and that he'd come to see her, grovelling for forgiveness. From the look of his studiousness, all her confession had done was enable him to focus on his latest project. Jessie set her jaw, the walls inside resurrecting as she watched him.

He's not worth it.

She sighed as she turned away. Maybe she should leave. Living across from Nate would be too painful… for her, at least.

Slipping out of her robe, Jessie picked up a comatose Cole and pulled him close as she crawled back into bed.

Chapter 66

Jessie's subconscious registered that something was amiss, but her slumbering mind didn't want to act; instead it ran through scenarios of what could be touching her face. She grumbled as she swiped it away, but whatever it was soon started again. Jessie tried to shift position, but found herself pinned to the bed, a weight on her chest holding her down. The surge of adrenaline that shot through her at the familiar threat ignited her brain synapses and her eyes flew open as she readied for a fight.

'Bloody hell, Cole, you scared the hell out of me,' she said to the cat sitting on her chest, his green eyes slits as he concentrated on tapping her face to wake her up. She stared up at the ceiling as she willed her heart to slow its pace. Cole nose-bumped her to get her attention.

'I'm guessing this is a request for breakfast, not a declaration of love?'

She ruffled Cole's fur as she nudged him off her sternum before she attempted to turn on her side, crying out as she did so. She'd forgotten to prop herself back on her side when she got back into bed the previous night, and now she was paying the price.

Jessie gritted her teeth as she eased herself out of bed.

How can a needle cause so much pain?

She plucked her robe off the bed, and limped over to the window, pushing the voile aside and gazing at the view.

All was still—the trees, the lake, the birds, even the insects—as if waiting for her to decide. Before she could stop herself, Jessie's gaze had slipped to the Lake House. All seemed quiet there too. Even Nate's car was gone.

A heaviness settled in Cole's place as she thought about Nate resuming his life as if she had been nothing more than a bump in the road.

'Meeoooowwww!'

Jessie turned to see Cole perched on the edge of her bed, clearly miffed by her distraction, and she smiled as a slow warmth nudged aside the heaviness.

At least I matter to someone, even if only on his terms.

Jessie eased downstairs and busied herself feeding Cole, before making herself some coffee and porridge; she needed to get back to her own routine. She carried her breakfast things to the table, settling as comfortably as she could, and spied a note from Ray. Jessie picked it up and read it: "Jessie, I hope you feel rested. Call me as soon as you read this. Ray."

She laughed and rolled her eyes. *Drama queen.* But she got a fuzzy feeling from knowing he, too, cared. She picked the mobile up off the table, where she'd deposited it on coming into the kitchen—she was getting used to technology again… unfortunately—and dialled the number Ray had written on the note.

'Hey, Bev, it's me… Jessie.'

'Jessie! How are you? How did you sleep?'

'So-so. I woke up on my back, which proved an issue when

I wanted to move, but I made it downstairs.'

'That's good. Listen, I'll pop round later, after school.'

'No, Bev, you don't have to do that. I'm fine, honestly. I'm only calling because Ray left me a note.'

Bev chuckled before responding, 'He's such a worrywart, but he does care about his patients. So, do you want me to bring anything later?'

'Honestly, Bev, I'm fine. To be honest… I just want to be on my own.'

'Why? What's he done now?'

'Who?'

'That son of mine. Who else?'

'Why would he have done something?'

'Because he came to see you last night?'

'No, he didn't.'

Jessie heard Bev cover the receiver and shout Ray's name. She could hear an exchange of words, but couldn't make out what they said. She got the impression Ray was getting a dressing down.

'Jessie, are you still there?'

'I'm here. Is everything okay?'

'Fine, fine. Listen, I've got to go. I'll let you off for today, but I will come to see you soon, okay?'

'Okay, I'll look forward to it.'

'Hmmm, I hope so. Ray? Come and speak to Jessie. I've got to go, otherwise I'll be late.'

There was a clattering of the phone, some muffled sounds, and then Ray's soothing voice came on the line.

'Good morning, Jessie. How do you feel this morning?'

'A bit sore, struggled to get up, but—'

'Strange. Did you sleep on your side like I showed you?'

'Ummm, for a while, but I must have shifted in the night. Woke up on my back.'

'Ah, that'll do it. At least you slept, though. That will have done you the world of good.'

'I suppose.'

'Well, I'll pop to see you sometime this morning. But you're not to do anything today, just rest.'

'It's not like I can do much, anyway.'

'I mean it, Jessie. Rest. Anything else can wait. Promise me?'

'Okaaaay, I promise.'

∞

Jessie stared longingly at the claw-foot tub. She would have loved to fill it to the top with jasmine-scented bubbles and slip into its warmth, but the thought of Ray having to haul her out because she couldn't get up soon put paid to that. Instead, she stepped into the shower, allowing the hot jets to massage her aching body. She closed her eyes; the water reminding her of Nate's gentle caresses and she shivered, goosebumps rippling across her skin despite the heat of the water.

She pushed the memory aside and concentrated on cleansing herself of the entire experience. He'd shown a different side to himself the previous day, one she was not about to forget.

Half an hour later, dressed in loose fitting sweatpants and a sweatshirt, Jessie dug a fleecy blanket out from under her bed and padded downstairs. Her movements were more fluid after her shower, and she hoped she wouldn't seize up again after a day spent curled up with Heathcliff and Cathy.

Humming to herself, she put the kettle on, deciding a huge mug of tea would complete her cosy plans, when there was a knock at the door.

He's early, she thought, not having expected to see Ray until much later.

Plastering a smile on her face, Jessie opened the door, the smile dying as she did so.

∞

'What are you doing here?' Jessie snapped as she took in his bedraggled look and the paper bag and coffee cups in his hands.

'I've come to explain,' Nate replied, giving her a half smile, his eyebrows lifting in question… or was it hope? 'I've brought breakfast.'

Jessie glanced from him to his offering before shaking her head.

'You made your views abundantly clear yesterday.' She turned away, pushing the door closed behind her, but something stopped it. She turned back to see Nate's foot in the way. 'Move your foot, Nate. I'm not in the mood.'

'Please, Jessie, give me a chance to explain. That's all I ask.'

'Give you a chance to explain!' she exploded, forcing Nate to take a step backwards. 'Give *you* a chance, when that's the very thing you wouldn't give me?'

She paused, her breathing heavy as blood thundered in her ears. She glared at him and he looked away, kicking the ground with his foot. Jessie's hand was throbbing, and she relaxed the grip she'd had on the door, feeling her nails withdraw from the wood.

Looking up at her, his chin still dipped, giving her that little boy lost look that Jessie had no doubt had worked wonders for him in the past, he said, 'Please let me explain. What you saw yesterday, the way I was, it isn't what you think. I promise you.'

'Really? So you weren't blatantly ignoring me as I poured the worst part of my life out to you? A part I *never* wanted to have to relive. A part I have *literally* spent thousands on in therapy to come to terms with.'

'No, Jessie, that's—'

'And in half an hour, you succeeded in sending me right back to where I started. You made me feel like the worst person in the world again.'

'That's not what—'

'Even after Beth told me I was no such thing, you, in your reaction to what I told you, shattered all that, blasted it to smithereens, seeing me as nothing more than a heartless bitch who'd given her child away because she didn't—'

'Jessie! Listen to me! For fuck's sake, take a breath!'

Jessie glared at him, her mouth open mid-sentence.

'You're right… hang on, let me finish,' Nate said, holding his hand out to stop her interrupting. 'In a way, you're right. My reaction was to what you *said*, but it wasn't aimed at you. In no way was it a reflection on you, I swear.'

Jessie watched as he clutched his free hand to his chest, the look on his face so earnest she felt her anger simmering down.

'So, what was it to?'

'It was a response to what that bastard did to you, to what your bloody sister did, and still is doing to you.'

Jessie reached her hand out to steady herself as her emotions warred within her.

'W-why didn't you say something? Why let me think it was aimed at me? Why let me leave and not stop me? Why leave it until today?' Jessie demanded, her voice growing angrier the more the questions came.

Nate hung his head and shrugged. 'I don't know. All I know is I wanted to kill him for what he did, and I didn't think my anger was what you needed.'

'It wasn't, but it would've made a difference knowing it wasn't me you hated.'

'I don't hate you, Jessie.' Nate stepped towards her, but Jessie backed away, her hand firmly on the door again. 'I could never hate you.' Nate didn't approach her further, and when she looked at him, the look on his face plucked at Jessie's heartstrings.

'Y-you should have told me,' she whispered, her voice hoarse.

'I wanted to. I came last night, but Dad wouldn't let me in. He said you were sleeping, and I wasn't to disturb you, so I didn't. I went home… I haven't slept all night Jessie, waiting to explain, to fix it.'

Jessie didn't reply, taking in his anguish.

'I'm sorry, Jessie.'

'So am I.' Jessie brushed a stray tear away with the back of her hand. Nate frowned, a puzzled look taking over.

'You have nothing to be sorry for. It's me who should apologise. I will make it up to you, I promise, I—'

'I'm sorry because it's too late, Nate.'

'Too late? What do you mean? It can't be too—'

'It is. I never intended getting involved with anyone when I came here, so maybe this is all for the best. I just want to be alone.'

'No, no, you don't mean that, Jessie. Please say you don't mean that.'

'I do mean it. Everything that's happened over the last few days has just been too much. I can't deal with us, with you, and with everything else. I just can't.'

'But you were coming to tell me about Owen. You said that. You said you wanted to share him with me, to make him part of *our* lives?'

'I know, and I was, but I didn't bank on how opening up to you, airing my dirty laundry, so to speak, would make me feel. It's not just you, Nate. I don't want to be with *anyone*.'

'No, no, no, this is all my fault. If I'd reacted differently, if I'd been more supportive, if I'd told you who I was angry at…'

Jessie shook her head as he spoke. 'You can't know that. Neither of us can. It's best to end this now before we get in too deep.'

'Jessie, no. I refuse to believe this is what you want, not after what we've shared. Please say you don't mean it. Please, Jessie… I… I'm in love with you…'

Jessie's heart skipped a beat at his words, words that would have made her ecstatic a few days ago, but which now did nothing but make her sad. She reached out and took his hand.

'I'm sorry, Nate, but I can't.'

She released his hand and turned away, closing the door behind her.

∞

The vibrations reverberated through Jessie's head as she stood, forehead against the door, tears rolling down her cheeks as Nate pounded on the door, all the while pleading for her to open up, to give him a chance.

As hard as she tried, she couldn't block out his voice, couldn't hide from his hurt and pain.

But he hurt me too.

The words rebounded in her mind, while the traitor in her chest yearned to open the door and rush into his arms.

Eventually Nate's knocking slowed and then stopped, and Jessie held her breath, waiting to see what he would do next. But as she heard his car door slam and his tyres skid as he pulled away, her aching heart grew heavy and she closed her eyes.

What have I done?

Chapter 67

Why did I listen to him?

Nate shook his head as he drove. If he'd ignored his father and gone to talk to Jessie, maybe things would have been different.

Or would they?

Nate recalled the look on her face as she'd dealt her blows—the hurt, the sadness, the pain—and his heart ached. It was how she'd looked that first day… only this time, he was the cause.

He thumped the steering wheel and shook his head. As he'd listened to her story the previous day, his anger and revulsion pouring from him in colourful slashes, it never dawned on him this would happen. All he'd fixated on was what he would do if he got his hands on the man who'd hurt the woman he loved.

There it was again—love. Once only a meaningless word, now an emotion Nate had never felt for any woman in his life before Jessie.

Nate stopped the car and as he stared through the windscreen, he realised he'd driven to the gallery. Not knowing what else to do, he decided it was as good a time as any to clear up the mess he'd left behind.

As Nate unlocked the door, he saw Em had beaten him in; the daily mountain of mail lay strewn on the counter. He absently picked through the paraphernalia, his attention drawn to a flyer for Potters Hole library.

Thanks to the damp issue I have finally raised the funds to fix, the library will be closed until it is resolved.

Have no fear, though, I will still meet your reading needs, although you will need to dust off your computers as the library is moving online.

Go to www.pottersholelibrary.co.uk for a virtual browse and easy to use check out service.

For those of you who know what you want, feel free to email me direct at libby@pottersholelibrary.co.uk. I will deliver your selections to your door.

Love, Libby x

'Good on you, Libs,' Nate murmured, smiling as his mind conjured images of Libby Jeffries and Cal Greyling, his high school friends; thick as thieves until that night. Nate shuddered and pushed the memories away. Libby was doing a fantastic job of dragging the library into the twenty-first century, but the building which housed it was in a shocking state of repair. He made a mental note to go and see her. If she'd not already contracted someone, he'd ask Mac and Johnny, as he knew they'd do it for a good price.

Folding the flyer and shoving it in his back pocket, Nate bounded up the stairs to find the door ajar and a plethora of colourful language emanating from within. Nate frowned and clenched his fists as he strode into the room.

'What the hell are you doing in here?' he demanded as he glared at Em, who was cursing as she shoved his detritus into refuse bags.

'Well, hello to you too,' she replied, dropping the bag and

squaring up to him, hands on her hips.

'You shouldn't be in here, Em. You know this is my space.'

'I'm fully aware of that, but who do you think clears up after one of your binges?'

'I clear up after myself!'

'Oh really? So, you pick up your empties and discarded bits of pizza?' She held the refuse bag up in front of her. 'And then change these?' Em pointed to the scrunched up bedding on the narrow cot.

Nate frowned, casting his mind back, searching for evidence to prove her wrong, but he drew a blank. 'Yup.'

'Ha, you do not! All you sort out are your precious canvases and paint. You *never* clear anything else up, believe me.'

Em returned to Nate's mess, while he slouched to the walls and began removing the chaos.

'So, how did it go?'

'What do you mean?'

'Oh, come on, Nate,' Em said, staring at him. 'Who do you think let Jessie in?'

Nate sighed and leaned against the gaudy wall, sliding down until he sat on the floor. He pulled his knees up before facing Em and shrugging.

'Jeez, Nate, what happened?' Em dropped the bag she was holding and came to sit next to him, her hand squeezing his shoulder.

Resting his head against the wall so he could stare at the blank ceiling, Nate relayed the events of the previous day, adding the morning's encounter, before dropping his chin, fixating on the floor between his feet.

'I don't really blame her, to be honest.'

'What? How can you say that? You *know* me, Em. You know what I'm like, how I react to things.'

'Yeah, *I* do, but Jessie doesn't.'

'What are you getting at?'

'Think about it. Put yourself in her shoes.'

'But I'm not her ex. I would never hit her. I'd never hit a woman full stop.'

'Abuse isn't just about the physical, Nate. Jessie saw your response to her words as metaphorical blows, hence why she feels the way she does.'

'That's what Mum said too.'

'Well, listen then. How would you have reacted if the roles had been reversed?'

Nate shrugged, his heart heavy.

'What do I do, Em? How do I fix this?'

'You can't. It's up to Jessie now. You've explained and you're just going to have to give her time.'

'How much time?'

'As long as she needs.'

'She said it was over though, Em, that she shouldn't have got involved.'

'And maybe she means it. If that's the case, you will have to accept it.'

Nate hung his head again as he whispered, 'But I can't. I love her.'

Em pulled him into her arms. 'I know you do, but it doesn't mean Jessie will reciprocate.'

'But I can't sit around and do nothing.'

'You have to. It's up to Jessie now.'

∞

Jessie sat on the sofa, legs pulled up to her chest, a blanket covering her as she stared into space. Cole nestled beside her, oblivious to the turmoil within his mistress. *Wuthering Heights* lay open on the coffee table, Heathcliff unable to keep her attention for once.

Nate's visit had wrong-footed her. She'd been so certain of what his actions had meant, yet his words that morning belied what she'd witnessed. Watching him hurl paint at the walls with such viciousness had brought to mind the times Matthew had hurled things—anything within reach—before he'd turned his anger on her. And that's what Jessie had been waiting for—what she was still waiting for—Nate to turn his blows on her. That's why she'd put her walls back up; she had to. She couldn't go there again. She deserved better.

But, am I wrong?

She wanted to believe Nate, but she'd made that mistake before, on more occasions than she could count. Jessie shuddered as Matthew loomed over her, his Jack Torrance look preceding the beatings, the cigarette burns, the accidental falls down the stairs. She'd believed Matthew over and over until that last time. Then it wasn't just about her.

Is Nate different? Is he telling the truth?

Jessie sighed and shook her head. She wasn't in the right frame of mind to answer. She needed to focus on herself. She needed to get back to work. She needed to consider Beth's offer.

Jessie reached out and buried her hand in Cole's fur, massaging him into a soothing purr.

Could she be part of Owen's life? Could she get close to him and not want him back, not want a second chance? The driving force behind her giving Owen up had been Matthew, and whether he would come looking for them. But the restraining order had kept him at bay, until his hospital visit, that was. Plus, he had a new family to focus on now. Jessie's stomach contracted as she thought of them, and she prayed they wouldn't have to endure what she had.

Her thoughts turned to Anita. Jessie felt terrible for what she'd said, but it had been a long time coming. Matthew's halo shone brightly in Anita's eyes, and Jessie had yet to find a way to tarnish it. She needed to try; she knew that. Anita was her only family.

If she was a friend, I wouldn't forgive her, Jessie thought, wondering if Bev would forgive her for dismissing Nate.

Cole stood up and stretched, readying himself for a change of position, but Jessie intervened. As she pulled him close and buried her face in his fur, there was a knock at the door. Not wanting to see anyone, Jessie ignored it, but whoever it was continued to knock.

'Jessie? It's me, Ray.'

Reluctantly, Jessie released Cole from purgatory and left the warmth of her blanket behind as she went to let Ray in.

'Sorry, Ray, I was miles away,' she said, smiling.

'Looks like someone wasn't as successful as me.'

Jessie looked down at the doorstep to see a paper bag, now greasy with its contents, and a coffee cup on the doorstep.

'Nate came earlier.'

'Did he now? I told him to leave you in peace. Just as I told my wife, by the way.' He held a bag out to Jessie. 'A week's worth of meals she just happened to have, so *you* don't have to worry.'

Jessie's eyes welled with tears at Bev's thoughtfulness, and she took the bag from Ray, who retrieved the offerings Nate had left and carried them into the kitchen. Jessie felt a pang of guilt for sending him away when his parents were taking care of her, but she pushed it aside. She had to learn to separate the two.

'Right, let's have a look at that wound of yours, shall we? How's it been today?'

'Good,' Jessie said, as she allowed Ray to inspect the puncture mark on her hip.

'The redness has gone and the swelling's gone down, which is great news. I think my work here is done.'

Ray smiled at her, patting her hand as he rifled through the medical bag he'd brought along.

'I'll leave these with you.' He handed her some clean dressings and antiseptic wipes. 'But I doubt you'll need them. If it stays dry overnight, you can take the dressing off and let the air get to it. If you can wear loose clothes for the next week or so, it will help.'

'That won't be a problem,' Jessie said, mentally rummaging through her wardrobe in search of anything fitting.

'I have no doubt you will see Bev soon, as she rarely takes heed of anything I say. I did try.'

'I'm looking forward to it, to be honest,' Jessie said, walking Ray to the door.

Ray stopped at her words and turned to face her. 'Jessie,

you don't have to worry. Whatever happens between you and Nate, Bev and I are always here for you. Okay?'

Jessie couldn't answer, the effort of holding back the tears rendering her mute. Instead, she nodded and smiled, before throwing her arms around him and burying her face against his chest. After a few moments, Jessie felt Ray's arms encircle her.

∞

After Ray left, Jessie unpacked the food parcels Bev had sent. Her mouth watered as she lifted the lids to see what was inside. Her stomach rumbled, and despite herself, Jessie emptied a lasagne onto a plate and put it in the Aga to warm through.

As she made space for the rest in the fridge, Jessie heard tyres crunching on the driveway, and her heart lurched.

Not again.

Determined not to answer the door, she held her breath as footsteps approached. But instead of the expected knock, she watched as a piece of paper was pushed through the letterbox.

Jessie exhaled as the footsteps retreated, not moving until she heard the car pull out of the driveway. She unfolded the note:

Give me a chance to explain. N x

Like you did me? Jessie crumpled the note and tossed it in the bin as she went to retrieve her dinner.

Chapter 68

'Get out, get out, get out!' Em yelled.

'Whoa, steady on there, Em. What have I done now?' Nate raised his hands in defence as she loomed over him, slumped as he was at her desk.

'What have you done? Have you looked in the mirror? You look like shit.'

'Gee, thanks, but you know—'

'If I hear you whinging because she's not contacted you one more time, I'll… argh!' Frustrated, Em turned her back on him and started to walk away, but changed her mind. She whirled around to face him, and Nate watched her face as she fought against her angst towards him.

'You need to go home, away from this place.'

'The gallery is where I always come when I feel like this.'

'Yes, but you're not usually cluttering up my domain, disrupting the chi.'

'I know, but I can't work, can I? Not with my hand like this.'

'Have you, I don't know, tried?'

'Of course I've tried. What do you take me for?'

'Just asking. And you're sure it's not broken?'

'Yep. Dad says I've just got to rest it, that I should have

thought of this before punching the wall.'

'He has a point.'

'Don't—'

'Oh, I have no intention of going there… for the millionth time… believe me. But one thing is certain, you're not staying here, not like this.'

'Why not? It's my gallery,' Nate mumbled, sulking as he crossed his arms over his chest.

'Not for much longer if you keep moping around. You're scaring the customers away. Look.' Em gestured around. The place was empty. Nate's gallery was *never* empty.

'Fine,' he said, pushing himself away from the desk. 'But what am I supposed to do?'

'I don't know, how about decide on a theme for your next collection?'

'I guess, if I can stop thinking about Jessie.'

'Nate!' Em shouted, making him jump. 'You have to forget about her. There's nothing you can do now except wait. So, find something else to do. Whatever it is, I don't care. Just find it away from here.'

Nate gave Em a sullen look as he passed her and saw the corners of her mouth twitch.

'Don't you dare go bothering her,' Em called after him.

'Right you are, boss,' he said, saluting her as he left.

∞

Why haven't you said something?

Nate stared across the lake at Bluebell Cottage, as he had for the last few days, ever since Em had sent him packing, but there was no sign of life. He'd even driven over to see if her car was there, which it was, but he'd resisted the urge to knock and see if she'd got his note. Of course she had.

He couldn't understand why she hadn't been in touch. He deserved a chance to explain.

Like you gave her?

Nate shook his head as his mind reminded him, just as his mother had, of his behaviour.

But I did give her a chance.

And this was what he kept coming back to. He hadn't forced her to leave, he'd just not responded suitably to what she'd told him. She had explained…

'Don't be a dick, Parker,' he muttered and shook his head, disgusted with his attempt at rationalisation. But he *had* been a dick that night, and now he was paying the price. She'd shared her story with him, her full story, and he hadn't been able to swallow his own emotions to be there for her.

Nate made fists with his hands, wincing as his injured one made it clear it was a mistake. He flexed it, studying the damage he'd done; damage he prayed would be temporary. The bruising had yellowed, but the swelling remained, the skin hot and taut.

He looked over at his easel, at his attempt to draw, and snorted. It looked like a kindergarten kid had been let loose on the page. He'd honestly believed nothing could stop him from drawing, so he'd tied a pencil to his injured hand, but his fingers couldn't hold the instrument, never mind grip it to create the quality images he was known for. Fancying himself ambidextrous, Nate had tried his other hand, the result of which lay before him.

How long would it be before he could draw again, before he could paint again, before he could capture the look on her face the morning after? And that's what it all boiled down to. He needed to commit to paper the way she'd looked before he lost the image forever.

Yeah, like that will happen!

'Argh!' Nate glanced around his studio, but everywhere he looked there was Jessie, still at various stages of completion. How could he not think about her when she was everywhere?

Grabbing his laptop, Nate left the studio and ensconced himself on the sofa. If he couldn't paint, he needed to find something to take his mind off her. He opened his laptop and stared at the web page he'd been wanting to build for a long time—his online shop. He'd bought the site and the web address, but he'd done nothing more to bring NP Originals to life.

What better time than right now?

Chapter 69

'Ben? It's Jessie... Jessie Ellis.'

'Jessie Ellis, Jessie Ellis...?'

Jessie rolled her eyes and shook her head at the estate agent's attempt at pretence.

'You sold me Bluebell Cottage, remember?' she prompted him.

'Ah, yes, Jessie Ellis. The woman with a dislike of technology. Forgive me for not twigging straight away. It's the use of technology that confused me.'

Jessie bit back a retort.

'What can I do for you, Jessie? It can't be about issues with the cottage, because I gave you a week to get back to me on those, and that expired a while ago.'

'I'd like to sell it.'

'You'd what? Sell? But you've only just bought it,' Ben Travers spluttered. 'What's happened? I thought you loved the place?'

'I did, I do, it's just...'

It's just what? I met someone, and it's not worked out?

'You won't get back what you paid for it, you know, selling it so soon, especially if you factor in the legal fees,' Ben said, stirring Jessie from her thoughts.

'I would think I'd get more, given everything I've done since

I've been here,' Jessie retorted, indignation rising as Ben devalued her beautiful cottage.

'I think *I* would know if you would get your money back. I *am* the expert, after all.' Ben's condescension made Jessie's blood boil. 'You haven't been in it long enough to add any significant value to it, it's as simple as that.'

'I don't believe you!' Jessie snapped, jumping up from the kitchen table and almost knocking over her coffee. 'Let me tell you exactly what I've done before you make such a blanket remark.'

Without waiting for an answer, Jessie launched into describing the modifications she'd done to the kitchen, the addition of the porch, which still had some work to do, and the swing. But as she talked, wandering through the cottage as she did so, all she could see was Nate: how he'd selflessly offered to help her without being paid, how he'd been concerned for her well-being from the day they met, how he'd been sensitive to her reaction to Anita's letters, accepting the explanation she'd given him without question.

Nate was everywhere as she informed Ben how she'd built bookcases into all the alcoves, and images of the fun they'd had filled her mind. Jessie traced her finger along the beeswaxed shelves until she stopped. Her voice caught mid-sentence as she stared at the copy of *Wuthering Heights* Nate had given her. She'd shoved it out of sight, but now, as she remembered the Nate she'd fallen for, the Nate she'd bared herself to, the Nate who'd known what this book meant to her without being told, Jessie plucked it from the shelf.

'Jessie, are you still there? Jessie?' Ben called, but she was no longer listening as she caressed the cloth cover.

'I… I'll get back to you,' she murmured and cut the call, before opening the cover. The note Nate had written drifted to the floor.

Jessie bent down to retrieve it, her gaze devouring the words he'd written:

For my Cathy,

H x

Her mind filled with memories of the night they'd spent together, of his tenderness as he'd touched her, of his concern as he'd entered her, of his anger at what Matthew had done to her. A sob escaped her throat as a hand gripped her heart.

Had he been telling her the truth after all? Maybe she *had* misunderstood his reaction. But the words he *had* hurled at her had cut her deeply.

Jessie sighed and laid the book gently beside her reading chair before walking back through the cottage and stepping outside for the first time in almost a week.

∞

Just as she had that first day, Jessie wandered down to the shore, drawing the sweet fresh air into her lungs. Her gaze devoured the view before settling, as always, on the Lake House. His truck was missing and a pang of sadness lurched into her chest, taking her by surprise.

Cole brushed against her legs and she picked him up, holding him close as she turned and took in the vista that was Bluebell Cottage. She smiled as she saw her longed for swing and she wandered over and settled herself on it, Cole curling up beside her. Jessie closed her eyes and gently rocked back and forth, allowing her senses to roam, calmness washing through her.

'I'm home,' she murmured, startling herself as her mind added, *And I'm not going anywhere.*

As the thought took root, Jessie felt like a weight had lifted. Potters Hole was where she'd chosen to start again, and Bluebell Cottage was the sanctuary she'd selected. Why would she leave? Why should she? She couldn't run away every time things got tough. Wherever she went, whoever she met, eventually, if she got close to them as she had with Nate, she would need to share her past; it was only fair. Secrets had a way of making themselves known, after all.

Jessie sighed as she watched the birds diving and soaring as they frolicked in the breeze.

Secrets led to webs of lies which couldn't be sustained. Being open, being honest, might be harder, but it was for the best. If people didn't like her when they knew the truth, then so be it, but at least she wouldn't be hiding any more.

Not that I should hide away. I have nothing to be ashamed of.

The thought surprised her, and she felt as if she'd emerged from a cocoon, her ears almost popping with the change. Despite all the therapy she'd undertaken, it had been Beth who'd finally made her see the truth.

Thoughts of Beth brought with them thoughts of Owen, and Jessie wondered how he was, a bubble of excitement tickling through her as she remembered she no longer had to wonder.

She jumped off the swing, eliciting an irritated meow from Cole, and raced inside to find the photo Beth had given her.

Chapter 70

'Hey Al, how's it going?' Nate said as he propped the door to Bennett's open and dragged a box of paintings inside.

'Well, if it isn't Potters Hole's own Michelangelo,' Al said, throwing his cloth over his shoulder as he came around the counter. 'I thought you'd got lost in other things?'

'Yes, and no,' Nate said, struggling to lift the box and not wanting to draw the inevitable Spanish Inquisition.

'What happened to your hand?' Al grabbed Nate's arm, examining the damage.

Nate, having given up on the box, pulled his arm away, stuffing his injured hand into his pocket. 'DIY.'

'Ah, helping that pretty young thing out, were you?'

Nate frowned, deciding to let Al's un-PC comment slide. 'Who are you talking about?'

'Oh come off it, Nate. I know you see a lot of young women, but this wasn't that long ago. She was late, you were waiting, ring any bells?'

Nate felt heat flood his cheeks, and he nodded. 'Yes, something like that.'

Al stared at him for a moment, but when Nate offered nothing further, he shrugged and picked the box up.

'So, what have you brought me?' he asked as he carried the box behind the counter.

'Nothing specific. I went for a selection of different themes, but all the required size.'

'Hmmm, good. Okay. I'll get these displayed as soon as that grandson of mine shows his face, and keep you posted.'

'Yeah, no rush. You still having trouble with him?'

'Yup. Likes to remind us we're not his parents, too, which upsets Jeanie.'

'Understandable. He'll be okay though, eventually.'

'Eventually may be a long time coming, but, yes, he's a good kid, he just needs to let go of his anger.'

Nate didn't respond, his thoughts turning to the anger he still harboured towards his birth mother.

'Any chance of a coffee… to go, please?'

'Sure thing,' Al said, slapping the counter with his cloth.

As Al busied himself, Nate noticed Libby's flyer about the library. With no other plans, he decided it was as good a time as any to pay her a visit.

∞

'Hello? Anybody here?' Nate called as he nudged the library door open. The sign informed him the library was closed to visitors, and he hoped he wasn't too late to be of help.

Nate heard footsteps, and he looked up as Libby appeared, dusting down her t-shirt and jeans, her long dark hair in an untidy knot on the top of her head.

Just like she always wore it.

'Oh, hey, Nate, isn't it?' Libby asked, dazzling him with her all too rare and familiar smile. It had always been a competition between him and Cal to see who could make her smile, her perennially sombre features departing like the clouds on a rainy day to let the sun shine through.

Nate coughed to clear the emotion and nodded. 'Yes, Nate Parker.'

'That's right, you're the big artist everyone talks about.'

Nate felt the lump rise in his throat and he looked away. He wondered if she would ever remember how close they'd once been. The doctors had said she would regain her memory, but almost fifteen years had passed since that night, and Nate was still just a resident of Potters Hole to Libby.

'Do you need a hand?' he eventually asked.

'Nah, I've got it. Just boxing the books up to move them before the work can start.'

'Oh, so you've got someone to do the work?'

Libby snorted and covered her face with her hand as her cheeks reddened, making Nate smile—another Libby gesture.

'I wish,' she said, glancing away as she brushed her hand across her lips. 'Council turned me down flat, said they had more pressing matters than a library to spend their money on.'

'There's a surprise.'

'Exactly! So, it's going to be down to fund-raising, which takes time to organise, then, once I've got the on-line lending library up and running, I can focus on that.'

'How bad is it?'

'Worse than I thought, to be honest. The damp has ruined some of the bookcases too, which are irreplaceable as they've been here since the library first opened its doors. I've moved the rest someplace dry, so hopefully they won't succumb.'

'Have you had any quotes yet?'

'Yep, had to, for the council, but they're huge, maybe because they thought the council was footing the bill.' Libby shrugged and shoved her hands into the back pockets of her jeans. 'Did you want something?' she asked.

'Sorry?' Nate said, puzzled.

'Well, you came looking for me, so I presume you wanted to ask me something… I don't see you as much of a bookworm.'

'Hey, I read!' Nate said, his affront making her burst into laughter.

'I'm sorry, a fault of mine… judging people too quickly,' she finished when Nate raised his eyebrows.

'So…?' she pressed.

'Yes, so, er, well, if you haven't got anyone to sort the damp out yet, I know a couple of guys who can help.'

'That's great, Nate, but, as I said, I have no funds to pay them.'

'You can sort that later. What's important is to get these doors open as soon as possible, as not everyone in town uses a computer.'

'Tell me about it,' Libby said, sighing as she rolled her eyes. 'All I've had is complaints about how I'm discriminating and being ageist. I mean, what else can I do? The mobile library is now part of the landscaping.'

'Is it okay if I have a look round? I can give Mac and Johnny a call and sort out when they can start.'

Libby stared at him for a moment and then shrugged. 'Knock yourself out.'

∞

Nate wandered through the skeleton of the library, memories of his mother taking him to story-time as a child filling his head. His gaze lingered on the antiquated signs, bringing him to an abrupt stop at "Classics". Nate's thoughts shifted to Jessie, and he wished he could have seen the look on her face when she found the book.

He sighed and turned away, a nugget of an idea pulling him up short. He turned back and stared at the sign again as his mind churned, a bubble of excitement exploding inside him.

'How're you getting on?' Libby said, walking into his thoughts and making him jump.

'I'm done. I was just having a look round. I'll give the lads a call and get them to liaise with you. Do you have a card?'

'No, but if you give me your phone, I'll put my number in it.' Libby held out her hand, but Nate hesitated. Before Jessie, he would have handed it over without a thought, but now…

For Christ's sake, this is Libby!

Chastising himself, Nate handed his phone over. 'And I've an idea of how we can get you the money you need.'

'Really? How?' Libby paused, her face suddenly full of hope.

'I can't say at the moment as I need to discuss it with someone, but I think it will work. I'll let you know.'

'Wow, my knight in shining armour.' Libby handed his phone back.

Nate opened his mouth to respond, but changed his mind.

'I'll get back to you, as will Mac or Johnny,' he said instead, waving as he left Libby to her packing.

Chapter 71

Jessie stared at the photograph, tracing her finger over Owen's face, absorbing once more how little he resembled Matthew. He was all her dad, and by default, all her.

How could I have thought I wouldn't love him?

The familiar guilt stabbed at her heart.

Maybe it's best if I stay away.

In the photos Beth had shared, she'd seen how happy Owen was with them, so why rock the boat? If she stepped into his life, it would complicate things, raise questions she may not like his response to.

What if he hates me? Jessie sighed, a stray tear plopping onto the photo. She brushed it away with her fingertip. *I couldn't handle that.*

She tore her gaze away from the photo and stared through the kitchen window, the beauty of the view soothing her anxious soul. Jessie cast her mind back to meeting Owen, how he'd turned his huge, doleful grey eyes on her as he thanked her for helping him, how Beth had told her she was brave and had given her and Adam the chance of a family. Jessie knew Beth would ensure Owen knew the truth as to why she had given him up.

'And it wasn't because I didn't love you… not really,' she

murmured as she looked back at his face. Being afraid she wouldn't love him if he looked like Matthew was only part of it. The real reason was the primal fear that Matthew would come and finish what he'd started. Jessie shuddered as she recalled the beating he'd given her, the beating that had changed the course of her life.

If she'd have kept him, if she'd have run away with him, she'd have spent her life looking over her shoulder, perpetually in fear for his life; the authorities always needing to know where children were. As for her, alone, no one really cared where she went or what she did, or decided she wanted to be.

No, I did the right thing. She nodded to reassure herself. She had given Owen the chance of a normal happy life, and that's all she ever wanted for him. As for herself, Matthew hadn't come looking for her after she'd moved away; he'd replaced her instead.

'Please don't let him hurt them too,' Jessie whispered as she thought of a demanding baby competing with the man who always needed to be the centre of attention.

But Matthew hadn't stayed away when, thanks to Anita, he knew she was in the hospital. Had Anita also told him where she lived? Jessie couldn't be sure, but it would be something her sister might do, given her unwavering belief in Matthew. That, in itself, was reason for her to move.

But why should I? Why should I have to live in fear?

The restraining order offered her some protection, but it was only a piece of paper. It wouldn't stop Matthew if he came after her. It wouldn't stop him punishing her for what she knew would be a mammoth list of transgressions by now, new family or not. Yes, breaching the restraining order would land him in court. His actions may send him to prison, but would she be alive to press charges?

Maybe I should *move, just to be safe*, Jessie thought, only this time, even Anita wouldn't know where to find her.

Jessie sighed again, her shoulders sagging under the weight of indecision. First things first, though; she turned the picture of Owen over to see Beth's number. Jessie picked up her mobile and dialled.

∞

'Hello!'

'Oh, hi Beth, it's—' Jessie started.

'Adam? Adam? Can you grab the bags?'

'Why can't you? I've got my hands…' Adam's voice tailed off as Beth moved away.

'Sorry about that.'

'I… it's Jessie, I—'

'Jessie! Wow, great to hear from you! How are you?'

'Is this a bad time? I can call back if you're busy.'

'Don't be daft, it's fine. Adam will manage, despite his grumbling.' Beth chuckled, making Jessie smile.

'I'm sure he will. I'm… I'm just calling to see how Owen is. Is he all better?'

'He's great, comes home tomorrow. That's what all this is about. We've just got back from the hospital and picked up a few welcome home things for him.'

Jessie could hear the grin in Beth's voice, and her heart swelled. She had made the right decision.

'That's fantastic. I can't wait to see him.' Jessie gasped, the words out before she had time to think. She held her breath, waiting for Beth to retract the offer she'd made at the hospital.

'Absolutely! We'd love to have you. You can stay here as we have a spare room, and I know Owen would love that. He seemed quite taken with his guardian angel.'

Emotion raced up through Jessie, rendering her mute, a lump in her throat threatening to reveal the truth.

'Jessie? Are you still there?'

'I-I'm here,' Jessie choked out.

'Are you okay?' Beth's voice was tinged with concern.

'Y-yes, of course, I-I'm more than okay. I can't believe how kind you're being, how lucky I am to have the chance to get to know him after everyth—' Jessie's voice broke, and a sob escaped.

'Don't cry, Jessie. You deserve to get to know him. You saved his life, don't forget that. It took a lot to do what you did.'

'Yeah, a real hero, running away.'

'Hey! Stop that right now. You did what you had to do. I understand that all too well. You didn't, and still don't, deserve to live in fear of that low-life. At least now you're free to live your life on your own terms.'

Jessie snorted, shaking her head.

'What was that for? Jessie, what's wrong? Has something happened?'

Jessie looked down at the floor and sighed. It felt strange to be telling someone she hardly knew about her past, and yet, Beth was the perfect person.

'He came to see me in the hospital.'

'Who did? Your ex?'

'Yep, the very same.'

'But how did he know you were even there?'

'That's the good bit. You see, my ever loving sister told him.'

'What? Why?'

'Well, let's just say she's always been a fan of Matthew. But that's not the worst of it.'

'Why?'

'She kind of insinuated that she'd told him where I live, which means I should probably think about moving.'

'What?! No. She wouldn't, would she? Surely not, not after what he did to you?'

'That's the thing. She doesn't believe me, never has.'

'I know, but you're her sister, and to put you at risk like that, whether or not she believes you…'

Jessie shrugged, not knowing what to say.

'Do you really think she'd do something like that?' Beth asked after a moment, and Jessie could hear her breath almost held as she spoke.

'I honestly don't know.'

'Why don't you ask her again?'

'Easier said than done.'

'Why?'

'Because I told her I never wanted to see her again.'

'Ah, Jessie, people always say things they don't mean in the heat of the moment. She's your sister, your family. Call her… talk to her.'

Jessie didn't respond. Deep down, she knew Beth was right.

She could call Anita, and she would. She just wanted her to understand how far across the line she'd gone.

'Are you unhappy where you live, Jessie?'

'God no, I love it, it's my little piece of heaven,' Jessie replied, gazing out at the lake as she spoke.

'Then why move?'

'Matthew… and… Matthew, why else?' Jessie corrected, not wanting to talk about Nate.

'Is that the only reason?'

Jessie hesitated. She didn't like lying, but she didn't want to share the other reason. 'Yes, of course.'

'Okay, has he attempted to contact you since the hospital?'

'No, not that I'm aware of.'

'I presume you have a restraining order against him?'

'Yes, of course, but it's hardly going to stop him if he really wants to find me.'

'I agree, but there are ways you can protect yourself—alarms, mace, self defence. Have you explored any of these?'

'No,' Jessie murmured, feeling as if she was being chastised, although this wasn't Beth's tone.

'Don't let him win, Jessie. You've come too far.'

Jessie didn't reply, Beth's words washing through her as resolutions surfaced.

'Promise me,' Beth prompted.

'I promise,' Jessie whispered.

'Hmmm, a little more conviction would've been good, but I'll take it,' Beth said then chuckled. 'It's been so good to hear from you. Let me know when you want to come, and I'll make the spare room up for you.'

'Thanks Beth, I really appreciate it, and thanks for listening.'

'Any time.'

Jessie rang off and pressed the phone under her chin as she stared out of the window, pondering Beth's words. She knew Beth was right. She'd walked away from Matthew to protect her unborn child. At the hospital, she'd stood up to him to protect Owen… again. So, if she could do it for Owen, she could do it for herself.

A bubble of excitement fizzed inside her as she thought of Owen and the opportunity she now had to get to know him. Jessie grinned and busied herself preparing dinner, her thoughts shifting to work; she'd kept Bev at bay long enough.

Chapter 72

'So, what do you think?' Nate asked, spreading his palms and raising his eyebrows as he finished telling Em his plan.

'Okay, let's recap. You have an idea for your next show, which is great, by the way, entitled Transformation?'

'Yep.'

'And you want to include *all* the paintings you've done of Jessie?'

'Almost all.'

Em looked at him but didn't respond, instead frowning.

'And you want to donate *all* the money raised to the library?'

'Yes, Libby needs funds, and I thought it would be a great way to raise some.'

'And why would selling paintings of Jessie be a good plan, might I ask?'

'Well, because she's a bookworm, and I think she would approve,' Nate said, toeing the ground as he wilted under Em's scrutiny.

'So, you've asked her then?'

'Libby? Not yet, I was—'

'Not Libby, Jessie! Have you asked Jessie, who currently hates your guts, if it would be okay to sell the intimate paintings you've done of her?'

'Ummm, not exactly.'

'Not exactly as in you have asked her, or not exactly as in you haven't?'

'No need to be like that, Em.'

'You forget, I know you, Nate Parker, and whilst your heart is *usually* in the right place, you can be a little misguided. So, which is it?'

'Well, she *did* say I could show the paintings, but…'

'But what?'

'She wanted first dibs on them, for the cottage.'

'And, has she?'

'No.'

'So, you haven't got her permission then?'

Nate didn't reply, staring at the floor as he saw his grand gesture on the verge of disintegrating.

'Oh, Nate,' Em said, rubbing his arm. 'Why, oh why, do you think exposing Jessie to the world like this will be a good thing?'

Tears brimmed his eyes as he looked at Em.

'Because she loves books and—' His voice broke, prompting him to clear his throat. 'And Libby's agreed to dedicate the classics section to her… as a thank you…' he tailed off, not having anything else to say.

'Urgh, the classics, seems a bit stiff,' Em said.

'*Wuthering Heights* is her favourite book,' Nate added with a shrug.

Em studied him for a moment, and he could see her wrestling with her opinion.

'She's going to have to be there to appreciate what you're doing,' she eventually said.

'I know.'

'And how do you plan on that?'

'I'll invite her.'

'That's no guarantee.'

'I know, but I have to make it right and I thought this… I thought this would be perfect.'

'It is, Nate. So, what do you need me to do?'

Chapter 73

Nate sat back, massaging his aching hand.

Maybe I should take a break?

He looked around his studio at the canvases lined up against the windows, their paint drying before he could pack them away safely, ready to transport to the gallery.

Nate looked back at the creation in front of him, studying the lines he'd sketched, capturing his last image of her the day she'd told him it was over. Despite the sadness and pain, there was a strength that hadn't been there before; a confidence and self-assuredness he hadn't seen before she went away. He hadn't noticed it that last day, too intent on getting her to hear him out, but the details had come back to him as he sketched, shining through her anguish.

Nate sighed and stood up, flexing his aching hand. He wandered to the windows and stared out across the lake.

But what does it mean for me? He shook his head and turned away, focusing on the paintings. He couldn't think about that now. He had a show to prepare, and if he didn't win her over then…

I'll have to admit defeat. He knew better than anyone that you couldn't make someone love you, no matter how much you wanted it.

Nate walked along the row of paintings, pausing before the two he felt sure Jessie would select, given she'd lingered over them the night he'd introduced her to his world. Nate smiled at the memory and reached out to touch the edge of the canvas—the paint was dry.

He picked up the first one and nestled it in the tissue paper he'd set out ready, securing the wrapping with a midnight blue ribbon. He repeated the exercise with the second painting before retrieving the invitation Em had sent over earlier.

Once Em had agreed to his plan, they'd settled on a date with Libby, and then Nate had left Em and Libby to draw up an invitation list.

Nate traced his fingertip across the silver embossing on the midnight blue card, the background sprinkled with stars and a crescent moon—the night sky they'd gazed at together that evening. He turned the invitation over and, with the silver pen Em had issued him with, he added a note:

Cathy,

Please come.

H x

Will it work? He shrugged. He honestly didn't know.

Nate slipped the invite into its envelope, inscribing her name in cursive on the front, and before he could change his mind, he loaded the two paintings into the car and headed to Bluebell Cottage.

He was grateful for the dry day as he rested the paintings on Jessie's doorstep. Her car wasn't there, and he only hoped she hadn't gone away again. *I'll keep an eye on them*, he thought, as he slipped the invitation through the letterbox.

Nate hurried back to his truck; he had to meet Mac and Johnny at the library and introduce them to Libby.

Chapter 74

Juggling a bouquet and the borrowed Tupperware, Jessie rang the doorbell.

'Jessie!' Ray said as he opened the door. 'Come on in. Bev! Jessie's here.'

'It's great to see some colour back in those cheeks,' he added as he ushered her towards the kitchen. 'How are you feeling?'

'I'm good, I think,' Jessie said, smiling.

'Excellent, and how's Owen? Have you heard?'

'He's home. I spoke to Beth a few days ago, and he's doing really well.' Jessie's smile turned into a grin.

'You know, that's the first time I've seen you truly alight, Jessie,' Bev said, wiping her hands on a towel as she came over. 'And it's great to see, isn't it, Ray?'

'It surely is,' Ray said, already retreating from the kitchen. 'I'll leave you ladies to talk. It's great news about Owen, Jessie, and you, of course.'

'Of course,' Jessie laughed, turning to Bev and thrusting out the bouquet. 'These are for you. A thank you for being there for me... and for looking after me,' she added, holding up the bag of Tupperware.

'I wasn't sure what you liked so—'

'I liked all of it, trust me.'

'I'm glad. These are gorgeous, Jessie, but you didn't need to.'

'Don't get excited. They're just some blooms from my fledgling garden.'

'Well, I love them, thank you.' Bev gave Jessie a hug and a peck on the cheek. 'Coffee?'

'Yes, thanks, that'd be great.'

'You really didn't need to shut yourself away from us, you know. We're here to help.'

'I know, and I'm sorry, but I needed some time… to think.'

'So, it wasn't because of what happened between you and Nate, then?'

Jessie felt the heat rise in her cheeks as Bev watched her.

'Why, Jessie? You and I were friends before I shoved you at Nate.'

'I know, but… oh I don't know, it just feels awkward to talk about him with you. I'm sorry, Bev. I didn't mean to offend you.'

'You've nothing to apologise for. If anything, I should apologise to you for Nate's behaviour.'

'Why? He's a grown man. You're not responsible for the way he behaves.'

'Maybe not, but I feel it reflects on how Ray and I brought him up.'

'It reflects on the way his birth mother treated him, not on you and Ray. I understand why he reacted the way he did.'

'He's mortified by his behaviour towards you. It wasn't directed at you, Jessie, you have to know that. It was—'

'… directed at Matthew, my ex. I know, he told me.'

'So, why won't you see him?'

Jessie flinched at Bev's directness, feeling her hackles rise as her body readied for attack. She closed her eyes and took a breath. *Bev is a friend.*

After a moment, Jessie opened her eyes and looked at Bev. 'I think you probably know the answer to that. Actions speak louder than words, Bev, and his performance was a stark reminder of the life I'd walked away from.'

'But you must know Nate isn't like that. He doesn't have a vicious bone in his body. If anything, he's always stuck up for the underdog. He was never a bully.'

Jessie nodded. 'I can see that, have seen that to a certain extent. But you have to understand that Matthew was the same when we first met. He couldn't do enough for me. I can't go there again, Bev, I just can't.'

'And you wouldn't be.' Bev patted Jessie's hand. 'But don't you see? You're doing to Nate exactly what he did to you.'

'In what way?'

'Tarring him with the same brush as Matthew, when they are both very different people, with diverse moral codes.'

Jessie fell silent, pondering Bev's words, and Bev left her to it, busying herself making the coffee she'd promised.

'I can't help it,' Jessie said as Bev placed a plate of muffins and a steaming mug in front of her.'

'You have to try. You both do,' Bev said. 'What else have you been mulling over during your sequestration?'

'Ummm, moving hou—'

'What?! You'll do no such thing!' Bev said, outraged, as she slammed her mug on the counter, spilling her coffee. 'Why on earth would you be considering something so outrageous?'

'Calm down, I'm not doing it, it was just something I'd considered.'

'But why?' Bev asked, settling herself back at the counter opposite Jessie.

'Because Anita, my sister, implied she'd told Matthew where I live.'

'Do you think she has?'

'I wouldn't put it past her, but I don't know.'

'Well, there's only one way to find out. Go and see her.'

'It's a bit of a long way, don't you think?'

'Not really, not when it's so important. Besides, you can tell better if she's lying to you when you're face to face.'

'I was face to face at the hospital when she said it.'

'Yes, but you had a lot going on. This time you'll be focused on her and her body language.'

'And if she has?'

'We can put things in place to stop him from hurting you.' Bev pushed away from the counter and picked up the flowers.

'That's what Beth said.'

'Who's Beth?' Bev asked as she busied herself arranging the flowers in a vase.

'Owen's mother. Anyway, I didn't mean to take up so much of your time. I only came to bring you those, and to say I'm ready to come back to work,' Jessie said, changing the subject.

'Oh no, you're not,' Bev responded, placing the vase on the windowsill.

'Yes, I am. I feel fine, and it would be a great distraction.'

'That's why you're not coming back yet. You need to see your sister and put some of your demons to rest. Ray and I will have Cole.'

'It's not that easy, Bev. Anita has never believed me about Matthew.'

'Have you shown her your scars? It's hard to disbelieve evidence.'

Jessie bristled as her defences readied themselves once more. 'No, I haven't. She didn't believe me when I told her, so why should I?'

Bev grasped Jessie's hands, forcing Jessie to look at her. 'Because she's your family, that's why, and because evidence is a lot harder to ignore than words.'

Jessie pulled away and stood up, wrapping her arms around herself. 'I don't know, Bev. I want to move on, to put it all behind me. Keep dredging it up will not help me.'

'You can't move forward until you've left the past in the past. You won't do that until you show Anita the truth.'

∞

Jessie stared at the paintings; their wrappings pushed down, creating a bed for them to rest on. She took in the details, now in full technicolour, just as she had the night they'd first captured her. Nate had shared with her a place sacred to him, a place no one else had set foot in, and he'd done it to show her he wasn't like Matthew. She recalled the broken mug, how she'd been terrified Nate would hit her, just as Matthew would have done. Instead, he'd waved it off as the accident it was, and brought her to his sanctuary.

When she saw his creations, the details had mesmerised her, the lifelike renderings still incomplete. Nate saw her in a way Matthew never had; he saw her as a person. To Matthew, she'd been a prize, a bauble, an object, but never a person.

Jessie remembered how she'd lingered before these two, seized by the image of herself gazing out of her bedroom window, tickled by the reminder of finally getting Cole to trust her. He'd remembered. Nate paid attention in ways Matthew never had.

She reached over the small pile of post she'd left on the table, and grabbed her mobile. Taking a deep breath, she punched in the number and waited.

'Roland? It's Jessie.'

'Jessie! how are ye? I didn't think we'd be hearing from ye… ye know… not after…' Roland tailed off into an awkward silence.

'Neither did I, to be honest, but it was never about you and the boys. She told you that, right?'

'Umm, no, no, she didn't. But that's good to hear. I know the boys miss ye. I do too,' he added quietly.

'How would you feel if I came to visit?'

Jessie heard a sharp intake of breath and knew Roland would be looking around him to see who was listening, as he always did when he was formulating a reply.

'But, I thought ye didn't want… ye know, ye and Anita?'

'I didn't, but I need to see her. I need her to understand the truth.'

'Aye, that she does need. When do ye want to come?'

'How about tomorrow? Will she be there?'

'I'll make sure of it.'

'Thank you, Roland.'

'Away with ye. Drive carefully.'

As Jessie disconnected, she caught Cole's slitted gaze as he appraised her.

'I'm sorry, but think about it this way; you get to laze on Uncle Ray's knee while I'm gone.'

Cole blinked and turned away, stalking from the room.

Chapter 75

'Hello Roland. Is she here?' Jessie asked, turning her back against the unseasonal wind.

'Aye, she is. Come on in out of the weather.'

Roland stepped aside and ushered Jessie inside the marble-floored hallway, her footsteps echoing up the sweeping staircase. Jessie shivered. She'd never felt at ease in this house.

'What are *you* doing here?' Anita's biting tone brought her shiver to a shudder, and Jessie took a deep breath before turning to face her sister.

'I've come to talk to you.'

Anita snorted and crossed her arms, defiance settling across her features. 'I thought you never wanted to see me again, let alone speak to me.'

Jessie clamped her mouth shut, killing the retort that sprang forward, and glanced at the floor before looking back at her sister.

'I have things I need to show you.'

'What things?'

'You'll see,' Jessie said, and placed her small case on the floor.

'I'll take that,' Roland said, whisking the case away. 'I'll put this in the guest room, and I've left ye both a bottle of red breathing in the drawing room.'

'Roland!' Anita snapped.

'Och, hear the lassie out, Annie. She's yer sister.'

Jessie watched Anita flexing her jaw as she glared at Roland's departing form. She then nodded and headed for the drawing room. Jessie followed.

∞

Jessie gulped down the glass of Claret Anita had thrust into her hand, wincing as the sharp taste brought tears to her eyes. She could feel Anita's glare boring into her as she gathered her courage.

'So, what's all this about, then?' Anita demanded, tapping her foot and pursing her lips.

'Sit down and I'll tell you.'

'I don't want to sit down. Tell me now, or show me, whatever it is you've come all this way to do, and then you can leave!'

'Sit!' Jessie ordered, her temper on the verge of bubbling over. 'I have a story to tell you and I'd like you to hear me out before you comment.'

'If this is about you and Matthew, I've heard—'

'Sit down!'

After a moment, Anita sat opposite Jessie and sipped her wine sulkily.

Jessie took a deep breath, rubbed her clammy palms against her thighs, and fixed on a point above Anita's head. She cleared her throat.

'Once upon a time, there was a young woman who met her Prince Charming,' Jessie began, stealing a look at Anita to see her rolling her eyes. *She's never going to believe me.*

'I'm listening,' Anita prompted, and Jessie nodded.

'Okay, well, the prince showered her with gifts and compliments, took her to all the best places, showed her off to his friends, praised her talents as a teacher, and admired her adventures before him. The—'

'Exactly, he's bloody perfect, so what's all—'

'Anita, please, just listen,' Jessie implored, as she locked eyes with her sister. The resentment she saw broke her heart, but she was here now, and she needed to go through with it.

After a few moments, Anita nodded her assent, her face relaxing as she settled back on her sofa to listen.

'Thank you,' Jessie whispered, gathering her thoughts before continuing. 'The young woman was bowled over by him, in awe of his high-profile job, turned on by his dashing good looks, and excited by the way he could get people to do whatever he wanted. So much so that when the prince asked if she would be his princess, she didn't hesitate to accept.

'It wasn't long after the wedding though that the princess noticed the gifts lessened, the compliments turned to suggestions, and he locked her in a gilded cage for his attention only. When the princess questioned any of this, or acted in a way the prince deemed unacceptable, he would punish her, reminding her it would not happen if she would only listen to what he asked, what he said, what he suggested, and she acquiesced.

'But no matter how hard the princess listened, it was never close enough, as the prince continued to punish her…' Jessie broke off and chanced a glance at Anita. Her sister was still attentive, although her lips were pursed once more, and she was tapping her foot.

Please hear me, Anita.

Jessie readied herself for the main part of her story, prepared to bare herself to Anita, just as she had to Nate. She just prayed Anita would finally see and understand.

Taking another deep breath, Jessie continued. 'He wrenched her arm up her back, shattering her elbow, because she was half an hour late home from work. The princess had to have a plate fitted to put it back together again.' Jessie paused and, without making eye contact, she removed her cardigan and showed Anita the scar zigzagging down her left arm.

'The princess had to have another plate inserted when he threw her down the stairs for daring to buy a new shade of lipstick to surprise him.' Jessie slipped the cardigan off her shoulder and revealed the scar along her collarbone.

'For not having his dinner on the table on time, he shoved the princess so hard she fell against the table, breaking several ribs and puncturing her lung.' Her hand shaking as she fought against the memories, Jessie lifted her shirt to show the scar on her ribcage where the chest tube had been inserted to re-inflate her lung.

'When the princess told him she wasn't up to accompanying him to a work dinner, the prince punched her so hard in the chest, he broke her sternum, causing both her lungs to collapse. This time the princess had to be intubated… a blessed stay in hospital…' Jessie tailed off as she fingered the scar on her throat; the relief to be away from him, no matter the reason, washed through her.

Shrugging out of her cardigan and unbuttoning her shirt,

Jessie pointed to various scars across her arms and torso. 'These tiny scars are from his cigarettes, a reminder to the princess to do as he said, to wear what he told her, to not suggest they watch boring programmes on the television. But all this paled into insignificance when the princess told the prince he was about to become a father…' Jessie's voice cracked as the memories came crashing in and the tears spilled over. Jessie brushed them away, only to have more take their place. She chanced another look at Anita, to see the rivulets in her make-up, the glass of wine discarded on a table.

She's hearing me.

'The prince was incensed by her news and called the princess a whore, accusing her of cheating on him, of spitting out the birth control he force-fed to her each night. The prince conveniently forgot how he'd given her food poisoning, deliberately, making her violently sick, before raping her one night. So angry at her news, the prince punched the princess in the face, knocking her to the floor, where he proceeded to kick and beat her, the blows to her stomach causing her to pass out. Leaving her for dead, the prince went out, seeking solace for the trauma the princess had put him through.

'When the princess came to, she dragged her bruised and bleeding body to the neighbours he forbade her from meeting. These strangers saved the princess's life.'

Jessie paused again and forced herself to look at Anita before she carried on. She wanted to see her sister's response.

'It was this attack on her unborn child that forced the princess to act. She couldn't allow the prince to abuse another soul. The princess turned to her sister for help, but her sister didn't believe her, saying the prince would never behave in such away…' Jessie tailed off again as a sob escaped Anita and she covered her mouth with her hand, rivers now running down her cheeks.

'But the princess had made up her mind, though she knew she couldn't risk the prince finding them both, so she did the only thing she had the power to do. The princess gave her son a chance at a life away from her, but more importantly, away from harm. If the prince was going to come after anyone, it would be her.

'If her sister had offered her protection, the princess may have been able to keep her son, but she didn't. Instead, the princess found a home for herself, but the prince found her and punished her for leaving. The doctors implored her to press charges, but the princess knew they wouldn't stick. The prince had friends on the force who would make sure of it.

'All the princess could do was move away and start again. A restraining order was the only protection she had. But then—'

'Stop!' Anita blurted. 'Please stop. I'm sorry, Jessie, I had no idea.'

Jessie stared at Anita, open-mouthed. 'Yes, you did. I told you everything.'

'But you didn't sh-show me…'

'I shouldn't have had to, Anita. You've known me my whole life and *know* I would never lie about something like this.'

'But Matthew was… is…'

'I know. I married him. But you're my sister. You're all I have. You should've believed what I told you.'

The sisters lapsed into silence, the occasional sniff the only sound in the room.

'D-did you tell him where I live?' Jessie finally asked the question which had been plaguing her since she left the hospital.

'God, no, I'd never do that,' Anita said, shaking her head.

'Then why did you say you had?'

'I don't know, I… Can… can you ever forgive me, Jessie?'

Jessie stared at Anita and sighed. She went and sat beside her, pulling her into her arms.

Roland chose that moment to come in, the grin that decorated his flushed face conveying his pleasure at the sight.

'Thank heavens! I was just making sure ye hadn't killed each other.'

The sisters looked at each other and smiled.

'So, can I interest either of ye in some cocoa?'

'Cocoa? After what we've been through!' Jessie burst out laughing.

'I think we'll stick with the wine, husband of mine,' Anita said, shooing Roland out of the room. She turned to face Jessie, wringing her hands as she formulated the words.

'I truly am sorry, Jessie.'

'I know.'

'But I don't know how I can make it up to you.'

'You can't. What's done is done. All we can do is move forward and find our way back to each other. For Mum and Dad.'

'And for us,' Anita whispered as she refilled Jessie's glass and handed it to her.

Jessie hesitated as she looked at Anita, the earnestness in her sister's eyes prompting her to nod.

'And for us,' she confirmed, clinking glasses with Anita.

Chapter 76

'Okay, out with it,' his mother said, laying her knife and fork down and crossing her arms, fixing Nate with her special all-knowing stare.

'Leave him be, Bev,' his father chided.

'He's been gloomy throughout dinner and I think we have a right to know why. We only see him once a week. Is it too much to ask for him to be cheerful?'

'I am here, you know,' Nate said, pushing his potatoes around his plate, chasing the broccoli.

'Oh you are, are you? You could have fooled me,'

'Beeeev,' his father warned.

'I'm only expressing concern about the welfare of my son.'

'Course you are, Mum. More like you're prying.'

'Well, if you bring your moping to the table, I'm entitled to know why.'

'I'm not moping,' Nate said, dropping his cutlery with a clatter.

'Nate Parker, don't you lose your temper with me,' his mother scolded, causing Nate to roll his eyes as he leaned back in his chair.

'If you must know, I left a couple of paintings for Jessie the other day and I haven't had so much as a thank you from her.'

'Is that all?' His mother tutted as she moved to clear the plates away.

'What do you mean, is that all?'

'Well, it's not surprising you haven't heard from her, given she's gone away. She'll probably reach out when she's back.'

'Gone away? Where's she gone?'

'Just up to Scotland. Hand me your plate.'

'Why Scotland? Is it Owen? Is he okay?' Nate asked, handing over his plate.

'Yes, yes, Owen's fine, as far as I know.'

'So?' Nate prompted when she didn't elaborate.

'So, what?'

'For God's sake, Mum, why has she gone to Scotland then?'

'To make peace with that sister of hers, that's all.'

'Why? It's her sister who should do the work.'

'That may be so, but sometimes you have to be the bigger person, Nate.' His mother raised her eyebrows and fixed Nate with a stare.

'What are you looking at me like that for? When will she be back?'

'I have no idea,' his mother said as Cole sauntered into the room and brushed up against his father's legs.

'Hello, Coley,' Ray said, the joy in his voice making both Nate and his mother smile. Ray leaned down and scooped up the once-feral cat.

'Not at the table, Ray!' his mother chided

'Oh, he's all right.'

'Maybe I should go up there too?' Nate interspersed.

'Go up where?' his mother said, frowning at his father as he fed Cole some scraps of chicken he'd saved.

'Scotland, where else? Just in case that ex—'

'Absolutely not!' his father burst, startling the others. 'Just leave that girl be. She has far more pressing issues to deal with than a spat with you. Besides, it will do you good to wonder about her for a change, given all the hearts you've broken over the years. If it's meant to be, son, she'll come around.' His monologue finished, he got up from the table and carried a purring Cole out of the room.

'Ouch,' Nate said, rubbing his arm as if his father had punched him.

'Well, he has a point.'

'Oh really? And how's that?' Nate muttered, more than a little put out that his mother hadn't jumped to defend him.

'It's up to Jessie now, not you, but don't get your hopes up.'

'What? Why? What has she told you?' Nate closed his eyes to steady his racing heart as he waited for her to explain.

'She just mentioned that she was thinking of moving.'

Nate felt his heart contract at his mother's words. 'Move? Why would she do that?'

'Because she's worried he knows where she lives.'

'But how could he… Anita?'

His mother nodded, clearing the rest of the table.

Nate was quiet for a while, processing what he'd been told, his body calming as he did so. 'So, that's why she's gone to see her,' he whispered.

'Sorry, Nate, I didn't catch that?' his mother called from the other side of the kitchen, where she was busy loading the dishwasher.

'That's why she's gone to Scotland, then? To find out?'

'Amongst other things, yes.'

'What other things?' But try as he might, Nate couldn't glean any further information from his mother before he left an hour later.

∞

Nate brooded on the conversation at dinner as he drove home. Moving away seemed extreme to him, but he hadn't been through what Jessie had, so what right did he have to judge her decision? She'd shared her scars with him, which had painted all the picture he'd needed.

Maybe I should drive up there. Where exactly, though? He laughed at his own bull-headedness. Scotland was a big place, and he didn't know where she was.

But I have to help her somehow. That bastard had no right to be dictating her life again.

But how? If she decided she wanted nothing to do with him, how could he help her?

As the roads blurred beside him, Nate's mind drifted to the gallery.

A few years ago, the daily tag of a street artist had bade good morning to him and Em. Nate had scoured the area, trying to find out who it was, but nobody was talking. Determined to catch the culprit red-handed, Nate had invested in some state-of-the-art cameras, which transmitted live feeds to his laptop.

He was putting the finishing touches to a painting in his studio one night, when his laptop beeped, alerting him to movement at the entrance to the gallery. Nate raced over in time to see an all too familiar face spraying his daily call sign.

'Got you, you sneaky bastard,' he muttered, recognising a local street artist called Rayon. A month later, Nate hosted Rayon's first show.

'Cameras it is,' he said to himself as he pulled his truck up snugly against the Lake House.

Chapter 77

Jessie laughed out loud, almost spitting her coffee on Anita's starched tablecloth as she watched her nephews playing football in the garden.

'What're you laughing at?' Anita said as she set a fresh pot of coffee on the table and snagged the last piece of toast.

'James's attempt at a foul. Ethan called him out on it immediately, and they've been arguing ever since,' Jessie said, raising her eyebrows as Anita slathered strawberry jam on her wholewheat toast.

'What? Everyone's allowed a sin in life.' She took a huge bite, the jam smearing over her upper lip.

'Such a lady,' Jessie said, laughing, and Anita grinned, strawberry seeds caught between her teeth.

'Remember when we were kids, and we'd sneak jam sandwiches?'

Jessie nodded. 'And we always got caught because of your seedy grin.'

'Harsh… but fair,' Anita conceded. 'So, what do you fancy doing on your last day, then? We've shopped, been to the spa, taken in the sights. Anything else you'd like to do?'

Jessie hesitated before replying, not wanting to tarnish the bond they'd rekindled. She focused on her nephews, argument forgotten as they rough and tumbled on the lawn, trying to find the words.

'I… I'd like to see Owen,' she finally said and turned to Anita, just catching the stiffness before it disappeared.

'Why?' Anita blurted.

'Well, because I'd like to get to know him.'

'Are you sure that's a good idea, Jess? After everything, is stepping into his life really the best thing to do for you… and for him?'

Jessie studied her sister, searching her face for the usual judgement and condemnation, but like her words, only concern shone through.

'Beth… and Adam… they both said they'd love me to be part of his life. It's a chance, Annie, a second chance…'

Anita came to sit beside Jessie and took her hand, forcing Jessie to look at her.

'I know it is, and you deserve that chance, but think about it, Jess. What if you became too attached? What if seeing him with the McKennas is too much? You can't take him back; that's not how things work.'

'I know that, and I wouldn't. It's just that… he's all me and… I don't know… I was wrong and… I'd like to make it right.'

'And how do you propose to do that?'

Jessie shrugged, tears brimming as she looked at Anita.

'Listen, whatever you want to do, I'll support you, but please Jessie, think it through first. You don't have to decide today.'

Jessie nodded, not trusting herself to speak.

'Right, I best get those two off to school, then I'm all yours,' Anita said, squeezing Jessie's hand.

∞

'Where are you going?' Anita asked as Jessie opened the front door.

Dammit! She'd hoped to sneak out before Anita came back.

Slowly, Jessie turned to face Anita and, keeping her voice light, she said, 'I'm going to see Owen. I rang Beth, and she invited me straight over. You don't mind, do you?'

Anita sighed, and Jessie watched her working her jaw as she pondered a response. Jessie braced herself, fully prepared to defend her position.

After a few moments, Anita exhaled and spread her hands wide. 'Just be careful, Jess, please. I don't want you to get hurt… again.'

'I will,' Jessie said, smiling as she turned to leave, but stopped. 'Thanks, Annie,' she added, glancing at Anita before hurrying outside.

Chapter 78

'I'm sorry Adam isn't here,' Beth said as she handed Jessie a steaming mug of coffee. 'Work crisis that only he can deal with.' Beth rolled her eyes, making Jessie smile, despite herself. 'Let's go outside as it's such a nice day. Owen should be awake from his nap soon.'

As Beth said this, Jessie's heart lurched and her mouth went dry, her eyes filling with emotion. Not trusting herself to speak, she gave a tight smile and followed Beth outside onto the decking.

The sun was at its peak, turning the tree-enclosed garden into a sun trap. Jessie gazed around at what could only be described as a child's playground: a sandpit, a swing-set, a trampoline and a part-built tree-house in the gigantic oak tree at the end of the garden. Everything a child could ever want.

My little boy is loved, Jessie thought, any doubts dissipating as she brushed away a stray tear, not wanting Beth to see.

'What's the matter, Jessie?' Beth asked.

'What makes you think something's wrong?' Jessie cleared her throat as she composed herself. She needed to say what she'd come here to say.

'You're not yourself,' Beth said, shrugging. 'I know we don't *really* know each other, but you seem on edge, upset even, when you have no need to be. Owen is just having a nap. You can see him when he wakes up, don't worry.'

'It's not that, honestly.' Jessie stared over the rim of her mug at the tree-house, remembering the one her father had built for her and Anita.

'Then what is it?' Beth nudged as she gently touched Jessie's arm.

'You love Owen, don't you… as if he were your own?' Jessie said without looking at Beth.

'Yes, of course we do. You know this. I told you—'

'And you would give your life for him if it came to it?'

'In a heartbeat, but I don't understand, Jessie. You're scaring me.'

'And no matter what his little heart may desire…' Jessie's voice broke, and she finally looked at Beth, tears brimming her eyes, '… or who he may choose to love, you will always support him, without judgement?'

'Jessie, what's going on? What's wrong?'

'Please, Beth, please just—'

'Always, Jessie. You have nothing to worry about, as far as Owen is concerned. He is part of us and we are part of him.'

A sob escaped Jessie's throat at Beth's words, the tears now unimpeded.

'Oh my God, Jessie! What on earth is the matter? Are you ill? Did you get an infection from the donation?' Beth dropped to the deck in front of her, her hands rubbing Jessie's denim-clad thighs.

'No, no, nothing like that,' Jessie said, sobbing and smiling weakly before grasping Beth's hands and looking her in the eyes.

'Promise me, Beth, promise me you will protect my little boy, our little boy, from everything that may bring him harm.'

'Jessie, you know we will. Talk to me. Tell me what this is about.'

Jessie looked away, gazing around the garden, before turning back to Beth. Squeezing her hands, she said, 'Then I am asking you not to tell him about me, about where he came from.'

'But why? I thought you wanted to be part of his life. Adam and I certainly want you to be.'

But Jessie was shaking her head as Beth spoke. 'Believe me, it's not because I don't want to, it's because I feel it would be better for Owen if I simply remain the lady who helped make him better.'

'I don't understand. What's happened? Has your ex—?'

'No, this has nothing to do with Matthew and, quite frankly, if he came anywhere near you or Owen, I would kill him with my bare hands…' Jessie paused, taken aback by the vehemence of her words as her heart thudded in her chest, her body readying itself for battle.

Matthew no longer frightens me, she thought, the emotions that coursed through her body supporting her words.

Clearing her throat again, she said, 'It's to do with the three of you.'

'I don't understand.'

'Beth, the three of you are a family, a blissfully happy family. I see it everywhere I look, and it fills my heart with joy to know I did something right as far as Owen is concerned. I couldn't have wished for better parents for my son than you and Adam.'

'Thank you, but I still don't—'

'You and Adam are his parents, not me, and I want it to stay that way. I want him to always know that and never have the pain of knowing I gave him up. I want him to always believe he is loved and was wanted, and that he is one hundred per cent your son.'

'But why?'

'Because I've seen firsthand the impact a mother giving up her child has on that child as an adult, no matter how loving and caring his adoptive parents have been. I don't want that for Owen.'

'But, Jessie… don't you ever want to see him again?'

'Of course I do,' Jessie said, tears flowing down both women's cheeks. 'But, for Owen's sake, I think it best I don't. Send me pictures, keep me updated, but I don't want to interfere with the beautiful family you have created.'

'Which *you* are part of.'

'No, no, I'm not.' Jessie held Beth's hands as she sat back in her chair. 'And that's a good thing. With me in his life, it affects you more than anyone. You're his mum, Beth, and that's all he needs to know. I'll love him from afar until the day I die. And if you need anything for him, and I mean *anything*, just ask me.'

'I… I don't know what to say.'

'You don't have to say anything. Just love him and keep him safe.'

'Always.'

'Good.' Jessie smiled through her tears. 'I have one request though…'

'Of course, anything.'

'I'd like to see him one last time, before I go… and before he wakes up.'

'I can wake him up and—'

'No... thank you... honestly, it's better this way.'

Beth nodded, and Jessie hugged her.

'Thank you for saving my life, Beth.'

∞

As Jessie trudged towards Owen's room, her steps growing heavier the closer she got, she saw evidence of a little boy, her little boy, wherever she looked. Toys were strewn around the floor, paintings occupied the fridge, and foot and hand casts adorned the walls alongside a gazillion photographs, charting Owen's life to date. And he was a happy little boy. His eyes said it all. And they were a happy family. Seeing these photos, Jessie knew she'd made the right decision.

She stood for a moment in the doorway, watching Owen as he slept, oblivious to the turmoil inside her. Tentatively, she approached his bed and reached out a shaking hand to stroke his dark-blond hair, smiling as his lips puckered in his sleep.

She couldn't stay long, she knew this. Her emotions fought to break free, but she needed to commit this moment to memory, to absorb everything so as never to forget.

Feeling herself teetering on the edge, Jessie bent down and kissed him, before whispering in his ear, 'I love you, little man. You will always be a part of me and hold a special place in my heart. Goodbye, precious boy.'

Jessie watched him for a moment before turning away, the tears streaming, her heart shattering into a million pieces as she gave up her son for the second time.

Chapter 79

With Jessie away, Nate decided it was the prime opportunity for him to put his plan in motion, stage one of it anyway. In between juggling Em and working on the pieces for the upcoming show, Nate set about ex-husband proofing Bluebell Cottage.

Knowing he still needed to bring Jessie in on his plan, or his mother did, depending on how things worked out, Nate decided it best to make the security cameras as invisible as possible, which would also work well should any intruder attempt to locate them. The trees surrounding the cottage provided the perfect locations, as Nate could install them at various vantage points so they covered the whole of the cottage and grounds.

Installing them isn't the issue, Nate pondered as he worked. Getting them working was. The system he'd bought was part of a bigger alarm system and would enable Jessie to view the feeds on a laptop or phone; he just needed to get her to embrace technology again.

As he worked, Nate forced his mind away from Jessie's technophobia and to the show he was planning. He was struggling with how to stage it, which was not usually an issue, yet no matter how he arranged the paintings, nothing seemed right.

The final camera secured, Nate climbed down from the

ladder and fished a beer out of his truck. He plopped himself down on the porch swing and stared out across the lake, pushing all thoughts of Jessie and the show out of his mind.

As his gaze wandered, the beautiful landscape around Bluebell Cottage chipped away, finally announcing its intention as he drained his beer.

Of course! Bloody hell, why didn't I think of it sooner?

Nate whooped, startling the birds from the nearby trees, as the paintings appeared before him, nestled amid the surroundings in which he'd captured her.

∞

'Em? Em? Where are you? I've had a breakthrough, I know how to do it,' Nate called as he raced into the gallery, startling the customers contemplating his work. 'Sorry, sorry,' he said, nodding and smiling at the familiar faces.

'Em?'

'What?' Em snapped as she emerged through the invisible door. 'What've you got yourself all riled up about?'

'I know how to stage the show. It came to me as I was at Jessie's—'

'What were you doing—?'

'It doesn't matter, just listen,' he said, grabbing her hands and pulling her into a corner out of earshot of his now curious clientèle.

'Well, you're going to have to calm down if you don't want everyone to hear you,' Em grumbled, extricating herself from his grip. She planted her hands on her hips, staring at Nate, eyebrows raised and lips pursed, until he stood still and took a breath.

'Okay, are you listening?'

'I'm listening.'

'Great… right… I'm going to recreate the surroundings of Bluebell Cottage—where Jessie lives—and position each painting in the place I captured it.'

'What do you mean?'

'Do you remember those sticker books when we were kids, the ones that had all the background filled in, but there were blank spaces?'

'Yeeesss.'

'And you had to buy the stickers each week and see if you could fill in those spaces to create the full picture?'

'I've already said yes, Nate. I'm not an idiot.'

'Well, that's what I want to do.' Nate clapped his hands and stood back, waiting for Em to capture his enthusiasm.

'But, clearly, *you* are,' she said, shaking her head. 'Have you completely lost your mind?'

'No, why? What's wrong with it?'

'Nothing, except we only have a few weeks and the gallery walls are made of glass.'

'Yes, I know, but I have a plan, oh ye of little faith?'

'Which is?'

'Mac and Johnny.'

'What about them? Aren't they busy drooling over Libby at the library?'

'Well, yeah, but all I need from them is some plasterboard and help to put it together.'

Em stared at him a moment before gesturing to the gallery.

'And where exactly do you plan on erecting this plasterboard collage of yours?'

'Right here?'

'But where do you propose putting the existing installation? And, come to that, how do you expect to do all this and stay open?'

'I've thought it through. Don't worry, Em.'

'Hmmm.' Em raised her eyebrows again, waiting for him to elaborate.

'This can all go upstairs in my studio.' Nate gestured to the main gallery.

'All this won't fit in your studio, for God's sake!'

'I don't mean that one.'

'What?' Em said, her blustering halted as she stared at him. 'But you don't let *anyone* in there, remember?'

'I know, but some things are more important.'

Em didn't respond, her mouth open as she continued to stare at him.

'It'll work. Look, people can come in the back way, enabling us to keep the show a secret.'

'But that studio is too industrial for these pieces.'

'I know, but it'll show them in a different light, maybe attract a new audience.'

'I'll have to get the walls painted to cover up your multi-coloured splatterings, which will—'

'No, you won't. Hang them amidst the chaos, and move the free-standing installations in there too.'

'Need I remind you that this gallery is all windows, so how are you going to keep it a secret?'

'Need I remind you I'm going to get the guys to help me erect plasterboard walls this weekend, then I can get to work painting them?'

'So, I have a day to relocate everything, do I?'

'No, you have a day to relocate everything and get the windows blacked out and decorated with the words: *"Transformation - Coming Soon"*, plus a countdown, which will need updating daily.'

'Anything else?' Em said, the sarcasm dripping from her words, but Nate ignored her; he knew she would embrace the challenge once she let it percolate.

'Ummm, oh yes, we need to add a web address so people can buy tickets.'

'But I thought this was an invitation-only show?'

'It is, but before I let any paintings go to their new homes, I want to run the show for a week afterwards, though ticket only.'

'You really like her, don't you?'

'No, Em, I love her. I just don't know if she feels the same way.'

Chapter 80

'Well, Coley Moley, I think it's about time I stopped moping around and did something productive, don't you?' Jessie looked over the rim of her coffee mug at Cole, who was conducting his morning ablutions on the kitchen table as usual. 'I wish you wouldn't do that here.'

Cole paused and glanced across at Jessie, tilting his head to one side as he appeared to ponder her words. He then yawned and returned to his preening.

'Great help you are,' she grumbled as she tidied the breakfast things away and readied herself for the task at hand.

Since she'd returned from Scotland, Jessie had insisted on returning to work, but hadn't wanted to talk about what transpired, regardless of how clever Bev's prying was; she was still processing it herself.

When not at work, she curled up with Cole and escaped to a different time or place, or went for long walks around the lake, allowing her thoughts to come and go as they pleased.

One thought which plagued her was the one thing in Bluebell Cottage which remained untamed—the spare room on the ground floor. When she'd moved in, Jessie used it for storage, and the last time she'd been in it was to free her library from its confines.

With her newfound connection with Anita, and the trust that Matthew was a threat she could more than adequately handle, Jessie felt it was time to reconnect to the world. The engineer was due in a couple of days to bring her online, so she needed to decide how the spare room—her study—would be best laid out.

Jessie grabbed a tape measure and wandered through the cottage. She'd decided on a study because it made sense to keep all the practical things together in one place, rather than strewn over the kitchen table, as they were currently. As she'd decided to invest in a laptop—emails were so much easier than letters—to go with the phone Nate had given her, Jessie thought it fitting that a suitable desk and chair should accompany it, turning the room into a study by their very presence. She just needed to measure up!

But as she opened the door, Jessie stopped in her tracks, her heart lurching, butterflies awakening in her belly.

I forgot about those.

∞

'Ew, it stinks in here, Parker!'

Nate raised the arm he'd slung across his eyes—the only relief he could find for his injured hand—and squinted at Em, her nose wrinkled in disgust as she proffered him a large cup of coffee.

'Gee thanks, Em. Nice to know all my hard work is appreciated.' He swung his legs off the cot and sat up. He smiled wanly at her and stretched out his aching back before accepting the welcome offering. He sipped his coffee as he watched Em inspecting his hard work.

'I have to say, I didn't think you'd pull it off,' she said, clapping as she spun around on her heel to face him.

'And yet I have.'

'Yes, you have, but at a cost by the look of it.' Em nodded towards his bandaged hand.

Nate shrugged. 'What do you think?'

'I think they look fantastic, I honestly do, but we still have a shitload to do before tonight.'

'Such as?'

'Well, let me see, Mr Organised. You need to hang the paintings in the glorious surroundings you've created, and the windows are still blacked out. I thought you were arranging for someone to clean them once the boards were up?'

'I was, but I changed my mind.'

'You changed your mind at the eleventh hour? Are you mad?'

'Just relax, will you? I've simply asked the sign writer to amend the wording to read "Transformation - A Journey to Self Discovery".'

'Hmm, fine, but what about the paintings?'

'Chill, Em, seriously, you'll give yourself a heart attack. I'm heading home now, with my coffee, to get them.' Nate leaned on his hand to push himself up and cried out, dropping back onto the cot.

'Let me look at that.' Em grabbed his rag-wrapped hand and unbound it. 'Jeez, Nate, you should have stopped. Look at the state of it!'

Nate studied his swollen hand for a moment and shrugged. 'It needed to be finished. I'll get Dad to take a look at it later.'

'Make sure you do.'

'Right, help me up. I best get on with the rest of my duties,' Nate said as Em allowed herself to be his fulcrum. 'Speaking of which, how's the rest coming along?'

'All in order, have no fear. All you need to do is hang those paintings and get yourself ready for tonight. That includes a shower because you bloody stink.'

'Forever the charmer.' Nate rolled his eyes before sobering. 'What if she doesn't come?'

'Then it's her loss.'

Nate's heart sank, his stomach hollow as he contemplated the prospect of Jessie being a no show.

'But I'm sure she will. Don't worry,' Em rushed, squeezing Nate's arm.

I wish I could believe that.

∞

Jessie finally let go of the door handle and stepped into the room. She hadn't had time to look at them before going to Scotland, so she'd put the paintings Nate had left in here, fully intending to hang them when she returned, but they'd slipped her mind.

With shaking hands, Jessie took them up to her bedroom and carefully peeled away the wrappings, her breath catching as she stared at the finished paintings.

Jessie plucked each one from its tissue bed and leaned it against the wall she'd earmarked. She allowed her gaze to roam over them as the morning light picked out the hues and brush strokes, following Nate's hand as he brought her to life in intricate and vivid detail. Jessie saw herself that first night, staring out across the lake, both elated and fearful that she was finally free. She smiled as she watched the moment Cole had permitted her to stroke him, laughing at the memory of an instant later when he'd expressed his displeasure and disappeared again. Jessie didn't need the memories though, Nate, had captured it all.

'Oh, Nate,' she whispered, remembering the night she'd first seen them, the night she'd bared her soul. Jessie shivered as she felt Nate's gaze caressing her scars as he whispered "beautiful" over and over. She gasped as her base throbbed and she evoked the touch of his lips, his fingertips, and the feel of him inside her as he gazed at her, concerned only that *he* wasn't hurting her.

Jessie looked through the window at the Lake House. It was time. She'd healed her past with Owen and Anita. It was time she saved her present and gave her future a chance.

Seeing his truck missing, Jessie scoured the glass house for any sign of life; there was none.

Dammit! Technology it is then.

Jessie raced downstairs before she changed her mind, deciding to text him and arrange to meet. She rifled through the paraphernalia on the table in search of the phone, toppling the pile of mail she'd been ignoring since her return.

Cursing, Jessie crouched down to gather the scattered post when a glitter caught her eye, and she retrieved a midnight-blue envelope strewn with silver stars from beneath some pamphlets, her name embossed in silver on the front.

Jessie peeled the envelope open and slid out an invitation,

the ornate silver lettering surrounded by the moon and stars glittering against the night sky:

You are cordially invited to a

Transformation

at the Nathaniel Parker Gallery…

As Jessie looked at the date and time, her heart lurched; it was that night.

No wonder he isn't home.

Jessie glanced at the clock, and her breath caught. She had less than three hours.

Chapter 81

Nate stood under the hot jets, allowing them to pummel his knotted, aching muscles, his mind elsewhere as he watched remnants of the rainbow swirl down the plughole.

The stage was set, and the show looked amazing. The panels he'd created provided an almost photographic backdrop to the images they showcased. Nate laughed to himself as he recalled Em's reaction.

'Nothing to say, Ms Nicholls? This must be a first,' Nate had quipped as Em stared open-mouthed at the lakeside tableau he'd created.

'I… I… Nate, it's stunning,' Em finally breathed. 'You have well and truly outdone yourself. Jessie will be blown away, I have…'

'*If* she comes, Em, and it's a big *if*.'

'So there was nothing when you got home?'

'Nope, not even a thank you note for the paintings I gave her.'

'I'm sorry, Nate.'

'It is what it is,' he said, swallowing the lump that filled his throat. 'To be honest, I don't even know if she's even there. She could still be in Scotland for all I know.'

'Have you asked your mum?'

Nate shook his head.

'Well, if anyone would know, she would.'

Nate had called his mother on his way home to "descale and fumigate", as Em had so eloquently put it.

'Yes, she's been back for weeks. Why?'

'Umm, well, she hasn't RSVP'd to my show, and the cottage looks pretty much abandoned.'

'I think she's got enough on her mind without worrying about coming to your show, Nate.'

'But she *has* to come.'

'Why?'

For a long moment Nate didn't answer, but then he whispered, 'You'll see.'

He'd cut the call before his mother could probe further.

Jessie, Jessie, Jessie, do you think about me too, or am I already part of your past?

Nate turned his face to the hot water, the drumming stimulating his nerve endings, waking him up. He was exhausted, but he needed to be at his best. He couldn't allow himself to be distracted tonight. Whether or not Jessie came, he had to be his usual upbeat self. Libby was relying on him and he had no intention of letting her down, not again.

Before his mind dragged him down another dark alley, Nate switched off the shower and wrapped a towel around his waist. He cleared the mist from the mirror and scrutinised himself, smiling ruefully.

I look like shit! His eyes were bloodshot, with dark circles underneath from lack of sleep, and his skin looked sallow from its lack of exposure to the outdoors.

I can't do much about that, but this…

Nate picked up his razor and attacked the Grizzly Adams beard Em had frowned over. He wasn't sure Jessie would approve, either.

An hour later, Nate inspected himself in the full-length mirror. He tugged at the collar of his white shirt, already feeling it was strangling him, and fixed his bow tie as loose as he could get away with without it looking wilted. Black tie wasn't his usual attire for a show, or anything for that matter, but tonight was a little different.

He looked up at his cleanly shaven face. Eye drops had softened the redness in his eyes, and he smoothed a stray hair back from his face, only just stopping himself from wiping his Brylcreamed hand on his trousers.

Nate grabbed his discarded towel and wandered over to the window as he cleaned off the hair cream. Bluebell Cottage was still slumbering.

Maybe I should call round. At least then I'll know. Almost as soon as he finished the thought, Nate dismissed it. The lack of knowledge gave him hope, which would sustain him through the evening, allowing him to be the perfect host he needed to be. There was much more than his personal life riding on this show.

Besides, he realised, glancing at the clock, he didn't have time. Em had informed him, under pain of death, that he had to be there an hour before the guests arrived, to make sure everything was in place. Plus, he'd promised to pick up his parents.

Guests! Nate laughed as he grabbed his dinner jacket off the bed. He'd never called attendees of his show guests before, but then again, he'd never before done anything like this.

∞

Her hair in heated rollers, Jessie stared at the contents of her wardrobe in dismay. In her panic at the little time she had to get to Nate's show, she'd almost missed the small print requiring black tie. There was a time, pre Matthew, when such events were a regular part of her life. Once he'd arrived on the scene, her attendance was surreptitiously whittled down until one day…

'You can get rid of all this crap now, as you won't be needing them any longer,' Matthew had announced, flinging open her wardrobe door and yanking out her beautiful dresses.

'W-what are you talking about? I wear them all the time,' Jessie had cried, grasping at her clothing as he tore them away from her.

'Oh, really?' Matthew stopped and raised an eyebrow, a sneer marring his handsome face. 'Do tell when the last time one of these saw the light of day?'

'Your office's summer ball last…' Jessie tailed off as she counted back on her fingers, massaging her thumb as realisation dawned.

'Exactly. Five years ago. No one wants you there, so there's no point you having them. Besides, I need the space for my suits.'

'You mean *you* don't want me there,' Jessie mumbled, tears filling her eyes as Matthew screwed her life into a shapeless ball.

'Same difference,' he said, slamming the wardrobe door.

'Please, Matthew, I spent a lot of money on those dresses. I love wearing them. If you'd only take… argh!' Jessie cried out, her hands flying to her face, shielding herself from more blows.

'Don't question me again, bitch. They're going in the bin. End of story.'

Jessie sat on the floor, sobbing, as Matthew regained control of the bundle and stalked from the room. She watched, breathless, as a sliver of silk slipped from the pile and slithered to the floor unnoticed.

She'd waited until he'd disappeared, before rescuing the dress and hiding it away, hoping one day she would get a chance to wear it again.

And here was her chance.

Is it a sign? she wondered, anxiety weaving its way through her body as she vainly searched for the elusive garment.

I have to find it. If she didn't, she had nothing else to wear. If she had nothing suitable to wear, she knew she wouldn't go, and if she didn't go, she would never speak to Nate. Given she'd made up her mind to do just that, she *had* to find the dress.

'Dammit! Where are you?' Jessie pummelled her fists into her clothes in frustration and a whisper of midnight-blue silk flashed in the light. She scrambled to follow it, discovering the spaghetti-strapped empire-line dress nestled amidst some nondescript shirts, exactly where she'd hidden it, with a lavender wrap twisted around the hanger.

Untangling the dress, Jessie held it up in front of her. The colour still flattered her, but she saw it was now too big, thanks to the enforced weight loss since she'd last worn it.

'What do you think?' Jessie turned to face Cole, the precious silk fluttering against her body. Cole appraised her from his position on the bed and dipped his chin before yawning, stretching, and settling himself down to watch her get ready.

'You're going to make sure I go, aren't you?' Cole blinked in response.

With time marching on, Jessie applied her make-up and removed the rollers, pinning her hair up, allowing soft curls to tickle her shoulders. As she stepped into the dress, the breath of silk sent a shiver across her skin, and a flicker of her former life rippled through her.

Knowing everyone at the ball would be dressed in more conservative attire, Jessie had chosen the daring silk dress deliberately. She liked to do her own thing, to not conform, and as she'd walked into the room, everyone had turned to look at her, especially the women, many of whom had complimented her later, confiding they too had wanted to dress differently, but they hadn't had her confidence.

Emboldened by the long-ago memory, Jessie stepped in front of the mirror and gasped, her hand flying to her mouth as her eyes filled with tears.

I can't go out like this. I'm hideous! Jessie shuddered as she stared at Matthew's branding, barely able to prevent the tears from ruining her make-up.

Her hands shaking, Jessie picked up the wrap and arranged it until she saw the Jessie she once was, a deep-seated longing stirring inside her as she wished she could turn back time. Her shoulders slumped, the lavender slipping and the angry scars reminding her of who she was now.

Except I'm not!

She wasn't the battered wife, too scared to leave her

husband. She was the survivor of a brutal relationship, the mother of a very special little boy, the new teacher at a delightful village school, the brave woman who's started her life over, who'd befriended a feral cat, who'd made new friends in a new place, who'd fixed her relationship with her sister, and who'd finally stood up to her ex.

As the thoughts raced through her mind, Jessie watched her shoulders straighten, her chin lift, her cheeks flush and the ghost of determination sparkle in her grey eyes.

I'm still the same person.

'One day, Jessie, you'll find your way back,' Dr Augur had said.

'Find my way back to what?'

'To yourself.'

And I have, I just lost my way for a while.

But with the help of Potters Hole, of Bev and Ray, of Bluebell Cottage and of Cole, Jessie had found herself again.

Staring at herself in the mirror, the scars dissipating as she focused on the woman looking back at her, Jessie realised she'd done something else she never thought she'd have the courage to do again. She'd fallen in love.

Chapter 82

'Wow, look at the ceiling! It makes you feel like you're there, in this magical place he's created. I…'

Nate smiled as he wandered through the crowd. It wasn't the first time he'd heard the comment, and he was sure it wouldn't be the last. Em had outdone herself in the hours he'd been gone.

He followed the images he'd created until they merged into the canopy of sky he hadn't thought to add, but Em had. This simple touch had transformed his show to yet another level, making it more immersive than he could have imagined. She'd also had the forethought to ensure the food and drink didn't mar the enchantment, concealing it and hiring servers—dressed to reflect the invitations—to drift amongst the guests.

'What would I do without you, Emily Nichols?' he murmured as he surveyed the packed gallery, his gaze lingering on the door, hope ricocheting through him as it opened, only to be dashed by unfamiliar laughter and chatter once more.

'You'd crash and burn,' Em said, startling him.

'Shit, Em!'

'Only answering your question.' Em followed his scrutiny of the front door. 'And, as to your second question… I don't know.'

'What do you mean?'

Em raised her eyebrows as she looked at him, her head cocked to one side, ruby lips pursed.

'Really? You forget, Nate Parker, I know you better than anyone, and I know exactly who you're wishing to walk through that door.'

'Yeah, well, doesn't look hopeful, does it?'

Em shrugged. 'Whether or not she comes, we need to get this show on the road, Nate. You've got over a hundred guests here, all champing at the bit.'

'Can we just—?'

'Nate, Nate!'

Nate turned to see Libby pressing through the throng, Mac and Johnny jostling each other in her wake. Nate chuckled.

Good old Libby.

'Hey, Libby.' He smiled as she paused before hugging him and stepping back, her cheeks flushing as she coyly averted her gaze.

'Sorry, I don't know what came over me,' she breathed, looking back at him and shrugging.

'It's fine, don't worry.'

'I'm just so happy with the work these guys have done. I wanted to thank you.'

'So they've behaved themselves, have they?' he asked, raising his eyebrows as he looked over Libby's head at his friends, who pretended not to know what he meant.

'Oh yes, yes, and the library looks wonderful. I even got them to help me put the shelving back *and* redecorate.'

'I'm sure you did.' Nate glanced at his mates again, and they grinned back. 'Is it all finished?'

'It certainly is. Ready and waiting for the grand opening and the special dedication,' Libby said, winking at Nate before gawking at the room. 'This place looks amazing. I can't thank you enough for doing this.'

'Don't thank me yet, we've got to sell something first!'

'Well, if the conversations I've overheard this evening are anything to go by, I don't think you need to worry.'

Nate smiled and glanced at the door as it admitted more guests, his shoulders drooping in response.

'Speaking of, where's Jessie? Is she here?'

'Nope, not yet.'

'She's cutting it fine, isn't she?'

Nate looked away and cleared his throat, not wanting Libby to see the tears that had sprung up.

'Sorry to interrupt, Nate,' Em cut in, tugging at his sleeve. 'I have some people I'd like to introduce you to.'

'Ummm, okay, yes, sorry Libby, would you excuse me?' Nate said, allowing Em to propel him away. 'So, who wants to talk to me?'

'No one, I just thought you needed rescuing. You need to pull yourself together, Nate. You have a room full of people who've all come to see you and your work.'

'But what if she doesn't come?' Nate whispered, his voice catching.

Em looked at him for a moment, her lips twisting and turning as she wrestled with how to respond. Finally, she said, 'Then you go see her tomorrow and tell her how you feel.'

'I thought you said I'd have to accept that she doesn't want to be with me and leave her alone?'

'Yes, well, I'm allowed to change my mind. Besides, I've *never* seen you torn up over a woman before, so you need to give it one more try.'

Nate nodded and gave Em a half smile. She reached up and brushed a stray tear from his cheek before linking her arm through his. 'Now, we don't need your muse to sell these paintings, do we?'

No, but I want her.

∞

Jessie stood across from the gallery, a bouquet clutched in one hand, her umbrella in the other. The place was packed, and her heart swelled for Nate as another sell out show looked imminent. The door opened, and Jessie caught the laughter and animation for a moment and smiled.

Maybe I don't need to go in. It's his night. It's not like he's expecting me.

She turned, ready to retrace her steps to the sanctuary of Bluebell Cottage. The thought of a glass of Malbec, of Cole, and of Heathcliff suffused her with warmth, but she forced herself to stop. She'd come to clear the air, to make things right. She had promised herself she wouldn't hide any longer, and that included hiding from Nate.

The rain had stopped, and as the evening sun broke through the clouds, Jessie folded her umbrella and tucked it under her arm. She caught prisms of radiant colour shimmering in a nearby puddle and looked up to see a rainbow arcing in the clearing sky, its pot of gold at The Nathaniel Parker Gallery.

Of course it is.

The warmth hit Jessie as she pulled open the door, her hands shaking, her breathing shallow.

I can do this; I can do this.

'Oh my God!' she exhaled as she stared at the paintings adorning the walls, the journey clear in the way he'd hung them. Jessie absorbed the pain and the sadness, the hope and the dreams, the laughter and the playfulness, the hurt and the isolation. She saw it all, just as he had. She'd lived it all, just as he'd recorded. The intimacy, the detail, the life and the feeling of each one took Jessie's breath away, just as the ones he'd left on her doorstep had.

'Stunning, isn't she?' a man said as he paused beside Jessie. 'Whoever she is, he's clearly in love with her to capture such raw emotion.' The man drifted away, merging into the throng without ever having looked at Jessie.

Suddenly, the enormity hit, and panic seized Jessie, squeezing her heart until she gasped. She reached out to steady herself against the wall, her umbrella clattering to the wooden floor, drawing looks of annoyance from the attending connoisseurs; looks which turned to curiosity, curiosity which turned to realisation, realisation which turned to movement.

As strangers edged towards her, Jessie lunged for the door, frantically pulling on the handle, her breath coming in short bursts, dizziness threatening to floor her. But the door wouldn't budge.

No, no, no, no, no. I need to go. I can't be here. This was a mistake. I'm not ready. I—

A large, tanned hand enveloped hers, barging into her thoughts.

'Don't leave,' he said, pulling her around to face him.

'I-I… I shouldn't have come. I…' she tailed off as Nate hooked his finger under her chin, tilting her head until she had no choice but to look into his cinnamon eyes.

'But you did, so stay… please.' He smiled that half smile that had reminded her of Elvis the first time she'd met him. So much had happened since then, so many bridges built, only to be burned by denial and misunderstanding.

'Look, Nate, I—'

'Don't go, Jessie. This is for you… this show. It's all for you. It's always been you. Ever since the day you moved in, nothing else has mattered to me, only you.'

'Nate, I…' Jessie floundered, not knowing what to say. 'These are for you,' she blurted, thrusting the bouquet against his chest.

'Coloured pencils…?'

'Paint-laden brushes would have been too messy.' She shrugged, making Nate laugh. 'Look, erm, I just came… Nate, I'm sorry I've been ignoring you these past few weeks. It's just that after that night… the way you were… I—'

'I know, I know and I—'

'Please, let me finish.' She rested her palm against his chest, feeling his heart racing beneath his shirt, its beat matching her own. 'It brought back all the shame. *You* brought back all the shame. I know you didn't mean to, but still… after everything we'd shared, it hurt. It hurt most that you would think me capable of such a thing.'

'But Jessie, I don't. I—'

'I know you don't, Nate, really I do. I just needed time. You weren't the only one, you know, tarring and feathering, I did it too. I kept thinking you were Matthew, and you're not, not by a long way. You're you, and I'm me, and neither of us are the people who hurt us.' Jessie fell silent. She'd said what she'd come to say.

Nate pulled her into his arms, peppering the top of her head with kisses. 'I've missed you so much, Jessie. I never thought I'd—' His voice broke.

'I've missed you too,' Jessie whispered, pulling away from him and looking up into his tear-rimmed eyes. Her heart swelled with emotions she never believed she'd feel again, feelings she thought Matthew had shattered.

She raised herself onto her tiptoes and pressed her lips to his, wrapping her arms around his neck. Nate pulled her close again, crushing his lips to hers, his need for her clear.

The sound of a throat clearing dragged Jessie and Nate apart, and Jessie's cheeks burned as she saw the amused grin on Em's face.

'Not that anyone minds watching you two lovebirds,' she said, cocking her head towards the ogling crowd, 'but we've got an auction to kick off.'

'An auction?' Jessie queried, puzzled.

'Yep, didn't you read your invite?'

Jessie blushed again and looked at the floor. She hadn't.

'Come on,' Nate said, pulling her towards the crowd. 'You might help us raise more money, given it's in your honour we're doing this, after all.'

'Wait… what? My honour? What are you talking about?'

'The Jessie Ellis Classics section of the library, but it won't get restored without funds.'

∞

'What have you done to your hand?' Jessie asked, feeling the distraction between them as Nate took her hand.

'Nothing that won't heal.' He smiled at her as he led her towards the middle of the gallery.

'Hang on, hang on,' Em called. 'Jessie, give me your coat and brolly.'

Still dazed by Nate's announcement, Jessie handed over the dripping umbrella she'd retrieved from the floor and shrugged her coat off her shoulders. As she did so, the wrap she'd taken care to arrange caught and slipped, revealing the scar on her collarbone.

She rushed her hand up to pull the lavender back into place, but Nate stopped her.

'You look beautiful,' he whispered, and heat suffused her face once more, but she persisted in hiding herself.

Again, Nate stopped her. 'You are so beautiful, Jessie. You don't need to hide.'

He kissed her on the lips as he gazed into her eyes, and Jessie shuddered as the fire ignited inside her.

'Relax and be you,' he continued, before turning to address the crowd.

'Excuse me, everyone, can I have your attention, please?'

Nate waited for the room to quieten, and Jessie willed herself to stay where she was—exposed—a smile plastered on her face, as over a hundred pairs of eyes turned to look at the two of them.

Jessie braced herself for the pointing, the revulsion, and the whispering, but there was none. Instead, she saw recognition as people glanced from her to the paintings and back, their faces illuminating with pleasure.

As she looked around the room, Jessie felt the tension ebb away and her wings unfurl once more, the wrap slipping to rest in the crook of her arms, where it always had in the past.

Nate squeezed her hand before letting go and stepping away from her.

'I'd like to introduce you all to a very special woman. A woman who changed my life in more ways than one the very first day I saw her. A woman you've all been admiring since you arrived. A woman who has been on a journey of her own—a journey back to herself.

'I'm honoured to introduce you to Jessie Ellis, my neighbour, my muse and the woman who has shown me how to love.'

Nate took Jessie's hand, turning to face her as he said in front of the packed gallery, 'I'm head over heels in love with you, Jessie Ellis.'

Before she could respond, Nate pulled her close, pressing his lips to hers as cheers erupted around them, and applause rang in Jessie's ears. For a moment, her stomach clenched as adrenaline built, ready to aid her escape, but then she slid her arms around Nate's neck and pulled him closer, her fear fading as the past evanesced, the future—their future—unfolding.

Releasing her, Nate grinned and turned back to their guests. 'Let the auction begin!'

THE END

Reviews are my life blood

As an indie author, it isn't just about writing a fantastic story that leaves you, dear reader, wanting more; I am also a one-woman publishing house—Scarygirl Ltd.

Being a publisher as well as an author means I have to pay for an editor, proofreader, and cover designer out of my own pocket. And then there's formatting, marketing, advertising, and distribution of physical copies to bookstores.

For me to succeed in the world of indie writing and publishing, I have to have the support of a great team, and I do.

And you, dear reader, are a vital part of my team.

To continue to write and publish the stories you love, I need to get word out about my books, and **reviews** are one of the best ways to achieve this.

So, team member, I am asking for your help.

If you enjoyed this book, it would mean the world to me if you would leave a review on Goodreads, your favourite reviewing spot, or on the site where you bought this book.

Thank you so much for reading my tales and for supporting me.

Love,

Marie

Join My Reader Club.

If you enjoyed reading CHASING RAINBOWS, why not join my Reader Club? As a member, you will receive a copy of my BONDS series prequel novella, THE CURSE OF SOULS, one of the FREE gifts available exclusively to those who join. In addition, you will hear about my latest news and releases, about offers I think you may be interested in, but more importantly, you will learn more about me and my life as we get to know each other.

After all, the very best thing about being an author is building a relationship with you, dear reader.

Just visit www.marieannecope.com to unearth more.

'Til next time,

Marie

Acknowledgements

The belief that I could write a romance novel came after reading Nora Roberts's Chesapeake Bay quartet several years ago. Not only did I not have to make my novel overly soppy, but I could add darkness to the stories, more in keeping with my natural way of writing—and with reality, if I'm being honest!

Once I realised this, the seed of creation germinated and whilst Mother Nature held us in detention for our crimes against the planet, I penned my first draft… longhand, of course. I can honestly tell you I have never been so excited to write anything as I was whilst writing CHASING RAINBOWS. I knew then that this novel was something special.

And so, that is the story of how Jessie and Nate came into being, and from their story, the next POTTERS HOLE tale has already begun.

I would like to call out two amazing people who have helped bring CHASING RAINBOWS to life: Steven Moore, for his incomparable editing skills, and for reminding me people don't blush as often in real life as they do in my novels; and David Berens, whose skill and mastery in translating my photographic collage into a face for my novel are second-to-none. Thank you both. I would also like to give a special shout out to Stephan J Myers for giving me the courage to publish this story.

As always, my thanks go to my friends and family for listening to me witter on about this story for the last few years and to you, dear reader, for spending your hard-earned money and trusting me to deliver. I hope I don't disappoint.

MARIE ANNE COPE lives in North Wales with her three cats and has been, at various times, a banker, auditor, yoga teacher, and a radio presenter. She is the author of the BONDS, ELLIE LAWRENCE CRIME THRILLER and TALES FROM A SCARYGIRL series and, writing as M. A. Cope, THE MISFITS series for children.

You can reach Marie at geni.us/MarieAnneCope
www.facebook.com/MarieAnneCopeAuthor
www.instagram.com/marieannecopeauthor

Printed in Great Britain
by Amazon

38132892R00225